The ONCE And FUTURE FLING

Leigh Heasley

The
ONCE
And
FUTURE
FLING

 by wattpad books

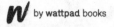 by wattpad books

An imprint of Wattpad WEBTOON Book Group

Copyright © 2023 Leigh Heasley

All rights reserved.

Published in Canada by Wattpad WEBTOON Book Group, a division of Wattpad WEBTOON Studios, Inc.

36 Wellington Street E., Suite 200, Toronto, ON M5E 1C7 Canada

www.wattpad.com

First W by Wattpad Books edition: November 2023

ISBN 978-1-99077-848-3 (Trade Paper original)
ISBN 978-1-99077-849-0 (eBook edition)

Library and Archives Canada Cataloguing in Publication information is available upon request.

Printed and bound in Canada

1 3 5 7 9 10 8 6 4 2

Cover design by Laura Eckes
Chapter images by Laura Eckes
Interior images by Creative Juice via Adobe Stock
Author Photo by Leigh Heasley

To my darling Sei'ne—
my joy, my laughter, my favorite storyteller, and my past.

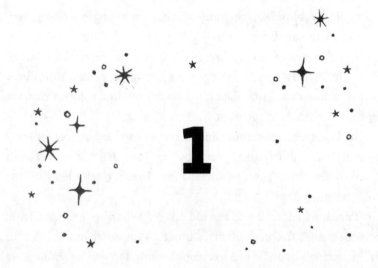

1

I was never much for gossip. Especially when said gossip concerned the lives of people buried about two hundred years before I was even born. But, well, when in Rome—or Regency-era London, as the case happened to be. If that meant feigning interest in small talk with Mr. Thomas Pickering as we floundered around the ballroom, so be it.

Unfortunately, I knew nineteenth-century social politics about as well as I did nineteenth-century waltzes. Not exactly something they teach you in European history class, believe it or not. Let's just say I found myself winging it on both fronts.

A faux pas was inevitable.

"Do you care much for Miss Lovell's singing?" Mr. Pickering asked. Kairos had done a good job with him. He was certainly handsome in a Jane Austen romantic lead sort of way. (The movies, I mean; I couldn't get into the books.) Wavy hair, classical features, endearingly crooked teeth. I just wish his personality had been up to par. Since the music had started, he'd done nothing but regale me with rumors regarding half of the party's guests.

If I had been introduced to a Miss Lovell, I certainly didn't remember her. Scanning the edges of the ballroom, I tried to glean which of the blushing, chignon-wearing girls might've been her. None of them stood out to me.

"I find it lovely." An embarrassed, happy giggle bubbled out of me as Mr. Pickering spun me once. As he took my hand to lead me through a line of waiting dancers, I hoped he didn't notice that my steps were just a beat too slow.

His laughter joined mine, but there was something patronizing about it that I didn't like. "Perhaps we have listened to different Miss Lovells, then. The one I heard last Tuesday sounded like one of my hunting dogs."

"Perhaps I subscribe to the old adage." When we emerged from the other side, the heel of my slipper came down on the toe of Mr. Pickering's boot. I'd like to claim that misstep was intentional—a gentle push for him to mind his manners—but that'd be giving myself too much credit. Our hands linked as we joined the arch. "If you cannot find something nice to say . . ."

"Suppose that is true, yes." The humor dropped from his face like he was a reprimanded child. I felt bad for ruining his joke. "I hear that Mr. Hennicker is giving her lessons in the art of singing during her season in London."

"Maybe she ought to get a new tutor, then." I'd learned from my first response that Mr. Pickering wasn't looking for pleasantries.

But it was immediately apparent that this, too, had been the wrong thing to say. Mr. Pickering's expression was stony. "If anyone can improve that awful crowing, it will be Mr. Hennicker. My good friend has quite the ear for music."

The promenade through the line of dancers was finished. It might have been my imagination, but Mr. Pickering seemed to spin me with much less care as we reformed the circle. His gloved hand caught mine roughly as the waltz resumed. At least now I was getting the hang of it.

The sounds of the string quartet filled the gap in our conversation as I searched for a less offensive subject. There were no answers in the glittering chandelier above us, nor consolation in the slow drip of its candles. Though we were upstairs now, the smell of roast turkey had followed us from the dining room. If there was anything universally understood, it was food. "What did you think of dinner?"

"It was fine." It was more of a begrudging grunt than an actual reply. "I liked the trifle."

I hoped there wasn't too much victory in my smile. "I thought that it was good too. A little heavy on the port, but one can never have too much of a good thing if you ask me."

Mr. Pickering's green eyes wandered. He broke into a rakish grin. "Yes. Yes, I can see that."

I could feel the good humor drain from my face. He was either ogling me or calling me fat. Maybe both, though I couldn't recall if the Regency period was one of those eras where the two intersected. For the moment, I decided to let it slide. "Of course, those are just my thoughts. For what it's worth, the kitchen is as comfortable to me as I suspect a place on horseback is for you."

We had reached the part of the evening where we exchanged outrageous lies about ourselves. While I might've received a constant IV drip of food porn via the Food Network, my culinary expertise was right at the box-cake level. It was a skill I wanted to pick up, though, so it wasn't a total lie.

"Can you read me so easily?" The warmth of his breath on my neck made me shudder.

Ogling. He was definitely ogling me.

"Like a book." That much was true, at least; I was so close that I could smell the hay and grass on his copper-colored tailcoat. "Men like you are my favorite subject to study, Mr. Pickering."

His lips were still dangerously close to my skin when he laughed a few dark notes. "Forgive me for being so forward, Ms. Blum, but I suspect you are not who you claim to be."

My heart nearly stopped.

I couldn't break character. It was part of the terms of service. "I am quite unsure of what you mean."

"I have watched you since your arrival. You struggled through dinner and now you waltz like a young girl first learning her steps." Mr. Pickering's fingers laced through mine and closed with a sense of finality. The dance seemed to speed up in my panic. I tried to look for the exit, but everything bled together, a ring of excited faces, emerald-green wallpaper, and velvet fainting couches. Around and around we went. "But perhaps the most obvious clue is the atrocious way you speak. Ms. Blum, you are no more from Yorkshire than I am."

Perhaps my put-on accent was less believable than I'd initially thought.

I stared, jaw working, but no words came. My thoughts raced through the contract I had signed with Kairos, trying to remember the protocol for something like this. Would I be fined? Or Retconned on my very first outing?

"Are you a Yankee?" His self-satisfied smile put a dimple in his right cheek.

The question pierced the mounting tension I'd felt since first arriving at the party armed with little more than some acting classes and a deep appreciation of period films. I smothered a relieved giggle—I still needed to play the part of someone who was sorry after all.

"Yes," I admitted, dropping the accent entirely as I ducked my head. "Yes, that is true, Mr. Pickering. From Virginia. I am the retiring sort and did not wish to call attention to my foreign status, so I thought it might be better if I played a game of make-believe tonight. My deepest apologies for deceiving you during our short acquaintance. It is wholly within your right if you no longer desire to speak to me after this dance."

Applause erupted as the song came to an end. An older gentleman in a puce coat called above the din of murmured conversation for the other male guests to join him downstairs for port. I drifted away, nodding my thanks to my dance partner.

"Perhaps I am not the only one who is so easily read," Mr. Pickering murmured. He swallowed hard before speaking. "Would a certain Yankee lady care to take a few turns in the garden?"

I have heard an innuendo or two in my day—and that was definitely an innuendo. With my best approximation of a demure expression, I looked up through fluttering lashes. "A certain Yankee lady would, yes, so long as you can guarantee Miss Lovell will not be serenading us."

Using the flurry of activity to mask our departure, Mr. Pickering took my hand and guided me through the townhouse: first down the steps, then through a well-appointed study on the ground floor that smelled of leather and old books. He opened a back door, peering into the blue of night for any potential onlookers.

"The garden, as promised," he said as he drew the door shut behind us. The night air felt coolly wet from the recent rain, a welcome reprieve from the drowsy warmth of the full ballroom. "Quiet and without a single bar so much as hummed by Miss Lovell."

The sight of the garden removed any doubt I had left of Mr. Pickering's true intentions. Small and boxy—it was in the heart of London, after all, where space was precious—the garden was decidedly ill suited for a moonlit stroll. There was a small square of fresh dirt that I assumed was a vegetable patch. A sundial was completely eclipsed by a young willow, and the walls were laced with climbing roses. Though it left something to be desired in terms of size, I had to admit it was very romantic.

"How lovely."

"Yes. Yes, it is." Mr. Pickering nodded, but unless a stray rutabaga had found its way into my cleavage, his eyes were nowhere near the garden. He took a step closer, a hand inching toward a boob before redirecting to the jeweled corsage pinned to my dress. "Forget-me-nots in sapphire."

I smiled down at them. "They were given to me. Do you like them?"

"I find them exquisite, just like you." The damp stone soaked through the back of my dress as Mr. Pickering pushed me against the wall. Our lips locked in a kiss that I probably would've enjoyed a great deal more if I had been anticipating it—or if there had been anything resembling buildup. All I could do was focus on the unpleasant moistness of his lips and the notes of garlic from dinner lingering on his breath.

"Are we just—" My question was cut short as he planted a hand on the back of my head and pulled me in again hungrily. "Mmmf."

It was probably a good thing his eyes were closed, so he couldn't see mine as they rolled hard in their sockets. Well, there were much worse ways of ending a dry spell. And it had been a very long, very dry spell.

My fingers tangled in the knot of his cravat. I worked at it desperately, not out of any real want but a hope that exposing Mr. Pickering's neck would give me respite from his mouth. As the last of the fabric came undone, and it fell somewhere in the grass, my teeth grazed him experimentally. His skin flushed with goose bumps. He gasped.

Mr. Pickering shoved all his weight against me, pinning me in place. The hem of my dress slid upward under greedy fingers. "Your thighs are so wonderfully creamy."

Since it was clear we were wasting no time, I grabbed a handful of his backside and pulled him closer, mentally thanking whoever invented fall front trousers.

Then I heard a shriek.

A young woman, mouth agape, stood in the doorway. From the small beauty mark on her lip, I recognized her as one of the servants charged with clearing away dinner—a process that was still ongoing if the bucket of kitchen castoffs was any indication. Her face was a kaleidoscope of expressions, shifting from surprise to hurt to anger before it finally hardened in resolve. She hurled the bucket's contents at Mr. Pickering. "Scoundrel!"

We were both soaked with what smelled like soured chicken stock. Mr. Pickering sputtered in disgust. The slick stump of a chopped carrot slid down his face.

Something drooped into my eyeline. I tore it from my hair, only dimly recognizing it as a curling potato peel before throwing it to the ground. "What's going on?"

"Nothing, not a thing," he managed, which got the bucket pitched at him as well. It smacked him in the face as he staggered back. "She is little more than a diversion."

"Nothing?" the servant echoed. "I mean *nothing* to you? How could you—"

Suddenly it was clear. I studied her heaving shoulders, the betrayal etched into her face, and smiled sympathetically. "Nice shot."

"Oh my god. No. You didn't." A brunet was practically broadcasting her phone conversation to the entire waiting room. Once or twice, I tried to make eye contact, hoping she'd get the hint, but so far she'd ignored me. A merciful beat of silence passed as she leaned in to her phone. I sighed in relief. Then she squealed, "Oh my god! You *did*? I can't even!"

A headache was definitely in my future, and it wasn't from switching to fluorescent lights after an evening in the lamplight of 1816 London, though that certainly didn't help. I glanced around the room searching for someone to commiserate with, but after the last call from the receptionist's desk, it was just the two of us.

The lobby was sparse and uncomfortable, lined with flimsy chairs that dug into my thighs. Unlike a doctor's or dentist's waiting room, there wasn't much to distract you. Not a single magazine, since a three-year-old Christmas issue of *Good Housekeeping* for one person could be from the future for someone else. I could only imagine the trouble there'd be if there'd been a television. So many spoilers.

There were only two real points of interest. The first was music, piped in through a small speaker. While media might have been time sensitive, "The Girl from Ipanema" was forever, apparently. The second was the far wall, the only one with any decoration or adornment.

Words in elegant black letters read THE KAIROS TEMPORAL MATCH-MAKING SERVICE. Beneath it was the agency's motto: WHAT IS TO BE WILL

BE, EVEN IF IT NEVER HAPPENS. The whole thing was framed by a wreath of forget-me-nots, painted in pale blue.

I wasn't sure when time travel had become a thing. Once it was invented, there wasn't anything preventing big business from bringing the technology back in time, as it meant a whole new means of undercutting their competition—not by price or by product but by whole years.

Money, of course. It always came back to money. Time travel, as it turned out, didn't come cheap. Even Kairos, whose rates were considerably lower than most other agencies, would have normally been well beyond my budget.

While business was newly regulated by the Twenty-First Century Fiscal Retroactivity Act, time travel for personal use had always been tightly controlled. The long-term effects of historical revision hadn't been thoroughly studied due to outcry from moral watchdogs, citing a potential butterfly effect. Visits to Nazi Germany were completely outlawed—Code Black—for just that reason.

Vacations were possible, of course, through packages to predetermined times and places based on popularity. Temporal immigration was much more affordable, but there weren't just legal hoops to jump through—it was a proverbial gauntlet, on fire, overlooking a tank of hungry sharks. Virtually impossible.

But there was a loophole. And I intended to exploit it.

"Ew. Hold on a sec, Jen." My heart stopped as the brunet sniffed the air. Her face scrunched unpleasantly as she looked at me. "Do you smell something?"

There wasn't any point in lying about it. I flashed my best approximation of a good-humored smile. "It's me."

Mercifully, I'd already changed back into my street clothes, but there were no shower facilities in Lockers and Wardrobe. That left me washing off chicken stink in the ladies' room with paper towels and hand soap. Though I'd done the best I could, I swore I could still catch whiffs of something rancid on occasion. Guess it wasn't just my imagination.

The woman looked at me like I had no fewer than nine venereal diseases.

"Gross." She scooted her Victoria's Secret handbag closer to her chair, as though my stink was contagious. Her phone conversation resumed.

I perked up at the swish of the receptionist's plexiglass window. He opened his mouth, reading off the clipboard, but stopped again. I had seen that look of trepidation many times before—the quiet horror of a man stumped by an unpronounceable name.

"Addy-lee-ah." He sounded the word out carefully, but from the furrow of his eyebrows he was clearly unsatisfied by the attempt. "Add-a-lil—"

"Adaliah. Ah-dahl-lee-ah," I corrected him as I approached the window, but from his thousand-yard stare I knew he had no intention of learning it. Sighing, I settled into a patient smile. "Just call me Ada. It's easier."

He nodded, relieved. "Ada Blum, the matchmaker will see you now."

"Thank you."

After the waiting room, the rest of Kairos was much more personable, painted in blue peppermint stripes. Even though my destination was just a few rooms down, I always lingered, distracted by the framed success stories along the way. Sometimes they were accompanied by photos, in color or black and white depending on the time period. Others were snapshots of painted portraits, some on display in modern museums. A few were people I recognized from my college history books, though I wasn't allowed to name names. The agency was very strict about the privacy section of its terms of service.

The door at the end of the hall was propped open. I stood in the threshold, feeling sheepish, but I didn't want to interrupt the matchmaker, Ms. Ellis Little.

The name suited her, as she was five feet if she stood on tiptoe. A tiny tea set on her headband bobbed like antennae as she waved through the holographic pages of her GlassBook. It was pretty much par for the course with her—each time we met, Ms. Little was wearing a new outfit, and it was always eccentric but disgustingly adorable.

I jumped when the book slammed closed. She'd finally noticed me. "Right, yes, hello! Close the door behind you if you would."

The office was comfortably cluttered, appointed with mismatched armchairs, a dozen wind-up toys, and a USB tea kettle. I sat on the edge of an oil-green wingback chair, not wanting to taint the upholstery with rancid chicken stock.

"So, what did you think?" The matchmaker propped her chin on laced fingers.

My nails clicked on the desk with agitation. "He's not single."

Ms. Little's face fell. A drawer whined open then she fanned through manila folders. "But, but—my records—"

"Are wrong," I said, trying my best to give her a reassuring smile. "I'm not upset, but you might want to strike him from the database. He has a mistress."

"Oh. Oh, crepes dear, I am terribly sorry." Once she had found Mr. Pickering's file, she scrawled a big *X* on the front with a flamingo-shaped pen, then tossed the whole thing over her shoulder. "To be fair, though, a mistress means he is *technically* single."

"Mm-hm." I was not amused.

The hope was snuffed out of Ms. Little's expression. Solemnly, she picked up a toy carousel from her desk and wound it. "Did you run into any other trouble? About, oh, an hour and fifteen minutes ago?"

"He suspected me."

"That certainly explains the vitals we recorded." She waved the idea away, eyes never leaving the toy as it spun in circles. "It happens to everyone on their first outing. Just learn from it. Keep your head down. There's a steep fee for Retconning timelines in the event that time travel is exposed in a protected era, per the Antiquity Protection Plan and Legislation Act—"

"APPL, yes. I'm aware," I said. "I'll make sure that it doesn't happen again."

She nodded. "Speaking of which, do you have your corsage?"

I reached into my purse, past my short-term temporal visa, and pulled out the jeweled forget-me-nots. A digital timer on the backing flashed 00:00. The corsages were Kairos's way of keeping track of its customers' whereabouts and well-being while in other eras. Ms. Little took the pin and locked it in another drawer.

"So, what's the next step of this process?" I asked.

"Let's take a look-see, shall we?" Opening her GlassBook, she summoned the glowing white outlines of a calendar. Each day was littered with appointments, but one date in particular flashed red. "Oh! It looks like I have a cancellation. Or will have, rather."

"'Will have'?" I repeated.

She smiled at me as though I was very stupid. "What is to be will be, my dear. How about him? He's from the 1920s."

"Isn't there that whole Great Depression thing right around the corner?"

"Cherry tarts, dear, you'll only have to worry about that if you marry him." She was already draped over the arm of her chair, digging through her paperwork for his file. "You could at least give him a try. It's sort of silly to swear off parsnip jam just because you've only ever tried strawberry."

I made a face. "I don't think that I'd like parsnip jam."

"That's because you've only ever tried strawberry," she said matter-of-factly.

"Well, I've never tried drinking bleach, either, but I don't think I should for novelty's sake." I sat back in the chair, the reek of bad chicken stock no longer my most pressing concern. "I'm seeking marriage, so maybe we could try another era? One that's slightly less volatile?"

"There's no time without its share of troubles, dear, that's the great tragedy of things." She paused, tilting her head slightly while studying me. "Can I ask you a question, Ms. Blum?"

"Sure."

The carousel's song began to slow down, prompting Ms. Little to pick it up and crank the key again. "Now, it's none of my business, dear, but whyever are you using our service in the first place? You have such a pretty face."

By now I was so used to hearing that line that I didn't even flinch. Of course, she had only said half of the usual sentiment: *You have such a pretty face, if only you would lose a few pounds.*

"So I've been told," I deadpanned.

She realized her error, eyes widening in horror as she scrambled to recover. "Er, that is to say—you could have any pick of your contemporaries, my dear! Why do you feel the need to go looking for one outside of your own time?"

"I could make some comment about men not being made the way they used to be, but that feels a bit clichéd, doesn't it?" I recited with a practiced smile. "I don't belong here. My grandmother used to say I was an old soul. Born in the wrong time. I'd never seriously considered it until she passed away a few years ago, but now I think she was right. I guess I'm just an Elizabeth Bennet looking for my Mr. Darcy."

Our conversation lapsed into silence as Ms. Little digested the answer.

"My dear," she said at last, "if you go looking, you'll find many answers here, but not to the questions you're asking."

I was starting to ask her what the hell she meant by that when the door creaked open behind us.

"Sorry, ladies," rumbled a male voice, deep and sweetly Southern. "Nobody was at the front counter—reckon they stepped out for a smoke—so I just let myself in. Didn't mean to interrupt."

My knuckles paled, nails biting into the arms of the chair.

"That's quite all right," Ms. Little replied, but her tired sigh said otherwise. "Just do make sure to sign the clipboard on your way out. Ms. Blum, this is another of our clients, Mr. Samson St. Laurent."

Despite my better judgment, I slowly turned in my chair to regard the man blocking the doorway. With election season underway, Samson's image had been inescapable: a stately, broad-shouldered gentleman in pricey suits and diamond cuff links, the honey brown

12

of his neat beard and hair at odds with his dark complexion. As I looked him over, it was obvious there had been some photo editing at work in those advertisements. His coat buttons weren't straining over his belly, per se, but there was less give than there should've been, and the sleeves looked like they pinched his arms.

A part of me wanted to smile but I pushed it back. "We've met."

"Oh." Ms. Little looked between the two of us, a finger curling at her lip. I don't think she knew what to say.

"We were just finishing up." I rose from my chair. "So, Tuesday next week, then? Same time?"

"Relatively speaking," the matchmaker said.

To my relief, Samson stepped aside as I approached the door, holding it open for me. He flashed a bittersweet smile. "It's good to see you, Ada."

"I wish I could say the same." It was difficult to hold his gaze. Through the stink of chicken stock I began to pick out the notes of his cologne, black pepper and bergamot. "Why are you here?"

"Same reason you are, I reckon." There was something sad in the silence that followed. He was the first one to end eye contact, sparing a glance back to the waiting room. Sam broke into a sly grin, but it was short-lived, evaporating with a single sniff. "Do you smell that? It's like—"

"Don't say it."

"Month-old chicken 'n' dumplings."

My hands balled into trembling fists as I stared back at him. He was acting so casual. Like it was all a joke. I needed a comeback. A good one.

"Shut up."

That was not a good one. Sam's shoulders shook with the beginnings of confused laughter. Too angry to continue our verbal sparring match, I turned on my heel and marched down the hall.

"Give me a ring later," he called after me. "We can do lunch."

2

By the time I got home, the aroma of rancid poultry and I had become old friends. Or at the very least, I had stopped paying attention to it.

The TV, still on from that morning, bathed the living room in eerie blues and twitching shadows. At least it saved me the trouble of finding the remote.

Some vapid celebrity chef started prep on a trio of autumnal meals while I shrugged off my jacket, kicked off my flats, and went through my nightly ritual of locking the door and sliding the heavy dead bolt—an additional security measure that probably violated my lease, not that I cared—into place. I belly flopped onto the couch with a groan, ready for an evening of living vicariously through people who ate way better than I did.

"The key to really good tortilla soup is the broth," the smiling brunet said from the TV. "Use chicken breast to make a hearty stock. Personally, I use bone-in 'cause it's fun to pick out the bones later!"

Never mind. Where did I leave the remote?

I patted around the coffee table blindly. Nothing. Then I weaseled my hands between the couch cushions. Still no luck. I grunted in frustration. Tearing apart my living room was the last thing I felt like doing.

The sudden buzzing of my phone threatened to vibrate my entire purse off the table. I dragged it from my bag as though it was made of lead. "Hello?"

"Heya, bosslady." Celena's Puerto Rican–tinged Brooklyn accent had taken some getting used to when we first met, but I gladly welcomed the respite from wallowing in my own self-pity.

"Hey, Cel. How'd closing go with the new girl?"

"It went fine." I could hear the frustration in her voice. "Woulda went better if she could stop texting for twenty seconds, though."

"Oh. She's one of *those*." I heaved a deep sigh. "And she interviewed so well."

"Twenty bucks says somebody was texting her the right things to say." The statement was punctuated by a devious giggle. "Okay, okay, enough shop talk. Did you bag Mr. Darcy?"

I rolled onto my back, rubbing at a temple. "Ugh. I really don't want to talk about it."

"Aw, c'mon, you can't do this to me," Cel whined. "Let me guess: you had a night of passion and now you're your own grandma."

"Okay, so maybe it wasn't *that* bad. The agency thankfully screens for things like that," I managed to say through sputtering laughter. "They just set me up with a total pig, that's all. One thing led to another and now I smell like that mystery tub of chicken salad in the break-room fridge."

"Hey, I'm telling you, it's not mine. I don't even like chicken salad."

"I seriously think it's been there longer than I have." A glance around the room showed no sign of the remote.

"Maybe *it* should be the bank manager. It has seniority," she said. "So, like, how does it work? Do the bachelors sign up for a match-making service, and they just don't know you're from the future, or what?"

"Not exactly." I considered how much effort it'd take to just get up and manually change the channel, but then immediately decided against it. "They don't know they're in the agency's database. There's too much potential for discovery. The agency vets them, though, and keeps tabs on their whereabouts in case they get picked from the pool of bachelors."

"Huh. That's a little creepy." She brightened as she continued. "Well, here's hoping the next one goes better, honey! It'd be cool if you could bring somebody to the Halloween thing."

"Okay, two talking points," I said, finally resigning myself to the current channel. At least the chef had finished her tortilla soup and had moved on to the most pretentious sweet potato casserole I had ever seen. "First, it doesn't work like that. It's a one-way deal. I can go meet them, but they can't come meet me."

"Aw, you're no fun."

"I'm your boss, I'm not supposed to be." Just when I thought I'd gotten used to it, I caught another whiff of bad poultry. I sniffed my shoulder self-consciously but didn't detect anything. "But seriously, historical integrity and all that. Imagine if somebody from a protected era went back to their own time with knowledge of smartphones and microwave dinners. It'd be chaos."

"Yeah, yeah." She sighed. "Okay, what's the second point?"

I wasn't sure if the headache I was developing was from the smell or the direction our conversation was heading. "I'm really not sure about Halloween."

"What? But—but you're like the only other person I know who can recite the entirety of *The Rocky Horror Picture Show*. Who's gonna help me lead the Time Warp?"

"I really don't want to hear about time warps right now, all things considered."

"Very funny," she said. "Come on. Please?"

"Binge drinking and strange men are scary enough the other three hundred and sixty-four days of the year." Heaving myself off the couch, I trudged down the hall, shrugging out of my clothes. A trail of coral-pink office casual stretched from the living room to the bathroom.

But Cel was insistent. "I'll be your best friend."

"You're already my best friend. Well, besides Teddy."

"He's your brother, he doesn't count," she answered. "Come on, please? Pretty please with Oreo crumbles on top?"

"Oreos, my one weakness." I lit a trio of candles, hoping they'd cancel out the reek of rancid chicken. A whimper on the other end crumbled my resolve. "I don't know. Call it a tentative yes—"

"*Yay!*" she whooped.

"—but I may have to back out."

"I've already got the perfect costumes picked out for us. I thought we could be Bugs Bunny and Daffy Duck—but, like, weirdly sexual, as is the trend for Halloween costumes." Cel paused thoughtfully. "You can be Bugs, 'cause I think he'd be the one with the bigger rack."

I was suddenly feeling very tired. "Honey, I've got to go. I'm in desperate need of a shower. I'm surprised you can't smell me through the phone."

"Oh, yeah, for sure. Go get cleaned up," she said. "I'll see you tomorrow for opening. Maybe it'll be slow, and we can pick out slutty tutus together."

"Looking forward to it," I lied. "Have a good night."

The call ended. I plugged the phone into the clock radio and scrolled through my music collection. A sudden thump and the muffled shriek of laughter from upstairs startled me. Staring up as though my neighbors could sense my annoyance radiating through the ceiling, I picked out a Peggy Lee album, put it on, and turned up the volume until it was all I could hear.

Satisfied, I tugged a makeup wipe from its plastic container. Something black clattered against the bathroom tile.

"What the heck," I muttered as I stooped to pick up the remote, half of my face scrubbed free of Regency-era rouge and lip paint. While I'd always been a little absentminded, this was an all-time low. Shrugging it off, I stood and finished taking off my cosmetics. I was checking my reflection for any smears of mascara when my stomach soured with a realization.

That morning, I had finished breakfast and turned off the TV. In my rush to get out the door, I'd dropped the remote on the couch.

Someone had broken into my apartment.

And, judging from the shadow lurking behind the shower curtain in the mirror's reflection, they had never left.

"Teddy?" I called.

There was no answer. I shivered at the sound of the curling iron sliding off the counter as I brought it in front of me like a club.

I wanted him to be the one behind the curtain. More than anything, I wanted this to be one of his thoughtless practical jokes. I wanted to scream four-letter words at him as he laughed until he hiccupped, red-faced and crying, and then we'd get dinner and watch bad movies like everything was okay. I wanted things to be okay.

But it wasn't Teddy. With his new job, my brother worked longer hours than I did. And the shadow was too short, too solid to be him.

"Teddy, please," I tried again, ignoring the desperate strain in my voice. "I'm not in the mood for this."

Once again there was no response. Peggy's cover of "Mack the Knife" came up on my playlist. I could call for help, but what would I say? Something told me the police wouldn't have much interest in a story hinged on lost remotes and boogeymen hiding in the shower.

Taking a deep breath, I studied the shadow. During our standoff, it had never moved. Not to shift its weight from one foot to another. Not to breathe.

It was ruling me, and I was letting it. This was all in my head. I swept the curtain back with the tip of the curling iron.

My invader stared back at me with empty eyes. A mannequin.

I didn't own a mannequin.

She leaned against the fiberglass wall, silk robe undone to give a coquettish peek at a familiar burgundy bra and panty set. Her hair was not the right shade of red—it was artificial, more plum than crimson—but it hung in loose, bouncing curls like mine. The rhinestone earrings Teddy gave me for Christmas the year before were jammed through her plaster ears.

The slightest touch sent the mannequin sliding to the bottom of the tub where it lay like a corpse in a casket. I stared at it for what felt like hours.

One of Peggy's torch songs died midnote as I pulled my phone from its dock and called 9-1-1.

I stood on the breezeway in a tank top and a pair of Hello Kitty pajama pants a female officer had rescued from the bedroom while the area was being secured. It hadn't taken long for them to determine that my stalker was long gone, but I still hadn't been given the okay to come back inside. Instead, I watched helplessly through the open doorway as people in uniform snapped dozens of pictures of my home, the comfortable clutter turned crime scene. In a way, it was almost as invasive as the break-in.

At first I had clung to the hope that the investigation would come and go discreetly. The last thing I needed that evening was to find myself the subject of building gossip on top of everything else that had happened. But as fifteen minutes stretched into forty-five, and more and more of my neighbors peered through their blinds at the flashing blue lights in the parking lot, I realized that, like it or not, this was becoming a spectacle.

People were subtle about it, at least. No one wants to let on that they're a rubbernecker. Under the guise of a smoke break or a trip to the mailbox on the ground level, they'd trickle from their apartments one or two at a time, lingering on my floor just a bit too long. They tried to piece together the story starting with me. They flashed uneasy smiles, searching my face for bruises from an angry boyfriend, or for a drug dog in my home. But they never asked me what had happened. Not once. It was easier, more interesting, for them to come up with their own stories. They could cast me as a villain or a hero over a cigarette or as they sifted through junk mail.

"Ms. Blum." The sound of the officer's voice dragged me out of my thoughts. Between his slow drawl and fading farmer's tan, he seemed more suited to mowing hay than overseeing the scene of a crime. "I'm Officer Toussaint. Bit chilly out here, huh? You want a jacket?"

"No, that's all right." I hugged myself tighter for warmth. "Have you found anything?"

He joined me on the breezeway. "They've got some partial prints, but if you handled the remote before you called, they may be yours."

I nodded, numbed by the surrealness of the situation.

"We checked all the windows, and you've only got the one entrance here," he said, jerking his chin to the doorway. "Nothing shows signs of forced entry. Could you have left your door open at any time, ma'am? Doing laundry, out on a quick errand . . . ?"

"*No.*" The answer came sharper than I intended, in equal parts indignation and revulsion. Officer Toussaint was clearly too stunned to respond. I forced a patient smile. "This isn't the first time this has happened."

The rising of his eyebrows put a wrinkle in his forehead. "Somebody broke into your place before?"

"No," I said on a deep exhale, shoulders dropping. "But I've gotten messages. Letters with no return address. Calls from unknown numbers, threatening emails. Things like that."

"Mm." He bit his cheek. "Can I see 'em?"

Dread pooled in my stomach. "I get rid of them. Delete them. Throw them away."

"What?"

"I know, I know." Taking a step closer to him, I pleaded with his soulful brown eyes, wishing he could just understand. "I thought that it was normal."

He shook his head, pulling a small notepad and pencil from a coat pocket. He started to jot down some notes, but his handwriting was so messy I couldn't make them out. "Ain't nothing normal about being harassed, Ms. Blum."

"I made some mistakes in college," I confessed. "And some enemies too. I used to call the station all the time, maybe before you worked there. They never took me seriously. I put another lock on the door and got over it."

"Mm-hm." He made another note. "Seems like an awful big thing to 'get over,' don't you think?"

I laughed in disbelief. "With all due respect, Officer Toussaint, I didn't have many other options. I can't spend my whole life wringing my hands in fear."

The pencil paused. "Do you have any names for me? These enemies of yours?"

"No." I shook my head. "They've always been anonymous."

With that, the notepad and pencil slid back into his pocket. His smile was tired. "Breaking and entering, but no forced entry. No stolen property. Perp no longer on premises. We'll take what evidence we got, ma'am, try to get some statements from your neighbors, but know there's not a lot we can do in these sorts of cases."

"I understand." I watched him step back into my apartment.

I couldn't do this anymore.

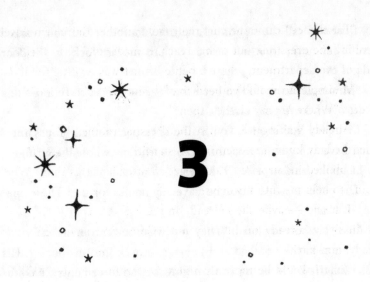

3

"Well, don't just leave me hanging." Teddy's widened eyes looked even larger when magnified by his horn-rimmed glasses. The lighting of Lockers and Wardrobe wasn't as flattering as his station back in Hair and Makeup. Here, he looked way too much like our mother, ashen and severe, though I'd have rather jumped on a grenade than tell him. "Did they find any prints?"

Sliding out of my flats, I placed them in the bottom of my assigned locker. "No, nothing. He wore gloves. Just like all the other times."

"Oh my god," he murmured sympathetically, a hand to his mouth. "It's like something out of a true crime show. I'm so sorry, puddin' pop."

I shrugged with a defeated smile. After a week of dwelling on it, the incident had lost some of its edge. "I don't even wanna know what he was going to do with the mannequin."

Teddy shuddered. "Or what he *did* with the mannequin."

"Thanks, that was just the mental image I needed to get me through the night." Our conversation was interrupted by a wheeled rack of empire-waisted gowns as it rolled between us. I was immediately drawn to a soft rose-colored one. "Are these for me?"

"Fat chance," came the curt reply from another Kairos employee, pushing the dress just out of my reach. It made its way to the other side of the department, where a petite brunet was waiting for it.

"A simple no would've been fine," I muttered before looking at Teddy. "Where *are* my clothes, then?"

"Already waiting for you in the dressing rooms," he answered. "Let the lady know if something doesn't fit."

I blinked in surprise. "I don't get an attendant this time? Who's going to help me into my stays?"

"I dunno—maybe she's already in the dressing room." He waved dismissively, already on his way out. "Come find me when you're ready, mm-kay?"

While I would be more than grateful for an evening that didn't involve squeezing into some kind of shapewear, something wasn't adding up. Shutting my locker with a shoulder, I watched my brother until he disappeared into the employee lounge. Hopefully he was right.

My path to the dressing rooms was blocked by a middle-aged woman getting a crash course on maneuvering in a hoop skirt. I waited as she bobbed and swayed through a few awkward steps before finally spotting an opening.

Each dressing room door was set with a tiny chalkboard with the name of the client it had been prepared for. I passed by three that were already occupied, marked with GALT, ARNETTE, and SCHEU. Yet another had been recently erased and the door left hanging ajar, but the fifth was clearly mine.

BLOOM, the chalkboard read in cutesy, curly handwriting. The attendant had even gone the extra mile of turning the Os into daisies, underlining the name with a leafy vine. Too bad they hadn't put the same effort into spell-checking.

Still, the Kairos dressing rooms were nice enough that I couldn't muster up much complaint as I locked the door, sealing the clamor of Wardrobe behind me. The small space was something like a well-appointed walk-in closet with its own antiqued dresser, plush ottoman, and full-length mirror. There was no attendant, however.

The right side of the small space was dominated by a well-stocked rack of long satin dresses and woolen coats in a variety of understated prints. A few shelves held folded garments—sweaters and long skirts, I quickly discovered—along with a stack of polka-dotted hat boxes.

I shifted through the collection of hats and jeweled head wraps, eventually settling on a brown velvet cloche. As I tried it on in the mirror, my reflection's faint smile soured with slow-dawning recognition. "Dammit, Ms. Little."

Thirty-five minutes later, I crept into Hair and Makeup like I was on a covert mission. Unfortunately, Teddy was waiting for me, lounging in his salon chair with a leg draped over the padded chrome arm. As we locked eyes, the idle swinging of his foot came to a sudden halt. His mouth opened, but nothing came except stunned silence.

"There's been a mistake," I announced.

"I'll say." He popped up from his seat. "I thought you wanted to get laid, not get help with your algebra homework. You look like a middle-school nightmare."

"That's not what I meant." I shot him a dirty look, but it withered under the knowledge that he was right. None of the dresses Wardrobe had picked out for me had been particularly flattering—long, shapeless, and oversized, they made me feel like I was wearing a tent. In the end, I had opted for one of the less-slouchy sweaters and a pleated skirt. "Is it really that bad?"

"No. It's worse." He *tsk*ed, and his eyes flicked down. "Are those support hose?"

The question made me self-consciously tug at one of the stockings already inching down my leg. "No, but they might as well be. An attendant caught me on the way out and forced them onto me. She wouldn't let me wear garters, Teddy. She said they were 'out of style' for the time. They're rolled to my knees. Rolled! Like knee-highs!"

"For Chrissake. You'll be tugging at your hose every fifteen minutes like a granny in church," he scoffed before a devious grin spread across his features. "Well, they'll be down around your ankles by the end of the night one way or another, mm?"

"Oh, hell no. I'm not going anywhere like this." I crossed my arms. "Something's up. Last time, Ms. Little was trying the hard sell on a bachelor from the twenties, but I told her I wasn't interested."

"Looks like she went with it anyway." Teddy tapped his chin thoughtfully before retreating to his station. Cracking open a makeup palette marked with Kairos forget-me-nots, he pulled out a small booklet and held it up. "Yep. This is a lookbook from 1922."

Squinting, I could just make out the half dozen watercolor models in fringe and feathered fascinators on the cover. "You know I like my Moscato way too much to live during Prohibition."

Teddy spun the chair toward me with a pointed look. "A single dry evening won't kill you."

"Unless this guy's so boring he drives me to drink." I glanced down the line of stylists hoping to find someone sympathetic to my plight, but Teddy's co-workers were all wrapped up with their own clients. "Couldn't you call Ms. Little? Tell her I want to go back to the Regency era instead?"

"Regency? After last time?" He arched an eyebrow. "You're hell-bent on being somebody's mistress, aren't you?"

"That's not funny. Please call her, Teddy. I've had a rough week."

He glanced at the clock. "I'm supposed to get you out the door in twenty-five. There's no way we can send you back to Wardrobe and get out of here on time. My supervisor will kill me."

"I guess I could cancel my appointment."

"And pay a last-minute cancellation fee?"

"Right. I'd forgotten." Resigned, I flopped down in the chair. "I guess there's no help for it."

"Oh, come on, it's not that bad." Teddy whirled me around once.

"Go out for an evening, have fun, boink somebody's great-grandpa. I'll take you out to dinner afterward."

"Hm, that's tempting." I tapped my lip in thought. "Does it have to be somebody's grandpa? I'm too young to be a grandmother."

"Sure, sure. Somebody's great-uncle, then. That better?" He unfolded a plastic cape and threw it over my shoulders. "It's not like you're stuck there forever, is what I'm saying. I've never understood that—the marriage-types, I mean. A night is one thing, but who wants to move to 1922 permanently? Who would want to live in a world without Netflix?"

I suppressed an uncomfortable squirm. "No Netflix means no Netflix and chill."

"Fair point." Teddy pumped the chair up until my reflection appeared in the vanity mirror. "Still, there's a reason I gave you my employee discount, and it's not just because I find Kairos's queer dating pool to be a little, well, shallow."

"You're still bitter about the James Dean thing, aren't you?" I asked.

"Yes, of course I'm still bitter about the James Dean thing." He took a comb from its jar of pale-green sanitizer. "You know, Elizabeth Taylor seemed pretty sure about what team Jimmy was playing for. I'm just saying that if they want to know for sure, I'd be glad to find out for them. But, no, suddenly we're worried about timelines and historical integrity."

"For what it's worth, they wouldn't let me see Elvis either." I sighed. "How many times have you watched *Rebel Without a Cause* this week?"

"I'll have you know I've only watched it three times, and once was while I was folding laundry, so it barely counts," he said between strokes of the comb. "So, what were you thinking about for hair?"

"No idea, considering I was supposed to go to the 1800s." I bit my lip thoughtfully. "Throw it in a bun?"

"I mean, sure, we could do that, if you wanna be boring." He toyed with my hair, folding it under so that it came my chin. "Since I can't cut it, how about a faux bob?"

"Sure. You know better than I do." I closed my eyes as he sprayed my hair. The taste of heat protectant settled on my tongue. "So maybe life in the past isn't for you. Have you ever thought about visiting the future? Things can only get better from here, right?"

"Mm, not necessarily. Things are always fluctuating." He clicked on the styling wand. "Most parts of 1920s America are Code Blue on the visitation advisory scale—relatively safe for marginalized people. By 1950, it's been elevated to Code Orange. Later doesn't mean better."

"Oh wow. Code Orange," I breathed. "Regency-era England was blue too. My hand still cramps up thinking about all the waivers I had to sign."

He sectioned off my hair and started curling. "Well, the bureau is always going to issue some special alert for women time travelers regardless of where you're heading. Bet you I wouldn't have a very hard time going back to ancient Rome, though."

"I'll get your toga ready."

"I was thinking about *pteruges*, actually." Once my head was full of curls, he tore open a pack of bobby pins and poked a handful past his lips.

"Excuse me?"

"Those leather skirts the soldiers wore," he said from the side of his mouth. He tied off the bottom layer of my hair and tucked it under, pinning it in place. "Sexy. Good air flow."

My face pinched at the thought. "Seems drafty."

"Then I'll wear a pair of printed leggings under it. Start a new trend," he said flatly. The pins rolled in his mouth as he worked, until finally the last one was in place. "What do you think?"

I reached up to touch the curls that framed my face. Only a practiced eye could've seen that it wasn't a real bob. "You've got to show me how to do this."

"It's nice, isn't it? The drama of a short haircut without the three years of intense regret," he said. "Let's get to work on your makeup. How's life at the bank?"

"Same as it always is." I braced my chin on a knuckle until Teddy shooed it away. "Corporate keeps pushing for more and more sales but the people over in Insight keep denying every mortgage, loan, and credit card application I send their way."

He shook his head, clicking open an eyeliner pen. "Using time travel to see who will default on their payments. That's so messed up."

"That's business." I drummed my nails on the armrest as I tried to stay still while Teddy dotted my lids with eyeliner. I breathed a sigh as he picked up the smudging brush. "This wasn't what I wanted to do with my life."

"So maybe it's not exactly how you envisioned things. You've done all right for yourself, though. There's tons of people in this world with college degrees who are stuck flipping burgers. I mean, hell, before I landed this job, I was barely scraping along renting a chair from Sassy Kutz."

"They're gone, by the way," I chimed in. "I stopped by the mall last week and it's a CBD store now."

"Finally. Love it when the trash takes itself out." Once the eyeliner was finished he tapped out some eyeshadow. "I'm going to work this a little farther up than what you're used to. Almost to the brow line."

"That's fine." I closed my eyes. His brushstrokes were faint against my lids. "And, yeah, I know I should be grateful. I just thought I was doing the responsible thing. People always joke about women's studies or liberal arts degrees, not law school."

"At least you had some help with paying off your student debt, mm?" He stopped his work as if to consider something. "Maybe I should have an affair."

"You snarky little bitch!" I hissed, eyes flying open, unsure if I wanted to laugh or punch him.

"What?" He hid behind the palette like it was a tiny makeshift shield. "How else would I be able to afford college?"

"Well, don't start a side hustle as a comedian, that's for sure."

"Sticks and stones, puddin' pop. Sticks and stones." He took a step back, tapping the excess off the eyeshadow brush. "Mm-kay, what do you think?"

A halo of gunmetal gray powder glistened around my eyes. "I like it. I would've never had the courage to do it myself. It's really heavy, but it looks good."

"Makeup was just becoming a socially accepted thing in the twenties, thanks primarily to the rise of the film industry." He picked up the mascara wand. "So, the trends of the day were inspired by the makeup worn in movies, which had to be a little over-the-top to stand out on black-and-white film. Look over my shoulder for me?"

"So, it was more like stage makeup." I stared over his shoulder until the vanity lights became unfocused. "In all seriousness, though—you really should pursue that history degree."

"Maybe one day." He dumped a trio of lipsticks in my lap. "Pick a color. Hope you remembered to bleach your teeth, they're all pretty bold."

I turned the lipsticks over in my hand, settling on a vibrant orange red. Holding up its tube to the light, I narrowed my eyes to make out the tiny gold letters on the side: Strawberry Spice. "Oh. Strawberry and parsnip jam."

"What?"

"Nothing." I passed it over.

"Mm-hm." He didn't sound particularly convinced as he deliberated between two shades of foundation. "How would you feel about moving in with me?"

An old-fashioned phone in the next room seemed to ring forever, unanswered.

"Oh, Teddy, I don't know . . ." I stammered. "You've always taken care of me. I really don't want to be a burden now too."

"You're never a burden, hon." He turned my arm over and dabbed a dollop of the lighter shade against my wrist, rubbing it in with small circles. "After everything that's happened, I'd feel a lot better if you did."

"But you and Antoine—"

"Are taking some time off," Teddy finished, looking away. "So, no, you won't be crashing our love nest or anything."

"Oh, come on. You guys are always doing this." I rolled my eyes. "In two weeks he'll be back and I'll be a third wheel. No thanks."

Satisfied with the way the lighter shade looked, Teddy sponged out a small portion on my forehead, cheeks, and chin. "I don't know this time. I think he's just out of my league."

"Shut up. You're adorable and you know it. And he knows it, too, if he's got any sense at all." The chill of the foundation made me shiver as Teddy applied it. "So excuse me if I don't bust out the cookie dough and breakup songs just yet."

"Jesus, girl, who needs a life coach when I have you?" The corner of his mouth twitched with an incoming smile. "Will you at least consider moving in? The nest egg won't last forever, especially if your trips with Kairos become a recurring thing. At least together we could save on rent."

"Okay, okay, I'll think about it." With that, our conversation lapsed, leaving me to stew in the silence. Even in jest, mentions of the affair—and the resulting money—made me uncomfortable. By the time Teddy finished outlining a cupid's bow shape onto my lips, I thought the words would burst out of me. "Have you seen Samson?"

"What?" Teddy slammed a drawer closed a little too hard. "Where?"

"Here."

"No, no, I haven't," my brother said in a hushed whisper, his tone growing darker by the second. The lipstick opened like a switchblade in his hands. "And he had better hope that I don't."

I stared up at the ceiling. "At the end of my session last Tuesday, the door opened and there he was."

"And you're just telling me this now?" He dabbed a fluffy brush into a bright-red rouge before applying it to the apples of my cheeks.

"I wasn't sure if it was worth mentioning." In reality, I'd been afraid that Teddy would overreact in typical big brother fashion—and it was clear from his expression that my concerns weren't completely unfounded. I tried changing the subject. "Shouldn't you be following the cheekbones? My face is round enough as it is."

"Round faces were preferred back in the twenties. Think of the big red circles on the face of a Raggedy Ann doll," he answered without missing a beat. "Did he say anything to you?"

For the thousandth time, I replayed my conversation with Sam, scouring each line for sinister intent. I still couldn't find any. "He was friendly. Told me to call him, that we'd get lunch sometime."

"He could stand to go without a few lunches, if you ask me," Teddy muttered. "Do you think he's stalking you?"

"Ms. Little said he was one of the clients here. That's a steep price tag just to stalk someone."

"That doesn't mean anything. You can't afford Kairos but you're here on my employee discount. The man has ways of pulling strings, and he's not exactly scared of burning money."

"But why, though?" I asked. "There are much more immediate ways of trying to reestablish contact. Social media?"

"Yeah, like Sam does social media. You know, that'd explain his money problems—he probably does his taxes on an abacus." He pursed his lips, lost in thought. "Ada. The break-in."

"What?" But as I held my brother's gaze, I knew exactly what he meant. "You think Sam was the one who broke in to my apartment?"

"Convenient, isn't it? Resurfacing on the same day." Teddy leaned against the vanity, arms crossed. "Almost as if he broke in to find out where you were, what you were doing."

"That'd make sense, but what about the mannequin?"

He shrugged. "Maybe Sam's into some kinky shit."

I snorted with laughter, but it was short-lived. "Could you look into it? Ask around, see where he's going, who he's seeing?"

He nodded. "Let me do some snooping. Figure out who his

Kairos stylist is, see what they know. I have a feeling it's probably Marcella or Ryder."

"Thanks, cuppycake. You're the best." I couldn't help but giggle as I stole another glance at my reflection. "I look like Betty Boop."

"That's the idea." He admired his handiwork, but his pleased smile faded after a moment. "Just promise me you won't take Sam up on his offer."

"Teddy . . ."

"Look, I'm usually down to encourage all your half-baked bad decisions, but there's a line, and Sam St. Laurent didn't so much cross it as pole-vault over it." His voice was firm. "And I know you're a big girl now, but you'll always be my baby sister. So humor me, all right?"

"All right, all right." I threw my hands up in defeat. "I promise."

"Good girl." Opening a drawer, Teddy produced a small plastic case. "Mm-kay, time for falsies."

I grinned. "Speaking of which—when is your next drag show?"

"Oh, that was smooth." He laughed. "You were saving that one, weren't you?

4

When I had first found out I'd be visiting 1922 New York, I'd envisioned an evening of secret speakeasies, Tin Pan Alley jazz, and moments stolen from F. Scott Fitzgerald novels. Instead, I watched as my date got punched by an old man during a game of chess.

At least, I assumed it was my date. He matched the picture Ms. Little had given me. Henry Levison. His black hair looked wet with pomade save for a single strand he'd seemingly forgotten, which curled like a corkscrew on his forehead. He was dark eyed and pale. One might've called him unremarkably handsome except for a distinct, twice-broken nose—which cracked under the old man's fist.

Chess pieces bounced and scattered across the leaf-plastered concrete. Henry reeled, both hands going for his nose as he gave a surprised bark of laughter.

"You got some nerve," the old man spat around ill-fitting dentures. "Hustling an old man out of his last dollar."

"Yeah, well, maybe you shouldn't have bet it on a game of chess." Henry's pained expression slowly unscrewed. "Consider it the price of a lesson. You play it too safe. It's a game of aggression, Pops, not dollies."

His words took some of the fire out of the old man, who straightened his houndstooth cap with a sense of finality. "I'll report you to the authorities."

"Sure." Henry's Brooklyn accent was rougher than Cel's. He didn't bother looking up from collecting chess pieces. "Give my regards to Officer Murphy while you're there."

Angry footsteps grew quiet in the distance as the old man's stormy departure bled into the sounds of Washington Square Park on a Saturday afternoon. With the last pieces righted, Henry scanned the area for what I imagined was his next match. His scuffle with the old man had caused something of a stir at the game across from him—between two NYU students, if their varsity sweaters were any indication—but since it was apparent that Henry would not be forcibly rearranging an old man's face that day, their interest had waned and their game had resumed.

Henry had no other challengers.

He slumped, chin braced on a knuckle as he plucked up a silver dollar, considering it before biting down. He seemed pleased with the mouthfeel and produced a mostly empty coin purse.

This was my chance.

The bench across from him squeaked as I sat down. "Hi. I promise I won't punch you in the face if you win."

From the look he gave me, I thought Henry would swallow the dollar whole. He stared for a full five seconds, surprise slowly draining from his expression as he smoothed back his hair. Pulling a handkerchief from his back pocket, he spit the coin into his waiting palm and started to clean it. "You, uh, you saw that?"

I smiled. "I did. Are you all right?"

"Yeah, yeah." A ginger touch of his nose made him wince. "I'll admit it—the geezer's got a mean haymaker for somebody whose biggest adversary is probably arthritis. So, what're we playing for?"

Well, he might not have been what I was looking for, but he was funny at least. "If you win, I'll take you to dinner."

His eyes never left me as he dropped the coin into his purse before tucking it and the handkerchief away absently. "Boy, lady, you don't mess around."

"Calm down. I don't expect you to win." Calling it an empty boast would've been an understatement. The last time I had played chess I'd been in high school. I'd learned the game exclusively so I could spend time with the class valedictorian. He was "a total doll baby," to borrow a phrase from Teddy.

"That so?" Henry seemed to be waiting on something. He finally nodded at the pieces. "White goes first."

"Oh. That's right." Heat washed through my face as I scrambled for an opening move. I took my knight and set it down along the outside of the board, trying to judge his reaction. "My name is Adaliah Blum. Everyone calls me Ada, though."

"Henry Levison." His expression was focused, unreadable, as his attention shifted from me to the chessboard. "And a knight on the rim is dim."

I quirked an eyebrow at his response. "That supposed to mean something?"

"Yeah." He picked up a pawn and moved it near the center of the board. "It means you're lousy at chess."

The next half hour would prove exactly how true that statement was. My knight gambit didn't pay off and I lost a third of my pieces in the process. "So, is this just a pastime for you, hustling women and the elderly?"

"Sometimes I'll squeeze in a kid too. Take his penny candy." Henry shrugged, flashing a boyish grin. "All things considered, I probably deserved to be punched."

His win was less of a victory and more of a mercy kill.

Through the tree line, I could see the pristine stone arch that served as the landmark for the park. Somewhere, jazz played, small and tinny on a radio, punctuated by the long squawk of a jalopy horn. One by one, I put the pieces back in a velvet-lined case Henry provided. "Should we be going, then?"

Draping an arm over the back of the bench, Henry packed a pipe with sweet-smelling tobacco. He took a thoughtful pull as he crushed a still-burning match under his oxfords. "I don't like charity."

"What?"

He took the pipe from his mouth, gesturing at me with the stem. "You threw that game on purpose."

"No, I promise I didn't." I laughed, shaking my head. "Either you're particularly good at chess or I'm particularly bad at it. Your choice."

"Let's make one thing abundantly clear." Henry poked the pipe back in his mouth and puffed a few times. "I'm not particularly good at anything. What were you expecting to get out of this?"

The lacquer of the chess case felt cool under my hands. "I wanted to get to know you. Honestly, Henry, haven't you ever had a girl show interest in you before?"

He went quiet at that, blowing out a slow line of smoke.

"Sure," he said after a moment, voice low. His gaze fell from my face to the jeweled forget-me-nots pinned to my neckline. "But none of them looked like you."

I wasn't sure if that was a good or a bad thing, but I pushed it from my mind as I stood. "Do you have a place in mind for dinner? I'm new to the Village. Maybe something cold for your nose, to keep the swelling down?"

"Oh, you're a real riot." Henry rolled his eyes, but something gave him pause. His expression softened the longer he sat there, stewing over his pipe. "How do you feel about chop suey?"

There wasn't much of a difference between 1920s Chinese restaurants and the ones back home. If anything, the one Henry took me to felt oddly authentic compared to its modern-day equivalents. There were no bright paper lanterns that seemed more IKEA than Beijing, no faded triptychs of the Great Wall, and no dust-covered, waving

Lucky Cat waiting by a plastic-wrapped register. The only indication that this was a Chinese restaurant was a few banners, gold on red, hanging from the support beams. The painted cement walls were empty.

I smiled at our waiter as two plates were set down in front of us, steam rising from vegetables and diced chicken in a glistening, syrupy sauce, but as he walked away, I was overcome with a sense of bittersweetness.

It was funny. People spent all this money trying to go back to the past, when food was the cheapest time machine I knew.

Across from me, Henry ate with enthusiasm. As he pulled his fork clean, his dark eyes darted from me to my plate. "Don't like the food?"

"Oh, no, the food's fine." I snapped up my fork and took a big, reassuring bite. It wasn't as cloyingly sweet as the Chinese takeout I was accustomed to. The vegetables had a snap to them, and the smell of bell peppers filled my nose.

He wasn't convinced, gaze dropping. "It's okay. An acquired taste, I guess. Try some of it with the rice, you'll like it."

"Nobody orders Chinese for the rice." My smile wavered. "I guess I'm just used to eating it with chopsticks."

He glanced up from his plate. "You know how to use chopsticks?"

"Sure," I said easily. "Doesn't everyone?"

"No." Henry laughed, but it wasn't the loud bark that I'd heard before. It was breathless, surprised. More genuine, in a way. He looked at me as though I was a completely different person. "No, they don't."

My cheeks warmed under his attention, and I suddenly felt very foolish. Chinese restaurants had always pandered to their American customers. Of course chopsticks weren't a readily available staple in 1922. The waitstaff here had probably never even heard of fortune cookies.

"I had a neighbor who showed me," I lied. "So, is chess your preferred method of swindling people or do you have other games that you enjoy?"

"You're changing the subject."

"I'm not—"

"Sure you are." Henry spoke over me. I went quiet at the force in his tone, and in the ensuing silence he tapped the tines of his fork against his plate thoughtfully. "But why?"

"Please, Henry, I'm not." I laughed, but I was sounding more guilty by the minute. "I'm really not."

"Yeah, but this," he began, outlining my rapidly warming face with a finger, "says otherwise. You didn't turn nearly this pink—real cute, by the way—when I accused you of throwing the match at the park."

"So I blush very easily," I admitted, too stunned to even acknowledge the compliment.

"Trust me, I noticed," he said dryly. "But you're more embarrassed now, which is interesting. Either you were pretty confident that I'd come to dinner with you, or you're lying about something now. Something pretty big."

I nearly choked on another bite of rice and vegetables. Under normal circumstances, I considered myself a difficult person to read, but this was the second time in just as many outings that a date had called me out on a lie. Worse, there was something much more concerning about the glint of recognition in Henry's eyes than Mr. Pickering's would-be sleuthing back in the Regency era. I felt vulnerable, almost naked, under his gaze—a sort of powerlessness.

As our waiter reemerged from the kitchen, Henry called out across the restaurant. "Hey, Ping Pong, c'mere."

Immediately, whatever spell Henry held over me shattered. I melted into my seat in a mixture of anger and embarrassment as the waiter, remarkably patient, made his way to our table.

Apologies poured out of me with every step he took. "I'm so sorry, what he just called you was ignorant and inexcusable—"

Once again, Henry's voice drowned mine out. "We need a pair of chopsticks."

"What are you doing?" I hissed through a fixed smile.

"Calling you out on your bullshit," he muttered.

"What?"

"You don't have to lie to make me feel better, Ada. Especially over something as dumb as chopsticks." Pulling out his coin purse, he slid fifty cents across the table, his attention returning to our waiter. "Should be more than enough for a pair of oversized toothpicks. I'll even give 'em back when we're done."

Our waiter, seemingly unfazed, rattled off something in what I think was Cantonese, collected the money, and returned to the kitchen.

My head swiveled to Henry the moment the double doors rocked to a close. "You didn't have to call him that."

"I'm sure he's heard worse. Besides, you know his name?"

"No, but 'waiter' would've sufficed." I realized from the looks of the other patrons that my voice was steadily rising.

"Whoa, easy there, *shiksa*." Henry held up his hands defensively. "I don't know if you've noticed, but this is New York. Everybody hates everybody else here."

I exhaled thinly, trying to rein in my anger. "That doesn't make it right."

His resolve seemed to break the longer I kept eye contact. Finally, Henry lapsed into a fit of quiet, nervous laughter. "What kind of girl *are* you?"

"The kind of girl who'll leave you with the bill if you don't stop acting like a Neanderthal. And I *do* know how to use chopsticks, thanks, but I hope you know I'm not obligated to prove that to you."

"Fine." There was something simmering just beneath the surface of Henry's expression as he sullenly went back to his chop suey. I ate, too, but our conversation had soured my appetite. My thoughts were dominated by a litany of better uses for my time. I could've spent the evening tangled up with some gorgeous Regency-era bachelor—provided he really was single this time. Stupid, stupid parsnip jam. Why would you eat it when you could have perfectly nonracist strawberry?

I let out a sigh of frustration. Henry looked up from his food.

"Listen," he said in a small voice. "You can just go if you want. These people know me. I'll pick up the tab."

"A promise is a promise, but I do think it's a good idea if I go." I was already counting out a dollar and twenty-six cents from my Kairos-appointed allowance when the door to the kitchen opened and our waiter returned with a pair of plain chopsticks, setting them on a cloth napkin between the two of us.

"Thanks," Henry said flatly. He slumped, chin on a knuckle as he played with his chop suey. He wouldn't look at me.

Dammit. How had Henry managed to make me feel like the villain in this situation? He was the one being a racist, presumptive jerk. I tried to drum up some excuse for him—he was a product of his time after all—but that didn't make it better.

"Well, what're you waiting for? Get on your high horse and get out of here," Henry muttered.

I should've walked out on him then, but I didn't.

At first, Henry feigned disinterest as I used the chopsticks to pluck a piece of chicken and eat it, but as I continued, his attention slowly migrated my way. His eyes widened. He reached out a hand, mouth forming a question before his eyes knitted together in stubborn resolution. His fingers closed into a fist.

Without a word, Henry went back to pushing food around his plate at a furious pace.

In spite of everything, I smiled. "Do you want me to teach you how to use them?"

There was a long pause. His fork clanked against the table. "Yeah, okay."

I took his fingers and started to shape them into the right position. Henry had musician's hands—long and elegant but hardened from regular abuse. His left hand was particularly rough. "You play?"

"Violin." He held the chopsticks easily enough, but when it came time to manipulate them, he struggled.

"Just use your middle finger to open them up. How long have you played?"

"Before I could read." There was distraction in his voice. He bit the inside of his cheek as he tried to do as he was told, face lighting up when he seized a slice of chicken. His triumphant smile was short-lived, though, as was his grip. As the piece slipped farther and farther, he raced to eat it. "Ma had plans for me to play professionally, but I'm not—"

The morsel dangled above him, dripping sauce on his chin. Henry flexed the chopsticks and the chicken dropped. He slurped it up, chewing smugly, like a cat with a mouthful of canary.

"I feel more cultured already." He preened before shifting his grip so that he held the chopsticks like ice picks. He stabbed the next piece and brought it to his mouth. "But this might be a little more efficient."

I tried to keep a straight face. "If we're talking about efficiency, you could just eat it with your hands."

"Come on, that's just barbaric." He wiped his chin on a wrist.

"And stabbing isn't?"

He thought it over, weighing invisible pros and cons with a chopstick as he chewed.

"No." Henry stabbed another piece for emphasis. "But it's more satisfying."

So maybe I would finish the date with Henry after all. He wasn't irredeemable, just in desperate need of some sensitivity training—and he wasn't hard to look at it either. Definitely the type of person who became more attractive with familiarity. I picked up my fork and speared some vegetables. "So, what type of music do you play?"

He cracked a shy grin, eyes flitting back to his plate. "That's a goofy question."

"How so?"

"Let me ask you this: What sounds do you make with your voice?" To my surprise, he kept using the chopsticks, silently mouthing the instructions I'd given him earlier. He tried to pick up a clump of sticky rice, but it fell with a splat against the plate.

I wasn't sure how to answer. "All of them, I guess."

He finally settled on picking up a single grain, studying it. "Same goes for a violin. My friends and I play *freilech*, sometimes. Weddings, mostly, as a favor to those who've been good to us. But people with money aren't too interested in that kind of music. They want Vitali, Bach. Old white men want to listen to older, deader white men."

"Didn't you say you weren't good at anything?" I helped myself to more rice and vegetables, though my eyes never left him.

"Trust me, I'm not." Henry tried a few more clumsy bites before he spoke again. "Say, can I ask you something?"

"You just did, didn't you?"

He swallowed, giving a dismissive wave of a chopstick. "Hey, I'm being serious for once. What do you want out of life?"

I faltered. "I'm not sure what you mean."

"Don't play coy. You know exactly what I mean. Every broad does," he said, staring down at his food. "It's usually a picket fence upstate. If she's ambitious, not too hard on the eyes, it's one of those new penthouse suites like they're building on Park Avenue. It's two kids, a girl and a boy, and diamonds on your anniversary. You get what I'm saying?"

The front door opened, spilling a cascade of dry leaves across the floor. A quartet of ratty-looking bohemians shrugged out of their coats as they placed their orders for chop suey. With a deep, stabilizing breath, I tried to gather my thoughts. "I guess I'm tired of fighting. I want something simple. Something real. Something easy."

He was silent for a long time after that. The bohemians were seated. Once they thawed, their corner of the restaurant filled with raucous laughter and cigarette smoke.

"Ada." Something about Henry's smile was sad. "Look. You seem like a swell gal, for a shiksa. You're pretty and you're not completely hollow headed, even if you're lousy at chess. But I'm not the guy you're looking for. In fact, if I were you, I'd make a point to never see me again."

I nodded slowly. The sting that normally accompanied these sorts of speeches was strangely absent. If anything, I felt numb. Henry was just another stranger from another time, another place. I'd disappear from his life and he would grow old and die long before I ever set foot in Kairos. It was strange to think about.

"I understand." It was the same tone I used when I explained to hopeful customers why their mortgage application was denied. Calm. Even. Professional. I even gave him a gracious smile as I rose from the table with the money for our meal in hand. "Thank you for the evening, Henry. I hope your career as a violinist goes well."

A blast of cool autumn wind threatened to blow off my cloche as I left. The late afternoon sky was tinged with pink. I had no idea how long dinner had taken, so I wandered to a nearby alleyway and checked my corsage. The timer flashed: 3:25. Over three hours until my chauffeur would arrive at Washington Square to pick me up. I sighed, leaning against smoke-stained brick.

While I wasn't particularly hurt by Henry's words, they were baffling. The date had gone bad so abruptly. Our conversation ran in circles in my mind, around and around like the horses in Ms. Little's carousel. A perfume advertisement plastered on the opposite wall caught my eye.

The young woman in the ad wasn't dressed too differently from me, in a sack dress and cardigan, but the clothes accentuated her thinner, more androgynous frame. Maybe that was why. Yes, Henry had called me pretty, but so had Ms. Little. It was a hollow compliment filled with hidden conditions. Even someone as unpolished as Henry probably had the good sense not to call a girl fat to her face.

Well, my love of Oreos was a lot stronger than my love of fitting into a size twelve. Maybe a trip to the Baroque period was in order. I might've struck out on my first two outings, but Rubens seemed like my kind of guy.

I walked to the corner. As a wave of Model Ts slowly puttered by, I planned a hypothetical late dinner with Teddy. A bright-yellow taxi rolled up to the sidewalk. I gave a reflexive smile, a polite refusal on my lips, when the back-seat window cranked down.

My stomach did a flip.

5

"Now, what's a nice girl like you doing in a time like this?"

Kairos hadn't had to do a lot to Sam to bring him up to the fashion standards of the day. Idly, I wondered if the seersucker suit was from his private collection—and if it wasn't, how in the world Wardrobe had managed to get one in his size on such short notice. But regardless of who was responsible, I had to admit it was a clever choice. The blue stripe of the material was a near match for his eyes.

He leaned one massive arm over the cab door, grinning at me in a self-satisfied way that I had to remind myself wasn't endearing anymore. I didn't dignify him with an answer.

"Aw, c'mon, sugar. That was a pretty good line. At least give me a smile." He glanced down the street. "Don't know where you're headed, but why don't you hop in? The meter's running."

"It's not too far away. I can walk." I could feel my stockings slowly rolling their way down my knees, but I couldn't dare touch them. Not in front of Sam. "Besides, I wouldn't want to keep you from your appointment."

"Appointment?" he echoed before nodding in recognition. "Oh that. Let's just say she wasn't my type. And if you don't mind me being a mite forward, if you're standing here, maybe your date wasn't exactly up to your standards either."

Sparing a glance behind me, I half expected to see Henry emerge from the restaurant. The street was crowded with unfamiliar faces. "I guess not."

"C'mon, Ada." Sam slid his bulk over. "For old time's sake. Promised you lunch, didn't I?"

"It's a little past lunch, I think."

"Then I'll buy you dinner."

I puffed my cheeks, buying myself some time to think of another excuse. "No. I can't, sorry. Teddy would be furious."

"Only if he finds out." Sam gave a diabolical chuckle. "Boy's still keeping you in line, huh? How is he?"

"Teddy's all right." I was hoping a short answer would end the pleasantries, but Sam just looked at me expectantly. "He's working for Kairos, actually."

He nodded. "Thought I might have seen him when I checked in. What department?"

"Hair and Makeup." I waved a hand over my face. "He was my stylist today."

"That's a relief. I was gonna have a few choice words if he was working in Wardrobe." His gaze dipped down to take in my outfit, lingering a little too long on the hem of my skirt. "I think a nun's habit would've been more provocative."

"Gee, you sure know how to make a girl feel special." Somehow, I managed to sound annoyed despite the telltale warmth spreading across my face. I shifted my weight, unsure if he was enjoying the view or if he could see that my stockings were slipping. "Look, Sam, I'm not sure what you're up to, but this isn't the time. I just got out of a bad date. All I really want to do is go home and eat my feelings."

"Sounds like fun." He extended his hand to me through the open window, expression softening. "Why don't you let me make it up to you?"

"What?"

"Seems a shame to let some no-account loser ruin your whole evening. C'mon." Sam patted the seat beside him. "I'll show you a good time. Maybe we'll find out why they call it the Roaring Twenties, huh?"

I hesitated.

It was a terrible idea, but the temptation was there. I'd seen Sam more in the past two weeks than I had the past two years and, perhaps against my better judgment, wanted to know how the time had treated him.

Moreover, I wanted to know what his game was. While I seriously doubted Teddy's theory that my ex was behind the break-in at my apartment, I did have to admit it wasn't totally unfounded. Sam had never been without an ulterior motive—a gleeful devilishness that I had always thought was more cavalier than malicious—and the coincidences behind our chance meeting were stacking up fast.

"All right." I opened the cab door and sat down. Despite the cool weather, the air inside felt uncomfortably warm. "But I've only got about three hours before I'm due back at Washington Square."

"You have my word."

I wasn't sure if I was ready to believe him or not, but at that point, my curiosity outweighed my concern.

Sam nodded at the front seat. "Driver, we're ready."

The car lurched forward, reentering the sluggish flow of traffic. Briefly, I made eye contact with our cab driver—a skittish-looking man who hid his red hair under a driver's cap—but it seemed like he was trying particularly hard not to eavesdrop. I searched for a seat belt only to remember they weren't mandatory yet. "Sorry, by the way. About before, in Little's office. You caught me at a bad time."

"I gathered." Though Sam draped a casual arm over the back of the seat, he was working the ring on his right hand in circles. He always did that when he was nervous. "Gonna guess that date didn't end as planned either."

"My 'eligible bachelor' turned out to be not as eligible as we thought. His lover threw a pot of spoiled chicken stock at me."

"Oh." Sam worked his jaw. "Yeah, reckon that'd do it."

The restaurant grew smaller and smaller behind us. Rows of laundry fluttered on lines stretched between buildings, dark shadows against the jeweled sky.

I cleared my throat. "So, I guess you're single again."

"Yeah." He stared down at his ring, straightening it. "Penny got the farmhouse."

My stomach dropped. "Oh, Sam. Your mother's farm. I'm so sorry."

It was strange to think that at one point, that farmhouse was almost ours.

"Don't be. Ain't the worst thing I lost in all this." He looked out the window. "If anything, I'm the one who ought to be sorry."

The last remnants of Chinatown had disappeared completely before I spoke again. "Why are you here?"

"Told you before."

"Yes, in that pithy one-liner double-talk you're so fond of," I snapped. "I wrote your speeches, Sam. I know bullshit when I hear it. Why are you really here? In 1922 New York?"

His shoulders sank with a deep exhale.

"Thought it was time for me to move on. But with my schedule, and my age, dating's been hard. Kairos fixes at least one of those problems. A whole evening out in just a couple minutes. Time travel is something else." He gave me some curious side-eye. "What about you?"

I couldn't tell him. The seat pulled at my skin like adhesive as I fidgeted. "I think I told you once about my grandmother."

He nodded. "The one you were named after, rest her soul."

My smile betrayed me. I hadn't expected him to remember such a small detail, though I should have. He'd always been good at making someone feel like they were the center of his entire universe. I guess it was a necessary skill for a politician. "Maybe she was right after all. About why all my relationships end in disasters. I was born in the wrong time."

"Maybe we both were." Sam thumbed his ring again.

"Really." I yanked at the tops of my stockings through my skirt discreetly. "Where do you think do you belong?"

His eyes rolled upward in thought. "Well, don't know if I belong there, but I think I'd have an awful lot of fun in old Vegas. Say what you want, but the mob understood class."

"I shouldn't be surprised," I said around a laugh. "That sounds just like you."

The corner of his mouth quirked in a smile that turned bitter-sweet as he looked at me. "Where do you think you'll end up?"

"Oh, well," I began, at a loss as to how to answer my own question. "I'm not sure. I'll know when I find it."

It was as though the words knocked the wind out of him. He settled back in his seat, breathing shallowly. A bead of sweat dripped from his hairline.

"Soon as I saw you in Little's office, I knew I was only kidding myself," he said, voice hoarse. "I thought I could just say good-bye, but—you, with somebody else. It'll kill me. I can't move on. I don't know if I ever will."

"Sam." Was I pleased or nauseated by his confession? "No. If you're looking to start over, you're about two years too late."

A single window—front seat, passenger side—had been cracked open, but the tepid breeze that passed through smelled of exhaust belched from passing cars. Sam took a handkerchief and dabbed at his forehead. "Better check your watch. I'm not two years too late. I'm about ninety years too early."

"You're being ridiculous."

"You know what's ridiculous?" There was a bite to his tone as he stuffed the handkerchief back in its pocket. "A girl going back a hundred years in search of a beau who's probably gonna choke on a goldfish with a flagpole up his ass, when she's got somebody right here. Somebody who loves her. Somebody who'd do anything for her. Even chase her across time."

"Maybe we have gone back in time, because I've definitely heard this story before, and I know how it ends." It hurt to see him flinch at my words, but I knew I had to stand my ground. "You made your choice."

"Adaliah, I am *sorry*." He reached for my hand but I jerked it away. His fingers curled closed, drifting back to his lap. "You were right. You were always right, you know, 'bout everything. But I was scared. No matter how much you love somebody, throwing away everything for 'em is a hard thing to do—"

"Unless you've got nothing to lose," I finished. It was a hollow victory to see Sam blink away tears. Soon I was blinking them away, too, the world outside the cab's windows turning to dripping oil paints. "Damn it. We can't do this. Things have changed too much."

"Can't we try?" he whispered.

The cab was pulling up to a tall building framed by the dappled hues of Central Park. It was like a fairy tale palace in the middle of Fifth Avenue. Its many windows and pearl-green roof glistened like a jewel box in the last lights of the day.

He reached for my hand again. "Please? Just a couple of hours. You deserve a lot more than whatever disappointment that sad sack doled out tonight. Let me do this. One night."

I tried to formulate a response, some reason to refuse him, but the stifling air of the taxi had turned my thought process to mush. His hand dwarfed mine.

"One night," he said again. He leaned closer, his deep voice so low that it registered in my core like the thump of bass on the dance floor. "And if you can so much as remember that boy's name in the morning, I'll never bother you again."

I shivered.

This was insane.

It was reckless.

And it was easy.

"Okay." I exhaled as the car came to a stop beneath the palace's awning. "Okay. One night."

Before I could react, he kissed my cheek. The world paused,

hanging on my halted breath. Stunned, I giggled reflexively, but it felt like it was coming from someone else.

Sam scrambled from the back seat, nearly hip checking a valet out of the way in the process. With a curled lip, the uniformed man backed off, lingering awkwardly by the gilded double doors.

The rush of cold air almost stole my breath as Sam held the car door for me. The color of early evening settled over him, painting the laugh lines at his eyes—creases I'd put there myself years before, when things were easy.

"Welcome to the Plaza Hotel," he murmured against my neck as I stepped out onto the pavement. "Let's go. The concierge has been expecting us."

Maybe we really could go back.

The hotel suite removed any lingering doubt that Sam hadn't known exactly what was going to happen that night. A fire glowed in the hearth. Tiger lilies, my favorite, covered the marble mantelpiece. A matching bouquet rested on the baby grand tucked away in the corner. White packages topped with turquoise satin bows overflowed the tufted settee and a pair of wingback chairs.

Sam had always been lavish with his gifts—especially for me, and especially when he was sorry.

His reflection grinned at me from the art nouveau mirror over the fireplace. With the *click* of the door behind us, he looked cartoonishly devious, as though he might swallow the key. "Like the arrangements? Not exactly easy to find here, but I think it was worth it."

I took off my cloche. Between it and the humidity of the taxi, my curls had turned to frizz. "Who did you bribe?"

Some of the smugness drained from his face. "You're killing me, Ada. The flowers came honestly. All this came honestly."

Scrunching my hair up did little to revitalize it. I sighed and threw the hat onto the entryway table. "I meant about Kairos. Whose palm did you grease to find out where I was going? Ms. Little doesn't seem the type."

He held up his hands defensively. "You know they keep their mouths shut over there. Terms of service and all."

"Then how? You can't expect me to believe you just so happened to be driving by that particular street corner, at that particular time, out of all the times and all the street corners in New York City."

"Stranger things have happened, haven't they?" He shrugged out of his seersucker jacket. Giving it a cursory glance, he beat the dirt off it before hanging it on a rack by the door. "You know, it's funny. This whole time travel dating thing's awful convenient, but it sure does take the magic out of chance happenings. Like when I met you."

With his outermost layer gone, I could tell that Sam was still every bit the oversized brute I'd met in my second year of law school during my internship at the offices of St. Laurent & Broux. A former golden boy gone to seed, Sam had never really adjusted to a life that didn't involve loading up on carbs before a game. His body was a knot of muscle that hadn't disappeared; it was just buried beneath years of sinful excess. Me and my food-blog-inspired midnight binges hadn't helped matters. And judging from the generous swell of Sam's belly that I didn't recall, the divorce hadn't either.

"I don't think there was anything 'chance' about us." My gaze finally met his. I was fairly sure I saw his cheeks deflate, like he had been holding his breath while I was inspecting him. Sweet, but Sam was a little bit past sucking it in. "You were in a bad marriage. If it hadn't been me, it would've been someone else."

"Now that isn't true. I wasn't some common philanderer looking for a side girl, no matter what the papers said." He leaned heavily on the back of the settee. "Ada, a fella thinks he knows what love is until he falls headfirst into it. I love you. And I miss you."

The silence grew so clear I found myself picking out the punch-lines from a radio show someone was listening to on the next floor.

I wanted to say that I felt the same way. That I missed Sam—big, wonderful Sam, generous Sam, Sam who was secretive and underhanded, Sam who always had something up his sleeve and was never without his bag of dirty tricks. And in a way, I *had* missed him. I missed how well he knew me, how safe and understood he made me feel.

But in that moment, standing in front of him, I wasn't sure if I *could* miss him, or just the things that he brought to our relationship. To miss Sam—to love Sam—would be to acknowledge the hurt and fear and heartbreak I'd harbored over the past two years and to accept them as necessary. That wasn't something I could do. Not yet.

I couldn't miss Sam.

I could only miss that he was easy.

The silence whittled away his smile until there was hardly anything left of it. He gestured to the presents spread out on the furniture. "C'mon, I wanna see your face when you open these."

The bow on the largest package fell away easily as I picked it up. Rose-scented perfume rolled from pale-pink tissue paper. Nestled inside was a dress.

The handkerchief hemline uncurled and pooled on the floor in soft chiffon and silk the color of peacocks. A smaller box revealed a matching feathered fascinator. Both were detailed with tiny gold beads and amber-colored stones that seemed to pulse in the ebb and flow of the firelight.

He looked at me with hopeful eyes. "You like it?"

I held the dress against me. Unlike the clothes Wardrobe had provided, this was not a sack. It was sleeveless, with thin, beaded straps. The back was scandalously low, even by modern standards, with nothing but a cape of gauzy material to lend me modesty. "You don't think I'll stand out too much in it?"

He picked up another box and sat in the space it had occupied. "As a matter of fact, I was hoping you would."

The next gift was a pair of silk opera gloves. Then stockings and a garter belt that provoked a blush from me and a darkly mischievous laugh from Sam. The rest contained jewelry—a choker and string after string of pearls dotted with pea-sized insets.

"Sam." I looked up at him, almost begging. "This must have cost a fortune."

"Yeah." He leaned back, arms folded over his belly. "But it's worth it. You know, I always saw a lot of myself in Jay Gatsby. Just a nobody chasing after unattainable women by throwing money at 'em till they can't help but trip over it."

"Or they're buried by it," I muttered, unable to help myself. "You know I never cared about the money."

He looked away and toyed with his ring. "Maybe not, but you were awful quick to take it when it was offered to you."

"I didn't see any other way." Closing the distance between us, I sat down on the arm of his chair. "I was a scared college kid with lots of debt and no career prospects, suddenly thrust into the public eye."

"True enough." The gentle weight of his hand on my hip coaxed me toward his lap but the flutter in my stomach told me that was dangerous. "You gotta forgive me, Ada. When the media pushes a story for so long, sometimes you start to believe it yourself."

"I know, Sam." I smoothed the pale-brown gingham of his bow-tie, ignoring the tears starting to blur my vision. "I know that all too well."

The far-off applause of the radio show gave way to the soaring sound of a big band. One of Sam's wingtips tapped to the rhythm absently in the ensuing silence.

That gave me an idea. "When was the last time you danced?"

He blinked in surprise, his eyebrows rising and falling in thoughtful waves. "I might have done the Electric Slide for the policeman's charity ball three months ago . . ."

"Okay, let me rephrase: When was the last time you danced, and it *wasn't* for a publicity stunt?"

Sam could see exactly where this was going as he pushed himself from the chair, wincing as his elbow gave a sharp crack. "That would be three years ago, at the townhouse. With you."

"That's what I thought." I worked the heel of one of my Mary Janes, kicking it off playfully.

With a wicked grin, Sam stooped to help me with the other. "It was your birthday, and we finally got around to those foxtrot lessons I'd promised you."

"It looked so much easier in *Dirty Dancing*—" I didn't get a chance to finish that thought, rendered speechless as I felt Sam hook his thumb beneath the roll of my stocking. I remembered how to breathe one inch at a time as the fabric slipped down my leg.

"You been fighting with these old things all evening, sugar," he growled slyly as he set to work on the other leg. His hands lingered on my calf just a moment too long, but I didn't exactly mind. "But as I recall, your dancing career came to a tragic end when you tried to two-step right through the coffee table."

"I might have come out of retirement last week." I cleared my throat, hoping it would return to its normal range. "I waltzed with my first Kairos date."

Sam's moustache twitched with a suppressed laugh. "Mr. Chicken Stock?"

I winced. "That's the one. He wasn't too impressed with my footwork either."

"That's only because you've never been taught." As he pulled me to my feet, Sam's fingers laced through mine. His other hand moved to the small of my back. "Of course, it might be a little more appropriate if I taught you how to Charleston."

"You know how?" I stifled a giggle.

"Not really, but I've seen enough to get the gist of it. There's a lot of head bobbing," he said as he took me through a few steps. Despite their simplicity, I found myself a beat off, dragged around more like a rag doll than a dance partner. "Posture, Ada. Keep your head up."

I threw my shoulders back and feigned a haughty expression. "And remind me why you went for football in college instead of dance?"

"Two reasons." Sam cracked a wry smile at me as he corrected my hand placement. "One: they didn't offer full scholarships for show choir. Two: Penny wouldn't have been caught dead with a theater kid."

My eyebrows clenched. "You know, most women would be thrilled to have a partner who would take them out dancing."

"Yeah, but Penny isn't most women," he said with a deep sigh, but he couldn't hide the grin that followed. "She said it was embarrassing watching a three hundred and fifty–pound man shimmy like a ninety-pound ballerina."

I tripped my way through another box step. "I prefer to think she just didn't like getting upstaged."

Sam rumbled out a laugh and pulled me in closer. "Why don't we pick up the waltz later? You go get changed, and we'll get a nice dinner. Got tickets for *Seventh Heaven*—"

"You really did plan a whole evening, didn't you?" I beamed up at him, but some of my enthusiasm faded as I started to add up the time. Thirty minutes to get here and thirty to get back. Twenty to get dressed. At least an hour and a half for dinner, knowing Sam. And a show on top of that? It wasn't adding up. "But—"

"But?" Sam pulled away, looking at me expectantly.

"The time. I've got maybe an hour and a half left."

"Right. The time. I was waiting until after dinner to ask you this, but—" His smile dimmed but wasn't completely extinguished, flickering between sentimentality and a tragic kind of hope. "Let's not go back."

I stared. "What?"

"We could stay here in the twenties," he whispered, a desperate laugh threatening to swallow his words. "Who needs a future when you've got a past? They won't find us. There's a statute of limitations on temporal crimes."

"An expired temporal visa is a class one felony," I hissed, mind racing. "That's ten to fifteen years in the pen, easy. I've never even jaywalked before, how can I—"

"If you're going to do something, don't be half-assed about it, I always say." The joviality in his voice drained the longer he looked at me. "It ain't as hard as you think it is. I've been gone for two days now. The feds have more pressing concerns than a couple of small timers like us."

"Two days." I sank into the settee with the realization. The radio upstairs still played, a single trumpet wailing forlornly. "You've been gone for two days."

He crossed his arms. "Look, I know you're upset—"

I raised a hand. "No, I'm not. I'm a little overwhelmed by this, that's all. I was willing to let bygones be bygones tonight, for old time's sake. But running away with you. Forever. That's different. I can't just forget what happened."

"I'm not asking you to." He brushed a strand of hair from my face. "I'm asking you to let me make it up to you. Let me give you the life you wanted."

"But here? In the twenties?" I gestured to our opulent surroundings. "In a few years, all of this goes away. The Great Depression, Sam? Remember?"

"Of course I remember." He cupped my chin and brought my gaze up to meet his. "That's the point. We know it's gonna happen. We can outrun it."

"What?"

"Economics, sugar," he said. "The Depression didn't hit everywhere at once, and not all of 'em got it as hard as the States. France doesn't feel it until the early thirties, and comparatively, they do all right. Unemployment is pretty on par with modern rates."

I nodded slowly. "So, we flee to France."

He gave a grim smile. "Told you I'd take you to Paris eventually."

"Fine." Pulling his hand from my face, I traced the deep lines of his palm until a second—and much larger—concern struck me. "But what about the Nazis?"

"What about 'em?"

"Paris falls to the Nazis in, what, 1940? Forty-one?" I lowered his hand. "We can't stay there."

"Already ahead of you. You can take your pick: both Sweden and Ireland proclaim neutrality during the war. Or, heck, we can just head back to the United States by then. Lord knows the government won't be interested in drafting a fat old bastard like me."

"I see," I murmured, still not entirely convinced.

He studied me for a moment, the last remnant of optimism fading. "It's hard throwing your whole life away, isn't it?"

"That's not fair. I gave you a lot more time to make up your mind," I shot back. He recoiled, fingers drifting away from mine. I sighed. "Dinner. Let me think about it over dinner."

"Of course," he said. "If I had my druthers, I'd give you all the time in the world."

"Thank you." Gathering up Sam's gifts, I made my way to the bathroom. Closing the door with a heel, I lurched to the sink, nails gripping either side of the basin.

I felt nauseated with indecision. This was everything and nothing that I wanted; a beautiful and surreal nightmare that I could wake from if I wanted to, but with the knowledge I could never dream it again.

Though I wanted to cry, the makeup staring from my reflection stopped me. I touched my cheek, outlining the rouge circles Teddy had applied. If I stayed, this would be the last tangible evidence of my brother—and it was something as fragile and ephemeral as makeup. I hadn't even told him that I planned to emigrate, hoping for and yet dreading the day that Ms. Little would find a match for me that didn't involve being someone's mistress.

Again.

I turned the tap on, then off again, unsure if the water was safe to drink, before finally deciding against it. Taking down the remains of my faux bob, I dampened my hands and finger combed my hair. There wasn't much I could do with it at this point, so I rolled it into a high bun and shoved a few bobby pins in to hold it.

I shrugged out of the ugly sweater Kairos had lent me before I began to pick my way through Sam's gifts. My hands acted of their own accord, layering on silk and chiffon, clasping strings of pearls and donning dangling earrings. Twenty minutes passed before I recognized the woman giving me a critical once-over in the mirror as myself.

It was so much easier to face the problem from behind a mask.

I heard a distant knock.

"That'll be the last of the deliveries," Sam called from the sitting room. "What's a reasonable tip in this day and age?"

I felt a second wave of guilt at the thought of yet more gifts from Sam. "A dollar should be more than enough."

The door rattled again. Curious, I peeked out from the bathroom just in time to see Sam jam his wallet back in his jacket.

"Keep your pants on, son," he muttered, a wad of bills in hand as he threw the door open.

A trio of shadows darkened the threshold. Their leader grinned at Sam but there was nothing nice about it—head down, teeth bared like an animal as he flexed his hand around a pair of brass knuckles.

"Evening, pal," Henry said.

6

Before Sam could react, there was a *whip-crack* of metal striking flesh. He staggered backward, a hand pressed to his bloodied mouth.

One of Henry's accomplices—a small hungry-looking man—lunged for the open door in an attempt to get into the room. Forcing the pain from his expression, Sam slammed the door into the man's face. I winced, but Sam only gave a nasty laugh, still pushing. He almost had it closed.

"How did I know I was gonna run into you, Henry?" Though his muscles strained, heels digging into the carpet, Sam wasn't making any more progress. I could only assume the men on the other side were fighting back. "Jehovah's Witnesses were a hell of a lot more insistent back then, weren't they?"

"Wrong faith, Methuselah," Henry grunted.

The phone, Sam mouthed to me. The door shook. He lost an inch. Planting his back against the door, he put all of his weight into another shove. The gap narrowed. *Call for help.*

There was a crack of timber as something was wedged into the doorframe. A baseball bat. Sam tried to force it back out but pulled back just as quickly when the bat smashed his fingers.

"Son of a—" Sam shook the pain from his hand before looking up at me. "Hurry."

I nodded, dropped to a crouch, and worked my way to the settee. Maybe they wouldn't see me.

"He's a monster in a suit," one of them grumbled.

"That's what Tommy said," Henry answered. A moment later he spoke again, voice raised. "I'm gonna level with you, mister. You got something we want. You give it to us, we'll leave you alone. Simple. Or we can keep playing red rover. Your choice."

I couldn't believe what I was hearing. Henry was robbing us. This was the man Ms. Little had set me up with? I was going to have some choice words for the matchmaker if we got out of this in one piece. *Parsnip jam, my pasty white ass.*

Picking up the phone with shaking hands, I dialed 9-1-1, muffling the sound of the rotary clicking back into place with the hem of my dress.

A wave of nausea washed over me. *9-1-1 didn't exist yet.*

Any luck? Sam mouthed, but he knew the answer as soon as we locked eyes. Hope drained from his face. The question that had lingered in the flex of his eyebrows finally solidified into an answer. "Make yourself scarce."

Dropping the phone, I frantically looked for a hiding spot. The sofa was too low to squeeze under. In desperation, I darted across the room and curled up beneath the baby grand, heart thumping in my chest. Sam flashed me a reassuring smile before he steeled himself.

"Tell you what, son," he said, "I'll pay up, but you gotta promise me you'll keep your hands to yourselves. Same goes for your boys. You got that?"

There was a pause before Henry spoke up again. "Yeah, okay. No funny business?"

"No funny business," Sam repeated.

My thoughts raced. Where were the Kairos field agents? They were supposed to intervene in emergencies. I reached for the jeweled corsage at my collar but only touched empty fabric. My stomach flipped.

The sweater. The corsage was still pinned to my sweater, thrown haphazardly over the towel rack in the bathroom. Sam obviously didn't have his if he was a temporal fugitive. Without those, Kairos had no means of detecting any trouble.

With a deep breath, Sam took a step back. The door opened wider, pushed by the tip of the baseball bat. Henry watched, apprehension slowly dawning on his features as Sam meekly reached for the wallet in his jacket before pulling a gun instead. I bit back a surprised shriek.

"Told you he'd be packing heat." Henry's expression was all flat lines, thoroughly unimpressed by the weapon. "Thought you said there'd be no funny business."

"Ain't nothing funny 'bout getting shot," Sam snapped back. "Now, you three hooligans get on back home to your mamas. Find a corner store to knock over, some mailboxes to smash, you hear?"

Henry studied him. A smile twitched at the corner of his mouth. "Do it. I got it coming anyway."

I swallowed painfully, my lungs a vacuum. Sam had done his share of morally dubious things, but I wasn't sure if he had it in him to shoot somebody.

Then again, up until a few minutes ago I hadn't thought he was the type to own a gun either.

We all waited for an answer.

"Go on," Henry said. "Send me to hell. That's where people like me go. Isn't that what they told you in Sunday school?"

Sam sucked in a shallow breath. He braced the gun with both hands but didn't pull the trigger. The barrel slowly lowered. "I can't."

A moment passed.

Henry shook his head, expression piteous. "C'mon, boys. I've seen enough."

With that, he closed the distance with a wide swing so obvious that even a man Sam's size could sidestep it, but it had only been a distraction. The heel of Henry's shoe came down hard on Sam's foot. Sam stifled a howl of pain and threw a fist into the smaller man's chin, following with a right cross with the pistol's barrel that Henry had no hope of countering.

Henry stumbled, eyes unfocused. His two friends rushed the room and swarmed Sam. The first swing of the baseball bat missed Sam's head by a hair's breadth, landing on his shoulder instead with a loud *smack*. The smallest of the trio piled onto Sam's back and went for his eyes. Sam grabbed the boy by a thin wrist and threw him to the floor.

That was the opening Henry was looking for. Sam staggered back as cold brass made impact with his jaw.

Then the man with the baseball bat ended it.

Sam's eyes rolled closed as he crumpled. The gun clattered to the floor.

I screamed. The robbers whirled around at the noise. I covered my mouth a moment too late, willing my sobs to come out silently. No one saw me. The radio upstairs played "Ain't We Got Fun."

"It's a game of aggression, Pops. Not dollies," Henry said mournfully as he looked down at Sam's prone form, stooping to pick up the gun. "He won't be out long, so we have to work fast. Pick him clean. Make him comfortable. We're not here to rub him out. You listening to me, Jake?"

The smallest one—Jake, apparently—had already grabbed Sam's wallet. He leafed through the bills with a low whistle before pocketing the whole thing. "You got it, boss."

The two accomplices grabbed Sam's unconscious form by the wrists. Reflexively, I shut my eyes, but the sound of his body being dragged across the suite was somehow worse than seeing it. I could still picture his slack, empty expression, like that of a body in a morgue. As I heard the bedroom door shut, I muttered a silent prayer that Henry was right, and Sam was only unconscious.

"Ada? Where are you?" Henry called, but I didn't dare answer. A beat later, he gave a deep sigh and pinched the bridge of his nose, muttering something under his breath before taking another look around the room. "Dammit. Tommy said she was here."

Every muscle tensed. My hand snaked through the legs of the piano to grab at the bench, testing its weight in my grip. It was heavy for its size, but I thought I could use it as a shield if I needed to.

"I heard you scream." Henry's oxfords drew closer to the piano. My hand tightened around the leg of the bench, edging it closer. He dropped to a knee. I clenched my teeth and took a sharp breath, braced for the worst.

But nothing happened. Henry observed me with a sympathetic expression. A nasty purple bruise in the shape of a half-formed gun barrel was already blooming near his left eye.

No brass knuckles. No gun.

"Hey," he said, voice tellingly hoarse. He cleared his throat and tried again. "Hey, you don't have to cry anymore. He's not going to hurt you."

I stared, fingers falling slack. My stomach felt completely, achingly hollow.

"Yeah, yeah." His gaze dropped as he ran a hand through his hair. Another curl popped loose. "I told you that you probably shouldn't see me again. But, well, I didn't say anything about me seeing you, yeah?"

I didn't respond.

He sighed. "Look, I'm sorry you had to see that. But Tommy just watched that drugstore cowboy pick up a sack of cash from Al Kingston himself."

I had no idea what Henry was talking about. "Who?"

"Tommy. You know, red hair, shifty eyes." He looked at me like I was stupid. "Your cab driver? We're pals. He keeps an ear to the ground for me."

Henry offered me a hand but I ignored it, using the piano bench to pull myself up. My arms felt like they were made of pudding. "And Al Kingston?"

"You really are new in town, huh?" Henry's disbelieving look flattened at my lack of a response. "Let's just say he's not a very nice guy. So, you gonna thank me for saving you from that creep or are we just gonna sit here and give each other moon eyes all night?"

"Get out," I spat.

He blinked twice, before pretending to clean out an ear with his pinky. "You wanna run that by me again? I'm a touch deaf in this ear."

"I said, get out." My raised voice trembled with the threat of more tears. "We thought you were robbing us. I don't know what your 'friend' saw, but you've got no right to come in here and gang up on poor Sam."

"What?" Henry's nostrils flared as he glanced at the bedroom door meaningfully. "You actually *like* this clown?"

The question made my stomach flutter with uncertainty. "Well, *like* might be too strong a word, but I don't think he deserved a baseball bat to the head."

Henry quirked a half smile. "Doll, we all deserve a bat to the head for something."

"That's not funny." Moving toward the bedroom, I came face-to-face with the man who had knocked Sam out.

No longer in the heat of a fight, I could make out the pockmarks on his face from acne scarring and realized he was barely a man at all—nineteen if he was a day. He looked right past me. "Got him all tied up and gagged. He's starting to come around."

"Thanks, Schlomo," Henry answered. "You wanna get back to that? I need to straighten this dame out."

Schlomo nodded, then slipped back into the bedroom. We were alone again.

Henry took two stiff steps to a wingback chair and practically collapsed into it. His hands went to the tie around his neck, undoing it in one well-practiced motion. "You know what it looks like, right? You've got to."

"No." I crossed my arms. "No, I'm afraid I don't."

"This Sam character climbs into Tommy's cab right out of Kingston's place and doesn't even have the sense to count his dough in private. Then he picks you up, right after you've been seen with me," he explained. His typical veneer of cynicism fell away for a moment, revealing a sincere desperation. "He knew my name. He was expecting me. Don't you get it? The gun, Ada. He was paid to kill you, to send me a message."

I rubbed at my temples. "First of all, calm down. We had dinner. It's not like we were engaged. I sincerely doubt that I matter enough to you to end up on somebody's hit list. Second, that would be a very long con, considering I've known Sam for almost five years now."

Henry peered up at me dubiously with his good eye; the other was swollen completely shut. "You got some history?"

"No, I just like to climb into taxis with complete strangers," I snapped. "Of course we do. His name is Samson St. Laurent. He's my ex."

"Ex? Ex-what?" he asked, giving a derisive snort. "If he had actually pulled the trigger on that gun, he might've been an ex-person by now."

I wasn't sure if Henry was playing dumb or if it was a term that hadn't been popularized yet in his time, so I decided to play it safe. "I mean that we dated for a while."

Henry's mouth opened but no sound came out for a full five seconds. "I never thought you'd be the type to have a sugar daddy."

"Like I haven't heard that one before." It was a herculean effort to conceal my eye roll until I was in the safety of the bathroom. I unpinned the Kairos brooch from my sweater and placed it on a shoulder strap. Hopefully I wouldn't be in too much trouble with the agency. "Very original. Next thing I know, you'll be telling me he's old enough to be my father."

"You mean he isn't?" Henry leaned against the doorframe, arms crossed, blocking my way out. "My apologies for coming between you two lovebirds, then. You do realize what he does for a living, yeah?"

"He . . ." I worked my jaw, at a loss for a cover story. Somehow, I didn't think telling Henry that Sam was a state senator from the distant future would go over very well. ". . . owns some land down South. A peach farm. Could you move, please?"

"Yeah?" Henry frowned but did step back, following me into the other room. "So, what's he doing making backroom deals with the Kings, then?"

"Would you listen to yourself? Hit lists, backroom deals, baseball bats, and brass knuckles—you sound like something out of a mobster movie." As soon as the words left my mouth, I knew I had made a mistake. Henry's weak smile only confirmed my suspicions. "Oh. Oh god. You're actually a gangster."

"What tipped you off?" Henry's shoulders dropped. "Honestly, I thought you knew. A girl like you doesn't just come on to a guy like me unless she knows."

I tensed as I heard Sam slur from the next room. He was coming around.

"No." I wasn't sure if the feeling in the bottom of my stomach was embarrassment or terror. I was stuck in a hotel room with a gangster. An actual gangster. Flinching, I turned to the bedroom. "No, I had no idea. Listen, I need to check on Sam, we should go—"

Henry held up a hand. "What, does this make me somebody different now? Somebody you should be afraid of? Ada, I came here because I thought you were in trouble."

I didn't look at him, fingers curled around the doorknob. "Forgive me if I'm a little apprehensive. Gangsters don't exactly have the best press where I come from."

Without waiting for a reply, I stepped into the bedroom. It was jarring to see Sam thrown unceremoniously across the canopy bed, the velvet curtains torn from their grommets to serve as impromptu binding for his hands and wrists.

Jake and Schlomo were perched on a small ottoman at the foot of the bed, each clutching a handful of cards. They'd helped them-selves to a now half-empty box of chocolates, undoubtedly another gift from Sam if the tiger lily attached to its lid was any indication. The two froze as they saw me.

"Untie him," I said in a tone that sounded braver than I felt. Neither of them moved, so I climbed onto the bed to do it myself.

"Lady, I don't think that's a good idea," Jake said around a mouthful of bonbon. Scooping up the box, he held it toward me, but I wasn't sure if it was an offering or a distraction to keep me from freeing Sam.

"No, thank you," I said, pushing it away. "I don't think you've got anything to worry about. He's been knocked senseless, and he looks like a trussed-up pig."

Sam giggled. "Gonna *feel* like a trussed-up pig after dinner."

Unable to help myself, I smiled. "There you are. That's my Sam."

"And that's my Ada," he mumbled. He winced as he turned his head. "You finally get through to the police?"

Schlomo froze. Jake finished the chocolate with a hard swallow.

While I didn't want to lie to Sam, I was worried that telling him the truth would only make him struggle more. He was in no shape to put up another fight. "Things are going to be fine."

The two grunts visibly relaxed. Jake picked up another candy and popped it in his mouth.

"Guess I really am starting to show my age." Sam groaned, giving a single lethargic wiggle against his bindings. It was useless, and he fell against the bed again with a sigh. "Twenty years ago I would've slobber knocked all three of them punks. I'm sorry, sugar. You really do deserve better."

"Shush. You did the best you could." I dug my nails into the velvet knot over his wrists and tore it loose, then made quick work of the bond at his ankles. "I think you may have a concussion, though. Can you walk?"

"*You* ain't gonna walk tomorrow," he said with a waggle of his eyebrows that might have been suggestive if it wasn't for their independent timing. "Not the first bonk to the noggin I got. I told you I'd show you a good time, so I'm gonna show you a good time."

His arms shook as he pushed himself up. Jake and Schlomo

reeled back in terror for a full five seconds before Sam collapsed on the bed again.

"Soon as I sleep this off," he muttered, eyelids fluttering.

I think we all breathed a sigh of relief.

"A night I won't forget, I promise," I reassured him, but I could feel my smile faltering. "I'm going to go back to Kairos now, Sam. You need medical attention."

"What? No." He floundered on the bed with renewed vigor. "This was my last chance to make things right by you. I'm not gonna mess it up this time."

"You didn't mess anything up." My hand slid across his chest. "We have a whole lifetime ahead of us to make amends."

Sam's breath caught. His eyes were wet and questioning.

"Let's do it," I whispered. A wave of uncertainty washed over me, but I could feel some fledgling sense of happiness in it—or at the very least, a finality to it. "Let's run away together. Let's go to Paris."

He blinked hard and fast. "You mean it?"

"I do." I squeezed his shoulder reassuringly, but I wasn't sure whom I was trying to convince—him or me. "We have to do this right, though. I need to get my affairs back home in order, and you need to see a doctor."

Sam struggled to kiss my hand. "You're killing me, Ada."

"Please. Two weeks." In reality, I had no idea if that was enough time to do everything I would need, but it seemed a good place-holder. "Two weeks and we can start over. I'll meet you at that same street corner, and you can give me that same lame pickup line."

A stray tear rolled down his cheek, darkening the soft cream of the duvet to a dull brown. "Promise me you'll smile this time?"

I nodded.

With a pained grunt, Sam rolled onto his side to face me. I thought he was twisting the ring out of habit until the gold band was pressed into my palm. A trio of diamonds sparkled in the low light.

"Know it's a mite too big for them pretty little fingers," he said, "but maybe you can keep it on a chain until I can buy you a proper one."

The lump in my throat made it hard to speak. "Oh, Sam."

I kissed his forehead.

He exhaled as he settled into the touch, deep and slow. He held me there, thumbs on my jaw and fingers in my hair, and for a moment we didn't need to go back—we had never left.

A heavy exhaustion seemed to settle over him, but he smiled at me regardless. "I love you. Now or in a hundred years."

"Just rest for now," I murmured, standing from the bed. "Things are going to be okay."

Sam slept.

In the parlor, Henry tapped out the rhythm to some unheard melody with his shoe. As I closed the bedroom door behind me, I wasn't sure if the look on his face was fatigue or regret. Maybe both.

"How is he?" he asked.

"I'm not sure." I stood on tiptoe to check my makeup in the mirror over the fireplace. Licking a thumb, I wiped away the faint tracks my eyeliner had left on my cheeks. "He's talking fine, but he wasn't coordinated. I wouldn't trust him to walk right now. He needs to see a doctor."

Henry blew out his cheeks, slumping back against the settee. "Dunno if you can find a doctor who makes house calls at this hour, but if you do, I'll pay for it."

I gave him a quizzical look in the mirror.

"What?" He waved vaguely at the air. "What do you want me to say? 'Sorry for knocking your boyfriend out, give him two aspirins and call me in the morning'?"

I turned to face him. "I'm just surprised, that's all. Didn't think you'd be that concerned for his welfare after the whole he's-working-for-the-Kings conspiracy from earlier."

Henry patted gingerly at his black eye and hissed in pain. "Yeah, well, for the record I'm not. But it's the least I can do, considering."

"Well, that's very magnanimous of you," I said thinly. "But it's not necessary. I'm just going to—"

There was another knock at the door. Staring at the entryway, Henry slipped the brass knuckles from his pocket.

"Who is it?" I called. There was no way in hell I was going to open it blindly after last time.

"This is management," answered a man on the other side. He had that same happily terrified tone of voice I heard Cel use sometimes when she dealt with particularly unnerving customers. I felt a twinge of pity. "There was a noise complaint—ah, a crash, a woman scream-ing? We just wanted to make sure everything is all right."

The little color Henry had drained from his face. He looked at me, breath held, but the sag of his shoulders told me he thought my answer was a foregone conclusion.

It would be a lie to say I didn't think about it. A single word to management and police would be swarming the suite. No more gangsters. More importantly, no more Henry.

"Oh, no. My husband was teaching me how to do the Charleston and I tripped over the coffee table," I said. "But we're fine now. My apologies if we disturbed anyone."

Henry's good eye widened in disbelief.

"Excellent, excellent," the man replied. It sounded as though he was already retreating down the hallway. "Glad to hear you are in good spirits. Do enjoy your stay at the Plaza!"

"Thanks." Henry's head rolled, staring up at the ceiling as he rubbed the bridge of his nose in thought. "I really mean that."

"You can repay me by looking after Sam." I picked up my clutch from the entryway table. "I'm not sure when I'll be back. How long does it take to get to Washington Square from here? Thirty minutes or so?"

"You're funny. Try doubling that."

"What?" I suddenly felt ill. Replaying the taxi ride over, the trip hadn't seemed that long.

"Rush hour traffic," Henry continued. "You'll be lucky to get there in an hour, provided some basket case hasn't caused a five-car pile-up on the way."

"The Model T had to be invented less than, what, two decades ago? How are there already traffic jams?" I snapped open the latch on my purse. There was a small interior pocket—likely meant for loose change—but I thought it would be good for keeping Sam's ring safe.

I had meant it to be a rhetorical question, but Henry's lack of a response gave me time to scrutinize my remark. Had I said too much? Did he know, or at least suspect, that I was a time traveler?

When I looked his way, Henry gave a dim smile, nodding knowingly at the piece of jewelry I was holding. "So that's what easy looks like."

I closed my hand, slipping the ring inside my purse. "Beg your pardon?"

"Our conversation at the Chinese joint," he explained, elbows braced on his knees. His eyes dipped down at his folded hands before meeting mine again. "Diamonds on your anniversary. Those *are* real diamonds, right?"

I scooped up one of my discarded shoes, wiggling my foot into its confines, but I didn't see its match. "I'm sure they are."

"See? Turns out we were talking about the same thing after all." Stretching over the arm of the settee, Henry picked up the second Mary Jane. He held it out with a mock flourish, like a surly Prince Charming, but I wasn't in any kind of mood to play Cinderella. I put on the remaining shoe in silence. "Anyway, the boys can watch Methuselah. A dame like you, *dressed* like you, wandering around the city at night? I'm going with you."

"I can handle myself, thank you." My heels struck the floor hard and fast as I made my way to the door.

"Oh yeah? Which way is Washington Square from here?"

I stopped at the threshold, hoping to come up with an answer.

"It's more than the Village you're new to, huh?" he asked with a wry smile.

"Is it that obvious?" My arms dropped to my sides in defeat. "Okay, fine. But we've got to hurry. I'm expected back by seven."

"I thought we were just hunting for a doctor." He stood. "You got a curfew too?"

"Of sorts, yes."

"Great. Just great." Henry didn't look at me as he stepped outside the suite. "We better take Jake's car, then."

We rounded the corner to the elevator. The crosshatched cage door opened to greet us, folding against the adjacent wall. A man in the Plaza's uniform nodded to us but shied away from Henry, likely to avoid drawing attention to his impressive shiner. "What floor, sir?"

"Ground."

The operator pulled the heavy switch at his side. There was a deep thrum from the walls as we lurched into motion. "Going down."

Four floors passed in relative silence.

I didn't mean to, but I found myself watching Henry in the reflection of the bronze-plated walls surrounding us. When left to his own devices, he curled in on himself, arms crossed, and chin tucked to his chest. He seemed tired.

"You really don't have to come," I reminded him. "You could stay."

"No." He shook the drowse from his head. "I messed this up for you, so I'm going to fix it."

Thirty seconds later, the attendant unlatched the elevator door. Murmuring my thanks, I stepped out but didn't make it far. A bellhop cut me off, sailing past on a wheeled luggage rack before disappearing into a hallway that branched from the main foyer.

It was a busy night. The brassy wail of a trumpet threaded through the hum of conversation. At the concierge desk, a man in a tailcoat rang the service bell once, then with a twitch of his well-oiled moustache, rang it again impatiently. The lady on his arm was in better spirits, cheeks pink from laughter as she snuggled deeply into the dappled fur stole around her shoulders. Old men with unfashionably long beards sat smoking in a circle of armchairs, telling stories, but their discussion lapsed as I passed by.

Suddenly, I was rethinking the choice of wearing the outfit Sam had bought me. While it suited me more than what I'd gotten from Kairos, the figure-hugging dress made me glaringly obvious among the petite flappers draped in loose, flowing lines and fringe.

"Don't worry about them." The close proximity of Henry's voice made my skin buzz. "It's just been a long time since they saw somebody like you."

I nearly backed into Henry as a man in a tuxedo emerged right in front of me from a side entrance obscured by tall potted palms. "A country bumpkin who clearly doesn't know her way around the big city, you mean?"

"No, I—" Henry's eyebrows wrinkled. "You know what? Never mind."

There was more to the conversation than that, I could tell, but any thought of pursuing it disappeared as I glanced through the French doors the man in the tuxedo had exited from. My breath caught.

They opened onto a ballroom, framed by elegant columns and more towering palm fronds. A band was playing. Dancing couples wove past scattered tables set with gleaming cutlery, all beneath an airy skylight window.

"The famous Palm Court," Henry explained. His smile was lukewarm. "Going to guess that's where you'd be right now if I hadn't ruined it for you—dancing the night away."

"I'm not sure about that," I answered. "Knowing Sam, he'd probably overdo it at dinner and spend the rest of the evening in a food coma."

A few servers crisscrossed the restaurant, carrying silver platters topped with steaming dishes from the kitchen. Predictably, there wasn't any alcohol being served—at least, not out in the open. As a tray passed, Henry snatched a cucumber sandwich.

"Speaking of dinner." He took a bite, expression souring as he slowly chewed. After a hard swallow, he opened up the crustless bread to stare at its contents. "Where's the rest of it?"

I laughed. "At least that's one thing we agree on."

Henry looked at me just a beat too long, smile warming, before he wedged the rest of the sandwich in his mouth.

"All right, let's go," he garbled. Before I could react, he took my hand, towing me through the commotion of the lobby. We attracted a few odd or worried stares, but Henry had a way of crowd walking that left us largely unnoticed. I gave a final glance at the Palm Court before Henry pulled me into the chilly October night air.

The valet nodded to me, but as his gaze traced down my arm to my hand linked with Henry's, it was like I became invisible. I hesitated.

"You think that stuffed suit would let a bunch of goons park here?" Henry dropped my hand. "Come on. It's not far. Half a block at most."

"For what it's worth, I think you're too well meaning to be a goon," I said.

"Well, I appreciate the sentiment, but pretty sure that's my job description." Henry kept his eyes ahead. "Wanted: one stupid goon. Tasks include making piss-poor decisions, beating up fat old men, and giving pretty girls the creeps."

"You know, self-loathing doesn't look good on anybody."

"I dunno." He bit the inside of his cheek. "I think it suits me."

I didn't know what to say to that, so we walked on in silence. The cold slowly worked its way through my limbs. I flexed the chill from my fingers, suddenly missing the warmth of Henry's hand. For a moment I contemplated asking for it, but decided it'd send the wrong message.

"So, did he really teach you how to do the Charleston?" Henry looked up at the store display we were passing: a quartet of barebones male mannequins in striped suits and boater hats. "That story you told to management seemed too specific to be a lie."

I tore my eyes away from the store window, the "gift" the stalker had left in my apartment fresh in my mind. "It was the waltz, actually. And I didn't fall over the coffee table. That was another time."

Henry ducked his head, biting back a round of surprised laughter. A single curl bobbed at his forehead, and he immediately scooped it away. "For what it's worth, I'm not too good at dancing either."

"I just don't have the patience for it, I think," I said. "Sam can watch any dance and have it figured out in just a few minutes, but when I try to do that, I end up bruising something—even if it's just my pride."

"So, if you and Sammy are so serious, what was going on between us at Washington Square? And Fong's?"

"We're not serious," I snapped before I could process what I was saying. Less than an hour ago I had promised to run away with Sam. My shoulders sank with guilt.

"Ada, he gave you a ring." Henry looked at me flatly. "There's only a couple of things more serious than a ring, and I'm not about to mention 'em, since there's a lady present."

"You didn't seem to be too worried about a lady being present when you beat the snot out of him," I fired back. We turned down a cramped side street.

He rubbed his cheek. "I said I was sorry. But for what it's worth, I'm still pretty sure he's on the Kings' payroll."

I exhaled in frustration but lacked the energy to argue with him. "Whatever."

"Just promise me you'll be careful, all right? Somebody like you shouldn't get tangled up in something like that." Henry blew into his hands before slipping them in his side pockets glumly. "Up ahead. Around the corner."

Henry's words at the Chinese restaurant came back to me. I tilted my head, trying to catch his gaze.

We both went rigid at the sound of breaking glass. He cringed.

"I hope that wasn't ours." I laughed.

Another crash of shattered glass.

"Wait till Levison gets a load of this!" a man shouted to a chorus of rough laughter. "He's gonna swallow his pipe, the rat bastard!"

"I hope he chokes on it," another voice chimed in, smaller, slimier than the first.

"No," Henry said with an infinitely deep sigh. "No, that's definitely ours."

7

There was a ring of them around the car. Men—boys, if I'm being honest—dressed in two-thirds of three-piece suits, mismatched and ragtag. Their shadows stretched long across the pavement, harshened by streetlamps. Like Henry's friends, they came armed: baseball bats and two-by-fours tipped with crooked, exposed penny nails. The passenger window was smashed, and the smallest among them had crawled inside to pick through the contents of the glove box.

"Jake's gonna be pissed," Henry whispered as we lingered at the corner. I took a shallow breath, surprised, as his arm looped around my waist. My knee-jerk reaction was to pull away from him, but I realized a heartbeat later that the arm was less of a gesture of affection and more of a protective measure, ready to yank me out of the way if anyone saw me. "Those are the Kings boys."

"What're they doing here?" Much like Sam earlier, I found myself sucking my stomach in, acutely aware of the soft crescent of my belly. I didn't dare look up, already imagining the look of disgust on Henry's features. My face warmed.

"I dunno. They might've been on their way to collect some protection money and recognized Jake's car." The arm around my waist squeezed once before releasing me. "New plan. Stick to the shadows. Hug the line of cars. Don't let them see you."

He dropped into a crouch, keeping well below the window line of the cars parked along the sidewalk.

"But—" I finally stammered. "But, Henry, we could just—a taxi—"

"Who wants Levison's pocket watch?" one of the Kings boys crowed. "Pure silver, it looks like—"

"Like hell I'm going to get a taxi now." Henry's voice was low. "Jake's car is one thing, but that was a bar mitzvah gift from my ma."

Farther down the line, another parked car was idling. The driver's-side window was cracked open. Henry bobbed out of his crouch to peek into the vehicle. Ducking down, he flashed a wicked smile my way. That was a little worrying.

He gestured for me to cross to the passenger side.

I felt the color drain from my face. "They'll see me."

"If they do, it'll be too late," he said, nodding to the other side of the car. "Go. Watch through the window. As soon as the coast is clear, open the door and hop in."

A moment passed as panic swelled in my chest. Henry's face darkened with determination.

"You can do this, Ada," he whispered. "Wouldn't ask you to do something I didn't think you could do."

I nodded with a hard swallow, mentally berating myself for going along with whatever stupidly dangerous plan Henry had cooked up. The body of the car was cool beneath my hands as I felt my way around the back.

"Think we should stick around, Frank?" one of the Kings asked from across the street. The cream paint job of Jake's ruined car came up in curls under a pocketknife dragged along the hood, spelling out a vulgar word. "Bet we could take 'em."

"Nah." Frank was a heavyset man playing a solo game of kick the can with the contents of an overturned garbage pail. He gave a glance at a silver watch before tucking it in his pocket. "It's a message, see. Let Levison get back to his people. Spread the word that this is our city and we'll take what we want. The Jews gotta know their place."

I turned the corner of the car, fingers hooked through the spokes of the rear hubcap. Inching toward the passenger door, I found myself checking over my shoulder constantly to see if I'd been spotted. But I was well away from the streetlamps, and the Kings boys were too busy talking smack to notice. With a deep breath, I inched just high enough to be able to look inside, poised to throw open the door at Henry's signal.

Inside the idling car, stretched across the whole of the front seat, was presumably the Kings' getaway driver. His back was braced against the driver's-side door, and his paperboy cap was slung low over his eyes. Asleep.

Through the glass, Henry grinned at me and struck a match. I had to bite my fist to keep from howling with guilty laughter as he fed it through the crack in the driver's-side window.

The lit match tumbled down the driver's cap, leaving a trail of blackened tweed in its wake. It finally settled on the man's chest, inches from his folded hands. The flame spread, eating the fabric and licking at the buttons.

I could barely breathe, waiting for a reaction. Ten seconds passed. The driver began to stir from the thickness of sleep. He clutched at his chest in confusion.

Something metal scraped along the asphalt, finally rolling to a stop at my feet. I tore my eyes away from the unfolding scene in the cab, trying to decipher what it was.

A metal can.

"What the—" Frank was right behind me. "Fellas, there's a dame here."

A panicked yelp drew Frank's attention to the car, where their driver was trying to pat out the growing flame with his hat. When that didn't stop the spread, he went for the door handle and, opening it, dove to the ground.

"Remember, smoking's a dirty habit," Henry deadpanned, using the man's back as a stepping stool to vault himself behind the steering wheel. The door slammed behind him. "Come on!"

"I don't think so, sweetie." Frank lunged for me, but I tore open the door and slammed it in his face as his grip left angry serpentines on my skin. He let out a string of obscenities. Blood wept from a shallow cut across his eyebrow.

I threw myself across the front seat. "Drive!"

Henry shoved the stick out of Park and twisted the wheel as hard as it would go. There was a crunch of metal as the car clipped the one in front of it. The floorboards rushed to meet me as Henry slammed on the brakes, then desperately tried to rev the engine. The car crawled forward.

Frantic, he searched the gearbox. "Shit, which one makes it go fast?"

I crawled back into the seat. "You mean you don't know?!"

"Look, I'm just a grunt." Henry tried another configuration. "This was always Jake's thing."

From my peripheral vision I caught glimpse of Frank going for the open passenger-side door. The pavement was a dizzying blur as I reached to close it. My nails scraped the handle. It was just out of reach. "And you thought now would be a good time to learn?"

"So, I've made some mistakes." On Henry's third attempt the car gave a tremendous backfire—going off like a shotgun—before rocketing forward. The door lurched an inch closer. I grabbed it and yanked it shut. Frank tried to pull it open but the car was too fast now, barreling past him and the rest of the Kings.

Overwhelmed by his success, Henry overcorrected and plowed through a set of garbage cans at the corner. A blackened banana peel splattered across the windshield and left a greasy smear.

"Oh, for goodness' sake," I huffed, scooting closer to Henry. "Move over."

"*You* know how to drive?" Without waiting for an answer, Henry squeezed past me, thighs brushing against the dash until he rolled into the passenger seat.

Taking the wheel, I flashed him a coy smile. "Sure. Doesn't everyone?"

It wasn't as easy as driving my hybrid back home. I had to use far more strength than what I was used to just to get the car back off the curb, gripping the wheel like one you'd find in a teacup ride at the carnival. There was an unfamiliar knock to the engine as I rounded the corner.

The main thoroughfare was choked with lines of puttering cars. I eased the brakes and inched into rush-hour gridlock.

Henry clawed at his hair, eyes wide. "What are you doing?"

"Not much point in escaping the Kings if we're killed in a collision," I answered. "You still have to obey the laws of the road."

"You got a screw loose or something?" Not waiting for a response, he pinched the bridge of his nose and shook his head. "Never mind. Don't ask a question when you already know the answer."

"Maybe we'll lose them in traffic." There was no rearview mirror, so I had to rely on the one mounted at the window instead. To my surprise, four of the Kings came into focus, weaving closer amid a chorus of angry honking. One of them had a gun. "Okay, maybe not. Get down."

Henry opened his mouth, but before he could complain I grabbed him by the shoulder and pushed him away as hard as I could. As he rolled to the floorboards, I searched for an opening, heart thundering in my ears. Finally, I saw one—like the parting of clouds after a torrential rain—but my hope was immediately dashed when I realized it was across the street.

"Shoot out the tires," one of the Kings shouted.

I had no other choice. As I mashed the pedal to the floor, the whole car rocked as we powered over the concrete median and into oncoming traffic.

The first four shots peppered the car's tailgate. My side mirror cracked and then shattered under the force of the fifth. The last one broke the rear window before embedding itself in the roof.

Henry stared at it from the floorboard. He swallowed uneasily.

A car broke from the next lane to pass, meeting us head on. Horns blared. Before I could process it, I had already veered away, throwing a just-recovering Henry to the floor a second time. I spent half a block frantically dodging headlights before I spied an opening to safety. Turning the wheel as hard as I could, I swerved back into our original lane, narrowly missing a stately bronze tower along the way. A moment later, I dimly recognized the red beacon hanging from it as a traffic light.

I had just run a red light.

In a stolen car.

With a gangster.

Sinking into my seat, I watched my shattered mirror as the last of the Kings grew tired of their pursuit, first jogging, then doubling over in the street one by one to catch their breaths. I slowed the car as I turned down another street. "I have no idea where I'm going."

"Take a right here, we're going the wrong way." Henry climbed back into the seat, shoulders moving in ragged waves as he peered through the gaping hole that was formerly our rear window. "So where are you from originally? By your accent, I'm gonna guess somewhere down South."

I thought back to Pickering's accusations on my first date. My Southern twang wasn't *that* bad, was it? My face warmed as I took the turn. "Virginia."

"It's cute." I didn't have to look over to know that Henry was smiling. "They all drive like maniacs down there, or are you just special?"

"Well, we don't normally have to flee gang violence." The gravity of what had just happened was slowly pulling me down. I felt sick. "Getting a taxi would've been easier."

"There you go again. Easy this, easy that." Henry threw his head back to stare at the small metal crater the bullet had left in the ceiling. "Nothing good ever came out of doing the easy thing. Easy is for cowards and quitters."

"Or for people who don't like making an enemy out of the mob," I muttered. "Why are you doing this?"

"Because I like you."

"No, I mean—" I blustered, throwing a hand up as though it'd help me pluck the words I needed from the air. "Why the mob? You don't have to do this. There's plenty of honest, respectable jobs out there. You don't have to live like a common hoodlum."

His gaze never left the ceiling. "Hang a right here. It'll get you back to Fifth Avenue. Then it's a straight shot to Washington Square."

That wasn't the response I'd been anticipating. His silence infuriated me more than any snarky comeback he had in his arsenal.

For a long time, the ride was a quiet one, swimming through the darkness of night, occasionally surfacing in the harsh light of passing streetlamps. In fact, we went so long without a word between us that I suspected he'd fallen asleep, but a quick glance across the seat proved otherwise.

Henry was staring at his side mirror, fingers tangled in his hair. No amount of pomade could save it now—a mop of black fly-away curls and wild corkscrews. The breeze from the cracked window caught the loose ends of his tie and made them dance like reeds along a lakeside.

"I wanted it once," he said in a small voice. "Easy, I mean. A wife, a brownstone, a trip across the ocean. Maybe a kid or two. Nothing too extravagant. But it wasn't in the cards."

"It's not too late to start over." I felt a sick flutter in the pit of my stomach as a policeman entered the reflection of Henry's side mirror. The officer made his way down the sidewalk and turned a corner. "The game of chess, that trick with the match back there—you're smarter than you think you are."

"No, Ada, I'm pretty damn stupid when you get right down to it." He gave an unsteady laugh. "Never quite good enough. Practiced violin my whole life. Can't even hear in my left ear anymore. NYU wouldn't take me."

"Why not?"

"How should I know? 'Better luck next time,' they say. Same story every year since I was seventeen." His laughter didn't die gracefully, reanimating in sudden, awful peals that shook his shoulders. "Not that I could afford it now anyway."

It was hard to keep my eyes on the road. The anxiety that sat in my stomach had soured into guilt. "Have you ever tried to get your name out there? Playing for tips, maybe?"

"Playing for peanuts, you mean. Nobody likes a charity case, me included." He snorted. "Could barely support myself, much less Ma. Tried factory work for a while. Didn't mind the long hours. Didn't even mind the lousy pay. But kids, Ada, they'd send kids down to fix the machinery and sometimes they'd forget and turn it back on—they were even younger than Estelle—"

"Estelle?" I repeated.

"My little sister. She's—" Henry waved it away. "Listen, I didn't start this to tell you a sad story. I started this to tell you I'm sorry. Back at the restaurant, I thought there was no way I could be the kind of guy you wanted. And seeing Sam, well, now I know without a doubt. I'm sorry for ruining your evening. For knocking Sam out. For stealing a car to get you here."

I smiled. "You forgot setting one of the Kings boys on fire."

"Now *that*," he said, jabbing a finger in the air, "that I'm not sorry about. Pull over. This is probably as close as we're gonna get."

Washington Square's iconic arches peered above a blanket of half-naked trees as the car slowed into a spot along the sidewalk. I was already bracing myself for the lecture I'd get from the poor Kairos employee forced to wait on my late return. Would they find out about the stolen car? Or did they already know?

"What are you going to do about the—" I tapped my nails on the wheel meaningfully. "This?"

"I dunno. Drive it into the East River maybe," Henry mused. I straightened with alarm, mouth agape, but he held up a hand to shush me. "Hey, relax—not with me in it."

With a relieved sigh, I cut off the engine and flopped back against the seat. Color finally returned to my knuckles.

Henry showed the beginnings of a hopeful smile. "Aw, shucks. Never knew you cared."

"Don't get too cocky." I waited for something else to follow in the silence, but I didn't know what. "Thank you for coming with me, Henry, even if the drive over probably gave me an ulcer. I would've gotten lost without you."

"Not if you'd hailed a taxi," he admitted. "But for what it's worth, I think you made pretty good time. So, you know a doctor near Washington Square or something?"

"Of sorts," I lied, biting my lip. "Henry, I've got to go. Somebody will be by to collect Sam soon, I'm sure."

"Right, yeah, of course." He nodded, forcing a dim smile. "Good-bye, then."

I popped the door open, but gave him a final glance, half lit by buzzing lights and flickering advertisements. Henry wasn't exactly handsome, but there was something unforgettable in the inky velvet of his good eye, his rumpled collar and undone tie, and his increasingly manic hair.

Without hesitation, I leaned in to kiss his cheek. He froze, whole body tense as I brushed his skin.

"Oh—" I immediately recoiled. "I'm so sorry—it's just—"

"No, hey, it's fine," he said, but his voice was tellingly hoarse. He cleared his throat and tried again. "No, really, it's fine. I just, I thought—"

"About me and Sam?" I interjected, shoulders dropping. "Really, Henry, I told you that we aren't serious."

"No, god, forget about that. I mean"—there was an uncharacteristic shyness in his smile—"I just thought that, you know, maybe we could do a little better than that, all things considered."

I started to ask Henry what he meant, but he made it quickly and abundantly clear when he leaned forward and kissed me.

Despite his uncertainty a breath ago, there was nothing unsure in the way his lips pressed against mine, desperate and impetuous, a hand snared roughly in my hair. I realized almost too late how rare this moment was—*I was kissing an* actual *gangster!*—so when he pulled away, I yanked him back by the collar to taste him again and again, until we were both panting and a little ashamed.

"You're a swell gal, Ada," he said between sharp exhales. "Good at driving. Bad at chess, though."

"Remember what I said. There's always time to start over."

He slid into the driver's seat. "Yeah, okay. Take care."

"You too."

Drawing closer to Washington Square, I noticed a familiar black cab with a wreath of pale-blue flowers painted on the back circling the park's tree-lined perimeter. Waving an arm, I chased it down until the driver stopped at a crosswalk. Breathless, I opened the door and slid into the back seat.

"Right on time, Miss Blum." My Kairos chauffeur smiled at me over the front seat, thumbing the brim of his black driver's cap, embroidered with more forget-me-nots. "Did you enjoy your evening?"

"Actually, there's been an accident. Can you help me?" I pleaded. "There was another Kairos client, he's been injured."

He sobered. "Of course. The safety of our clients is always our top priority. You leave it to me."

As the car pulled forward something in me unknotted, comforted that Kairos would take care of the situation. Still, I had to remind myself that it was Ms. Little's fault everything had happened in the first place.

A gangster. She had set me up with an *actual* gangster.

Slowly, I turned in my seat to peer out the back window. Through the tree line, I thought I could make out a pair of headlights starting and stopping awkwardly as a car pulled onto a backstreet. I smiled.

Maybe parsnip jam wasn't so bad after all.

8

There was a reason I never looked forward to the return trip to Kairos. Going back in time was virtually painless, but going forward felt like a full-body version of the way my stomach rose and fell with the sudden start and stop of an elevator. I always felt queasy afterward, and my return from 1922 was no exception.

The chamber opened with a hiss. My chauffeur offered me a hand up and a sympathetic smile. "You'll get over it eventually."

"I don't know about that." The room didn't quite spin as I planted a foot on the linoleum tile, but the colors did seem to bleed together in my peripheral vision. My knees trembled and I put more weight on my chauffeur's arm than I would have liked. "Could I get some water, please?"

"Sure." He led me to one of two spartan-looking office chairs. Other than the half dozen time dilation chambers, they were the only furnishings in the room, making it feel even more hollow. "Wait here."

Nodding absently, I sank into a seat as the door closed behind him.

I didn't like leaving Sam in the past. The night had stirred up some confusing feelings, some better than others, but regardless of their outcome, it felt like I was abandoning him, no matter how many times my chauffeur assured me otherwise.

Opening my purse sounded like a bomb going off in the quiet of the room, and for a moment I hesitated, holding it tight against me in fear that the room would flood with Kairos employees. No one came, so I wedged it open a little farther.

Three diamonds sparkled from a pocket. Taking Sam's ring, I tried it on my fingers one at a time, but it felt dangerously loose, even on my thumb.

Shadows passed under the door gap. Hurriedly, I slipped Sam's ring back into the purse and closed it.

My chauffeur handed me a glass of water and a clipboard. His smile was apologetic. "Because there was an incident today, you'll need to fill out a report. Take your time. One of the technicians will be with you shortly for your exit examination."

I took a long, grateful sip. "And Samson?"

"Two field agents are in the N-Energy chambers now, ready for a trip back," he explained. "You said he was at the Plaza, right?"

"Yes, room 504. October 9, 1922."

He nodded. "Thank you for coming forward about this, Miss Blum. I hope it didn't spoil your evening here at Kairos."

I smiled, but it felt fake. "Of course not. It wasn't the agency's fault. It's a gamble you take, time traveling. Things are bound to go wrong occasionally."

He turned to the door. "Let us know if you have any questions or concerns. We're here to help."

The moment he was gone, I tilted back the glass and drained it in five big gulps. The colors started to recede. I clicked the pen open and started filling out the incident report. It wasn't too different from the one we had for outages at work. It was nice to get lost in something monotonous, ticking checkboxes and filling in blanks until the final question gave me pause.

Was the incident caused, in whole or in part, by one of the bachelors or bachelorettes from our database? Yes/no.

Reporting Henry was the right thing to do. I knew that. Sam might've been breaking the law—and he still had to answer for the gun—but there were much less violent ways of dealing with him if Henry thought he was up to something suspicious. If I didn't say something about Henry, what was the likelihood there'd be a repeat episode with another Kairos client? I twisted the pen apart and back together in consideration.

The door suddenly swung open with such force it struck the wall with a bang. I barely kept my grip on the clipboard, slowly untensing as the technician in SpongeBob scrubs laughed at me.

"I scared ya, didn't I?" she asked, rolling the other chair over and sitting down to face me. She set down a plastic bin filled with the contents of my locker, a second clipboard resting on top. "I heard from Mel that you had a time tonight, Miss Blum. That so?"

"A little," I admitted.

"Explains the spike in vitals 'round twenty hundred hours," she noted, picking up the clipboard from the bin. "We lost contact with you for about fifteen minutes."

"I took off the cardigan I'd pinned the corsage to." I grinned sheepishly, lifting a handful of the handkerchief skirt on my dress. "I was gifted a new outfit while I was there."

"Contraband." There was a sharpness to the technician's tone as she kicked the plastic bin with her dirty sneaker. "You're going to have to turn it in before you go. All of it. You know the rules. Where's the outfit Kairos lent you?"

Heat flushed my face. "Back at the hotel."

"Mm-hm. Wardrobe isn't going to like that. You're going to get charged. Can I see your visa?" she asked, flipping a page. "Get any kinda injury? Scratches, bumps, bruises . . . ?"

"None that I know of," I answered, producing the required document from my purse. "Here."

"Thank ya." She splayed the book, barely glancing at its pages. "Up-to-date on your vaxes, but you're due for a booster in two months. Don't let it lapse."

"Yes, ma'am."

"All right, then. You know the drill. Change out. Place your contraband in here." She gave the bin a shake before standing. "You may be privy to a random search before exiting so don't go trying to sneak out nothing, okay? Keep your corsage for your follow-up appointment with Little. You done with that incident report?"

"Almost." I'd nearly forgotten about it. I circled *no* on the last question before passing it over. "There we go."

"Thank ya kindly, ma'am. Now, I'll give ya some privacy so you can change back into your civvy clothes," she said, backing out the way she came.

Once I was alone, I started peeling off layers. It was bittersweet, piling turquoise silk and chiffon in that cheap container. If there was one thing that Sam took pride in, it was gift giving, so I had no doubt that he had spent significant time and money on every detail, down to the last string of pearls. I almost suspected there was an entire suitcase of dresses waiting for me somewhere in that suite. He really had intended for us to run away that evening.

The last to go was my purse.

It didn't feel right to turn in the ring. It wasn't contraband—it had come from the present—but it also seemed dishonest to just walk out with it. I stared at the door, trying to imagine what the technician's response would be, before saying to hell with it and dropping Sam's ring into my cleavage.

Better to ask for forgiveness than permission.

After adjusting my décolletage, I made a final pass for anything I'd forgotten before stepping into the next room, bin in hand.

I faced a receptionist's window, but the lights inside were off and there was no one behind the desk. A narrow hallway branched to three doors. The first one, exit only, would lead me back to the waiting room for my follow-up. At the opposite end of the hallway was a door that would take me to Hair and Makeup. I wasn't sure of the third one, but it was ajar, and I thought I could make out notes of burnt popcorn and cheap office coffee.

Definitely a break room, then.

"Hello?" I called, taking a step toward it.

"Oh, you're done." The technician's voice carried from the break room. I angled myself to see into the room better and spotted her sitting at a folding table, transfixed by an old wall-mounted CRT TV. "Just leave your tub on the counter, honey. You can head out now."

Breathing a sigh of relief, I dumped the contraband at the window and made a mad dash for the waiting room before there were any more questions.

It wasn't long before I was called in for my follow-up with Ms. Little, but it was enough time to rehearse what I needed to say with the matchmaker. This turned out to be rather fortunate, because I had a great deal more feedback to share than I had originally thought, and none of it was particularly positive.

"What sort of fly-by-night operation are you running here?" I asked the moment I'd settled into the wingback chair in her office.

Ms. Little was gracious enough to pause, midrummage through one of her desk drawers, in order to give me an incredulous look. "Come now, dear. Kairos prides itself on offering very flexible hours of operation. We're open all hours of the day, not just nighttime."

"That's not what I—" I stopped myself, chin falling on a knuckle as I realized it was useless. Sighing, I tried another angle. "Ms. Little, correct me if I'm wrong, but I believe during our last meeting I made it abundantly apparent that I was not interested in seeing any bachelors from 1922."

"Yes." With a triumphant noise, the matchmaker pulled a round tin from the drawer. She dug her nails into the groove along the lid but struggled to pull it open. "And?"

I stared, unable to believe I had to spell it out for her. "You sent me to 1922."

The tin clattered to the table, still unopened. "I did no such thing."

"Yes, you did."

"No, I didn't." Sitting on the edge of her seat, the matchmaker strained to reach for her GlassBook. With a tap, the space between us was filled with a glowing projection of appointments. Ms. Little flipped through pages until she stopped on one with today's date. "See? I have you down here for a date with Wilhelm Willoughby from 1816."

Sure enough, there it was, hovering in front of me in white fluorescent lettering. *Blum and Willoughby, 1816.* I gaped. "But—but Wardrobe, and then Teddy's lookbook—"

"That *is* very curious, isn't it?" Ms. Little tapped her chin in thought, studying the calendar. A moment later, she straightened, a light of recognition in her eyes. "Ah! There's the sticky widget."

With a wave of her hand, she centered in on an appointment a few entries below mine, flicking her fingers to enlarge the text. *Bloom and Levison, 1922.*

"Oh." Suddenly I was feeling very foolish. I slumped into the chair, face flooding with heat. "So that wasn't a misspelling in Wardrobe after all."

"Clearly not." Ms. Little went back to working on the metal tin. "Still—no harm done. The technicians really ought to have caught the mistake before sending you back."

"Still." I drummed my nails on the chair's arm in agitation. "I think you forgot to mention a few key points in Henry Levison's dossier."

"He's a bit shorter than what you expect, isn't he? I think it's rather charming, actually. So many of our bachelors are such impossibly huge, strapping things." With a final, desperate pull on the lid, the matchmaker collapsed in defeat, dropping the tin to the table. "Crepes, it's like they make these hard to open as a deterrent. I bought these because I wanted biscuits, not a diet aid. Could you be a dear?"

She slid the tin across the table. I'd never heard of the brand before. "'Glitterbombs'?"

"They're new. Very new." Her smile turned shy, fingers pressed together as she watched me pry the lid open. "Try one! They make your teeth twinkle."

"No, thank you." I set the cookies back down in front of the matchmaker. "Henry Levison works for the mob."

"Yes." She snapped up two of the Glitterbombs, one for each hand, and took a big, happy bite. "And?"

At first, I thought that the cookies—pale snickerdoodles—were filled with sanded sugar, but on closer inspection I was thoroughly convinced actual glitter had been baked in. My stomach churned. It took me a second to remember the topic of our conversation. "That might be something to mention in someone's dossier."

"Purely an oversight." Finishing off one of the cookies, Ms. Little sucked the glitter from her fingers. "Normally, a Kairos client would be well aware of Mr. Levison's, ah, less than legal activity going in, as they would've specifically requested that."

I blinked. "You mean someone *asked* to be matched up with a gangster?"

"Of course, dear, of course." Ms. Little examined the cookie in her other hand, turning it so it sparkled in the light of her desk lamp. "Why in the world would anyone go through the trouble of traveling all the way to 1922 to date, say, an accountant? Or a store owner? Or a thousand other mundane occupations that you can find perfectly well here in the present?"

"I hadn't really thought of that."

At that, Ms. Little set down her cookie and folded her hands on the table. "People don't use Kairos because they are searching for love, Ada. They are searching for an experience—a fantasy. They travel to 1860 or 1922 because they want an evening with a cowboy or a gangster, not a lifetime with Henry Levison, a would-be violinist with crippling depression who moonlights as a knee breaker for the mob."

I frowned. "That doesn't seem right."

"Doesn't it? But didn't you ask for a Regency-era bachelor last time? 'I guess I'm just an Elizabeth Bennet looking for my Mr. Darcy,' I believe was how you phrased it." There was a subtle but striking shift in Ms. Little's expression that grabbed me by the heart. It was like catching a strange glint of sentience in a doll's eyes. "So, I suppose that brings me to my next question. For your upcoming appointment, would you prefer Mr. Willoughby of 1816, or would you like a second try with Mr. Levison?"

A minute may have passed, but it felt like hours, staring at the holographic appointment book until the letters lost all their meaning. I thought of Henry, then my promise to Sam. "I think I'd like to go to 1922 again, but my upcoming schedule is pretty busy. Is there something available two weeks from now? Same time?"

The matchmaker nodded. "Relatively speaking."

"It's a pretty slow day today, so you can have your pick," the waitress said as she walked past a row of booth seating. "Y'all wanna sit in the Godzilla or the King Kong section?"

"Is there anything left in the *Citizen Kane* room?" Teddy asked as he ducked under a particularly low wall-mounted, top-hatted moose.

She smiled over her shoulder. "Not unless you want bar seating, sweetie."

"Aw, shucks."

I pinched his side in passing, eyes never leaving the waitress. "Either is fine."

After everything that had happened in 1922, I had completely forgotten about Teddy's offer to take me out to eat. During the drive we had tried to pressure each other into picking the destination before mutually deciding on Mack's. It was a local watering hole with a comfort food menu almost as varied and quirky as its decor.

It was also Sam's favorite restaurant. Our favorite restaurant. I couldn't count the number of times we'd gone to some new fusion restaurant in the DC area and been disappointed by the thumb-sized portions, only to find our way back to Mack's with a plate of deviled eggs between us.

As my brother and I slid down a pair of long, wooden benches, I tried to push the memory from my mind.

Teddy snapped up the drink menu. "I'll have a beer. You want anything? I'm buying."

"Hm?" I tore my attention from the scale replica of King Kong's fist jutting from the wall overhead. "Right, sorry. A sweet tea, please."

He stared at me, oblivious to the waitress turning back to the bar. "Wow, the twenties must have been a hell of a ride. Turned you into a teetotaler in a single session."

"Oh, stop." I picked up the dessert menu and smacked him with it. "I'm driving, remember?"

"Yeah, yeah. But it's been a whole hour since you left, and you haven't dropped a single detail about this 'Once and Future Fling' of yours," he said. "The mind wanders. Was he cute?"

"Um. He was—" Though I had anticipated the question, it still somehow caught me off guard. I struggled to find a word to describe Henry, but all I could think of was the shiner Sam had given him. "Good looking enough, I guess. Black hair, dark eyes. Pale."

"Muscular?"

"Not really, no," I answered. "Thin. Wiry. You know me, I thought he could've used a sandwich."

"Of course you did." Teddy's fingers drummed on the table. "Does he have a name?"

"Henry." I thanked the waitress as she returned with our drinks, then took our orders. "Are we done playing twenty questions?"

"Not quite." My brother took a particularly loud sip of his beer. "What's he do for a living?"

"He's a violinist." The quickness of the lie startled me, so I said it again to cement it. "He plays violin in a band. *Freilich*, I think he called it? I don't know. He's Jewish, for what it's worth."

"I wonder if that's anything like klezmer." Teddy toyed with an extra straw the waitress had left, lifting one end to his mouth to shoot the wrapper at me like the dart from a blow gun. It bounced off my forehead. "Do you like him?"

"I don't know." I picked up the wrapper and tied it into a knot while trying not to think about the way Henry had kissed me. "He's troubled."

"Well, yeah," Teddy said flatly. "He's a Jewish guy living in 1920s New York. Of course he's troubled. Antisemitism isn't exactly limited to Nazi Germany, you know."

The wad of paper lowered in my hand. "I hadn't really considered that, no."

"It was alive and well here in America too," Teddy continued. "Heck, I read some listicle the other day that said colleges had caps on Jewish acceptances back in the day."

"Really." I tore the wrapper into little pieces to sate the growing anger in the back of my mind. "Why?"

"Same as it ever was," Teddy said with a roll of his eyes. "They were scared that the Jewish people would overtake the economy if they got too educated. Classic gatekeeping."

"That's awful." I searched for some other sentiment, but the sheer ignorance of it rendered me speechless. "That's just awful."

"Yeah." Teddy's phone, facedown on the table, lit up and blared one of the default ringtones. He grabbed it and swiped. "It's Antoine. He's sent me a link to a video."

I was a little relieved to change the subject, a small seed of guilt blooming in the pit of my stomach at the thought of my earlier conversation with Henry. "Is it that all-corgi remake of *Lord of the Dance*? Cel showed me that on my lunch break."

"No." The glare from his phone reflected off Teddy's glasses, completely obscuring his eyes. "It's a khopesh demonstration. You know, my favorite weapon."

"Right, yes, the khopesh." My eyes fluttered closed as I thought back to the hundreds of hours I had patiently sat through my brother's sermonizing about the Egyptian sword. "How could I ever forget?"

"That's so hot," he breathed. He watched the video several times in silence, poring over every detail. "Look at the way he uses it to trip this guy—"

"It's very effective," I said with a smile that I hoped felt encouraging. "Is that 3D printed or hand forged?"

"Oh, it's obviously a machine-made reproduction," he huffed, giving me a look that said I was very stupid. "But what does it mean, Ada?"

"It . . . means that Antoine thinks it's a cool sword too?"

"No, *his* favorite weapon is the katana," Teddy explained in a mocking tone. "We had an argument about which was better a couple of days before we broke up."

I nodded sagely. "Right. I can see why you decided to take a break now. Katanas are so overrated."

"Yes! Thank you!" Unfortunately, Teddy's vindication was short-lived. "Wait. Are you patronizing me?"

"No!" I blurted, but a wave of giggles betrayed me. "Relationships are only as sturdy as the swords they're built upon—"

"You tubby little bitch, shut your mouth!" He picked up what was left of the straw wrapper and threw it at me.

It landed in my cleavage.

We fell silent for a whole two seconds before erupting into even louder laughter.

Teddy slumped over the table, the tremble of his shoulders punctuated by a sharp hiccup. "I hate you so much."

"Love you too, cuppycake," I answered with a grin.

"Seriously, though." He pushed his glasses back up the bridge of his nose with a finger and started the video again. "What does this mean? Is he apologizing?"

"You know, most people would apologize by saying the words *I'm sorry.*" I looked around for any witnesses before shoving a hand into my boobs. "I wish you two would just sit down and talk. Use your words, figure things out. Does he make you happy?"

"His delts make me happy."

"You know that's not what I meant. You should—" As I fished out the straw wrapper, my finger brushed against the warm metal of Sam's ring. My train of thought promptly derailed. "You should . . ."

Teddy looked up from his phone. "I should what?"

"You should—" I plucked up the straw wrapper and threw it away, hoping it'd buy me time to remember. "You should reflect on why these petty arguments keep happening. Are there real differences or are you just looking for a reason to be angry with him?"

"I dunno." Teddy blinked rapidly. "He just has this way of making me so mad, you know? Like, I know I don't have my history degree yet, but I've done tons of independent research."

I nodded. "It's part of your job description."

"Right, yeah, Kairos requires a certain working knowledge of history," he said. "But Antoine just talks over me sometimes. Tells me I'm wrong 'cause he saw something on the History channel once—"

"And I know how you feel about the History channel." I flashed a commiserating smile.

"Mm-hm, it's not real history anymore. It's all reality TV and crackpot theories." He glanced down as the waitress slid a plate of fried catfish and okra in front of him. "I just wish he was as passionate about learning as I am."

"I'm sorry, hon." I picked a few stray chunks of olive off my muffuletta and popped them in my mouth. "That has to be frustrating."

"Yeah." He crunched on a bit of battered fish. "So, speaking of learning—I did a little bit of snooping and found out what Sam's been up to."

I froze, midbite. A spoonful of tapenade fell from my sandwich, landing on the plate with a thick smack. "Oh?"

"Well, apparently Kairos field agents recovered him with one hell of a concussion," Teddy said. "And he had a massive overage. Two whole days."

"Wow." I tried to sound surprised. "Will he be in a lot of trouble?"

He shrugged. "Pretty unlikely. Kairos is mostly concerned about liability. He signed the waivers, of course, but the fact that field agents took that long to find him might attract attention from the Bureau of Temporal Anomalies. That could've become a situation real fast."

"Isn't a couple of days a little too small-time for something like the BTA?" I asked hopefully.

"I don't know. I'm just repeating what Marcella told me. She heard it from Ryder." He dunked his fish into a ramekin of tartar sauce. "None of us know where they found him, though. Let's just hope it was decades away from 1922, huh?"

Nearly choking on my sandwich, I grabbed for my glass of tea and chugged it.

"Yeah," I sputtered, swallowing hard. "Here's hoping."

9

"Thanks, mister. Have a great evening." Cel watched as a rusted-out truck sped out of lane two with a cloud of exhaust. She muted her mic, spinning in her chair. "So, hypothetically, this time travel dating thingy. Could you date royalty? A real, live prince? Asking for a friend."

Maybe Ms. Little was more right than I realized.

I wish I could say I'd spent the past two weeks soul searching, that on the day of my next Kairos appointment I was prepared and confident in my plan to run away with Sam to 1922, but at best it would be a bit of an exaggeration, and at worst it'd be an outright lie. Between the raging shitstorm that was working at the bank and my tendency to procrastinate on anything that wasn't actively killing me, I was no surer I was making the right decision than I'd been in the moment I made the promise to Sam in the first place.

"Maybe. Apparently, some clients request cowboys or gangsters. I don't think a prince is too far-fetched." I grabbed a clear tube that shot in from lane three and sighed at the rattle of loose change inside. There was a leather pouch included for change, but no one ever bothered to use it. Unlatching the tube, I emptied the contents into my hand. Three hundred dollars, twenty-two cents, and one cigarette butt. "That's attractive."

"Hey, at least it's not a dead mouse this time," Cel said cheerfully as she counted her debits and credits for the day. "I'm not a history nerd or anything, but it'd be nice to play princess for a while. My last boyfriend called me a feminazi when I asked him to pay half the rent on the apartment. You know, since I was also paying the utilities, the grocery bill, his car payment, his credit cards . . ."

Originally, I had planned to call in sick on my final day in the present in hopes of making some last-minute plans, but a cursory check of my phone that morning put the kibosh on the idea. One of my part-timers had texted to say she was out with a hangover (I had to admire her honesty), while my loan officer was at home with sick triplets. There was no way I could call out, too, and leave Cel to deal with the fallout. Especially since I knew there was a real possibility that I'd never see her again.

"Oh, honey." I processed the deposit and sent the tube back with a receipt, then pumped a glob of hand sanitizer into my palm. The smell of artificial apple tinged with disinfectant filled the air. "You really know how to pick 'em, don't you?"

"It's my secret superpower. Put me in a room of available men and I'll find the jerk." She eyed the clock on the wall. "Five minutes until closing and I haven't seen a deposit from the Healing Light today. I swear to god if they drop it off now, I will crawl through the drawer and strangle that patchouli-huffing hippie with her own dreads."

In a way, I was thankful for the bank's special brand of organized chaos. Staying busy prevented me from dwelling on the things I hadn't done, the good-byes I'd never said. It was only when most of the tellers clocked out at five o'clock and I was alone, closing with Cel, that my worries caught up with me.

"Easy there, tiger. Go ahead and pack up. If she comes, I'll process it." I rubbed my hands together, vigorously at first, but slowing as I considered how to break the news. "What would you do if you really liked him, though? Would you leave everything behind for him?"

She pulled the cash box from her drawer and flipped through the keys on her bedazzled lanyard. "I dunno. That's hard."

My heart sank. An airbrushed unicorn greeted me as the Healing Light's company minivan rolled around the corner and into lane one. I sighed. "Right on time."

Cel emerged from the vault. She pointed to her eyes, then to the driver, as if to say, *I'm watching you.* "Yeah, that's right. You keep singing along with that Celtic Woman CD. You may live today, Starwonder, but next time I make no promises."

I snorted. Thankfully the customer couldn't see her.

Per usual, the total on the deposit slip was wrong, so I struck through it and wrote the correct amount. Starwonder didn't notice the difference—also per usual—and as she rolled away with her receipt, I pulled the shades and turned off the lights. It was time to face the music. "Cel, there's something I need to tell you."

"Uh, okay?" She emerged from the vault, pulling her bottle-blond hair down from its messy bun since we were off the clock. "I'm not in trouble, am I?"

"No, it's nothing like that." Closing my eyes, I braced myself for the impending storm. "Do you remember Samson St. Laurent?"

"The married guy, right?" As close as I'd gotten to Cel, I'd made a point not to share too much of my romantic history with her. People had turned on me for lesser reasons, and I liked her too much.

"Yes, that's him." I winced. "I . . . might have run into him recently."

"Oh?" She pressed her badge to the card reader and left the teller line. "Was it bad? Do I need to cut a bitch?"

"No." I laughed uneasily at the thought of tiny Cel taking on anybody, much less Sam, who had a foot and several hundred pounds on her. "The divorce is finalized. He wants to get back together."

"Oh." She heaved a deep exhale, settling into a relieved smile. "Gosh, you really had me there. The way you were building it up, I thought you were about to drop something cataclysmic on me.

I mean, if he makes you happy, hon, who cares what anyone else thinks? You should go for it."

"That's not all." My smile was tight. "He wants to run away with me. To 1922."

"Oh," she murmured again, this time struggling to slump into a chair in the lobby. "Oh, wow. That's . . . that's definitely something right there. When?"

"Tonight."

"*What?*" Even the knitted cat on the front of Cel's sweater seemed to frown as she slouched, chin in her hands. "But—but Ada, *no*, you can't just leave me—what happens if my next manager is psycho?!"

"Well, that's part of why I wanted to tell you." I locked up my money and carried it to the vault. "You're a great worker, and I'm not just saying that because we're friends. You're reliable. You show good leadership when I'm not here. I obviously won't have any say in it, but I really think you should apply for my position once I'm gone."

"Me? Bank manager?"

"I think you're a shoo-in for it, honestly." The vault door closed with a heavy clang. I keyed in a security code and badged out. "Besides, the bank is always looking for ways to cut corners. If they hire you, they'll only have to pay for half the training."

"Well, thanks. That *almost* makes it better." Cel gave me the tiniest of smiles as I joined her in the lobby. She puffed her cheeks. "Still, running away to 1922. That's . . . kinda illegal, isn't it?"

"One of the many reasons I'm still not sure about it." I heard the fax machine in my office whir to life. Probably another rejection from Insight. "We could apply for a permanent visa, but that process takes years—and it's still not guaranteed we'll get it."

"That's tough," she murmured.

"I know. Originally, I'd planned on marrying someone from a protected era to get one, but better the devil you know, huh?" I moved toward my office. "I'll be right back. Just have to get my purse."

"Wait!"

Turning on a heel, I looked at her expectantly.

She bit her bottom lip. "But—but what about Halloween?"

I wilted against the doorframe, pinned in place by a tsunami-sized wave of guilt. "I told you I might have to back out."

"But—but can't you wait? Who else will be weirdly sexual Bugs and Daffy with me? What happens if you get caught by the BTA and you get hauled off to time jail?" With each new question, her voice rose in pitch until it was an almost inaudible squeal. "They don't have Halloween in time jail, Ada!"

"You'll just have to bust me out, I guess. Bake a file in a cake." I stepped into the office and shut the door behind me, still fighting off the urge to smile.

I was going to miss Cel.

It would seem suspicious if I cleaned out my office, I had decided, so my desk was still littered with personal effects: last year's birthday card from Teddy, a novelty candle made to look like a margarita that I'd bought at a festival with Cel a few months before, and a picked-over dish of candy meant for customers that sometimes served as a stop-gap measure when I didn't have time for lunch. Looking at it all made me homesick for a place I hadn't left yet. I'd even miss the van Gogh reprint, the one with the sunflowers hanging on the far wall, a holdover from the previous bank manager.

For the millionth time that day, I thought about taking the card. At first glance, it wasn't anything special—glitter and gold-leaf flowers on the front—but my brother had left a long message on the inside, and sometimes I would reread it when I was having a bad day. Of course, it would be considered contraband once I entered the '20s. If I was ever discovered, it could easily add ten years to my sentence.

My bag was hooked over the back of the chair. I threw the strap over my shoulder but didn't leave, tracing my fingers over the front of the card. My eyes stung. There was no way I'd be able to make it through my makeup session with Teddy without bursting into tears.

I braced my hand against my collarbone. Beneath the thin

material of my button-up, I could feel the impression of the silver chain that held Sam's ring.

Across the room, the fax machine was still going. A growing stack of papers sat in the tray, waiting for someone to pick them up. Even mortgage contracts weren't that long. Was Insight sending me several at once? I moved closer, thankful for a momentary distraction.

Normally, the fax would finish a job in less than a minute, but whatever it was processing had slowed the machine to a crawl. The most recent page inched from the mouth of the printer, dripping with ink.

It wasn't from Insight. It wasn't even a document.

Someone was sending a photograph.

I watched in horror as more and more of the picture fed out. It was of me, but I had never seen it before, though I recognized the outfit as one I'd worn to work a week earlier. I was climbing into my car, still in the bank parking lot. Whoever had taken it must have been across the street. My eyes had been obscured by a black text box.

Soon, it read.

Swallowing back the urge to vomit, I snatched the paper and tore it up, but there was another waiting just beneath it. This one was a blurry picture of me at the supermarket. *I will make you scream.*

"Like hell you will." I tore that one up too. And the next one, and the next one.

I don't know when I started crying.

"Hey, bosslady?" Cel's voice was small from the doorway. "Is everything okay?"

"It will be." My hands shook as I picked up the stack of papers. "Could you take this to recycling for me?"

"Sure, but I . . ." She took a few steps into the room but moved no farther, her eyes searching mine. "Are you crying? What's wrong?"

I tried to answer but all that came from my mouth was an ugly croak. Shaking my head, I dumped the faxes into Cel's waiting arms, hoping it would be enough of an explanation.

"What are—" Her jaw went slack as she eyed the top picture. She flipped through several more before dropping them on the desk in disgust. "Who's doing this to you?!"

"I don't know," I whispered around aborted sobs. "It's been happening for two years, a little longer. Since the affair went public. It was in the newspapers. Strangers—they don't know what really happened, what we were—"

"Shh, hey, now, you're gonna look like a raccoon if you don't calm down." Cel's smile flickered as she pulled out a tissue. She dabbed at my eyes, picking up what little mascara had already started to run. She looked away, her eyebrows knitted together in understanding. "That's why you want to run away."

"Yes." Saying it out loud sucked the last bit of strength out of me. I swallowed back a mouthful of bile, teetering unsteadily on the balls of my feet. "People tell me I deserve the harassment, that I brought it on myself because I'm a home-wrecker. I used to fight it, I used to try to explain that there was no home to wreck—but I'm tired, Cel. I'm so tired."

"People are sick." She sat on the edge of the desk, watching her dangling feet with a sad smile. "Buncha basement dwellers, probably. Lonely. They're just jealous you didn't have the affair with them."

"You're too good for this world, honey." I sniffed, reaching for another tissue. "But it's too late. They win. I just want to go away to a place where it hasn't happened yet, and I don't care how. That's why I went to Kairos. That's why I'm going tonight."

A long silence stretched between us.

I checked the time on my phone. "I should go."

"Why does it have to be tonight?"

The question made me hesitate. "I'm not sure I'll get another opportunity like this. Sam loves me, and I loved him. I think, given enough time, I could love him again. It could take months for Ms. Little to pair me up with the right bachelor. Maybe years. And the sessions aren't exactly cheap."

"Yeah, but, like, a phone call could fix all this." Reaching up, Cel finger combed the bedraggled curls framing my face and pushed them back behind to better study me. "If Sam loves you, he won't mind waiting, and he won't mind trying to find another option, you know?"

I considered the phone again, unsure if I even had Sam's number anymore. "Maybe you're right."

"I mean, if this is what you both want, go for it. Who doesn't want to be a time traveling Bonnie and Clyde? But you seem hesitant."

My shoulders dropped. "I can't leave Teddy behind."

"Oh, and not your bestest friend, Cel?" She feigned offense, pressing her hand to her chest. "I see where I am in the rankings now."

Despite everything, I laughed.

Encouraged, she continued, "But seriously. You should call him. He'll understand. Please?"

"I will." We hugged. "Thank you, Cel."

"Yeah, yeah. Let's get out of here—I don't want a call from the regional manager bitching about overtime tomorrow." She patted me on the shoulder. "Oh, but if you really do decide to run away, at least wait until after Halloween, okay? I already bought the tutus."

10

There were few women in Chinatown, and children were even rarer. Standing at the street corner, I couldn't see any families. Borough natives—always men—passed me on their way home, wearing ill-fitting suits sweat stained from a long day's work. While they didn't speak to me, their eyes were talkative. To some, I seemed to be an outsider. To others, a curiosity. And to others still, whose gazes lingered the longest, I wondered if I wasn't a reminder of the wives or sisters they'd left behind.

Though it was approaching the end of October, the evening was unseasonably warm, and the air stank with day-old meat from the cart across the street. It didn't pair well with the occasional spew of car exhaust and the lingering hint of hot cooking oil, presumably from Fong's. For the fifth time, I unpinned the corsage from my sweater to check its digital clock.

Digging through years-old text messages on my phone, I had managed to find Sam's number from a group text at work. I had tried to call him a dozen times from the bank's parking lot, but he hadn't answered. At first I had wondered if maybe he had changed phones, but the voice mail was unmistakably his. As it stood, I wasn't sure if I had been too late and he was already on his way to Kairos or if he'd completely forgotten the promise we'd made and was somewhere else. Either was a possibility, considering the amount of head trauma he'd received. It seemed like I had no other option but to go ahead with my outing to the '20s.

My hair and makeup session with Teddy had been spent only half listening to Antoine's most recent cryptic texts, instead imagining conversations I'd have with Sam over a nice, completely gangster-free dinner. Without the pressure of running away, I found myself looking forward to spending an evening with him. If there were two things to be said about Samson St. Laurent, the first was that he was a lot of fun.

The second was that he was perpetually late. This evening was no exception. According to Kairos's timer, I had already been waiting for twenty-five minutes.

It took several tries but I eventually found a passerby who spoke enough English to direct me back to the Plaza. My heart stopped at every taxi on the street, hoping I'd see Sam's profile through the darkened windows, but I was met with empty back seats and unfamiliar faces.

I needed to calm down. I was overreacting. Sam was only a little late. After all, it had taken me an easy twenty-minute walk from the docks at South Street—where my Kairos driver had dropped me off for my pretend date with Henry—to Chinatown after finally getting my bearings. Twenty-five minutes late wasn't all that unreasonable.

Or maybe he had forgotten. Maybe something had come up. My mind kept going back to that fax machine spitting out candid photo after photo of me. Sam could have been a target too.

People stared as I ran past, but I didn't care anymore. Two, then three blocks passed, a blur of concrete stoops and fire escapes, then I lost track. I only stopped for traffic, and when I eventually ran out of breath, I stopped, bracing a hand against the post for Canal Street.

My mind was still spinning as I recounted the directions. I needed to head toward Bleecker Street—or was it Baxter Street? The sign above me said neither.

A lavender sky was settling over the city as afternoon aged into evening. The lamps hadn't come on yet but they would within the next hour. Night would complicate things. Trudging forward, I looked for another person to ask, or better yet a taxi. Around me, shop assistants hung black streamers from store windows and taped paper pumpkins to the glass.

I was debating entering a pharmacy that looked like it was on the verge of closing when I noticed the tall glass box perched near the mouth of the nearby subway entrance. Outside of the movies, I had never seen an actual telephone booth, so it took me a moment to register that the middle-aged man just inside the booth's folding doors was making a phone call.

As soon as he was finished, I darted inside and scooped up a handful of coins from my purse, feeding them into the slot frantically before dialing the operator.

"Hello, switchboard, how can I direct your call?"

I slumped against the inside of the booth, exhausted. "Could you connect me to the Plaza Hotel?"

"Yes ma'am," she answered. "Hold please."

I held my breath in the silence.

Someone picked up. "Hello, you've reached the Plaza Hotel, how may I serve you?"

That voice I *did* recognize. It was the manager who had investigated our noise complaint. "Hello, sir. I'm not sure if you remember me but this is Mrs. St. Laurent. My husband, Samson, had reservations with you two weeks ago."

"Yes, yes. It is a joy to hear from you again, Mrs. St. Laurent," the manager said eagerly, but I wasn't sure if he truly recalled me or if he was just paying lip service. "What can I do for you?"

I paused, formulating a story I hoped wouldn't sound too suspicious. "Samson was so pleased with your service last time he told me he was going to book the Plaza a second time. Can you tell me what room we'll be staying in?"

"Of course, yes, I would be thrilled to." There was an uncertain pause. "Er, Mrs. St. Laurent, a thousand pardons but it seems that your husband has not yet placed these reservations. I don't see his name anywhere in our books. Perhaps I could book the room for you now?"

"Oh, no, that's not necessary." I forced a laugh. "That's my Samson, always waiting until the last minute. Thank you very much for your time, I'm sure he'll be calling to make a reservation very soon."

I hung up before he could respond. Someone else was waiting to place a call, so I left the booth, unsure of what else to do. While it was just like Sam to be fashionably late, we'd never once waited in line at a restaurant or relied on cancellations for a hotel, no matter how exclusive. He always had reservations, and I couldn't imagine tonight would have been any different. In all likelihood, he had just forgotten our date.

Maybe he'd come down with a case of cold feet too.

A quick glance at my corsage said I had a little over three hours left. It was a lot of time to kill, and I still couldn't shake the feeling that something was wrong—that Sam was lost in 1922 and somehow it was my fault. I needed help.

Turning a street corner, I saw a flash of yellow from a passing taxi, but I no longer searched for a certain politician in the back seat. Instead, I flagged it down and climbed inside, sliding across the leather upholstery.

"Where to, lady?" the cab driver asked. His cigar glowed in the coming night.

I rubbed at my temple, already regretting what I was about to say. "South Street Seaport."

As the cleaver came down on the shad's head, separating it from its body, I realized that Ms. Little was absolutely mad. The South Street Seaport was not an ideal location for a romantic rendezvous. In fact, the South Street Seaport was not an ideal location for anything or anyone, unless they happened to be a sailor or a fisherman, and even then, I had my doubts.

An elderly woman in a lumpy shawl counted out pennies as the fishmonger finished deboning her purchase. Feeling queasy, I stepped away from that stall and tried not to look at the dozens just like it that lined the Fulton Fish Market.

Though it wasn't a large stretch of land—no more than a few blocks—the seaport churned with activity. In addition to the comings and goings of the market, tall sails and columns of dark smoke denoted the presence of ships new to the nearby docks, where teams of delivery men unloaded cargo. Some goods were passed onto trucks waiting on South Street, while others found a home in the half dozen warehouses that called the seaport home.

I had no idea why Henry would be here. More importantly, I had no idea where to begin to look for him. Across the way, a mountain of emptied shells marked the entrance to an oyster house. It seemed like a much more sensible place to meet someone. I took a step toward it, then stopped. Oysters weren't kosher.

"Get out of the way, lady," a man behind me barked. I whirled to face him, wide-eyed, only to come face-to-face with the massive wire crate of live lobsters he was carrying over his shoulder. His muscles strained against the weight. "Are you deaf or just stupid? I said move!"

"Sorry." Scrambling out of the way, I stepped into the path of a group of men lugging a pallet of green bananas. A mix of catcalls and jeers sent me running from them too. Without a clear objective, I fell prey to the flow of the crowd, bounced, shoved, pushed, and trampled like a particularly apologetic piece of driftwood in the throes of an advancing tide. "Ack, oops, sorry, pardon me, sorry—sorry, I didn't mean to—"

Eventually, I found shelter under the eaves of a warehouse at the far end of the docks. It was already closed for the day, massive wooden doors crisscrossed with chains and secured by a grease-covered padlock. The din of the market was punctuated by the sound of distant fireworks, though I didn't see the telltale sparkle anywhere overhead. Probably blocked by the city skyline.

There was no way I could find Henry at the seaport, provided I hadn't already missed him while waiting for Sam. I choked back bitter laughter. Two dates lined up for the same night and I'd managed to miss both.

Not that Henry was exactly a date. Fistfights and high-speed chases weren't my first choice for an evening out.

Exhausted, I sat down on a crate that once held MADELINE'S SUPERIOR APPLES, if the faded logo was any indication. I checked my corsage again. It would be a couple of hours before Kairos expected me back, but I had no idea what to do until then.

Somewhere, a car roared past, leaving a vacuum of silence in its wake. I weighed my few remaining options. Sightseeing was a possibility, but I struggled to remember which landmarks had actually been built now. Even a dubious dinner back at the oyster house was starting to gain appeal.

"Not as though anything else could go wrong tonight," I muttered.

Footsteps crunched against gravel, retreating into the darkening twilight. Someone screamed amid the crack of another round of fireworks.

My heart hammered in my throat as I pulled myself up on shaking legs.

Those hadn't been fireworks.

I pressed into the shadow of the warehouse. Something inside me screamed to get away, but I couldn't move, terrified of making myself a target. If I stayed still, maybe I could wait out whatever gang violence I had stumbled into.

Oh god.

Henry. He was still here. And somehow, I knew he was involved in this.

I had to find him.

With a deep exhale, I tried to still my heartbeat to better pick out the footsteps again, but I could only make out the sounds of the market. Had anyone even noticed?

The corner of the warehouse was maybe fifteen feet away. Ignoring my sense of self-preservation, I edged toward it and into the alleyway, where I thought the gunshots had originated.

The alley reeked of waterlogged garbage. The flotsam and jetsam were ankle deep, though at times when my footing was less sure, I'd sink until it reached my knees, and I clung to a rusty drainpipe just to keep my balance. A pack of cats—or at least I hoped they were cats— scattered at my approach. Something viscous seeped into my shoes. I tried to not let it bother me.

Finally, I reached the end. Flattening myself against the building once more, I risked a glance into the street.

To my relief, there were no shadowy figures with guns and base-ball bats waiting beneath the glow of a dying streetlamp, no strong hands emerging from the shadows to pull me out of my hiding place.

There was only a lone figure lying facedown on the worn cobble-stones. Too big and too well dressed to be Henry, his cream-colored jacket was already soaked with blood. He didn't stir at my approach. He didn't move when I stood over him, my voice small as I touched his shoulder, like he was only sleeping. "Sam?"

He didn't answer.

I dropped to my knees. Loose gravel bit into my shins but I barely registered it. It was as though every sensation, every emotion I should've felt in that moment had drained from me. There was no urgency, no anger or sadness that I could reach. Like I had forgotten how to grieve.

Placing my head between his shoulder blades, I listened for a heartbeat that I knew wasn't there. The fabric of Sam's coat was already cool to the touch.

I'm not sure how long I sat there with him. Humming Peggy Lee, I stroked his back absently and ran my hands over the rolling hills of his shoulder blades. I traced the words *I love you* across his spine and left rust-red fingerprints on his neck as I combed his hair.

Dimly, I recognized that what I was doing was insane. Discovering the body would paint me as the prime suspect, and I was actively incriminating myself by touching him, my hands stained with his blood. But the lawyer section of my brain wasn't in control at that moment. Another part of me was, and it was trying to process that Sam had died.

"What happened to you?" I whispered.

I had avoided touching the wound in some ill-placed belief that he could still feel it, but it was clear he had been shot. Swallowing back a mouthful of bile, I slowly climbed to my feet in search of the bullet. I didn't see it in the immediate area, but I did notice a long smear of blood leading from the body. The trail ended about thirty feet away. Sam had been dragged, presumably to be disposed of in the river, but something had prevented this.

A stiff wind moaned to life, sending loose newspapers rolling across the dull cobblestones. One of the funny pages plastered itself against Sam's side. I stared at it, half expecting Sam to peel it loose, before I balled it up and threw it off the dock. The paper bobbed in the dark, choppy waters before finally disappearing.

It was getting colder.

The distant wail of a police siren jarred me back to reality. This was a crime scene. Sam had been murdered, and whoever had pulled the trigger was still out there.

My thoughts raced as I ran between dingy pools of flickering streetlamps. I had to find help, to tell someone—Kairos, the police, anyone—that there was a killer on the loose.

That Sam was gone.

To my left I heard the crack of wood and glass, followed by a round of curses and coarse laughter.

"Hello?" I called. The conversation stopped. Tentatively, I rounded the corner, hoping for the best but fearing the worst. "Please, can you help me?"

A handful of workmen stood around a shattered crate of jars. In the harsh light, I couldn't make out their eyes, hidden in the shadow of heavy brows and flat caps.

"Hey, doll, this ain't exactly Fifth Avenue." The oldest of them, ill shaved and with salt-and-pepper hair, pushed off from a door marked for employees only.

I forced a weak smile. "I know, but—"

"Ah, Johnny, stuff yer gob." A man shot him a dirty look before hopping off the pickle barrel he'd been using as a makeshift seat. "It's plain to see she's been scared witless. Nothing to worry, miss. We don't mean ya any harm."

"Oh, thank goodness." I nearly collapsed from relief as the Irishman took me by the arm and led me back to the barrel. My knees shook as I sat down, head in my hands. "Please, it's my boyfriend—"

A third ashed his cigarette. "He pull a knife on you or something?"

Shaking my head, I tried to explain, but my throat closed tighter with every attempt. Tears stung my eyes. Sam was dead.

The eldest stole a glance to the right and left before removing a flask from his pocket. He passed it and a handkerchief over with a knowing look.

The Irishman took it with a nod, offering it to me. "Here, miss, it'll settle your nerves."

"No, thank you," I murmured, not really in the mood for bathtub gin.

He shrugged before dabbing the flask's contents into the rag, gesturing for my arm. The alcohol felt chilly against my skin.

"Can you tell us where he is?" the eldest pressed.

I swallowed hard. "He's—"

"Jesus," the Irishman hissed, dropping my hand with a revelation. "Covered in blood but there's not a scratch on her. Take a look for yourselves!"

There was a rumble of apprehension. I felt so small under the weight of their combined gaze. The sympathetic smiles were all gone.

"Thought you were in trouble," the smoking one said.

"Please, I am, I'm definitely in trouble—it's not what it looks like—" I begged, voice thick with tears. The Irishman edged away, and I dove for him, hands buried in his coat collar. "It's my boy-friend, he's dead. I loved Sam, I'd never hurt him, I'd never hurt anyone—"

With a muttered oath he tore loose from me, looking paler by the minute. He didn't say another word but backed up slowly, like I was some sort of wild animal. There was a fresh, bloody handprint on his coat.

"*Lizzie Borden took an axe . . .*" the eldest half sang, half muttered under his breath.

I stumbled from the barrel. "No, it's not like that. Please, I can show you—"

"Leave me the hell alone." He slapped me hard. The sound hung in the air of the emptying alleyway. I stopped, stunned, my cheek and nose pulsing from the blow. A tear rolled down my face, but he only sneered. "Stop your crocodile tears or I'll really give you something to cry about."

Teeth digging into my bottom lip to stifle another sob, I watched in terrified silence as they dispersed.

"*She gave her mother forty whacks,*" one continued, singsong. "*After she saw what she had done, she gave her father forty-one.*"

Once I was sure they were gone, I lurched back to the barrel, using it to brace myself as I assessed the damage. My nose wasn't bleeding but the skin of my cheek still prickled with heat. I looked down the alleyway blearily, knowing I needed to keep going if I was going to find help, but when the workmen had left, they had taken the last of my strength with them. My knees buckled.

I laid my head against the barrel and cried the way I should have when I found the body. Big, ugly, red-faced crying. Gasping crying. Hiccup crying. I cried until the sounds of my sobs stopped making noise, and when I was done with that, I choked back another round of vomit and screamed, fist pounding into the wooden lid.

It wasn't fair. Sam wasn't allowed to waltz back into my life and carry on like nothing had happened. He shouldn't have been able to build up my hopes with apologies and promises and words I'd waited years to hear just to die like a dog in some dirty street that stank of fish and rotting trash without reason or explanation. We had been so close to being happy.

I had been so close to being happy.

Footsteps echoed behind me but I didn't look up. I didn't care anymore. They grew closer and closer until they stopped just short of where I was. I should've felt scared but I couldn't summon it—my sense of fear had gone to the same place my grief had hidden before.

"Ada?"

Parting the curtain of my hair, I peered up at the long shadow addressing me. "Hi, Henry."

He looked a great deal better than the last time I'd seen him—but then again, that wasn't saying much. The shiner had fully healed, his tie was done up properly, and the manic curls I'd seen before were crushed under what had to be half a tin of grease, but he was still ghostly pale and new dark circles rimmed his eyes. Henry gave an aborted smile, swaying with indecision as he nervously passed his violin case between hands. "What are *you* doing at the fish market?"

"Originally? Looking for you," I admitted, peeling myself from the barrel.

"Now, why the hell would you wanna do a thing like that?" he joked, the corner of his mouth twitching. As I flipped my hair from my face, his eyes widened. He dropped his violin case, a hand going for my cheek. It stopped just before it touched me, his fingers hovering so close I could feel the radiant warmth on my skin. "Are you okay?"

"No." I sighed so deeply it made me cough. "No, I'm not."

"Got a bruise on your cheek and"—he gave me a once-over—"you look like you took a bath at a slaughterhouse. What happened?"

"Sam's been murdered." I tossed an irritated glance down the alleyway before tapping my cheek. "And this? Well, let's just say chivalry is dead."

"Tell me something I don't know," he said dryly. "But Sam's been bumped off? You know who did it?"

"I think I heard it happen but I didn't see anything." I looked down at my hands. The drying blood had turned my palms brown. "Can you take me to the police so I can file a report?"

It seemed like the right first step. Any direction was better than just sitting idle.

"Uh—yeah, sure, I can get you to the station." His jaw flexed with uncertainty. "But first, don't you think we oughta get you cleaned up? With the way you look, the brass'll probably think you did it."

My arms dropped in defeat. "I had a feeling you were going to say that."

"Well, right now, you're not doing yourself any favors." Tapping his foot in thought, he surveyed our surroundings, eyes finally settling on the pickle barrel. "I'm gonna guess that given the impromptu nature of our boy Sammy's departure from the mortal coil you didn't exactly bring a change of clothes with you."

"Please don't joke about it like that." I inspected the hemline of my skirt. It had gone relatively unscathed. "But, no, I didn't."

"You know, Ada, there's a lot of bad things in this world, and you can either laugh about 'em or cry about 'em." He sized up the door next to us before trying the handle. It rattled, locked. "That's stupid goon rule number one: if you're going to get bloody, bring a change of clothes."

"I don't know, that doesn't sound like a stupid rule to me." I watched with interest as he pulled out a set of keys. He considered each one, checking them against the lock, then flipping them on the ring. By the time he got to the fourth one curiosity got the better of me. "What're you doing?"

His eyes flicked to the barrel. "So they're making pickles here, yeah? Pickles gotta be brined in something—usually vinegar."

"And?"

"Vinegar gets blood out of clothes." Finally, he found the one he was looking for. At first glance it looked like an ordinary key, but as he held it up to the light, I noticed that most of its teeth had been filed down. Next came a Chinese good luck coin from his pocket. He fed the key through the hole in the coin, then slipped it into the lock. "For what it's worth, I'm sorry for your loss."

The alleyway blurred as I blinked away more tears. "I just don't understand why it happened. Why here?"

"Because this is where you go when you want somebody to disappear. There's things to be bought and sold at the Fulton Fish Market, and I don't just mean the catch of the day." Patting himself down, Henry took out his pipe and held it like a hammer. He turned the key and smacked it with the pipe's bowl. Nothing moved, so he tried it again. "I got a pretty good idea who iced Sam. Let's hope I'm wrong, for your sake."

I stared. "You don't still think he was working with the Kings, do you?"

"You got any better theories?" On the fifth turn the lock's pins fell into place. He held the door open for me with a flourish. "Ladies first."

"And I thought we agreed that chivalry was dead." I forced a thin smile as I stepped inside.

Though operating hours were over, the air of the cannery was still stifling—and, as Henry predicted, acrid from hours of boiling vinegar. The three massive vats used for brining and sealing were barely visible, their stainless-steel rims glowing like slim crescents in the dim light let in through grimy windows. More barrels lined the walls. Long tables were set up for assembly, speckled with crates half filled with the same kind of jars I'd seen broken outside. The wooden rafters were exposed, strung with wires and naked lightbulbs.

He set his violin case on an empty shelf and shut the door behind us. "Dark in here."

"Do you see a switch?"

"No. Probably best if we keep the lights off anyway." The telltale scratch and sizzle of a struck match echoed through the quiet. Henry offered it to me, then lit a second one. In the flickering light, his eyes looked like black marbles, glossy and fathomless. "Look for some water. We need to keep the stains wet."

Hand cupped around the flame, I hugged the wall in search of a sink or a spigot. "So, what were you doing at the fish market?"

"Huh?" Trying to look up at me, Henry hit his head on the underside of the table he was investigating. "Ow, shit."

Smothering back an apologetic laugh, I peered into a corner between two shelves. Water glittered from a mop bucket, but as I moved closer, I could see that the surface was brown and cloudy with dirt. "For some reason, I find it hard to believe that you just happened to be in the neighborhood."

There was a long pause. "I was busking."

I glanced back at him.

"There's always time to start over, I guess." He offered me a limp smile. "Who needs NYU anyway?"

I should've felt happier for him, but I couldn't help but remember Teddy's history lesson at Mack's. "That's wonderful. I'm so proud of you."

"Yeah, yeah." His match flickered as he waved me off and then turned away shyly. "Maybe I'll cut you a deal for your next birthday, but first let's make sure you don't spend it locked up."

"I'd like that a lot." The shelf next to me was filled with bright aluminum cans advertising WORLD'S BEST DILL SEED and MOTHER'S OWN MINCED GARLIC. "I mean that. I'd love to hear you play sometime."

The second pause was even longer. "Tried writing down some of the music in my head recently."

"You compose?" I combed through the spices, attention finally settling on a glass gallon jug. "Found the vinegar."

"Whoa, nothing so serious. Composing, that's powdered-wig, frilled-cravat kinda stuff." His free hand slid down the corner of a wheeled wire rack that towered above him. He gave it a cautious push, watching it drift away from him. "Sometimes I'll hear bits and pieces of a song, but I never know how to finish it. Not a composer."

"Maybe you just need the right inspiration." The flame was

getting too close to my fingers for comfort, so I blew it out and hefted up the jug.

"Yeah. Something like that." Henry planted his foot against the rack and launched it across the room, revealing a dingy industrial sink. "Ta-da. Now, go ahead and take off your shirt."

The jug threatened to slip from my grasp as I came to a sudden halt. "Excuse me?"

"Surely even a country bumpkin from Virginia knows you can't wash your clothes while wearing 'em." He stamped his match out and lit another, smiling above the flame mischievously. "Not the first time I've seen a woman's underthings, Ada."

"And it won't be the last, I'm sure," I said dryly, motioning for him to turn around with a finger. "A woman needs her mysteries. She's not interesting without them."

He rolled his eyes but made a show of rotating in place until his back was to me. "So that's why you're so secretive."

I unsnapped my Kairos corsage, repinned it to my skirt, then wiggled out of the blouse. "That's silly. I don't keep many secrets."

"Bullshit." He tested the sturdiness of an overturned washtub. "When you showed up, it was like I had wandered into a play I didn't have the script to. You're very careful to keep the audience's attention somewhere else."

The faucet squealed on with a hard turn. The material of my shirt darkened with cold water. "You talk about me like I'm an entertainer. A magician."

"You are, in a way." He sat down and used the new match to light up his pipe. "So, uh, Ada, I realize this may not be the time but . . ."

"But?" I echoed.

"Last time, when we uh—" Henry paused to nervously puff on his pipe. "When we—when we kissed, I just—"

"I don't want to talk about it right now."

"Don't want to talk about it right now," he repeated, nodding fervently. "Yeah, okay."

I let the sound of running water fill the silence. At the bottom of the sink I found a small nub of soap and used it to scrub down my arms and hands. Rivulets of old blood dripped down the drain. "Your employers, are—were—they good to you?"

"Better to me than I deserve." He shrugged, blowing out a thin line of smoke. "You're gonna wanna add the vinegar now. Mix it with water. You might have to work it in a little bit."

I uncorked the jug and followed his instructions. "But they didn't hurt you, did they?"

"Got socked in the face once or twice when I screwed up. If I didn't get a payment, sometimes I'd get my ears boxed," he admitted. "Nothing too serious. Jake and Schlomo, though, they're good friends. They look after Ma and Estelle."

It might have been the poor lighting, but when I lifted the shirt up for inspection, I swore the stains were significantly lighter already. "That sounds terrible. No one should be treated that way. Do Jake and Schlomo know about that?"

"Well, yeah, I guess they would considering it happens to them too." He shifted his weight on the washtub. "You're doing it again."

"What?"

"The thing where you redirect the conversation," he said.

My blouse dropped into the suds. I took a careful breath. "Henry, has it perhaps occurred to you that I'm looking for a distraction from a terrible tragedy?"

He took a long drag. "Yeah, well, maybe I am too."

Staring at the back of his head, I tried to imagine his expression in hopes it'd help me decipher that statement. But I drew a blank. Irritated, I sloshed more vinegar onto the shirt. "You want to know about me? Okay, fine. My favorite color is pink."

"What an earth-shattering revelation. I finally see the real you," he deadpanned. "And anyway, if that's the case, how come I always see you in turquoise?"

"Just because it's my favorite color doesn't mean I have to wear it. In fact, it's a general fashion rule that redheads don't wear pink." I examined the shirt again. The stains had been reduced to faint ghosts on the fabric—only noticeable because I knew what to look for. I wrung it out, clearing my throat to keep from crying again. "Sam liked me in turquoise."

"Oh."

"It's okay. You didn't know. But I hope you understand what I mean now. There's so much of me that's still tangled up in him. I've tried to move on, but I don't know if I ever will." I squeezed more water from the fabric. "I think this is as good as it's going to get."

"I'm sorry we don't have the time to hang it up on a line somewhere." He stood. "It's gonna get cold. You want my coat?"

"Won't that call attention to it? A dry coat over a wet blouse?" I wormed my way back into the shirt with a grunt. The material clung to my sides and felt oddly claustrophobic. "Besides, it'll just keep it from drying."

"Sure." He put the pipe away. "Is it safe to look now?"

"Yes." My eyes met his as he turned around. "You know, a lot of guys would've tried to catch a peek. Thank you for not being a creep about this, Henry."

"Don't know if I need to be thanked for being a half-decent person," he said, voice low. Crossing the room, he picked the violin case up off the shelf and opened the door. He edged onto the stoop. Distracted, I trailed behind him, peeling the damp material from my skin until I bumped into his outstretched arm. He was blocking the way.

I peered over his shoulder. "What's—"

"Shh." Henry ducked back into the cannery as a long shadow stretched across the worn cobblestones. "Somebody's coming."

"Ada Blum?" the figure called. As he stepped into the dying lights of the alleyway, I could just make out the embroidered forget-me-nots on his collar. He glanced down at something in his hands—probably a tracker—before advancing our way. "Ms. Blum? Are you there?"

Every muscle on Henry seemed to tense at once, like a dog with its hackles raised. "Do you know him?"

"Yes," I breathed. I could only imagine my vitals must've been off the charts since discovering Sam's body. "It's fine. He's been sent for me."

Henry looked at me sidelong. "First a curfew, now a babysitter?"

"In a way, yes." Explaining the role of a Kairos field agent would definitely be a violation of the terms of service. Reluctantly, Henry let me move past. I waved the Kairos employee down. "Hello—here I am."

"Good evening, Ms. Blum." The man thumbed the bridge of his hat to me. "Have you been in distress?"

"Yes. There's been another incident." I took the cannery steps two at a time. "A homicide. Can you help me?"

He blanched but offered his arm. "Of course, yes. Come with me."

As we turned to go, I glanced at the cannery, hoping to thank Henry for his help and say good-bye. But to my surprise, he was nowhere in sight. The cannery door was closed. I frowned, debating the merits of looking for him, but if he had disappeared that quickly I could only imagine he had a reason to hide.

"We'll get it sorted," the Kairos employee murmured as he pulled me away, but I wasn't sure who he was trying to convince—me, or himself. Homicide probably wasn't something covered in basic training. "What is to be will be, even if it never happens."

"I hope so." Looking behind us, I thought I saw a wisp of smoke curling from the corner of the building. "I hope so."

11

"So let me get this straight." The policeman tapped a stack of papers against his desk. The vibration sent his coffee sloshing at the sides of his NASCAR mug. "You're here to file a report about an alleged homicide. You didn't witness the murder and didn't see a suspect. And this all happened in 1922 New York."

All things considered, I think Officer Toussaint was just as glad to see me as I was him. In other words, neither of us were very keen on spending much time together in that closet-sized room he called an office. But my town's police force was notoriously small, and he was the only one available to take my statement.

I folded my hands and flashed my most tolerant smile. "That about sums it up, yes."

"Mm." Putting the stack of papers away, Officer Toussaint took out a pen that had somehow migrated from my bank, if the green and tan design was any indication. He clicked it a half dozen times but never actually put it to the legal pad that sat in front of him. "And you do realize that's just a touch out of our jurisdiction?"

"Yes." I flopped back in exasperation. The cheap wooden chair they'd brought out for me squeaked in protest. "Of course I realize that. Originally, I had planned to file a report with the 1922 Seventh

Precinct of Lower Manhattan, but Kairos insisted I file with you instead. A potential APPL violation, they said."

"Calm down, ma'am." He held up a hand, voice infuriatingly slow. "Rightfully, I don't know if I would have done anything differently myself, had I been in similar circumstances. But I am telling you to have realistic expectations. We'll do everything we can to investigate, but there's just not a whole lot to go off here."

I drummed my nails on the table. "It feels like we've had this conversation before."

"Beg your pardon?" From the flash of warning in Mr. Toussaint's eyes, though, I could tell he'd heard what I had said perfectly well.

"Have you called the BTA?"

"Yes, ma'am." He took a sip from his mug. "We've been on the horn with 'em since you filled out the initial report, but they're stretched awful thin up in Washington."

I nodded, unhappy but placated.

Recognition stirred in the officer's features. He clicked the pen again. "Blum. You know, I thought I recognized you last time we met, but I didn't know from where. You were in the newspapers, weren't you? Few years back?"

It had been a long time since someone had recognized me, but it still made me sick just the same. "Yes, that was me."

"You had an affair with him," he said, more for his benefit than mine. "Senator St. Laurent. With all due respect, ma'am, the stories didn't exactly paint a pretty picture of you or your relationship."

"With all due respect, that wasn't very respectful at all," I answered with a sarcastic batting of my eyelashes. "They were stories. Fabrications. I was demonized by the media. People see a young woman with an older man and their minds conjure a very specific narrative."

It was clear from the thinning of his lips that Officer Toussaint also subscribed to that theory. "Mm."

"You ever notice the words that get thrown around when an affair goes public?" I felt a bitter smile forming. "A man is called a cheater. It's a fair, accurate term; he cheated on his partner. But a woman? She's a home-wrecker."

"If you're going to get upset over name calling, *Ms. Blum*, maybe you ought to have thought about that before you got involved with a married man." He shielded the legal pad with an arm so that I couldn't see what he was writing. "It's a small world we live in, ain't it? Of all the places and times you could've been, you both wound up in New York, in 1922, on the same evening, at the same fish market."

"First of all, no, I'm not upset over name calling. I got over that the first time someone spray-painted *cocksucking whore* on the side of my car." I straightened in my seat. "Secondly, I know what you're insinuating, but wouldn't it be a little counterintuitive on my part to go through all the trouble of filing a report?"

He smiled, self-satisfied, as he leaned back and turned to a fresh page. "I wasn't insinuating anything, Ms. Blum. Just carrying on a conversation. That's an awful interesting direction you took it, though."

On any other day I would have suffered through the rest of Redneck Sherlock's spontaneous interrogation with polite smiles and a request to call a lawyer. But Sam was dead, and I was the only person in the world who seemed to care. The sadness and confusion I had felt since finding the body had worn away. I was left feeling raw, angry, and apparently very, very stupid.

I snatched the man's legal pad and tore a chunk from its pages, sending them up into the air like so much confetti. "Listen here, you—"

The door opened. I turned and saw a cheerful woman who was a little smaller than I was, but her ample curves were exaggerated by an uncomfortably tight-looking uniform. She waved but was quickly distracted by the flutter of yellow papers. Her mouth opened to form a question but she shook it off. "The BTA just called. There's no record of a homicide matching that date and time in their databases. A follow-up call found the alleged victim alive and well at home."

A paper drifted down to land on my head. I brushed it aside. "What?"

She smiled warmly. "Senator St. Laurent is currently at his town-house in the capital."

The world stood still. I heard the words but couldn't understand them.

"You've had a long day, Miss Blum." Officer Toussaint balled up some of the discarded paper and did a bank shot into the wastebas-ket. It was as if all his suspicions about me had suddenly evaporated. "You're free to go."

"All right, then." I picked up my purse with a fixed smile, des-perately trying to ignore the ever-growing twitch of my left eye. "Thank you so much for your time, Officer Toussaint. Have a good evening."

I wandered through the labyrinthine halls of the police depart-ment as though in a trance. If anyone spoke to me, I didn't hear them, and for the life of me I can't completely recall how I found myself back in my car, key in the ignition.

Nothing about this made sense. I put the engine in Reverse but didn't take my foot off the brake, unsure of how to proceed.

On the passenger seat, my phone lit up and vibrated its way across the leather upholstery. I picked it up and immediately felt a sense of dread. It was an unfamiliar number.

Normally, I wouldn't have answered it, but for some reason I felt like I had to. "Hello?"

"Hello, dear." Ms. Little's voice took on an odd, robotic quality when filtered through my phone's speakers. "I'm very sorry to bother you right now, I know it's a bit late—but it seems you left Kairos before we could have our follow-up appointment."

I shifted the car back into Park. "My apologies. There was an emergency."

"Cherry tarts, dear, I hadn't heard." There was a brief burst of static on the line. "Is everything all right, then?"

"Well, yes and no." I rubbed my eye, hoping that the jumping nerve causing the twitch would calm down. "While on my date with Henry, I discovered a dead body."

"No!"

"Unfortunately, yes." A small but loud suspicion struck me. "I'm surprised no one told you, considering it was another Kairos client. Samson St. Laurent."

"Oh." There was a long pause. "How very peculiar."

I snorted. "That's an understatement."

"I suppose it is, yes, considering I canceled Mr. St. Laurent's membership with Kairos after the previous incident in 1922." I thought I heard the shuffling of pages. "Upon further investigation, we learned that Samson removed his patented corsage to prevent being tracked for extended periods of time, which is firmly against our terms of service."

"What? But—"

"That's why I wasn't alerted, dear." She sounded immensely regretful. "He must have been using another time travel service when it happened. Still, my deepest condolences."

"Thank you, but it's not necessary." I checked my eyes in the rearview mirror. The twitch wasn't nearly as noticeable as it felt. "After filing the police report here per my chauffeur's recommendation, they told me that Samson is very much alive and well."

"How very, *very* peculiar," Ms. Little murmured.

I ran a hand through my hair in exasperation. "I know what I saw, but I don't know what to do about it."

She hummed thoughtfully. "During your follow-up appointment a few weeks ago you mentioned that you knew Mr. St. Laurent. Do you know where he lives, by any chance?"

"The police said he was at the townhouse," I answered. "I've been there."

"Well, while I normally wouldn't advise dropping in unannounced, perhaps you could pay him a visit?" she said. "I don't know about you, but it'd certainly make me feel better than just taking what the police said at face value."

There was a flutter of anxiety in my stomach. "It's been a long time since I've been there."

"Might I suggest bringing a cake?" she asked. "Uninvited or not, I always welcome a guest who brings cake."

I smiled but it felt bittersweet. "I'm sure Samson would feel the same way."

"Then it's settled." There was a note of triumph in her voice. "I won't keep you from that much longer, dear, but I do need to touch base about Kairos. I understand, given the circumstances, if you want to take a break from our sessions."

"I think that would be for the best, yes."

"Right, of course," she said. "I've taken the liberty of freezing your account with us. You can resume your sessions at any time. No expiration dates. I've also comped your last session. A refund will be wired into your account within five to seven business days."

"That's very kind of you." I put the car back into Reverse. "Thank you for calling, Ms. Little."

"Of course, dear. Your happiness is my priority," she said warmly. "If you need me again for any reason, you can contact me at this number."

"Noted, thank you. Have a good evening." I ended the call and backed out of my parking place. The highway was only a few miles away, but first I'd need to make a stop at the bakery.

It had been two years since I had last visited Sam, but it was as though I had never left. His place was nestled in a row of near-identical townhouses, their aged brick and dormers painted in muted primaries calling back to Georgetown's colonial days. The morning glories Sam and I had planted early in our relationship had continued their climb up the building's corner but had been trimmed before reaching the roof. Even the two sconces that flanked the friendly red door were still lit, as they always were—Sam never remembered to turn them off.

Unfortunately, the parking situation hadn't improved. I circled the street twice looking for an empty space before finally snagging a metered spot a few blocks away.

Rain speckled the plastic window on the cardboard box I carried. A dozen donuts shifted inside, their glaze still wet. They'd been out of cake but I didn't think Sam would mind.

If he was even home. I knew the police had no reason to lie about that phone call, but I was still plagued by the mental image of Sam on the docks. Climbing the stone steps leading to the entrance, I was suddenly convinced that someone else would answer the door.

At the welcome mat, I double-checked the four gold numbers over the mailbox and felt like a fool when it was, of course, the right address. I knew this place, I reminded myself. For several years, this had been my home away from home.

With a hard swallow, I knocked.

Then I waited, practicing smiles in the silence.

After a minute, I tried again. A droplet of rain pooled on the donut box.

No one was home. Trying to silence a thousand intrusive thoughts, I turned to go.

The storm door swished open. "You're liable to get soaked out there. Don't you wanna come in for a spell?"

I gripped the wrought iron balustrade to ground myself. Though my back was to him, I knew the deep rumble of his voice better than my own. All the tension I had been holding on to since returning from 1922 was suddenly gone, and I threatened to crumple like a puppet without strings.

"You all right?" he asked.

"Yes, I'm fine," I managed to say around the beginnings of delirious giggles. I blinked away tears. "I'm just so glad you're here. I thought I was going to have to eat these all by myself."

"Well, you know I'm always happy to oblige," he joked as he held the door. Sam's eyes searched mine as I drew closer, his lips twisting into a confused smile. "Ada, I—well, I'm hardly complaining, but why are you here?"

How was I supposed to explain this? There was no way to tell Sam that I'd discovered his corpse without sounding like a crazy woman.

"I needed to see you." Heat rushed to my face as the words hung in the air longer than I had meant them to, giving us both time to dwell on them. "I tried calling you but you didn't answer."

"I'm sorry, sugar," he said, eyebrows furrowed in concern. "I didn't recognize the number—heck, I'm surprised you still have mine, all things considered."

"I had to do some digging," I confessed. "Please, I know I'm not supposed to be here, but I need to talk to you. Can I come in? Please?"

He hesitated, eyes scanning the street behind us as though he expected paparazzi to spring from behind every tree and bush, before finally relenting.

"You know I never could tell you no," he said, stepping aside. "Let's get you inside."

The entry hallway was a tight fit with the two of us. I was so close to him, bombarded by a thousand memories, a thousand emotions—of once loving Sam, of losing and finding Sam all in the same day—that I couldn't help myself. With the silk of his tie knotted around my fingers, I pulled him down to my level. My lips met his.

It was a bad idea and I knew it, but I couldn't help myself. That's how it always was with Sam; around him, I surrendered to my vices, to all my bad decisions, and he loved me for it. I kissed him and he could only resist for a moment before his hands were on my hips, the past as easily forgotten as the donuts on the console table behind him.

"Poor thing. You never did like the rain." He wound one of my deflated curls around his finger, laughing sympathetically when that did little to revive it. "Let me take your coat."

As he peeled the water-dappled blazer off my shoulders, I was transported to a dozen other rainy afternoons just like this one, a kiss in the doorway that led to puddles of clothes trailing up the stairs to the bedroom.

He hung the jacket on the coatrack and picked up the donuts. "You know what goes well with donuts?"

"Coffee?" I asked hopefully.

He nodded. "Just so happen to have some brewing now. Come on."

I wandered behind him. In the kitchen, steam coiled from the coffeemaker that was dripping its contents into an already half-filled pot. Two mugs waited on the counter, as though he had been expecting me. Sam stared into his refrigerator for a moment before pulling out several bottles of flavored creamer. I frowned as my gaze fell on a sad pile of blue and pink packets stuffed into a napkin holder. "Artificial sugar? Really?"

He cracked a sheepish smile, sliding a hand over the curve of his belly. "Gotta watch my girlish figure."

"Oh, shush." I threw one of the packets at him with a laugh. "So donuts are fine but two teaspoons of sugar, that's where we draw the line?"

"Gotta offset the donut," he said as he poured the coffee.

"Yeah, that's some sound logic." I emptied two packets' worth into his mug and added creamer. "But what about your guests? Surely you don't expect them to use the fake stuff."

"Don't get many visitors these days." His gaze drifted away, and I knew, somehow, I had wounded him. "Sugar's in the cupboard."

My smile shrank. I dug two clumpy spoonfuls of sugar from a barely opened bag, swirling them into hot coffee until they dissolved. I couldn't avoid it any longer. "We need to talk."

Sam took a seat at the island. His eyes looked past me. "I think you're right."

"You're not going to believe everything I tell you," I began, carrying his coffee over. "And I don't expect you to, not at first."

"That's all right. I've been known to say an outlandish thing or two in my time." With a kind smile, Sam took the mug.

Heavy diamonds glistened from a band on his right hand.

I thought I would choke on my heart. Trembling, I pulled the chain from beneath my shirt, where an identical ring swung like a pendulum.

He stared at the two rings, trying to make sense of it.

"You," I rasped. "You're not the same Sam."

"I'm hoping you don't mean there's two of me running around," he said, taking a long, loud sip of his drink. "Don't think the world could handle two Samson St. Laurents."

"No, I mean—" I shook my head and sat down next to him. "You haven't gone yet. It hasn't happened."

"What hasn't happened yet?"

I turned in my seat, fear rising in my chest. "Please, Sam, you have to listen to me. Do not, under any circumstances, go anywhere near the Fulton Fish Market in New York. Not in the present, not in 1922—not ever. Promise me."

He blinked. His hand drifted back to his side, donut temporarily forgotten. "That's awfully specific."

"Please." I grabbed his lapels in desperation. "You *must* believe me. I found your body in 1922 New York at the Fulton Fish Market. I know it sounds crazy, but it's true. I tried to file a police report but they told me you were here—"

"I wondered what that 'wellness call' was about," he murmured.

"Yes," I whispered. "Please just promise me you won't go there."

He brought me in close, and I buried my head against his neck, willing myself not to cry again.

"Don't ever let it be said I didn't do everything you asked of me, sugar." His voice buzzed along my scalp as he brushed his cheek against my hair. "I promise. Nothing's going to happen to old Sam anytime soon, don't you worry."

Smiling at him, I tried to keep my expression fixed, but a tremor of tears welled in my eyes. I lost it, sobbing against him until the shoulder of his dress shirt was soaked through. But he patiently sat there with me, stroking the back of my head. He hummed absently, the sound like the purr of an oversized cat.

Eventually, I pulled away with a sniffle. "Sorry, I'm going to get snot all over you."

"Don't you worry about it. Adds character," he said with a slowly softening grin. "Now, why in the world were you all the way back in 1922?"

Swallowing thickly, I tried to formulate the words to explain what had happened. About meeting Sam in 1922, a different Sam, about the dress and dancing at the Plaza, about running away. But the longer I looked at the man sitting next to me, the more I doubted that it had happened—or that it ever would. Maybe by coming here I had prevented everything.

His expression shifted to one of sympathy.

"That's all right. You can tell me about it later," Sam said, pushing some of the hair from my face. "Time travel, calls from the police—it sounds like we've both had quite a day. Why don't you head on upstairs and have yourself a long soak in the tub? Take a nap?"

I nearly melted at the suggestion. "That sounds really nice."

He smiled warmly. "When you wake up, we'll have a late dinner. Order some Chinese—Gold Dragon, just like we used to. That's still your favorite, right?"

"I never get the chance to go there anymore since I moved." I bit my lip, eyes rolling at the thought. "Oh god. I had forgotten about their kung pao."

"Honey, I am fat," he joked. "I never forget."

"And extra rice?" I added. "I loved their fried rice so much."

"Nobody orders Chinese for the rice, Ada," he said, tapping my nose. "But, yeah, I reckon that can be arranged. Now, you sit tight here while I go get the water running for you, all right?"

I nodded and took a long, stabilizing drink of coffee, relishing its warmth. I knew it was a bad idea to go along with this, that this evening together would only further complicate things, but the familiarity of Sam was such a comfort. Everything with him was so easy.

Then a thought hit me. "Wait—sorry, I can't. There's no way I could get to work on time with a DC commute."

"That's all right." Sam stood from his seat. "Why don't I walk you to your car, then?"

"Sure, but—I just got here," I said, staring down at the pastries between us. "You haven't even had a donut yet."

"Well, I am on a diet," he said sheepishly.

"Oh, bullshit." I laughed, in spite of myself. "You've never said no to a donut, Sam. That's not like you at all, why—"

I caught him looking past me and followed his gaze to the clock in the hallway. My jaw dropped with the revelation.

"Are—are you trying to get rid of me?"

"Aw, shoot, sugar, you know I'd never—" Sam insisted, but the damage had already been done.

As I studied him, the pieces started to fall into place. Even with Kairos's time hopping, the evening had gotten away from me. It was nearly ten o'clock and Sam was still dressed for a night on the town.

"Oh wow," I murmured, cheeks warming. "I really *was* interrupting. You should've told me. Let me get out of your hair."

"Now, Ada, I ain't trying to get rid of you." There was an urgency to Sam's voice that verged on panic. "It's just that—"

From the hallway, there was a frantic rapping on the storm door. *"Bonsoir, mon joli bijou!"*

I suddenly felt ill. There was only one person I knew who was so completely, pretentiously French.

"Evening, Penny." Sam's shoulders dropped in defeat.

Penelope Jackson, his ex-wife, was no more French than my big toe, but after two weeks in Paris on their honeymoon, she had fully embraced her inner Parisienne and had never looked back. It took every ounce of willpower I had not to giggle when she entered the room wearing a black beret and a striped batwing dress. All she needed was a baguette.

"I am so, so, so sorry I am late. There was an outstanding turnout at my sculpture class for the homeless and we ran over the allotted time." She made a point of not acknowledging me as she swanned over to a seat at the island.

"Oh, an art class." I mustered a polite smile. "I'm sure they enjoyed that."

She squealed in fake surprise, a hand pressed to her chest. "*Mon dieu, vous m'avez fait peur!*"

"Good to see you too," I deadpanned.

Penny recovered quickly, fanning herself. "Oh, my apologies. As a bilingual person, sometimes I lapse into French when I'm caught off guard."

"It's interesting how you forget your native language." I took another sip of coffee. "It's good to hear you're still creating. You're an absolute visionary."

Sam looked at me as though I had just poked a sleeping wolverine.

"Well, I have always strived to be a patron of the arts." The empty flattery had done its job, distracting Penny from the snark. She leaned in with interest, pushing the bridge of her horn-rimmed glasses back into place. "We even had a few of the underprivileged model nude tonight for my lesson on sculpting the human form. *Quelle torture, quel sacrifice!* They will make great art. Can you imagine, some of them have never even thrown a pot before?"

I blinked. "Yes. It's amazing how the other half lives without such basic human experiences. I hear some of them even drink tap water."

"Disgusting, no?" She wrung her hands in discomfort, looking up at Sam. "Speaking of which, I have a few pieces I would like to gift to you, Samson."

He flashed a nervous smile. "Oh, Penny, that's awful kind of you—"

"Think nothing of it!" Penny waved dismissively. "But they are quite sizable. Could you help Trevor unload them from the car?"

"Be glad to," he said, already moving toward the door, but I was fairly sure he was just looking for a way out of the conversation before he could be dragged into the thick of it.

"*Merci beaucoup!*" Penny called after him, waving. She sighed in satisfaction as the door closed behind him. "I trained him so well. Life hasn't been the same without Samson, it really hasn't. That's why I hired Trevor."

I avoided giving a response by draining the rest of my coffee. "So you're teaching a class in DC? I thought you were still busy with the farmhouse renovations."

"Oh, *oui*, I am just taking a month's vacation while the painters do their work. I had my boudoir painted black and now the rest of the farmhouse is no longer in harmony. *C'est la vie*," she said with a dreamy sigh. "So while I'm in town, Samson invited me to dinner."

"Really? He invited you?" I tried not to sound surprised.

"He did, yes. He's been wanting to work through things for a while." Penny's face pinched as she spied the donuts between us. She pushed the whole thing, box and all, into the waiting trash with a dramatic sweep of her arm. "No *wonder* he hasn't been losing weight—all he eats is trash."

I was too stunned to stop her. The rest of her low-carb, low-fat ranting became indistinguishable background noise.

He'd been wanting to work through things for a while.

They were getting back together.

I stood, trying to keep my tone even. "Well, I hope that you and Sam have a wonderful time together. I really ought to be going since I have work in the morning."

"I am so thankful I never knew that life." Penny sighed before flashing me a renewed smile. "It's been so good to see you again, Delilah."

"That's 'Adaliah.'"

"*Peu importe*," Penny said with a self-depreciating wave of her hand. "Adaliah, yes. It's been some time since Samson mentioned you, so it's easy to forget. But thank you for stopping by. I know our previous exchanges were a little—ah—tense, but time certainly does heal all things, oui?"

"Sometimes," I said. "But sometimes it makes things more complicated."

Stepping out of the kitchen, I came face-to-face with a modelesque blond puffing his way down the hallway. A life-sized human sculpture was tucked under his arm like a football.

"Trevor, I presume?" I asked.

He grunted in affirmation before dragging the thing into the parlor.

Sam propped the storm door open with what looked to be a second near-identical sculpture.

I gawked. "Oh my god. Really?"

They were both statues of Penny.

"I've heard of artists putting part of themselves into their work, but this is ridiculous," Sam muttered under his breath.

"It's an uncanny likeness, for what it's worth." Shaking my head, I navigated past Sam and gave him a smile I hoped didn't look as hurt as I felt. "Thank you for the coffee."

"Didn't mean to chase you off. You don't have to go if you don't want—we really didn't have much of a chance to talk." He set the statue against the wall with a grunt, only for it to slide onto its side with a crack. Its plaster nose bounced across the floor. We both stared at it in horror. "Uh-oh."

"What was that?!" Penny screeched from the kitchen.

"Seems like you've got your hands full." I turned to look out the storm door. The rain had come to a stop and a few lonely stars dotted the night's sky. "Maybe some other time. Good-bye, Sam."

"G'night, Ada," he said distractedly as he picked the statue up and fruitlessly tried to jam the nose back onto the sculpture. "Wasn't nothing, Penny! Don't worry your pretty little head 'bout it."

I grabbed my jacket and opened the door but paused as a familiar sight on the key hook caught my eye.

It was a novelty spare key, the kind you could get made in five minutes at a big box store, topped with an enamel donut. I'd had it made for Sam as a joke when we were still together.

A key to my apartment.

It had been years since our affair went public and we'd lost contact.

Why did he still have it?

Trying to push the thought from my mind, I stepped out into the night air, but I couldn't help but feel like maybe there had been some credence to Teddy's theories about my stalker after all.

The walk seemed longer on the way back. Twice I stopped, wanting to look behind me in hopes that Sam would still be standing at the storm door waiting, but I knew that was foolish. Everything about this was foolish.

When my car came into view, I sighed. A bright-yellow slip of paper fluttered under the windshield wiper. A parking ticket.

As if the day could've gotten any worse.

"I swore I put in enough coins," I grumbled as I pried the paper loose. The green flag on the meter stood out in my peripheral vision. According to the gauge, there was plenty of time left.

Confused, I turned the paper over. It held only two words: *Keep Running.*

I had to. There was no other choice.

12

"Hey, bosslady, I—" Cel stalled in the entrance to my office. "Whoa, is that a bag of croutons?"

I slowly withdrew my hand from the resealable pouch next to me, my smile an even mix of guilt and embarrassment. "Yes, yes it is."

"Hey, I'm not judging," she hastily added, throwing both arms up in a gesture of neutrality. "Just, you know . . . by themselves? You're not gonna put them on a salad or *nothing*?"

"Really, I'd love to put them on a salad, but that would require more prep time than I had this morning," I explained. "Yasmin was scheduled to open today, and she's still out with her triplets. I had to fill in at the last minute so I didn't have time for breakfast, much less time to pack my lunch, so I just grabbed what was portable—"

"And that happened to be zesty garlic croutons. Say no more." She nodded knowingly.

"And I had eaten all the good pieces from the candy dish by nine." My head dropped in shame. "God, I am such a failure."

"Aw, sweetie, no." She hip checked the door behind her. "If it makes you feel any better, I'm wearing one black and one navy sock this morning, and I did that shit on *purpose* 'cause I couldn't find their matches and didn't think anybody would notice."

"Did they?"

"The moment I walked in." She sighed, flopping into the chair across from mine. "You coulda called me, you know. I'd have come in. You probably coulda used the extra hour of sleep after your date last night, am I right? Eh? Eh?"

To emphasize her point, she leaned on my desk with interest, chin propped on both knuckles. She batted her eyelashes expectantly, waiting for a story. With a tired sort of acceptance, I minimized the spreadsheet I was working on.

"Let me spare you some of the gory details." I unscrewed the cap on the lukewarm Coke on my desk and took a sip in preparation. "I'm pretty sure Sam thinks I'm crazy, and he's getting back together with his wife."

"What? But—but after all that? The whole 1922 thing?" Her hands thumped against the table in shock. "What a primo, certified douche."

"There's more to it than that. A lot more to it than that. But the full story requires a setting that sells alcohol in large quantities." I drummed my nails against the desk in thought. "Speaking of which, have you taken your lunch hour? We could go at the same time. Garlic croutons just aren't doing it for me today. My treat."

"Well, I'd love to," Cel began, twisting in her seat with uncertainty, "but there's kinda a person you need to see first."

"Oh?" When the fax suddenly started up, I jumped, but I was expecting more papers from my underwriter. "Another creep in the lobby? Are we being robbed? That'd certainly be a fine capstone for this shitstorm of a week."

"Not exactly." Giving a conspiratorial glance around the room, Cel leaned in to stage whisper. "It's the Feds."

My eyes widened. "What, like the FBI?"

"No, the BTA," she answered. "It's a special agent. Do you think they know you were trying to sneak off to the twenties? Are we gonna have to pull a *Thelma & Louise?*"

"I don't think so. It's probably about the police report I filed last night." At Cel's visible alarm, I added, "It's part of the longer story I mentioned. Things got a little trippy last night."

"Oh wow. Now I definitely want to hear about this later. This is getting juicy." A sly grin shifted across her features. "Speaking of which—this guy's a total hunkasaurus rex."

"No one actually says 'hunk' anymore, do they?" The fax had finished, so I gestured for her to pass the documents over. I spun in my chair until I faced the filing cabinet. A drawer in the bottom contained blank manila folders.

"No, but I'm trying to bring it back. Join me, Ada, and we will bring forth a glorious hunk-filled future!"

With folder in hand, I wheeled back in time to see her fist pump into the air. I bit back a laugh. "I'll pass for now."

"Well, okay, but you're missing out." Her hand drifted back to her side awkwardly. "For serious, though, I would let Officer Muffin-Pecs check my prison pocket anytime."

"Prison pocket?"

"Yeah. You know. Prison pocket. Bronx wallet?" She looked at me incredulously then shook her head. "Eh, forget about it. You want me to send him in?"

I wasn't sure what a prison pocket was, but knowing Cel, I had my suspicions. "If you would. I'm going to mute my calls during this, but if there's anything urgent, just knock."

Saluting, Cel turned on a heel and marched outside. The quiet of my office buzzed with a nervous energy as I waited, straightening and restraightening the same mortgage paperwork to keep my hands busy.

The second rattle of the doorknob caused me to drop the files back into the folder and slam the whole thing in a drawer. The contents of my desk shuddered under the force.

"Oh, I'm sorry. I didn't mean to scare you." Though the man standing in my office was not much taller than Henry, he was fleshed out with an easy twenty pounds of muscle. His black hair was tousled with sweat, while his prominent cheekbones and nose were flushed pink in contrast to his otherwise porcelain complexion. The motorcycle helmet under his arm made me think of him as a modern-day knight. To Cel's credit, he *was* a hunk—but it felt cheap, an understatement, to describe him that way. He was absolutely, classically beautiful. "Ada? Ada Blum? Is that you?"

He was also frustratingly familiar.

"Guilty as charged." I waved him in, still trying to place him. "Please, have a seat."

"Officer Muffin-Pecs" offered a shy smile as he closed the door behind him and sat down. "No offense, but might that be a bad turn of phrase, all things considered?"

I blinked. "I'm not sure what you mean."

The smile faltered. "'Guilty as charged'? Considering that—"

"Oh. *Oh.*" The weight of his words hit me, and I pushed back from my desk to put distance between us. Had the BTA taken Officer Toussaint's theories about me seriously? "But I didn't do anything—"

"Sorry, no, that was a terrible joke. You're not in any trouble." He let out an embarrassed laugh, a hand braced bashfully to his mouth. My heart skipped a beat as his eyes met mine. "It's good to see you again, Ada."

"Thank goodness." I practically melted against my chair, shoulders slumping in defeat. "I'm sorry, I know that I know you, but I'm not sure from where. Who are you?"

"I'm Rowland Fairchild. I was in your Timeline Causality and Ethics class."

Immediately, I could picture him sitting three desks away from me in the lecture hall. I wondered how in the world I had managed to forget him. How many lessons had he derailed debating the moral principles of time travel with our professor?

"Yes, of course, I'm so sorry," I said quickly. "It's great to see you again too. You're with the BTA now? Cel mentioned you're a special agent."

"I just graduated from the academy last year," he said. "In all honesty, I'm a little surprised to find you here of all places. You always gave such eloquent speeches—I thought for sure you'd end up working in temporal tort."

"I thought about it, but in the end, I just don't have the heart for it. I did pass the bar exam but—" I paused, not wanting to give out my life story. Besides, if Rowland paid any attention to the news at all, he probably already knew. "Well. Things change."

"An unfortunate truth, Ada. A very unfortunate truth," he answered, sobering. "I wish I was just here on a social call with an old classmate, but I'm afraid I need your help. Senator Samson St. Laurent is currently under investigation for unauthorized temporal insider trading and money laundering."

I could barely breathe. "What? I'm sorry, I don't understand."

Light-green eyes, almost mint colored, studied me from above steepled fingers. "We have evidence that Senator St. Laurent has used a third party to dabble in the stock market circa 1922 or 1923."

"So, basically he's telling someone what stocks to buy because he already knows the outcome." I opened the vertical blinds behind me, flooding the room with sunshine. "That's not illegal, though, is it? Our Insight department uses time travel to deny borrowers all the time."

"You're right. It's not technically illegal," he said. "What's trouble-some is that he's trying to hide his earnings from the government to avoid taxation and regulation. This is prohibited under the insurance and lottery provision of the Fiscal Retroactivity Act."

"And you're hoping by monitoring his accounts here at the bank you'll find where the money is going." I watched the wind tug at a stubborn autumn leaf still clinging to the tree outside my window. "I agree that sounds very on-brand of Sam, but why is he doing it? What's his motivation?"

"The going theory is that he's trying to reconcile with his wife," he said. "Senator St. Laurent's money problems are already well known among Washington insiders, and Penelope Jackson is not a cheap woman to court."

"I knew it." I made a sound that was somewhere between a laugh and a sob. "That's why she was at the townhouse with him yesterday."

He nodded. "This is a very serious crime, Ada. Some economists believe that temporal meddling just like this might have had a hand in the stock market crash of 1929."

"The Great Depression," I murmured, turning back to face him. "Does this have anything to do with the police report I filed yesterday evening?"

"A report?"

"I've been seeing someone from 1922 via a temporal dating service." It felt strange, almost wrong, to say I was seeing Henry. "Yesterday, during my session, I found Sam's body. He had been murdered. When I filed a police report, your organization said that there was no crime associated with that date and time."

"Interesting." Rowland tapped the helmet in thought. "Our databases are infallible. As gatekeepers, we have to keep the most accurate records possible. You mentioned Senator St. Laurent was at his townhouse—I assumed you made contact, then? Did you alert him of what had happened?"

"I did, yes, but I don't think he believed me." I frowned. "What's going on? Did it happen? Am I crazy?"

"I doubt that. There's a simple explanation," he said. "By telling Samson what was going to happen, you've changed the course of events. That said, I'm willing to wager it will come to pass again if you don't help me."

I bit my lip. "Well, I guess going to jail is better than dying."

"Believe it or not, it really is the better of two options." He reached out to rifle through the candy dish. I tried to look innocent when his hand came back empty, disinterested in any of the pieces I'd left behind. "Senator St. Laurent is getting into matters far over his head. Temporal criminals are the worst sort. They're well funded and ruthless. Like cockroaches under a light, once you've found them they scatter across the centuries again. I would hate for this matter to fall to the ORAE."

"Right, of course. It sounds like he found himself at the wrong end of a bad deal." Henry's theory about Sam working with the Kings was gaining more and more traction. "I'll look into it, but I really can't share any information with you unless you have a warrant."

"Let me give you my contact information. Give me a call when you find something, no matter how small." Rowland pulled a sleek black card from his pocket and slid it across the table. "Anything you can do to aid us in this investigation is appreciated, Ada."

"Thank you." I took the card. Above his phone number and email address, a holographic clock was imprinted into the heavy card stock. Its hands seemed to race as I tilted the card. When I looked up, the BTA agent was staring. I blushed, flattered at first—but grew increasingly uncomfortable under his gaze. "Is something wrong?"

He shook his head as if coming out of a daydream. "Are you a fan of van Gogh?"

"What?" I asked before turning. "Oh, the painting. I love the colors."

"I like most of his work, but I think his sunflowers are subpar," he explained. "They always look haggard to me. Like he needs a better gardener. Monet's *Sunflowers* is much better—easier on the eyes, in any case."

"I don't know," I said. "I guess people have an assumption of what flowers should look like. Bright, healthy. Uniform in their beauty. It's nice to see a painting of what sunflowers would look like if I tried to keep some."

There was an emerging edge of politeness in Rowland's smile that said he hadn't appreciated my joke. "Please consider what I've said. It's none of my business, but, out of everyone, you've got the most reason to punish Senator St. Laurent—for the things he's done to you."

Sam's ring burned like a brand beneath the neckline of my dress.

"I'll be in touch," I said "Have a good evening."

From my office, I could see across to the teller line. As Cel counted out money to an elderly man, her attention was elsewhere, following the BTA agent all the way out the door. The moment the transaction was finished she scampered across the lobby. "So, how'd it go? You gonna be his prisoner of love?"

"Not exactly. Officer Muffin-Pecs wants my help with an investigation." My stomach growled loudly enough for both of us to hear it.

Cel giggled. "Gonna guess that means you're ready for lunch now?"

"Mm-hm." I finished off my Coke in hopes it'd tide me over for the time being. "Go ahead and balance your drawer. I need to send off an email, then I'll be ready."

With another salute, she was gone, leaving me to my thoughts. I didn't know how to feel or what to believe anymore.

Teddy had warned me that Sam would only hurt me, but he had seemed so sincere when we had met in New York. Obviously, I had watched him lie before, clearing his schedule for "an important client" that was really me. Telling his constituents that he grew up "on a small farm with nothing but a lean-to and a peach tree." Calling Penny to let her know that he was "working late."

I guess I had just never seen Sam lie to me.

Feeling sick, I pulled up the bank's database on my computer and put in my credentials. A cursor blinked in the search field, waiting for a client name.

St. Laurent, Samson, I typed in with shaking fingers.

A page of results loaded.

While I didn't want Rowland's accusations to be true, the numbers in front of me didn't lie. Sam was a full month behind on his credit card. There was a delinquent loan. His checking account showed overdrafts for eleven months out of the past year. His savings was completely drained, closed out a year ago due to a zero balance.

What credits he had to his account were deposits made in cash, personal checks from names I didn't recognize. What was Sam's game?

Well, whatever it was, I wasn't playing anymore. I closed my workstation down and searched through my phone for Ms. Little's number.

"You've reached the Kairos Temporal Matchmaking Service," she answered on the second ring. "What can I do for you, dear?"

"It's Ada Blum. I think I'm ready to come back. When's your earliest appointment?"

"Mm-hm." There was a brief pause. "How does tomorrow at seven o'clock sound? With Henry?"

"That's—" My heart sank. While I liked Henry, I knew there was no future with him. I wasn't exactly gangster moll material, and the Great Depression was only a few years away. It was back to my original plan. "Not for me, sorry. The appointment time is fine, but no more gangsters, no more 1920s. I'd really like to get back to the Regency era if it's possible."

"Of course, dear. See you soon."

"Oh my god, Jen, I know. Like—" The brunet crossed, uncrossed, then recrossed her legs. She juggled the phone from hand to hand as she resituated. "I know! Oh my god, just, like, I know. I *knowww*."

It was just the two of us in the waiting room again.

I was running out of options. Earlier, I had tried to pass the time by pulling up an e-book, but I had been jarred out of the opening paragraph by a sudden bleat of laughter. After several more failed attempts, I tried some mindless game from the App Store and got a game over in record time, still unable to block out the conversation I was unwillingly eavesdropping on.

"Oh my god, no. What did she say?" She let out a small gasp, hand cupped to her mouth. "What did you say back? And then what did she say? And you said—oh my god, Jen, I know!"

Earbuds. I dimly remembered carrying some convenience store earbuds when I used to hit the gym on my lunch break. Unzipping a side pocket, I shifted through crusty pennies and old receipts, hoping I hadn't thrown them away.

"Are you for real?" Grabbing herself by the ankles, she pulled herself into a cross-legged position, feet somehow tucked under her in the cramped seat of the waiting room chair. "Ugh, yes, I know."

I had just found my earbuds— a snarl of white wires and slick plastic—under an empty travel-sized box of tissues when the brunet's phone call came to an abrupt end. That was when I made my first mistake of establishing eye contact.

She was looking at me. Great. Tuning her out would feel pointed.

Forcing a polite smile, I started to work my way through the tangles. "So, where—or I guess, when—are you going to today?"

"The 1920s."

"Ah." I dug my nails into the wires to loosen up a particularly stubborn knot. "The makeup from that time period is really interesting. I hope you enjoy it."

"Yeah."

Well, I'd given it the old college try. If Gossip Girl didn't want to make small talk, I wasn't going to drag it out of her. I uncoiled an earbud from its mate.

"Where are you going?" she continued a minute later—maybe when she realized I wasn't going to carry the conversation by myself. "Ye olde Ireland? 'Cause, like, you look super-Irish."

"Close." My smile felt strained. "Great Britain. Regency era."

"Like, Shakespeare?"

I stared at her in disbelief, barely managing to keep up the facade. "Close again, but not quite. Think Jane Austen."

"Oh. We were supposed to read *Sense and Sensibility* in high school." She chewed on her lower lip. "But I thought it was boring, so I just watched the movie instead."

I felt a pang of guilt and made a mental note to prioritize Austen in my reading list, no matter how dry she was. "Ah, I see."

"So, what's he like?"

"Oh, I haven't actually met him yet." I worked one wire through a loop in hopes it would thin the knot, but it only made it worse. "What about you?"

"So, like, originally? I was paired up with this guy from 1965," she explained. "I *love* hippies, so I thought it'd be superchill, but he ended up being military and—ugh, no. He was so depressing."

I nodded slowly. "Well, the Vietnam War was a really tough time for our boys . . ."

"Yeah, but he didn't have to like, dwell on it, you know?" She rolled her eyes with a noise of exasperation before waving the idea away. "So I did a hard pass on him. But this one I'm superexcited for. I love bad boys, and the matchmaker? She says he's a real, live gangster. Total badass."

My heart was coming to a slow stop. "Really. What's his name?"

"Oh, shit. Henry"—she tried to jog her memory with a snap of her fingers—"Henry Leverson?"

The tangle of wires fell into my lap. "Levison."

"Hey, that's right. You know him?" Her overplucked eyebrows rose in recognition. "Whoa, like, you aren't a thing, are you?"

"No." The answer came almost too fast. A moment passed as I thought about amending it, finally settling on, "He wasn't exactly my type."

She settled back in her chair, relieved. "Cool. Didn't wanna make things weird."

Her phone vibrated with an incoming text message, sending her whole bag shivering against the floor. Our conversation was over.

It wasn't any of my business, I told myself. I'd repeatedly expressed disinterest to Ms. Little about Henry and, understandably, the matchmaker had adjusted accordingly. It was selfish to think of him as untouchable, even if I personally thought his new match was a catastrophically bad one. She wouldn't see Henry— she'd see a gangster, a fetishized piece of history, and he was too lonely to care.

I knew I needed to let it go, but as the minutes ticked by, my thoughts kept coming back to Henry. Guiltily, I pulled out my phone.

It was against Kairos's terms of service to research anything about their bachelors and bachelorettes. Ms. Little had likened it to reading the end of a book first, and frequently reminded us that the information available might not be entirely factual, details lost or distorted over the years. But since I no longer had any stake in Henry's future, I didn't think it'd hurt. I just wanted to see if he'd ever gotten that wife, brownstone, and trip across the ocean like he wanted.

I pulled up my phone's browser and typed his name in the search bar. Though I didn't expect helpful results for a self-described "goon" like Henry, time travel had caused the internet's repository of historical records to swell, so it was possible. To my surprise, the first page was filled with hits—the very first link a Wikipedia page for Henry Levison. I bit back a smile as I clicked it, idly wondering if I'd read the life story of a Mafia don or a concert violinist. Knowing Henry, maybe both.

Henry Abraham Levison (November 1, 1896–October 1922) was an American gangster responsible for . . .

Though I read farther, the words on the screen lost all meaning. My eyes hung on that date. October 1922.

We met in October 1922.

I tried to rationalize it. Another Henry Levison, maybe—Henry was a pretty popular name in the '20s, if I recalled correctly. But the picture that stared back at me from the article was the same one I'd been provided by the agency. Despite the warmth of the waiting room, my breath shuddered on the exhale.

I tapped the Death hyperlink.

Levison's body was discovered in the East River on April 10, 1923, but contemporary records indicate that he may have gone missing as early as October 23. The frigid waters of the Hudson helped preserve Levison's body, which was reportedly so mutilated that it went unclaimed in the morgue for ten days as a John. It is suspected that Levison's death was retribution for . . .

A sudden squeal of laughter made me drop the phone. The brunet was furiously tapping out another text. I wondered if I should tell her. Would she even care?

Closing my eyes, I tried to talk myself out of the bad idea brewing at the back of my mind. People died every day, good people who didn't deserve it, but there was rarely a valiant time traveler willing to intervene on their behalf. I was tired of gangsters and car chases, mannequins and temporal capers. I just wanted to bag a Mr. Darcy and travel back to the 1800s where nobody had heard of Samson St. Laurent and the underpaid intern stupid enough to believe he'd ever leave his shrew of a wife for her. I didn't want to fight anymore, and even if I did, there was no way that the plan I was piecing together wouldn't end in spectacular failure.

But dammit, I had to try.

"You know," I said, waiting for a lull between messages, "before you go on a date with him, there's something you should know about Henry."

"Yeah?" She didn't look up from her phone.

I pressed on. "He has the greasiest hair. It's nasty. He tells people it's pomade but I'm pretty sure he just never washes it. I wouldn't touch it if I were you."

Well, it wasn't a total lie.

She made a face. "Ew. Okay, so the first order of business is a shower. Thanks for the heads-up."

"Not a problem. Just looking out for you." My nails clicked in thought against the armrest as she got another text message. This wasn't working. I needed another deal breaker. "Oh, and there's the whole car situation, but that probably won't be a problem."

"What car situation?" she asked. The screen slowly lowered from her face.

"Hm, I don't know." I pursed my lips to avoid giving myself away with a grin. "I've probably already said too much. You know the terms of service discourages outside research."

She gave me a sharp look. "Girl, you can't just hint at the tea and not spill it."

I pretended to consider my options, rolling my eyes to the ceiling before finally relenting.

"It's just that he doesn't have one," I answered nonchalantly. "So be prepared to bum a lot of rides from his friend Jake. He's a nice boy, you'll like him. It's a little cramped with Schlomo in the back seat, too, though. That's another of Henry's friends. They're sort of a three-for-one deal."

"But, like, taxis were a thing back then, right?" she asked. "We could just take a taxi."

The door opened. Panic welled in my chest as I waited for one of the receptionists to call us back, but it was just another Kairos client heading home after a session. Regardless, I was running out of time. I needed to go for the hard sell.

"Well, you could, but you're going to be the one paying the fare." Digging deep, I channeled as much as I could from Teddy and Antoine's wicked gossip sessions. There was almost always some angle of pity worked in. "I had to pick up the tab for dinner, bless his heart."

"Oh, wow."

"I know. You'd think that the mob would pay more." I smiled in sympathy. "But, well, he wouldn't really be a bad boy if he had a stable income, would he?"

The reception window slid aside. "Auri Romero, proceed to Lockers and Wardrobe."

I held my breath.

Still sparing the occasional glance at her phone, the woman across from me stood and, to my disappointment, moved to the door. "Thanks again for the warning."

I offered her a tepid smile. "It was the least I could do."

So much for that. It had been a stupid idea anyway. In the end, I couldn't really fight fate, could I? After all, I had already read it. No matter what I did, it had already happened. Henry was dead. He'd been dead for over a hundred years.

My head sank into my hands. I stared blearily at my shoes, overcome with guilt. Why couldn't I have signed up with Tinder? It might not have been any easier, but at least every third date didn't end in temporal paradox.

I'm not sure how long I waited. One playthrough of "The Girl from Ipanema" bled into the next. Maybe that was the point. Like Las Vegas casinos, Kairos wanted its patrons to lose track of the time spent in their waiting room. I pulled out my phone to check the time: 6:45. I had been waiting for twenty minutes.

A minute passed.

The clock rolled over to 6:44.

I hated time travel.

The plexiglass window slid open. The same receptionist stared down at his clipboard, still perplexed by my name. "Ms. Blum, proceed to Lockers and Wardrobe."

"Really, Ada is just fine," I offered reassuringly.

Walking down the long hallway, I lingered as usual on the framed pictures and success stories of the clients who'd come before me—or maybe after me, I wasn't sure anymore—but I wasn't trying to learn their faces or glean the secrets of their storybook romances anymore. I was waiting, maybe delaying, though I wasn't sure for what.

The last door on the hallway opened. Auri Romero stepped out, Victoria's Secret bag thrown over her shoulder. I felt a flutter of hope.

"A refund will be wired into your account within five to seven business days," Ms. Little said, just a step behind her. Her eyes met mine briefly before settling on the brunet with just a ghost of a smile. "Minus the applicable fees, of course."

"Got it." Auri waved as she passed me, disappearing back into the waiting room.

Stunned, I waved back a beat too slow, staring unfocused at the space she had occupied. Then I bolted for the matchmaker's office. "Excuse me, Ms. Little—"

"Hello, dear." She took a step back to allow me entrance, expression curious. "Have I got my times mixed up again? Shouldn't you be in Wardrobe by now?"

"Don't talk to me about getting time mixed up right now," I said dryly, flopping into a wingback chair across from her. "I need to make an appointment to see Henry Levison."

The matchmaker took her seat, fanning out the yellow gingham of her dress. "Henry Levison? Forgive me, dear, but I believe you said—"

"I know what I said," I interrupted, cringing. "But I've changed my mind. I want to give him another chance. Mr. Darcy can wait."

"Are you sure, dear?" She folded her hands. "After all, you said it yourself. You're looking for a less volatile time period, and the Great Depression is right around the corner—"

"I don't care." My knuckles turned white as I gripped the arms of the wingback. "Please. I'm willing to pay a fee, reschedule for another day, whatever it takes. But I need to see Henry again."

There was a long pause. Ms. Little paged through her GlassBook with an air of quiet disapproval. "Well, luckily for you there's that cancellation I mentioned."

I stole a glance around the back of the chair, at the door, before looking back at the matchmaker. "But that was weeks ago."

"What is to be will be, my dear." Her smile was cryptic. "Given Ms. Romero's sudden and inexplicable change of heart, we may be able to work you in today. Proceed to Lockers and Wardrobe."

My shoulders sank with relief. "Thank you."

"My pleasure." She shut the GlassBook with a flutter of pages and slid it aside. From a side drawer she produced a small cross-stitch frame, half finished, and a few spools of bubblegum pink and mint green embroidery thread. She tutted, feeding the needle through the cloth. "Though, really, I don't know what you see in the boy. He doesn't even own a car."

13

"Mm-kay, puddin' pop, I see two problems here." Teddy held up two fingers, folding them down one at a time. "A, I'm not part of Wardrobe. B, I go on break in five minutes."

"Those are your only concerns?" I asked. "I'm surprised. I thought you'd be more worried about the potential prison time. Not to mention losing your job."

"Oh, trust me, I'm acutely aware of those possibilities, but they hinge on whether or not this half-baked scheme of your actually works," he hissed, eyes darting to the line of makeup artists behind him, waiting with bated breath to see if they'd somehow overheard our conversation. "It's much more likely that this is going to fall apart long before you smuggle your boyfriend into the present."

"Can we not call him my boyfriend?" I crossed my arms but relented a moment later. "Cuppycake, I hate to put you on the spot like this, but I'm running out of time. Wardrobe's going to come looking for me any minute now."

He blew out his cheeks. "Fine, I'll help you. But you owe me. If this works, we're marathoning the entirety of *Forged in Fire*—"

"I thought you didn't like the History channel anymore?"

He gave me a sharp look. "Are you refusing the terms?"

"No," I said quickly. "*Forged in Fire*, got it."

"*And* you're buying dinner for the next month. My choice," he continued. "And taking a trip to Colonial Williamsburg. In costume!"

I nodded. "Anything else?"

"Let's just say the full terms and conditions of this agreement will be determined as needed," he said.

This was absolutely going to come back to bite me in the ass, but I didn't have much of a choice. "Sure, okay. So, you understand the plan?"

"Yeah, yeah." He leaned in for a brief hug, a maniacal edge to his grin. "I've got the director's cut of *Ocean's Eleven*, *Twelve* and *Thirteen* on Blu-ray. That practically makes me an expert in this sort of thing."

Some of the enthusiasm drained from my smile. "I have the utmost faith in you."

With that, he backed away from me and pressed himself tight against the wall of the staff's break room. As he slipped farther inside, I tried desperately to ignore the fact that he was humming the *Mission: Impossible* theme and headed to Wardrobe.

Knowing that Ms. Little had made a last-minute alteration for me, I had half expected not to see my name among the chalkboard signs that lined the dressing rooms, but there it was—the last on the line, and it was even spelled correctly. I locked the door behind me and immediately set to examining the purses I had to choose from, hung from a row of brass hooks. The majority of them were hand-sized clamshell purses, too small for my needs, but I eventually found a tall leather handbag I thought would work. I put it aside.

The clothes Kairos had selected for my 1920s outing hinted at significantly colder temperatures than my trips before. I scrolled through hangers drooping with heavy wool coats with enormous lapels made of mink, picking out the least ostentatious one I could find.

There was a trio of knocks at the door. That was Teddy with the signal.

I grabbed a navy-blue dress from the rack and cracked the door open.

"Everything okay, hon? I've been waiting for you in Makeup for a while," he said, just as we'd rehearsed. That meant he'd found what he was looking for.

"Oh, it's fine. I just had my heart set on this dress, and it won't fit," I answered with a sigh, showing him the garment. "I guess I'll have to settle on another one."

"*My* sister? Settle?" He puffed up theatrically—maybe a little *too* theatrically—as he snatched the dress from my grasp. "Nonsense. Let me see if anybody can find it in a size up."

"A size up? I thought we agreed I'd need to go a size down?" I whispered.

"I thought a size up would be more realistic," he muttered, leaning in. "I mean, let's be honest. That's not all water weight, sweetie."

I stared at him, trying to fight the urge to laugh. "You're not going to win any Oscars for this performance, you know."

"You wound me, Ada."

"Just stick to the plan, okay?" I started to close the door. "No more ad-libbing."

"Fine. Sheesh, everyone's a critic," he said, heading out with my dress in tow.

Once he was gone, I turned my attention back to the rows of clothing behind me and picked out my actual outfit—a long burnt-orange dress that was nearly the color of my hair and a pair of cotton stockings that threatened to cut off the circulation to my thighs, but I hoped they'd actually stay up that way. I was layering on handfuls of beaded necklaces when Teddy knocked on the door again.

"Here's the dress, hon," Teddy said, his smile curling deviously. "I got the biggest size I could."

"I hate you," I answered through a gritted smile, both hands out to receive the folded clothing in his arms.

"Excuse me." A voice three stalls away grabbed my attention. Another Kairos employee stalked toward us, the heels of her pumps clicking a furious rhythm. "Sir, you need to return to your own department. These are the ladies' dressing rooms."

"Yeah, I get that," he said. "I was just helping my sister find this dress in the right size, since there weren't any attendants available."

She looked sternly over her glasses. "Be that as it may, your presence here is going to make some of our clients uncomfortable, I hope you understand. Besides, it looks like she's already found another outfit."

Teddy's eyes narrowed. "Honey, if some lady thinks I'm lurking here to catch a peek at them, they're only flattering themsel—"

"We're sorry," I said firmly, grabbing the dress. "I'll be sure to alert an attendant next time."

She held out her hand. "I can take that dress back for you, if you'd like."

"Oh, no, that's not necessary. I might try it on and see which one I like best." I slammed the door and practically slid down it in relief. "Thank you for your time, I'll let you know if I require anything else."

The dress felt heavy in my arms. Unfolding it revealed that a man's double-breasted overcoat and driver's cap, both embroidered with forget-me-nots, had been tucked inside. Just like I had planned.

Teddy really was the best brother—not that I'd ever admit it to his face.

Opening the handbag I'd found earlier, I shoved the coat and hat inside, disguising them by wrapping them in a long scarf and a pair of gloves before heading out.

Teddy was waiting for me at his station in Hair and Makeup. He grinned as I sat down, then threw the plastic cape over my shoulders. "How was that for a performance?"

Despite my annoyance, I smiled. "I'll give it three out of five stars."

He made a face. "Yeesh. Tough crowd."

Dear Santa, the ad began, words stretched over the woodcut illustration of a beleaguered-looking urchin. *For Christmas this year, I'd like the day off. Please think of our delivery boys and shop girls—do your Christmas shopping early.*

I folded the copy of the *New York Herald* and laid it on the leather upholstery beside me. "And here I thought Christmas creep was a twenty-first century problem."

My chauffeur chuckled from the front seat, but his eyes never left the crowded streets of New York's Lower East Side. "No ma'am. Believe it or not, the push to get holiday shopping done early started out as a humanitarian effort. Without regulated workdays or child labor laws, the lower class would often be pushed to the point of exhaustion in the last few weeks before Christmas."

"That doesn't sound too different from working in retail now," I murmured.

"That may be true, but at least in the present day it usually doesn't end in a case of tuberculosis." At the corner, he took a hard right. Run-down shops and boarded-up taverns gave way to the smoke-stained brick of tired townhomes. The car was slowing down. "The Bowery is a rough neighborhood, Ms. Blum. I know it's not my place to say, but it doesn't seem right to match up a nice girl like you with the criminal element."

I thought back to my earlier conversation with Ms. Little. "It seems silly to go through all the trouble of traveling to 1922 to date an accountant."

He considered that with a slight bob of his head. "I see your point. Still, you don't have to go through with this if you feel uncomfortable."

I gripped my handbag. "This is where I can find Henry Levison today?"

"Yes ma'am." The car came to a stop.

"Then I'm going in." I opened the door and studied the row house in front of me. There was a deep crack in its cement foundation, and a third-story window was patched with butcher paper. "Thank you for your help, Mister—?"

"Jonathan Harvick. It was my pleasure," he said, tipping his hat to me. "I'll see you at eight o'clock, ma'am."

"Eight o'clock," I repeated.

If everything went according to plan, I'd be back at Kairos by six.

I walked up the stoop, stealing glances at the black car hovering at the curb. The driver seemed intent to stay until I was accounted for—normally a sweet gesture, but that day it felt distrustful, as though he was fully aware of what I was up to.

With a deep breath, I knocked on the door. Somewhere, a baby wailed.

Two minutes passed. A sharp wind, a precursor of the New York winter to come, cut through the warmth of my woolen overcoat. I nestled farther into the protection of the tall, slouchy collar, suppressing the chatter of my teeth. The baby kept crying. I debated letting myself in as I approached the five-minute mark.

The door finally flew open. An unshaved man stared back at me wordlessly before he looked down at his clothes—a yellowed undershirt, a pair of trousers with pink suspenders, one hanging listlessly from its buckle. Something nasty solidified in his expression, as though I had intentionally caught him in a state of undress. "Well? You gonna stand there?"

Sparing a final glance to my chauffeur, I took a step inside and closed the door behind me.

The entryway was claustrophobic. There was an odd hump in the floorboards that seemed to carry over to the crooked stairwell that dominated the main hallway.

"Rooms are a dollar a week, due on Sunday or you're out. Breakfast is at six, first come first served." The man took a few barefoot steps to the stairs, timber creaking worryingly under his weight. "First week needs payment up front. You got it?"

I tore my attention away from the bald patches in the plaster walls. "Henry Levison. Does he live here?"

My would-be landlord sighed and jerked a thumb upstairs. "Third door on the right. Tell him to can it with the damn violin, would ya?"

I thanked the man as I squeezed past. With each step, the infant's cries grew softer until they disappeared entirely into the lonely notes of a violin. The song filled the whole hallway, everywhere and nowhere at once. My steps grew slow, reluctant, as I left behind the first door, then the second. The vibrato swelled.

Interrupting seemed criminal, like painting over the work of an old master. I waited outside, listening for a break in the music, unsure if I wanted to smile or cry.

This was what Henry was meant to do. I had heard the shy hope in his voice when he had mentioned composing, the flicker of interest when we had talked about his music at Fong's.

He was good. He was *really* good.

But because of who he was, and when he was born, no one else could hear what I did. If I didn't do something, he would die without ever knowing how talented he was, and his body would be tossed into the East River like so much garbage.

Swallowing thickly, I found the courage to knock.

"Goddammit." The song died midnote, followed by a string of sour sounds. Footsteps stormed my way. Before I could react, Henry stood in the threshold, inches away from my face. "Listen, old timer, you want me to stop playing, then do something about the baby. Hell, I'll take her for a while if—"

His eyes met mine.

I smiled. "Hi, Henry."

At first glance, it looked as though I had caught Henry in his pajamas—a ribbed cotton onesie the color of oatmeal. Completely baffled by this choice in sleepwear, I gawked, on the verge of laughter, until I remembered a picture from one of my history books in school.

He was wearing a union suit.

I had caught him in his underwear.

He hesitated. Slowly, his fingers uncurled from the sides of the doorframe. I could see it in his expression, the wheels of his mind turning, processing what to say to me. "Nope."

The door slammed in my face.

"Oh, come on!" Howling with surprised laughter, I pounded on the splintered wood that separated us. "So me taking my shirt off at the cannery, that was fine, but your union suit is too much?"

"Ada, your unmentionables are one thing." Fabric rustled on the other side of the door. "But there's a certain level of embarrassment associated with being caught in anything that has an ass-flap."

"For what it's worth, I think it's cute?"

"Yeah, you would." The eye roll in Henry's statement was almost audible. "Anyway, you'll recall that I let you have your privacy."

I laid my head against the wall. "You're not even showing anything. Let me in."

"How about a rain check?" There was a muffled squeak of hinges and the clap of wood. Maybe he was putting his violin away. "I can work you in, uh, how does 1935 sound?"

My voice grew urgent. "Henry Abraham Levison, if you don't let me in right now, you may not *see* 1935!"

There was an abrupt and thundering silence. Downstairs, the baby was still crying. I knocked a few more times, arm drifting down to my side from exhaustion. "Please?"

The door opened tentatively. He was mostly dressed now—same tired trousers, same ill-patched and rumpled shirt—but his expression was somewhere between that of an ashamed child and an abused dog. Whatever humor remained in the situation evaporated.

He scanned my face questioningly. "How'd you know?"

"I—I beg your pardon?"

His hand clamped down on my shoulder and yanked me inside. Henry kicked a chair beneath the doorknob as a barricade.

"There." Satisfied, he turned his attention back to me, arms crossed. "Now. I'll ask you again: How'd you know somebody's been trying to kill me?"

My smile trembled under his stare. "Lucky guess?"

"Ada." Then both hands were on my shoulders as he looked up at me with sad amusement. "Please tell me you're not a setup."

"What?"

That was clearly the wrong answer. His head dropped, then his arms followed suit. He picked up his pipe and jammed it in his mouth, a twisting trail of smoke fluttering from it as he turned on a heel. There was something cagey about the way that Henry paced, like a sparrow that had found its way indoors but wasn't sure how to get out.

While watching him weave erratic circles around the room, I became increasingly aware of how empty it was. The walls were bare, save for cleaner, square patches in the paint—ghosts of artwork, photos that had once hung there, probably from the previous tenant. There was a single threadbare rug tacked over the lone window. Wires crisscrossed the floor, leading to the few things that ran on electricity: the radio and a bare light bulb. He had a bed and a pile of books that served as a nightstand. A clothesline stretched from one end of the room to the other, sagging with wet clothes, presumably from the metal tub still filled with dingy water.

"Sorry. You caught me on wash day." He stopped at the only other piece of furniture in the room, a shallow table that held a basin and overlooked a frameless mirror. Dunking both hands in the bowl, he splashed his face and clapped the hollows of his cheeks to wake himself up. He stole a glance at me, shaking his head. "Like sending in a cream puff. Maybe that was the point. Cream puffs can be poisoned. Wouldn't see it coming from a dame."

I lurched after him, on the verge of breaking into bewildered laughter. "You—you don't think I was sent to kill you, do you?"

"We keep running into each other, and your man was on the Kings' payroll. At this point, nothing surprises me anymore." He found a can beside the basin and twisted it open. "Did you ever find out anything about the murder? Something funny going on there."

"Oh?"

"Yeah. I combed all of the seaport, but I never found a body that night," Henry said. "I hate to say it, but something tells me he's sleeping with the fish now."

I tried not to smile. Rowland was right, I was sure of it. Somehow, I had changed the course of events and saved Sam's life.

"I think you were right. Sam"—I paused, catching myself before I used the wrong tense—"was working for the Kings in some way. It looked like a deal gone wrong."

"I'm going to be gracious and not say I told you so." The air became a mix of dying tobacco smoke and something like glue as Henry smeared his hands with product and set to straightening his hair. "Anyway, even if you aren't here to bump me off, the last thing I need right now is a broad on my arm."

My reflection smiled at him knowingly from the mirror. "For somebody who doesn't want to see me right now, you sure are gussying yourself up. What's the occasion?"

He stopped, midcoif. The pipe rolled in his mouth as he searched for an answer, but the look on his face said he'd been caught red-handed. "Ma would kill me if she knew I was half dressed in front of a lady. Even a shiksa."

"Where *is* your mother? I was hoping I'd get to meet her."

"You know, I was joking about you being fast before, but this is just getting ridiculous." His laugh was uneasy as he slathered on more pomade while trying to straighten a stubborn curl. "She lives in Brooklyn. Moved her there myself a couple years ago."

The windows rattled under a strong wind. I shoved my hands into the coat's pockets. "From the way you talked before, I was sort of under the impression you lived with her and Estelle."

"Nah. I pay their rent, Estelle's bills, send gifts for their birthdays. They live a lot nicer than I do, I make sure of that." He set down his comb, inspecting his hair in the mirror. There was a brief facsimile of a smile before his expression fell slack, unimpressed. "I see 'em two, maybe three times a year. It's better that way."

He washed his hands in silence, then threaded the tie through his shirt collar.

"Run away with me," I whispered.

His reflection looked at me dubiously. "Yeah, sure. Where we going, the Catskills?"

Setting the handbag on the bed, I opened it and took the overcoat and hat from their knitted hiding place. "I mean it. Come with me. You don't have to live like this anymore."

He spared a quick glance over his shoulder as though he was confirming my existence—that I wasn't just some trick of the light on the mirror. His smile was bittersweet as he put down his pipe. "Ada, I . . ."

"Please." I took a step toward him. "You can start over. *Really* start over. A place where nobody's ever heard of Henry Levison and the mob is just a memory. Your violin, the way you play . . . it's amazing. People will love it."

"Hey, listen—" He turned to face me.

"They'll love *you*, Henry." The words echoed off empty walls, and I wondered if I'd said too much, but didn't care. It was true, regardless, and once I said it the rest of the words came out at a desperate pace. "I don't know what we can do about your mother and Estelle. You take care of them, I understand that. You don't want to abandon them. We'll figure out how to make sure they get what they need. Money, a PO box, anything. It may be hard, but we'll think of something."

Henry was quiet. He gestured for the coat and hat, looking them over for a long time.

"What happened to 'easy'?" The husk of his voice made my skin break into goose bumps.

"I'm tired of doing the easy thing," I said. "I want to do the right thing."

Puffing his cheeks, he took stock of the room around us—the warped mirror, the mountain of books at his bedside table. He stared at the rug, as though he could see beyond it to the other smoggy townhouses that crowded the Bowery.

He smiled. "Yeah, okay."

"Really?" I searched his face for any inkling of his usual sarcasm, but there was none. "I—wow, I wasn't prepared for this. I thought for sure you'd try to fight me."

"That's what I was trying to tell you. At this point, I'm living on borrowed time. Anywhere's got to be better than here." Tentatively, he tried the cap on and checked his reflection. "So, what's with the getup? Worried I'm gonna catch cold?"

"We don't have time for the full explanation right now." My grin broadened as he shrugged into the Kairos overcoat. It wasn't a perfect fit—Henry was a great deal slimmer than most Kairos field agents—but I didn't think anyone would notice. "In short: it's a disguise."

There was a glint of recognition in Henry's eyes. "This looks familiar. That guy who came looking for you before, this is his."

"Mm-hm."

He started fastening buttons, eyes dipping back up to mine every other one. "Uh, should I be concerned right now? 'Cause the laugh is a little worrisome."

"No, it's just . . ." Fighting back another peal of giggles, I straightened his collar, tracing the embroidered wreath of forget-me-nots. "You look great. This might actually work."

"That's what I'm worried about. Why do I feel like I'm being roped into something stupid?" His eyes rolled to the ceiling, as though expecting the heavens to open and provide him with an answer. "So, uh, who exactly am I trying to fool?"

"The Kairos Temporal Matchmaking Service." I circled around him for inspection. The double-breasted cut suited him. Henry looked dignified, worthy of more than a run-down bedroom in a roach-infested tenement. He needed only one finishing touch.

"That's a mouthful. The Kairos . . . temporal?" He craned his neck as I fussed over his tie. A rare bit of color rose to his cheeks. "Like tempo. Time?"

"I thought I said we didn't have time for the full explanation." Tucking the twin tails of his tie into his lapel, I smiled up at him, satisfied. "Pack your things."

He gave a quick glance at the clothesline over our heads. "What about the laundry?"

"Leave it. We can buy you more clothes when we get there," I said. "But if it's important to you, take it. I'm not sure when we'll be able to come back."

Under his gaze, the weight of my words suddenly struck me like the pounding of a wave on the surf. I had been so caught up in the moment, the fear of losing Henry like I had—hadn't?—lost Sam, that it didn't occur to me how much he stood to lose in the process. So much had changed since the 1920s. Everyone he'd ever known would be dead and gone.

"I know this is a lot to ask of you." I bit my lip, unable to look at him. "If you need more time—"

"No. This is fine. Better than fine." He took my hand in both of his. "I don't know how I'll make it up to you, but I'll do it."

"You don't have to do anything," I said. "I know what it's like to want to start over."

He nodded at the bed. "All I need is my violin case. But before I go, I'd like to write a letter to Ma and Estelle. I feel like, after all the lies I've told them, they deserve to know the truth."

"Of course. Take all the time you need."

And in that moment, I wondered if Henry Levison hadn't been waiting his whole life to run away.

14

Though I tried to give Henry his space as he wrote the letter, perched at the opposite end of the bed, I couldn't help but admire his penmanship. He wrote in tight, neat print, all uppercase—like an architect—but signed with a looping cursive that was much prettier than the scribbles I churned out whenever I was asked for a signature. "You have very nice handwriting."

The corner of his mouth twitched. "You don't have to humor me."

"What? I mean it." I nodded at the still-wet ink. "Mine looks like chicken scratch by comparison."

He blew on the paper. "Was the worst in my class. Teacher tried to get me to learn with my right hand, but I couldn't hold it right. Just hope Ma can read it."

"Oh, come on, now you're just being dramatic." I held out my hand. "If it'd make you feel more comfortable, I could take a look to make sure it's legible."

He shied away, folding the paper into thirds. "That would make me feel worse, actually."

"All right, all right. It was just a suggestion." I watched as he slid the letter into a waiting envelope, already addressed, before putting the whole thing into an overcoat pocket. "Have you ever been told you're your own worst critic?"

"Don't know about that. I'd say I'm a mediocre critic at best." He ran a hand over his sole piece of luggage, the violin case. "Besides, I'm pretty sure my worst critic was Mrs. Fetterman."

"Who?"

"An old biddy. Lived two floors beneath us when I was a kid. She was my first violin teacher," he explained. "When I played badly, she'd threaten to cut my hands off. Kept a knife in her knitting basket and everything."

"That's . . ." I blinked. "Terrifying. And explains so much."

"Yeah, well, don't start psychoanalyzing me now," he said, shaking his head. "Freud would have a field day."

I jolted from my place at the bleat of a jalopy horn. It stood apart from the rest of the city's ambient noise, as though it was right outside, honking on and on until it settled into a single, blaring note.

Henry folded back the rug to peer into the street below. "Jake's here. Maybe he can give us a ride to—where we heading to?"

"Midtown."

"And this Kairos place is there? High class." He let out a low whistle, dropping the corner of the rug. "Who knew there was so much money in matchmaking?"

"It's a lot more expensive than you think," I said before I could help myself, moving toward the door. "Ready to go?"

He took a deep breath, gripping the violin case by the handle. "Yeah. Yeah, I think so."

In the hallway, he took out his keys and looked them over. He went as far as to put one in the doorknob, but he didn't turn it, a slow-dawning laugh overtaking him.

"Why bother. Not like I plan on coming back to this dump," he muttered before brightening with a glance my way. "So, you work at this matchmaking operation?"

"Hm?" I took the stairs two at a time. "Oh, no. I'm a banker."

At that, he stopped short. Heavy eyebrows knitted and flexed as he pointed to himself, then to me, then back to him. "I—but you, and the banking, and the mob . . . oy vey."

"What's the matter?"

"Oh, nothing's the *matter*." He gave an innocent shrug as he trotted down the steps. "I just thought, you know, given the circumstances it might be a little *unwise* of you to associate with people like me. Like a cat and a canary."

I rolled my eyes. "Honestly, Henry, it's not like I knew."

"But you found out soon enough. Still, I'm thankful you decided to look past my goonish exterior to see the sentimental schmuck within," he said with a dramatic flourish, head held high. A beat later, an eye cracked open to appraise me. "So, who's the lucky guy?"

"What do you mean?" I had to tug on the front door with both hands to open it.

"This is a matchmaking operation. If you don't work for it, you must be using it, right?" he asked, taking the handle from me. "Then who is it?"

Originally, I had every intent of hurrying past Henry onto the stoop, but the question froze me in my tracks. It had been so easy to flirt with him over chess when he had been nothing more than a way to spend an evening, but now I couldn't even form words, staring up at him helplessly.

His confused expression melted in my silence. A smile twitched at the corner of his mouth, small but hopeful. "It's me, isn't it? They set you up with me."

I laughed nervously in response and ducked my head to hide the heat flooding my face. My fingers laced through his as I ran for the cream-colored car idling in front of the boarding house.

He kept pace, eyes never moving from the sidewalk. It was clear that he was going through several emotions, but the rapid-fire shift of his expression said that he wasn't sure which one was the most appropriate. He settled on a goofy grin as he came up to the passenger window of Jake's car.

"Hey, pal," he said, rapping his knuckles on the glass, "when did you get this heap patched up? Last time I saw it, the Kings—"

I hadn't realized just how dark it was getting until snickering figures melted from the shadows of the street. We were hemmed in by a trio of thugs in ill-fitting suits. I was sorry to say I recognized at least one of them.

"—still had it." Henry deflated with a sigh. His head was cocked dangerously as he turned, voice colder than the autumnal gust that tore through the street. "Frank, you better be here to give me my watch back."

Something flashed from Frank's pocket, reflecting what little light the dim lamps of the Bowery provided, but it was no watch. "Got something even better to give you, Levison."

Henry tensed like a cat about to spring, but he stopped as he glanced at me, his jaw tightening. "What do you want?"

Frank flashed a nasty smile as he gestured to the rear door of the car with his pistol. "We're taking a little ride."

One of the thugs held the door open while another slid inside. Henry's eyes met mine again, looking tired. Defeated. "Thought you said you weren't a setup."

My heart dropped, my stomach churning. "Please, I have no idea what's going on."

I couldn't stop him from climbing into the car as the Kings goon turned the barrel of the gun on me.

"Don't worry, doll, you're coming with us. You can ride on Frankie's lap and if you're good, I might even 'plug' ya . . ." He leered as he ran his tongue over his teeth. Whiskey rolled from his breath. "If you ask *real* nice."

I blinked, vision blurring with angry tears. "I'd rather take my chances in the trunk, thanks."

He slapped me hard enough to turn my head. I sniffled but refused to cry. Not here.

"Suit yourself, ya fat bitch."

With a nod, one of Frank's lackeys made good on my taunt,

binding my arms behind my back with a necktie. I was dragged to the back of the sputtering car, struggling uselessly against the big man.

Automobiles of the 1920s didn't have built-in trunks like the cars of present day. Instead, extra storage came from luggage or crates strapped or bolted to the bumper. In the Kings' case, they had what looked like a large dresser trunk that had been emptied of its interior shelves. I was probably not the first person they'd transported this way.

As the guy pulled the trunk open, I made a desperate attempt to drive my heel into the thug's instep, but it only served to throw me off balance, pitching me straight inside. I landed amid empty sacks of what looked to be cement, my shoulder coming down hard on the handle of a mud-encrusted shovel.

In that moment, I understood. Fate wasn't something to be toyed with, a story to be rearranged because I didn't like the ending.

I had tried to save Henry, and now I was going to die with him.

The lid came down. I screamed wordlessly as my world went black.

We lurched into motion with a chorus of slamming car doors, leaving me to twist blindly in the confines of the trunk. I kicked and bucked against the lid, but without my hands, I could do little more than wriggle like a worm on a hook.

After several agonizing minutes of thrashing, I slumped against the floor of my prison, sobbing bitterly. I wondered if I would be the first casualty among Kairos's clientele. The corsage would ensure they'd find me, but at the speed we were going it would probably be too late. I'd be reduced to some footnote in Henry's Wikipedia article.

Also, Adaliah Bloom—misspelling my name, naturally—was found floating in a steamer trunk in the East River. She was survived by her brother, Teddy, and Auri Romero, who had the good sense to cancel her Kairos appointment.

Oh, hell no.

I wasn't about to be outlived by Gossip Girl.

Somehow, this revelation brought clarity to my racing thoughts. I needed to get my hands free.

The steamer was already a tight fit, but I managed to bring my knees up to my chest, taking ragged, shallow breaths. If I got out of this, I told myself, I was going to take up yoga.

Okay, so let's be honest: I was going to binge on Oreos for six days and *then* take up yoga.

Curled into a ball, I shimmied down the length of the trunk, pressing myself against the side nearest my feet. I plucked at dusty paper sacks, hissing as something hard dug into the tender flesh beneath my thumbnail—the blade of the shovel.

The car slowed. I heard the thrum of traffic as we entered some crowded street while I worked, flexing my shoulders in a shrug, dragging the tie along the length of the muddy spade. The car slowed and accelerated with the ebb and flow of traffic as I cut my way free.

Once my hands were loose, I pulled off the wreath of forget-me-nots at my lapel. The timer glowed dimly in the interior of the trunk.

I had to make a decision. If I kept the corsage on, Kairos would intervene, provided they got to us in time. It was probably the safer, easier option, but any hope of smuggling Henry into the present would be gone. Without the corsage, I would be on my own to get us out of here, for better or worse.

It was clear what I had to do.

The walls of the trunk flexed as I pressed my hands against them. They were soft, but I wouldn't be able to burst them with strength alone.

I twisted myself, wriggling until I could get the shovel from beneath me. After what felt like an eternity, I managed to pull it in front of me, hands wrapped around the splintered handle and feet planted along the back of the blade.

The car lurched to a stop, even though I could still hear the sounds of puttering engines all around us. We must have been at a traffic signal.

I couldn't have asked for better timing.

Drawing a deep breath, I kicked down with all my might, the blade of the shovel biting through the flimsy plywood of the trunk. Three more thrusts and I could wriggle out of the side of the chest, blinking beneath the streetlamps of the Lower East Side. Nobody in the car had noticed me yet.

I pitched the corsage into oncoming traffic. It shattered into a handful of glittering pieces.

The signal overhead clicked lazily to green. I had to act fast.

Before the car could start moving, I hauled the shovel back and brought it in flat against the back of the car's ragtop. In retrospect, I was lucky I didn't hit the frame, instead connecting solidly with the back of Frank's head.

He didn't even have time to make a noise, and slumped onto the front seat. The shovel clattered to the floorboards as I stood there, shocked.

"Did you—did you just knock Frank Kingston out cold? With a shovel?" Henry asked in the stunned silence. The thug to his left stirred into action, but Henry cut him off with an oddly nonchalant elbow to the nose. "Remind me not to get on your bad side."

"Could you be a little less pithy right now?" I yelled over blaring horns. The car started to pull away.

Seconds later, one of the rear passenger doors opened as Henry climbed over Frank. He squirmed free, arms folded around his violin case as he tumbled from the car. I rushed to meet him as he rolled to a stop with a pained groan.

I grabbed him by the arm and did my best to pull him to his feet. Jake's car sped down the street, weaving through traffic as it made a getaway.

"That's New York for you. Heaven forbid an attempted murder interrupt your daily commute," Henry muttered as we retreated from the street to a chorus of angry honks and rude gestures.

We raced down the sidewalk until I was out of breath, and even then, Henry towed me along, our hands locked in a white-knuckled grip. I tried to find anything to break the tense silence. "Are you all right?"

"Yeah, I'm fine. Kicking myself for not getting my watch back from Frank, though. How about you?" he asked. "You were like some kinda maniac with that shovel."

Looking back on the past few minutes, it felt unreal—like someone else had been in control of my body. "I didn't want anything to happen to you."

We made our way through the Lower East Side, Henry's grip slowly relaxing as we began to blend in with the crowds as best as we could with mussed hair and clothing.

"Ada." He worked his jaw, staring at the passing shop fronts to avoid looking at me. "I'm, uh, I'm sorry. About thinking you were a setup."

"It's okay," I said a little too quickly. "You haven't known who you can trust for a long time."

"It's just that"—his voice cracked, and he swallowed thickly—"anything too good to be true usually is. And you're definitely too good to be true."

I smiled, shaking my head. "Henry, don't be silly."

"No, I mean it." His eyes rolled to contemplate the sky. "This mystery woman just walks into my life like she knows me. Takes me to dinner, talks to me like a person. Puts me in my place—"

"I still don't approve of you talking to the waiter like that," I added.

"Yeah, yeah. I know. I got to thinking and—well, yeah. It wasn't funny. Sometimes you just do things because everybody else is doing it, you know? But that doesn't make it right. I deserved to be called out for it." His guilty laughter dwindled to a vulnerable quiet. "But I don't deserve you. You saved my life, Ada. In more ways than one."

I didn't know how to respond to that, so I just squeezed his hand, swinging it playfully. "So, I don't know about you, but these pumps are killing me."

He grinned. "I dunno, I've never worn pumps."

"Shut up," I laughed, nudging his side. "I mean—how are we going to get to Midtown from here? Because I'm not walking."

"Well, when you put it that way . . ." He nodded at a yellow checkered cab parked a little farther along the street. "We're hitching a ride with this guy, whether he's taking fares or not."

As we neared the taxi, Henry opened the cab door wordlessly, nearly startling the sandwich out of the driver's hands.

"Can't ya see I'm on my lunch right—well, if it ain't ol' Hank!" The driver craned his neck to smile at us as we slid into the back of the cab. He tore into the sandwich, washing it down with a gulp of Coca-Cola. "How ya doing, ya crazy bastard?"

"Hey, Tom. Look, I hate to cramp your dinner plans, but we need to get to Midtown toot-sweet," Henry said. "And if you're anything like the last ride we had, you're not getting paid."

Tommy started the engine as he studied us in the rearview mirror. "What's with the getup? You look like one of them hotel doormen and—wait, is this the dame from the Plaza? Spill it, Hank."

Henry made a face. "Please don't call me that."

"Yeah, yeah, whatever, Hank," the cab driver said with a dismissive wave of his hand. "C'mon, you gotta tell me what's going on."

I flashed a tired smile. "It's a long story."

"It's a long drive, lady," the driver said as we pulled away from the curb. "We got plenty of time."

I only hoped that he was right.

The Kairos headquarters in New York wasn't terribly impressive. To the casual observer, it looked like the service entrance to one of the numerous jazz clubs that called the theater district home. The only clue that anything was amiss was the facade of an always-closed mechanic's garage that housed the 1920 division of Kairos's motor pool and a faded forget-me-not wreath painted on the brick above a sign that read AUTHORIZED PERSONNEL ONLY.

Henry watched Tommy's cab merge with the rest of New York traffic, seeing him off with a halfhearted wave before turning to the alleyway. Though he did a good job of hiding it, I could see a glimmer of fear around his eyes. "So, this is it?"

"This is it." I climbed the cement steps. "Before we go in, let's get our story straight. You're my new chauffeur, training under Jonathan Harvick."

"Harvick, got it," he muttered.

I nodded. "If anyone asks, my date ended early and you went out to retrieve me."

Henry raised his hand as he trailed behind me. "I have some concerns? As in, I'm not entirely sure what's going on. What's the backup plan for when I screw this up? 'Cause, uh, telling you now: I'm gonna screw it up."

"You'll do fine. I'll do all the talking." Giving him a once-over, I flattened his collar and dusted off the road debris from his overcoat. He tensed under my hand, breath seizing. I smiled sympathetically. "I wouldn't ask you to do something I didn't think you could do, Henry."

"Oh, yeah, sure. Throw my words back at me." His exhale was shaky as he looked up at the third-story windows, but slowly his expression gained some resolve. "Yeah, okay. Let's do this."

We went inside. The small corridor terminated in a maintenance elevator spray-painted with more forget-me-nots. A small box equipped with a speaker and a call button hung on the wall by the door.

"This isn't like any matchmaking service I ever heard of. You sure it's not a speakeasy?" His dark eyes swept from corner to corner, skepticism building in the flat line of his mouth. "A real high-class one where you gotta know the password?"

I pushed the button. "Not quite."

There was a crackle of static from the speaker. "State your name and purpose."

"This is Ada Blum, returning from her date with Henry Levison," I said. I swear Henry squeaked behind me.

"Back so soon, Ms. Blum? We weren't expecting you for another hour," the speaker said. There was a thrum of machinery as the elevator doors opened. "You may proceed."

I moved inside, but Henry hung back, face knotted with apprehension. "Uh, you know, I'm starting to have some second thoughts."

"Oh, don't be such a baby," I said, grabbing his hand to pull him in. "It's going to be fine. Relax."

"Relax?" he echoed as the doors shut behind us. "You lead me through some real cloak-and-dagger shit and now I'm going down a rickety elevator to only god knows where—excuse me if I find it a little hard to relax right now."

"Henry, please." I squeezed his hand as the elevator took us down. "I can explain everything once we're out of here."

"No, Ada, I'd kind of like an explanation right now." He tore his hand from mine. "How does Kairos know who I am? I didn't sign up for any matchmaking service, and, well—if this was Ma's doing, she woulda just found me a nice Jewish girl like she's always going on about."

I paused, unsure of how to proceed. Any answers I could give Henry at this point would only lead to more questions, and I couldn't risk blowing our cover in front of the technicians.

He shook his head, expression somewhere between annoyance and disappointment.

"This is how I die, isn't it?" he said in a low voice.

"No." I rolled my eyes. "Henry, the scene outside your place, with the Kings? *That* was how you died. Or would've died. But this—"

We came to an abrupt halt. The doors squealed open. A column of artificial white light flooded the elevator.

I smiled. "This is how you live."

It took a moment for our eyes to adjust to the brightness. I walked out first, then Henry, but his steps were hesitant and his expression deeply mistrusting, as though every square of linoleum tile held some secret trap that would bring about his immediate demise.

One of the technicians smiled at us over her book of crossword puzzles. "No more incidents today, Ms. Blum?"

"No, everything went according to plan," I answered. Technically it wasn't a lie. "I'm sorry for being so much trouble before."

"Hardly trouble, hon." Knitting needles clicked in the other technician's hands. "That's what we're here for. Besides, trouble's kinda nice in its own way. Broke up the monotony of the routine. Speaking of which, you wanna get 'em? I'm in the middle of a row."

The first technician nodded and marked her place in her puzzle book. She pushed off her desk and rolled halfway across the room before bouncing out of her rolling chair. Unlocking another door with her badge, she beckoned us into a longer hallway. We weren't too far in before she glanced over her shoulder at Henry. "You're new here, aren't you?"

"Yeah," he answered distractedly, his eyes still drinking in his surroundings.

"Well, I'm Sheila. The other tech at the counter is Linda." She smiled. "And you're . . . ?"

The question caught us both off guard. I stared at Henry, willing him to say *anything* but his actual name.

"Uh, Hank." He winced. "I've been training under Jonathan Harvick."

"Oh, John! He's a sweetheart," Sheila gushed as she led us into a room filled with N-Energy chambers. "We always miss each other. We're either on different shifts or I'm on duty in 1922 and he's off in 1888, that sort of thing, you know?"

Henry shot me a wide-eyed look when the technician's back was turned. "Ah, yeah. Like two ships passing in the night."

"Exactly!" As she double-tapped a green button on the wall, two of the pods hissed open. "Well, I won't keep you. Head on in, make yourselves comfortable. Tell John I said hi, okay?"

Henry flashed a thumbs-up. "Sure thing."

When we took to our chambers, I breathed a sigh of relief. The carbon fiber lids slowly descended as the green button lit up and began to pulse. I looked over at Henry to make sure he was okay. He was clutching the armrests like he was preparing to go into space.

What the hell have you gotten me into? he mouthed.

My giggles echoed off the walls of the pod as it secured around me.

15

Henry scrambled out the moment his pod popped open, hugging his violin case tight to his chest. He looked every bit as bad as I felt; pale, disoriented, his shoulders rising and falling in time with his with terrified breaths. "What just happened? I—I feel like I just got off the Loop the Loop at Coney Island."

"Don't worry, 'Hank,'" I said, swinging my legs over the side of the pod. It felt good to have my feet back on solid ground. "I've been told you get used to it."

"Ugh, not you too. I hate 'Hank.' It was just the first thing that came to mind." He took off his cap and fanned himself with it as he scanned the room around us. "It felt like we moved, but we didn't go anywhere, right? This is the same place."

"Well, we didn't go any*where*, no." My smile was apologetic. "It's really more like we went any*when*."

"'Anywhen'?" As he realized what I meant, I worried that he was going to slide down the wall. "So I didn't mishear what that broad said—1922, 1888. This is like something outta that H. G. Wells book. It's time travel."

"I did tell you I could take you to a place where nobody has heard of Henry Levison." As I stood, the room spun around me like a carousel. I closed my eyes, trying to steady myself by leaning on a folding chair, but I came up short. Henry grabbed me by the waist. I tensed, and his eyes met mine. "And outside of a few notes in an obscure history book, I doubt anybody here has."

"Ada, I . . ." He bit his cheek, looking for the right words. "I mean, it makes sense. But why didn't you tell me?"

"Because I'm not allowed to." The smell of stale pipe smoke and tobacco burned my nose as I hugged his neck. "Any citizen from a protected era is forbidden to know about the existence of time travel. Henry, I meant what I said before. You were supposed to die, but I couldn't let that happen. Even now, your existence here is a violation of dozens of federal laws, but—"

"But you brought me here anyway." He brushed the hair away from my face with a smile. "You know, for a banker, you'd make one hell of a criminal."

I grinned. "Well, for what it's worth, I originally planned to be a lawyer. The two are surprisingly similar."

Footsteps passed by the door. Reflexively, I pulled away from Henry's embrace. For a brief second, he seemed wounded, arms drifting back to his sides, but there was no time to reflect.

"You need to get out of here before the other technician shows up with my clothes from Lockers and Wardrobe." I cracked the door open. Just as before, the office on the other side of the hallway was dark. Canned laughter leaked from the employee lounge. It was a clear shot to the exit. "Head that way. You'll pass through a waiting room. The parking lot is just outside. Wait for me. I may be a while, but I'll join you as soon as I can."

"Anything else I should know?" he asked.

I checked off a mental list. "Oh, if something happens and you don't feel comfortable outside, go to Hair and Makeup and ask for Teddy. He's my brother, he'll take care of you. Now go."

With that, I shoved Henry out the door and sank into the folding chair. The reality of what I had done was finally catching up to me. My vision blurred with tears. I had broken so many rules. I had cheated fate twice in a single evening. Hell, I had knocked out Frank Kingston with a shovel. But most importantly, I had saved Henry.

It was easily the greatest thing I had ever done.

It was also easily the most stupid.

"Hey, there, handsome. Where ya going in such a hurry?"

I froze as I heard the technician's voice on the other side of the door. My knuckles turned white as I gripped the sides of my seat and prayed she was talking to somebody, anybody, other than Henry.

"Sorry, lady, but my shift was over fifteen minutes ago," Henry answered.

It was a nice recovery, at least.

"Small world. My shift's almost over too. Me and some folks were gonna go get drinks after work." She was getting closer to the door. "You wanna come with?"

"Maybe some other time."

I debated opening the door to distract the technician, but I wasn't sure if it would be too obvious a ploy.

"Suit yourself. I didn't even know they was hiring new chauffeurs," the technician remarked. "Feels like the ones we got been here since Jesus was a boy. What's your name?"

"Hank," Henry said. "I'm training under Jonathan Haverick. Can I go now?"

"Yeah, sure, Handsome Hank. Just a minute." There was a long pause. "Just one more question. What year is it?"

I swore under my breath, leaping from my seat.

"You don't know what year it is?" Henry's comeback made me breathe a sigh of relief. It sounded so natural. "No offense, but are you senile or something?"

All joviality dropped from the technician's voice. "Listen, honey, I'm gonna need your employee ID number or I'm giving the boys at the BTA a call."

Unable to wait another second, I tore the door open, desperately trying to invent some kind of cover story for Henry. Anything just to get him out of the room and away from the technician. There was an emergency, or maybe Ms. Little needed him—

Ms. Little. As though on cue, the matchmaker stood at the threshold of the employee lounge, a delicate floral teacup perched on a saucer in hand.

I was going to be sick. There was no question—Henry was going back to his original time, and I was going to rot in jail for smuggling in a temporal alien from a protected era. What had happened to my simple plan of marrying a Mr. Darcy and reenacting my favorite Jane Austen movies for the rest of my life?

"Oh, there you are, Henry." Ms. Little broke into a pleased smile. "I see that you've returned from your first assignment with Ms. Blum—and she's in one piece too. Quite an improvement from her last venture to the 1920s, if I might say so. Very good."

In that moment, I forgot how to breathe.

The technician looked between Henry and the matchmaker. "So, he's fresh blood? For real?"

"Why, did you think he wasn't?" Ms. Little tutted at the other Kairos employee. "Really, dear, we are running a time travel dating service, not some—some sort of underground criminal operation."

"Well, okay, then." The technician eyed Henry warily. "But he still needs to learn some manners if you ask me."

"Yes, yes, of course. All part of employee training, dear." Ms. Little blew at the steam rising from her teacup before taking a tiny sip. "Speaking of which—I was on my way to collect you, Henry. I thought you could shadow me as I meet with Ms. Blum for her follow-up. It's best if an employee is familiar with every step of the process. Er, if you don't mind, of course, Ms. Blum. This meeting is typically confidential, I realize that."

I was caught off guard by the question, and could only stammer. "Oh, uh, of course not."

"Good, good! I'll have you sign a waiver before we begin."

Ms. Little laughed sweetly, toddling back into the employee lounge like one of her wind-up toys. "Come along, Henry. There's quite a lot you need to learn."

Henry looked at me, terrified. I bit my lip, but there was nothing I could do to help him while we were under the watch of the technician. Reluctantly, he moved to follow the matchmaker.

"Kids these days don't got upbringing at all," the technician huffed as she shoved a plastic crate in my direction. "I can see why you use our services, Ms. Blum. In my time, we knew better."

"I have no doubt." With a weak smile, I took my clothes and closed the door.

The instant I signed in at the receptionist's desk, I was called back to Ms. Little's office. On the one hand, I was grateful that the matchmaker was giving me no time to dwell on what fate awaited me in that office at the end of the hallway. But it also meant I'd not been given enough time to come up with a proper defense for my actions. I would have to settle for telling the truth.

Henry was already waiting for me by the door. We exchanged a wordless smile as I took a seat at the desk, but I was sure he could see the fear in my eyes, just as I saw it in his.

"Ah, hello again, Ms. Blum! Do close the door, Henry, if you would." Ms. Little's request felt more like a death sentence, the sound of the door entering its frame like the fall of a guillotine's blade. Her intervention with the technician had only been a temporary reprieve, likely just to save face in front of her employees, and now our punishment would be dealt privately.

"I'm sorry." It seemed best if I started things off with an apology and an acknowledgment of my wrongdoing. I'd still go down in flames, but maybe the matchmaker would take pity on me for being honest. "I'm fully aware of how illegal this was—is—but he was going to die. I know it's the law, there's government mandates, a million pieces of legislature, but it doesn't seem right."

"Ms. Blum—"

But I wasn't done yet. "He's not 'an experience,' for god's sake, to be rented out by a string of vapid trust fund babies looking to satisfy their gangster fetish. He's a human being—"

The matchmaker tried again. "Ms. Blum—"

"—with hopes and dreams and problems. You said it yourself, there's no time without its share of troubles." My voice threatened to break with tears. "How is it that we can interfere with their lives, shoving temporal tourists at them right and left, toying with their emotions, but we can't show them the common decency of oh, I don't know, warning them about the Great Depression that's coming in a few years?!"

By this point, Ms. Little had resigned herself to being an unwilling audience to my little rant. She picked up her cross-stitch and went back to work on a half-finished posy. "Are you quite finished, dear?"

I took a deep breath, collecting my thoughts. Truthfully, I had been hoping to get some sort of reaction out of the matchmaker, even if it was anger. Her lack of response had knocked the enthusiasm out of my sermonizing. "Maybe. But it's not right. You can send me to jail, that's fine. But this system is not right."

Ms. Little didn't look up from her threadwork. "Naturally, there's a fee for losing Kairos property. Those corsages aren't cheap. The price of chronium's gone up, you know."

"What?" I blinked.

"In addition, Henry will need to arrive at eight o'clock tomorrow morning. He needs to here on the hour, sharp." As Ms. Little stitched another petal, I caught the briefest glimpse of a smile. "For vaccinations and orientation."

"Uh." Henry raised a hand. "I'm sorry. Is there a gas leak? Vaccinations? Orientation?"

"For your job here, of course." The matchmaker flipped the

cross-stitch over and set it aside. DAMN IT FEELS GOOD TO BE A GANGSTER, it read in cheerful cotton-candy-pink letters. "My dear Mr. Levison, you can't rightfully expect to work for Kairos as a field agent without proper training, can you?"

"But—but why?" A delirious laugh escaped me. I could barely believe what I was hearing. "How—why did you—why are you doing this?"

Ms. Little plucked a Glitterbomb from an open tin, taking a happy bite from it. As she smiled, her teeth twinkled metallic pink. "What is to be will be, my dear. Even if it never happens."

The present-day branch of Kairos was smack-dab in the middle of a dying strip mall; specifically, it was a former Blockbuster Video, bookended by a Little Caesars and a sketchy Chinese restaurant that, despite its grimy exterior, made the most amazing dumplings ever.

Henry outpaced me easily, happily leaping from the sidewalk to the pockmarked hardtop. The sea of empty parking places gave him pause. "Did a bomb go off or something? There's nobody here."

"No, that's pretty par for the course." I stepped down behind him. "Throughout the 1900s there was a massive retail boom. Stores cropped up all over the place only for the market to drop out at the start of the new millennium. Even when the economy picked back up, brick and mortar stores never really recovered, primarily because of a thing called the internet."

"Are those what pass for cars these days? They look like tuna cans." Henry played off a flinch when I unlocked my little silver four-door, the flash of its cat-eyed lights catching him off guard. "What's the inner-net?"

"One future-history lesson at a time." I popped the trunk.

"Okay, fair." He hemmed and hawed over putting his violin case in the trunk, finally settling on a place far, far away from the spare tire. "So, what's the first lesson, then?"

I jingled my keys. "Get in. You're going to drive us home."

"What?" He gave the car a double take. "Oh, no."

"Oh, yes. Don't think I didn't notice you driving the Kings' car like a little old granny after I left that night." I waggled the keys once more for emphasis. "Everybody drives these days, especially people who don't live in big metropolitan areas. You need to learn."

"There's a big difference between driving a stolen car and driving *your* car, Ada." He slammed the trunk shut. "For example, I don't think you want this one to take a swim in the East River."

My smile slipped as I was briefly reminded of Henry's Wikipedia article. I made a mental note to check if it still existed, and if it did, I was curious what it would say. "Practice makes perfect. We can teach you the basics here—the parking lot's huge and there's nothing to hit."

Henry crossed his arms in response, frowning at the car.

"There's no way you can screw this up," I said.

"That a challenge?" He quirked an eyebrow. "Don't take a sucker bet."

"I like my odds."

He took a step toward the driver's-side door but reconsidered. "This is the future, right? Why don't we get one of those self-driving cars?"

"How do you know about self-driving cars?" I cocked my head.

He shrugged. "I read about it in one of Estelle's science fiction digests. Speaking of which, we got flying cars yet?"

"Not yet. Teddy thinks it's a government conspiracy meant to keep the man down, but I just don't think it's practical." I tapped my foot, growing impatient. "Do I need to remind you we've already cheated death once today?"

"Exactly," he snapped.

"Come on, Henry, don't be stubborn." I took his hand, folding his fingers around my keys. "Cars have come a long way since your time. There's power steering and antilock brakes, for one. After what we've been through today, driving will be a piece of cake."

There was a crack in the stone of his expression as he looked down at our hands, but he said nothing.

"I wouldn't ask you to do something I didn't think you could do," I said with a small smile.

"Oh, goddammit. Fine." His expression crumpled into one of resignation as he climbed into the car. "But if you use that line on me one more time, I'm going to time travel back to the twenties and prevent myself from ever saying it, you got that?"

"Thank you," I said as the car door closed behind him. The engine hummed to life as I moved to the passenger side. I gripped the handle but didn't get in, my attention stolen by the sign flickering across the parking lot, wreathed in blue neon forget-me-nots: KAIROS—WHAT IS TO BE WILL BE, EVEN IF IT NEVER HAPPENS.

I didn't know what to make of Ms. Little. Her cryptic answers and eccentric behavior made it difficult to pin down her motives. Whatever her endgame was, I was thankful for what she had done for Henry. Even still, as I replayed the evening's events in my mind, the matchmaker's sudden appearance seemed a little too serendipitous.

Had she known the entire time what I was going to do?

Or stranger yet, had she orchestrated it?

I jumped as Henry beeped the horn. Though he couldn't be heard over the sound of the engine, I could see him laughing through the passenger window. Shooting him a dirty look, I got in and buckled up.

"Think the horn's the only part that hasn't changed in these things." He drummed his fingers on the wheel. "So, a couple of laps around the parking lot to get my bearings. Provided we don't die in a horrific accident, where to after that?"

"Home, Henry." I smiled. "We're going home."

16

It wasn't exactly a death-defying trip back, as Henry drove exactly like a man of his age. By that, I mean his technical age of well over a hundred years old. I'm fairly certain we were passed by an old lady on a mobility scooter at one point.

Matters were only complicated when Henry started fiddling with the buttons along the center console at a red light. Before I could stop him, he had activated the car's Bluetooth. I tried desperately to defend my phone's music collection—Josh Groban and 98 Degrees were incredibly formative and influential to my development as a person, *thank you*—but so long as whatever I had on offer wasn't klezmer or grainy coverage of the New York Yankees, I think he still would've griped about it.

"Well, there's no accounting for taste," I murmured after his most recent and colorful critique of Sara Bareilles, wincing as he skipped an entire album's worth of her songs. "Take the next right. We're here."

Baby steps, I told myself.

The breezeway was choked with fallen leaves that crunched beneath our feet as we made our way up to the second floor. I fumbled with the lock, barely able to determine one key from another in the dim glow from the overhead light, the belly of its plastic case a graveyard for moths.

Henry didn't seem too bothered, though, looking over the balcony at the other apartments in the complex, their windows glowing in the oncoming twilight. "You got a nice place here. Private. Lots of space."

I opened my mouth, a counterargument on the tip of my tongue, but thought better of it. After seeing Henry's home in the Bowery, I had to agree this was an improvement. "Maybe too much space, sometimes. It gets lonely."

"Yeah, I could see that."

Turning on the light, I stepped inside and kicked off my shoes. He followed just behind, but curled in on himself almost warily, as though the slightest touch would destroy any of the furnishings of my apartment. I couldn't help but laugh at how gingerly he sat down on the couch, tucking his violin case behind his legs. "You don't have to be so gentle. I promise it's not made out of glass."

He smoothed his hand over the turquoise pleather, visibly relaxing. "It's just really nice, that's all."

I ducked into the kitchen and opened the fridge for a cursory inspection. It had been a while since I'd gone grocery shopping. "Are you hungry? I could order us something. What do you like on your pizza?"

"Uh, I dunno. I've never had it."

"What?" I was already pulling my phone from my purse. "Okay, we have to rectify this situation immediately. You need pizza *stat*."

After placing the order, I joined him in the living room. During my time in the kitchen, Henry had slowly migrated to the edge of the sofa, ever closer to the dark screen of the television, but played down his interest once he noticed I was watching. "It's a movie screen, isn't it? Just smaller. Where's the projector?"

"There isn't one, technically. It's a TV. The pictures come from inside." I sat down next to him. "You can turn it on, if you want."

He looked at me sidelong, clearly dubious. "You're messing with me, right? The thing's too skinny to have pictures in it."

I laughed and passed him the remote. "No, I promise. Technology has advanced a lot since your time. We might not have flying cars yet, but everything's been streamlined. Condensed. That little box I just used to order pizza? That's a phone."

He studied the remote, rolling it from one hand to another until he finally gathered enough courage to press the power button. As the screen lit up to show a celebrity chef putting the finishing touch on a pan of shepherd's pie, Henry let out a low whistle. "It's—it's in color and everything. It's even got sound. That's . . . that's really something."

I swore my heart would burst. Biting back a smile, I showed him the volume buttons, then how to change the channel. "I know it's a lot to take in, but if you're ever curious about what something does, let me know. I can't always explain how something works, but at the very least I can show you how to use it."

He gave me a knowing look. "That's gonna get old real fast. It'll be like having a toddler always asking why."

"No, I promise it won't. You're much smarter than you think you are," I said. "In fact, let's get started now. Do you have any questions for me?"

"Yeah." His smile broadened. "What's a guy gotta do to get a drink around here?"

"Okay, future-history lesson number two will cover the women's lib movement."

"Women's lib? What's that?"

"It means you get your own damn drinks." Batting his shoulder playfully, I stood and padded to the kitchen. "What would you like? I've got sweet tea, coffee, some off-brand soda. I think Teddy might've left some Moscato—"

"Moscato? As in wine?" He turned in his seat to look at me, arms folded over the back of the sofa. "*Tsk, tsk*, Ada. Never woulda pinned you for the type."

"What? I—" The realization stopped me in my tracks. "Oh, Henry. The Eighteenth Amendment. They repealed it."

His jaw fell. "You kidding me? When?"

I tried to remember. "Sometime in the early the thirties, I think. It's been a long time since I was in a history class, you'll have to forgive me. You're welcome to a glass of wine, though. I think it'd be a fine way to celebrate your first night as a free man in the present."

"Can't believe it. I almost made it." He sulked. "Coffee's fine. Two sugars."

My coffeemaker rattled to life as I poured more water into its reservoir. "No cream?"

"Well, if you got it, sure, but I don't wanna put you out," he answered bashfully. The cooking show went to a commercial break. "Okay, serious question. Chronium. The matchmaker at Kairos mentioned it. What's it do?"

Opening a cabinet, I spun the carousel that held my hoard of coffee pods, considering which one to use for Henry. "Oh, it's a metal that resists the force of time travel. It's more technical than that, I'm sure—I was never very good at physics. It stops clocks from going haywire during the process, that much I know."

"Sounds pretty important." There was a brief pause. "So, when did the whole time travel thing start?"

"That's the thing," I said. "I'm not sure. Once it was discovered, it was suddenly everywhere. I've heard they've even been working on portable units. No more using pods like you saw at Kairos."

"That's . . . worrying," Henry replied. "All right, next question. This brother of yours, older or younger?"

"Older, but not by much." I settled on a plain dark roast. "He'll probably tell you otherwise, though. Publicly, he's been twenty-eight for the past two birthdays."

"Don't know what it is about people and getting old. It happens to everybody," he said. "He good to you?"

I watched as the machine let out a trickle of steaming coffee into a waiting mug, then added some sugar and flavored creamer. "He's either the best or worst brother, depending on his mood. Sometimes he's both at the same time."

The grin in Henry's voice was almost audible. "That's family for you."

Once I made a second cup, I carried both drinks back to the couch and sat down. The previous show had ended and a new one, a baking competition, had started. Henry watched it with rapt fascination, taking his mug from me with a barely murmured thank-you. It was only when he brought the cup to his lips and took a sip that his attention was pulled away from the television.

"It tastes like chocolate," he said, pleasantly bewildered, before taking a second sip to confirm. He gave me a curious smile. "Chocolate and peppermint."

"It's the creamer," I explained. "Sorry, I should've warned you. It's what I had on hand."

"No, it's fine. It's better than fine." Holding the mug in both hands, Henry tipped it back and had a longer drink. He looked so satisfied I thought he'd melt between the couch cushions. On the TV, a woman was making impossibly beautiful flowers out of gum paste. He shook his head in disbelief. "And people actually eat this stuff in the end?"

I nodded. "The cakes are graded for taste and appearance."

"Just seems kinda weird to eat something so pretty, you know? Especially after they've had their mitts all over it while putting it together," he remarked. His eyes looked distant as he stared into his mug. "Estelle used to bake sometimes. She had this cake recipe, I think she came up with it herself . . . Ma sure as hell didn't show her. The cake always came out looking like shit, but it tasted great."

"I guess that's all that really matters in the end, if it tastes good." The coffee was still a little too hot for my taste—I didn't know how Henry could stand it—so I put it down on a bedazzled coaster. "Do you remember the recipe?"

"Nah. Never could cook. Can barely boil a pot of water without finding some way to screw it up."

"That makes two of us." I laughed. "Watching these shows always makes me want to try. They make it look so easy, but everything I touch ends up as some lopsided, overfrosted mess."

He smiled. "Maybe it tastes great, though."

"Maybe." We both cringed as one of the bakers took a dive, splattering cake everywhere. "I know it won't exactly be the same, but maybe I can make you a cake sometime. We could work on it together."

"With our pooled talents, we'll have all the ability of one semicompetent baker." As his shoulders shook with laughter, a single corkscrew popped free from the pomade's hold, bobbing at his temple like a spring. "But, hey, sure. I'll try anything once."

We lapsed into silence. He was quickly absorbed by the bake off, but I struggled to focus, too distracted by the man sitting next to me. Over the course of a single evening, I had seen Henry transform from a career criminal out of hope and out of options into a completely different person. There was a shy softness to him, an innocence I hadn't been expecting. My heart hurt for him, but at the same time, I was happy.

It was like I had finally done something right, something meaningful with my life. And I knew then I'd do anything I could to give Henry a second chance.

"Okay. One more thing." He spoke up again after I don't know how long. "Why me?"

"What?" I asked, though I was fairly sure I knew what he was going to say.

"I mean—" He turned to face me, the TV and all its wonders seemingly forgotten. "You could've gone anywhere, any time. People talk about meeting somebody like it's a once-in-a-lifetime kinda thing. But you. You had several lifetimes to choose from. Whole eras. Hell, whole centuries. And you still picked me to bring here."

"I don't know if I had a choice in the matter," I whispered. "Honestly, Henry, it just sort of . . . happened."

"God, I want to kiss you again." He drew closer. "I did a lousy job last time."

"I don't know," I said with a soft snort. "I thought it was fine. More than fine, actually."

"No, I'm telling you, it was lousy. I didn't think I'd get another shot, so I didn't take my time. But now—" His five-o'clock shadow grazed my cheek, ending with his lips so close to mine that I could almost imagine them, an ache like that of a phantom limb. "Now I got all the time in the world to do it right."

But patience had never been one of my virtues. His words hung in the air for only a breath before I kissed him hard, arms thrown around his shoulders. He tasted masculine, a sweet blend of old tobacco and coffee and just the ghost of chocolate.

Henry was surprised but eager, fingertips pressed to the softness of my hips until they hit bone. A guttural moan rattled from what seemed to be the very core of his being.

Then there was a knock at the door.

Henry went stock-still. I wasn't even sure if he was breathing. "Should—uh, should we get that?"

"No," I answered him, grabbing his jaw to guide his lips back to mine. "It's just pizza. It can wait."

17

I have to admit I was impressed. I would have never guessed that wiry little Henry could pack away an entire veggie pizza on his own, or that he would do it with so much enthusiasm. Or so quickly, for that matter. By the time I was on my third slice he was completely blissed out on the couch, sucking the last bit of sauce from his thumb.

"So, what are your feelings on pizza now that you've experienced it?" I nudged his empty pizza box. "I'm going to wager a guess that you don't totally hate it, at least."

"Is there always this much food in the future? I feel like I've just come home from a trip to Bubbe's."

I patted his shoulder sympathetically. "Wait until you try McDonald's."

There was another knock at the door. Henry rolled his eyes toward the entryway but didn't stir. "If that's more pizza, I'm gonna need another notch in my belt."

Before I could answer, the door was suddenly booted open. My brother navigated the threshold awkwardly, both arms looped through half a dozen shopping bags, with a bottle of wine precariously balanced on top. "The welcome wagon has arrived!"

"Teddy! Oh, let me help." I leaped from my seat to greet him, taking as many bags as I could manage. "You could've texted me. You know I'd have met you outside—"

"And ruin the surprise?" Teddy heaved a huge sigh of relief as he dumped the remaining bags on the coffee table. He looked at me sidelong, eyebrows waggling. "Besides, I thought you might be a little *preoccupied* with your new houseguest."

"Teddy, please." I shot him an indignant look while surreptitiously checking to see if my shirt was completely buttoned. "He's right here."

"Hello." Henry waved from his place on the couch.

"Oh my god!" Teddy squealed, hands clapped to his cheeks. "Look at you. You're just like James Cagney in *The Public Enemy* but you don't die at the end."

"Uh." Henry blinked. "What."

"Oh, Ada, he's so cute. Totally worth the prison time if you ask me." Teddy tapped a finger to his lip in consideration. "But you know, I thought he'd be taller."

"Ms. Little said the same thing," I said.

"Now listen here"—Henry stiffened with righteous indignation—"I'm five foot ten. Okay, maybe five foot nine, but still. That's not short. Besides, you're not exactly a Grade A specimen yourself."

"Boys, boys," I said, putting myself between them. "Can we save the bickering for after introductions? Teddy, this is Henry Levison."

"Charmed, I'm sure," Henry deadpanned, crossing his arms.

"And, Henry, this is my brother, Teddy." I flashed a patient smile at my brother. "Have you eaten dinner? There's plenty of pizza left."

"Please eat it," Henry said in a small voice.

"Oh, I guess I could have a slice or two." Teddy climbed over the back of the couch, flopping down in front of the remaining pizza with a dramatic sigh. "Since you're twisting my arm and all. Gives me something to do while you open your presents."

"These are for me?" Henry asked, surprised.

Not even bothering with a plate, Teddy chowed down on a slice of pepperoni straight from the box. "Well, yeah. We can't have you looking like an extra from *Angels with Dirty Faces*, sweetie. So I got you a little care package. Some clothes, toiletries, a few movies that I thought might be relevant to your interests. That sort of thing."

As he took a bag from the table, Henry seemed lost. "Thanks."

"It's the least I can do. Ada did the real heavy lifting today. I'm just an accessory to the crime," Teddy said around a mouthful of mozzarella. "I wasn't sure what size to get, so I got a range. Don't like it or it doesn't fit, leave them in the bag and I'll take them back."

Curiosity finally getting the better of him, Henry opened the first bag slowly, as though it contained live snakes. He removed a stack of fitted tees, two long-sleeved Henley shirts, a pair of dark-washed jeans, and a pack of socks—which, oddly, he seemed to be the most excited about, tearing through the plastic to pull out a set. It was only after he'd kicked off his oxfords that he seemed to remember he wasn't alone. "Uh, is this okay?"

Teddy rolled his eyes. "No, I wanted you to wear them on your hands and put on a show for us. Of course it's okay."

"Thanks." Stripping off his old socks—wool, thin with age and in desperate need of darning—Henry put on the new pair. He wiggled his toes with a dim smile. "I mean it. For everything. You really stuck your neck out for me. I don't know why you did it, but I'm grateful anyway. For Ada, I guess it makes sense, as much as anything she does makes sense, but you don't even know me, Ted."

"I don't have to." Teddy wiped his hands on a napkin. "You mean a lot to Ada, so you mean a lot to me too. That's how it works here."

There was a wet glint to Henry's eyes. Not wanting to embarrass him, I nudged another bag his way. He pulled out movie after movie, reading their titles aloud in an increasingly confused tone. "*Back to the Future I, II*, and *III*? *Timecop*? *The Terminator*? *Time Chasers*?"

I gave my brother a flat look. "I'm sensing a theme."

"What? I thought he'd relate," Teddy offered with a shrug. "Besides, there's so much pop culture he needs to catch up on, and movies are a great place to start."

Henry pulled out the last movie. "*Superman*?"

"Oh, there's a scene at the end—he spins around the Earth really fast to reverse time," Teddy said. "It's pretty much the best part of the whole movie, you'll love it."

"O . . . kay." *Superman* did not join the other movies, taking up residence in Henry's lap. "This is a movie? Can we watch it now?"

"I *guess* we could." Teddy looked at me. "Though Ada *did* promise me we'd marathon *Forged in Fire*, I guess that can wait for an evening when you're working at Kairos."

"You heard about that?" I asked, slumping into the seat beside Henry. "I can't believe Ms. Little is in on this."

"Heard about it? She's the one who told me about the 'new hire,'" Teddy said, complete with air quotes. "I swear she has to be senile or something. So, has he been vaxxed yet?"

"Uh, no," Henry answered. "That's tomorrow, after orientation."

"Fair warning: you're going to be sick as a dog. But it's a necessary evil when you work with time travel." Teddy picked up another slice of pizza. "The germs in your time and our time are superdifferent, and there's so many diseases that we don't even worry about anymore."

"Like what?" Henry looked up with renewed interest.

"Oh, you know, like some types of cancer, chicken pox, shingles . . ." Teddy pursed his lips. "Sis, help me out here."

"Measles," I added. "Oh, and polio."

"Polio." The little color in Henry's face drained. His voice grew strangely quiet. "You—you have a cure for polio?"

"We do." I gave him an uneasy smile, worried by his tone. "It was developed ages ago. Polio's been eradicated in the US for years."

"Estelle has polio. Has since she was a little girl." The pleather upholstery squealed under Henry's fingertips as they curled into fists. "You have a vaccine, but this is how you use time travel? For a goddamn matchmaking service?"

His head fell in his hands.

"Oh, Henry, I'm so sorry." I tried to place an arm over his shoulders but he flinched away. "Please, I didn't know—"

"You didn't know what? That polio is a thing?" he barked. "She's a good kid. Smart. Patient in a way that I never was, gentle in a way I couldn't be. You know how many evenings I had to carry her up all those flights of stairs, and she hated it, she hated depending on me—and there's so many other kids just like her who could use that vaccine. And I'm the schmuck you decide to save?"

I tried to answer but my throat was quickly closing.

"It's not like she could just pop off to the twenties with a case full of syringes." There was a protective edge to Teddy's voice. "It's illegal to bring certain things with you when you time travel. Anything that could accidentally advance that era's tech is strictly prohibited. Causality's a bitch, honey."

Henry shook his head. "I don't understand."

"Let's say that Ada did go back in time with the vaccine," Teddy began, his expression cool. "She cures everyone and wipes out polio in the process. When the 1950s roll around there's no need to research a cure for polio, because it's already been wiped out. So where did Ada get the vaccine from?"

Henry didn't answer.

"We're still learning about the long-term effects of time travel." Teddy's second slice of pizza was abandoned. "But there's a lot of research to support that unstable time loops, like I just described, are really bad news for reality as we know it. So the government tries to limit the scope of what things people are allowed to do with time travel."

"It's still not right," Henry growled.

"Metaphysics doesn't care if something's right or wrong," Teddy snapped. "Watch any of the movies I bought you and you'll notice a recurring theme. Make a change, even a seemingly benevolent one, and you'll start off a horrible chain reaction. Before you know it, you're ruled by damned, dirty apes."

Henry glared at him.

"That's from *Planet of the Apes*," Teddy explained with a know-it-all smile. "Another one you need to see. Not the Tim Burton one, though. Yuck."

"Please, Henry." A few stray tears rolled down my face. "I know you love your sister, and I wish I could help, but I'm not even sure what the repercussions are from bringing you here."

"Then why did you?" Henry shouted. "If it was so much trouble, why didn't you just leave me to die like I was supposed to? If you're so concerned about doing the safe thing, the *easy* thing, why didn't you just stick with your sugar daddy Sam?"

There was a long, uncomfortable silence. I could feel the weight of Teddy's gaze as he turned to face me.

"What's this about Sam?" he asked.

18

My mouth opened but no words came. I knew I couldn't outright lie to Teddy, and even if I could, Henry knew the truth, and he didn't exactly seem like he'd back me up right now. There was only one option, then. Taking a deep breath, I dabbed at my eyes with a napkin and hoped I didn't smudge my eyeliner in the process.

"I wanted to tell you before, but the timing didn't seem right. We were having such a good time and I just . . . couldn't." Glancing down at my folded hands, I tried to force a smile, but I could already feel it crumbling. "I know where Sam went, Teddy. He was in 1922. With me."

"What?" Teddy murmured. "What happened to him?"

"Me, that's what," Henry answered, gaze buried in the carpet, elbows braced on his knees. "I interrupted their little lovers' rendezvous at the Plaza. My buddy Schlomo knocked him out with a baseball bat."

Teddy took a sudden, sharp inhale. His voice was barely a hiss. "You got back together with Sam, didn't you? After I expressly told you to stay away."

I bit my lip. "Listen, I—"

"Oh, they didn't just get back together." Henry looked up with a smile that was equal parts sad and cruel. "The boys told me about the conversation in the bedroom, Ada. How you were going to run away to Paris."

It felt as though I'd just been stabbed.

"And you weren't even going to tell me, were you?" Teddy vaulted up from his place on the couch, shaking his head. "No, no, of course you weren't, because you've never had the cojones to just face a problem. You're always running away."

I grabbed for my brother's arm as he made his way to the door. "Teddy, please—it's true, I did think about running away to Paris with Sam, but I changed my mind. It was wrong. I couldn't just leave you forever."

"And it has absolutely nothing to do wifth Sam being dead." Sarcasm dripped from Henry's words.

Teddy whirled around, tearing his arm from my grasp. "Sam's dead?"

"Not . . ." My head dropped. ". . . exactly, no."

Henry looked as though he'd seen a ghost. "He isn't?"

"It's confusing, I know. I found Sam's body on my second trip to the twenties. He had been shot." I dug my hands through my hair, trying to collect my thoughts. "I came home and filed a police report, but they told me Sam was at the townhouse. When I went there, the Sam I met—it hadn't happened yet. So I told him not to go. I think I stopped it from happening."

I couldn't bring myself to tell them about Rowland's suspicions. There were some things better left unsaid.

"I can't believe you. Ada, you mean *nothing* to Sam. He's gone to great lengths to show this to you. You were just a kid, a law school intern, and he was a dirty old man who took advantage of you," Teddy snapped. "If he dies, that's his own business. Why would you even try to—"

"Because he's a human being!" I was stunned by the volume of my own voice, taking a deep, calming breath before continuing. "I know you've never liked Sam, especially after everything that happened between us. But he's still a person, and I loved him. I have to get over him in my own way, on my own timeline, not yours. My way doesn't involve drumming up a lot of pointless vitriol."

Teddy rolled his eyes. "Oh really? And where does running away with him fit into this healing process?"

"It was a mistake. To be honest, it wasn't even about Sam. He was just convenient. You're right, I really do just run away from my problems." My shoulders slumped. Any hope of salvaging my mascara was gone as the tears fell freely. "You want to know the real reason I wanted to sign up at Kairos? I wasn't looking to 'boink somebody's great-uncle,' or whatever it was you said. I thought if I married some Mr. Darcy from the 1800s, I could emigrate. Start over. Nobody would know about the affair."

"But"—Teddy's face tightened in confusion—"I offered you a room at my place. You know I would do anything to help you forget that chapter of your life."

"I know you would, and I appreciate that," I answered, rubbing my temples. "But you're going to get back together with Antoine, let's be real. You always do. And even if you didn't, what happens when I go to work and get harassed? Or the grocery store? You've always been my big protective brother, Teddy, but you can't shield me forever."

"So what? You'd rather enter a marriage of convenience to some dick from 1800? Forget Netflix, he probably doesn't even understand basic hygiene," Teddy spat. "I know it's a real challenge for you to think about other people, Ada, but did it ever once occur to you during your little scheme that you're the only family I have left?"

"Yes," I said hoarsely. "Of course it did, but I—"

"But you what? You didn't care?" He shook his head. The anger drained from his expression. "I guess I shouldn't be surprised. Everyone else turned their back on me when I came out. It was only a matter of time before you did too."

"You know that's not true," I whispered.

There was a rush of cold night air as Teddy stepped outside. "I thought I did."

Silently pleading for him to come back and talk, I reached for my brother with an outstretched hand. But I was too late. The door slammed closed. My fingers curled into a fist.

Across from me, Henry sat unmoving, still staring at the floor. If his words before had felt like a betrayal, his silence now was like a murder.

"Why did you have to tell him?" I asked.

"Because I don't want you to make the same mistakes I did." He slipped on his shoes. "You're a magician, Ada, but the show has to come to an end eventually."

I sniffed stubbornly, rubbing my eye with a wrist. "I don't understand."

"And you probably won't for a while." He got to his feet and took out his pipe. He didn't look at me as he packed it with tobacco. "Tomorrow, I want to go back to 1922. Permanently."

"What?" I gaped. "But you'll die—"

"Yeah. But when I do, it'll be for a good reason." He struck a match. "Life's already shitty enough as is. I don't need to live in a world where some government stuffed shirt from the future gets to decide if my sister walks or not 'cause he's afraid of what's going to happen."

"I'm sorry, Henry." Smiling through my tears, I stood up from the couch. "I really was trying to do the right thing by bringing you here."

"Yeah, well, maybe you should've stuck with the easy thing." Smoke curled above his head. "You deserve it. I'm going for a walk."

I watched him go. Once I was completely alone, I tried to surrender to the tears I had been fighting for the past half hour. But I felt strangely numb. There were no more tears left to cry.

Instead, I busied myself quietly tidying the apartment. The pizza boxes were broken down and left by the garbage to be taken to recycling. All the leftovers fit into a single Tupperware container, stashed in the fridge. There wasn't enough to do an entire load of dishes, so I washed the few plates and our empty coffee mugs by hand. I gathered up all the shopping bags and grouped them together on the entryway table, along with Henry's violin case. There was something comforting about the monotony of housework—a sense of normalcy that I hadn't experienced in what felt like ages.

When I ran out of things to clean, I brought out some linens from the hall closet and made Henry a bed on the couch, topping it off with my favorite Disney Princess blanket. Looking through the clothes Teddy had picked out, I found a pair of pajama pants and an undershirt and left them folded on the coffee table.

At eleven thirty, I stepped out onto the breezeway for a moment, but there was still no sign of Henry. I managed to hold out for another hour, watching late-night TV with a sleeve of Oreos before I had to finally call it a night.

"Good night, Henry," I said to the empty hallway, turning off the light.

I took off what remained of my makeup and threw on an oversized T-shirt. As the hemline brushed my thighs, I was struck with an intense memory of Sam. I always borrowed his shirts on those late nights that turned into impromptu sleepovers. Tentatively, I brought the collar to my nose, strangely hoping to get some ghost whiff of his cologne, but all I could smell was detergent.

And maybe a little BO if I was honest. It had been a long time since my 7 a.m. shower, but I was too tired to bother. I lit one of my scented candles—toasted marshmallow—before crawling into bed. It was only once I had settled in and gotten comfortable that I realized that every last inch of me ached.

Remembering my conversation with Auri, I pulled up a digital copy of *Pride and Prejudice* on my phone. I must have read the first page of the first chapter a dozen times, teetering in and out of consciousness, until the phone case slipped from my hand, and it seemed like too much effort to pick it back up. As I finally drifted off, I realized that once again I had tried and failed to get into Jane Austen.

I slept soundly until something in my subconscious reminded me of my fight with Teddy and that Henry would die—would already be dead and gone for a hundred years—by this time tomorrow. The green numbers of the digital clock glowed like a cat's eyes from across the room: 3:34 a.m. My chest rose and fell in shallow strokes, as though I had awakened from a nightmare. But sleep had been a comfortable void for me, an escape from the bad dream of reality.

The room was darker than I remembered. The candle's wick had drowned in its wax and the air still held a tinge of smoke. Feeling for my phone, I plugged it into the charger on the bedside table. I thought about checking on Henry in the living room, if he'd even bothered to return, but my body felt like lead. Rolling onto my side, I made silent bargains with myself, counting down the hours of sleep I'd get if I got up to check for just five, maybe ten minutes.

Behind me, the bedroom door creaked open.

"I'm so sorry." I breathed a sigh of relief, propping myself up on an elbow. "But I meant what I said before. We'll figure out a way to get your sister what she needs. Hell, if I can sneak someone out, how hard can it be to sneak something in?"

The only reply I received was a squeak of the bedsprings as he sat down next to me. His fingers combed through my hair.

"I waited for you," I continued. "You had every right to be mad, but next time could you try to be back before midnight? I was worried."

He still didn't answer. Annoyed, I turned to face him.

I screamed.

It wasn't Henry.

I flung myself off the other side of the bed, but the intruder's hands were knotted in my hair. My nails left trails in the bedsheets as he dragged me back by the scalp. I kicked blindly behind me, a tangle of blankets and pillows. Somehow, my heel struck his chin. "Leave me alone!"

He reeled and his grip on my hair loosened. Seeing an opening,

I kicked again, going for his stomach. Just before I made the connection, he recovered and grabbed my ankle. He folded my leg back on itself and pinned it in place with his weight. The other leg soon followed suit. I squirmed, desperate to crawl out from under him, but he was too heavy.

Straining, I looked over my shoulder, trying to memorize his features. His dark clothes and black ski mask blended with the shadows of the room. I could only discern that he was tall and much, much stronger than I was.

And that there was someone else in the doorway.

"Hey, pal," Henry snarled. "Gonna give you three seconds to—"

He didn't get a chance to finish. My assailant whirled on him. I rolled off the far side of the bed, hitting the floor just in time to see Henry collide with the wall. Blood trickled from his nose.

"That's it?" His shoulders heaved with the beginnings of unhinged laughter. "C'mon, buddy. I've gotten better haymakers from my friends."

Heart thundering in my ears, I looked for something, anything, that I could use to help Henry. Cords from the blinds brushed against my skin. I grabbed them and pulled, flooding the room with artificial light from the parking lot.

The man in the ski mask glanced at the window only for a second, but it gave Henry just enough time to pick up the still-liquid candle from my dresser.

"Let's see what's under the mask," Henry muttered as he splashed the hot wax across the intruder's eyes.

Howling in pain, the man clutched at his face while blindly fumbling for the door. Just before he grabbed the doorknob, Henry seized the man's arm. In one fluid motion, he brought the arm back, and there was a single, awful crunch. The man in the ski mask crumpled against the door with a whine.

The anger in Henry's expression dissolved. Coldly, calculatingly, he raised his fist to strike the man in the back of the head.

The man in the ski mask slipped into the hallway as the door whipped open unexpectedly. Henry struck it instead. Swearing, he pulled his hand free of the hole he'd made in the flimsy pressed wood and gave chase.

Scrambling upright, I grabbed my phone on the bedside table and followed them. By the time I got to the living room, it was only Henry, panting and damp with sweat, arm braced against the back of the couch as he stared at the open front door.

"Are you okay?" I asked in a small voice.

"Yeah," he said between deep gasps for air. "You?"

"I'm fine."

He closed the door in response, then slumped into a seat on the couch. "Who the hell was that?"

"I don't know." Blood was still dripping from his nose, so I ducked into the kitchen for some paper towels. "But it's not the first time he's been here, and it probably won't be the last."

"Why?" He looked at me questioningly as I rounded the corner. "I mean why you, of all people? You're a cream puff."

"Hey, I'll remind you I'm a cream puff who knocked out Frank Kingston with a shovel," I joked as I sat down beside him, but it fell flat. "Here. Lean forward and pinch the soft part of your nose with the paper towel."

He followed my instructions. "Thanks."

I turned the phone over in my hands. Calling the police wasn't really an option anymore, I decided; aside from the obvious problem of Henry's undocumented presence in the present, my track record with Officer Toussaint left me less than confident that anything would come of it.

It was almost four o'clock. Three more hours until I needed to get up for work. There was a part of me that was surprised I was even considering going, after everything that had happened, but there was a conference call that the higher-ups had repeatedly told me I absolutely could not miss unless I wanted a visit and a write-up from the district manager.

If I had any plans of being functional, I needed to sleep, but that wasn't about to happen.

"Sam and I met when I was in my third year of law school," I began on an exhale. "I had an internship at his firm. It was hard work. Maybe not as hard as factory work, but the hours were long. It's not a job you can just drop at five o'clock, but Sam did his best to make sure everyone got off at a reasonable time—even if it meant he needed to stay late."

Henry gave a slight nod. I couldn't tell if he was really listening.

"Everyone loved Sam. He was generous. Thoughtful. A lot of fun. I don't think he ever forgot a name or a birthday and he would buy us all lunch at least once a week," I recalled with a smile. "But he was lonely, I could tell. He had a wife, but I never saw her, and she never called. When her name came up in conversation, everyone at the office had this tone. There was something wrong."

He briefly unplugged his nose to see if it was still bleeding. "Wrong?"

"It was a poorly kept secret that Penny had fallen out of love with him. They'd married while he was still in college." I stared up at the ceiling. "I've seen pictures. Sam looked like a god back then. He was gorgeous."

Henry snorted derisively, pinching his nose again. "Yeah? What happened to that?"

I gave him a sharp look. "He tore his ACL his senior year. Sports injury. Put on lot of weight—that's when the trouble started. I always thought it was sad. He's not an unattractive man, even now. He's got amazing style, and he has this warmth and charm that makes him handsome. She was his wife. He should've been more than numbers on a scale to her, though I guess I'm not in a position to talk."

There was a flicker of remorse in Henry's expression, but it briefly passed. "So, how'd you end up together?"

"He was campaigning for reelection when his speechwriter got outed for plagiarism," I explained. "He was so stressed out. Everyone could feel it. I offered to write him a new speech—I didn't think it'd go anywhere, but he loved it. I always wrote his speeches after that. We started spending a lot of time together then. Dinners after work, late-night calls. He was so much older, I didn't think we'd have so much in common, but we did. He was smart. Totally underhanded and not afraid to break the rules if he thought he could get away with it, but I even admired that about him. He'd drive me home after work and we'd sit outside my apartment for hours, laughing, talking about nothing in particular. I didn't want to leave, and one night, I didn't."

Henry swallowed hard.

"I didn't want to love Samson St. Laurent. He was married, he had a career. I don't think he wanted to love me either—he knew what people would think. But it happened anyway, so we made plans to do the right thing." I pushed my hair out of my face. "He already wanted a divorce from Penny. She never came to see him, not even for Christmas, and she was draining his finances remodeling his farmhouse in Georgia. A total travesty, by the way. It's a farmhouse, not a French château. Sam told me once we were married, we could take a year off and restore it together."

"So why didn't it happen?" Henry asked. "The way this story's going, you should be married and living in Georgia right now."

"Sam was a fairly well-liked senator. One thing led to another, and there was talk of a presidential run. He didn't really want to do it, but there was pressure, so he threw his hat in." I bit my lip. "So of course, when the other party started looking for dirt on him—"

"They found you," Henry finished.

"Sam never made it out of the first primary."

The paper towel lowered from Henry's nose. It looked like the bleeding had finally stopped. "But that shouldn't have stopped you from getting married."

"It was more complicated than that," I said. "There was a media circus. My face was all over the news. They called me a gold digger, said that I was some plant from the other party sent to influence his views. People found out where I lived and I started getting harassed. Telephone calls, packages filled with shit and semen—they even vandalized my car."

"Damn," Henry murmured.

"For what it's worth, Sam tried to do right by me, in his own way." I felt like I should've been crying but my eyes were dry. I had recited this story so many times it felt almost clinical, like I was talking about somebody else. "If Sam's got a problem, he just throws money at it until it disappears. He wrote me a really generous check, and I left town."

Henry's gaze darkened. "Hush money?"

"He didn't call it that, but—yes, essentially. His PR team went into damage control. They decided the best course of action was to put distance between us, and that was the best way forward," I answered. "But I never wanted the money, Henry. I just wanted him to tell people the truth."

"But he didn't. He hung you out to dry." Henry shook his head. "I'll kill him. I swear to god, I'll kill him."

The early autumn chill was starting to creep into my apartment. My hands slid between my knees. "It was getting better for a while. I got a PO box, changed my phone number. People forgot. But for the past year, there's been someone—I don't know who he is, but he knows me. Where I work, where I go shopping, everything. He seems hell-bent on punishing me for the affair."

Henry ran a hand through his hair, by now nothing more than a slick mess of curls. "I'm sorry, Ada. I didn't know."

"Don't apologize. Every time has its troubles." I stood and headed for my bedroom. "You should probably get some sleep. Thank you for listening to me. And for saving me back there. I don't know what he would've done if you hadn't been there."

"Nah. I shouldn't have been gone so long." He rolled a shoulder bashfully. "I kinda got lost."

"Oh no, I'm sorry," I said, unable to hide the smile in my voice, but it slowly drained as I saw the digital clock in the bedroom. I was running out of time. "Sleep well, Henry. For what it's worth, you won't have to worry about getting lost for much longer. You'll be home soon."

"Huh, yeah." Henry seemed almost surprised by the notion. "Home."

19

That morning's conference call, like the countless other middle management pep talks that had come before it, was entirely pointless. Once attendance was taken and the passive-aggressive suggestions on how to increase credit card sales started, the conversation became little more than background noise.

I caught up on my emails and made a list of business-account holders who needed a follow-up call. When that was done, I put together starter kits for new accounts—my least favorite task as bank manager and one I'd normally delegate to the tellers, but I was desperate for a distraction from the lack of texts from Teddy that morning and the fact that Henry was gone. He had climbed out of my car that morning and walked into Kairos without so much as a good-bye.

Stubborn asshole. I should've made him take the bus.

"—so to conclude our conversation today, let's do a fun quick-fire review!" Brad, one of the lackeys from Engagement, enthused in a way that was entirely artificial. "Ada, let's start with you. How do you plan to motivate your staff into getting thirty-five percent more credit cards sales?"

I was not in the mood to play along. "I don't know, Brad,

maybe I'll force my tellers to cold call people at eight in the morning, because that worked out really well when you made us do that last quarter. Everyone knows customers feel like signing up for a card with twenty percent APR before they've even had a cup of coffee."

"Um." Brad cleared his throat. "That's certainly a, um, a strategy, Ada—let's move on to you, Stephanie. How do you plan to get more sales?"

Fairly confident that I wouldn't be called on again, I grabbed my empty coffee cup and went to the lobby for a quick refill. Caffeine was the only thing keeping me afloat.

"Heya, bosslady." Cel waved from the coffeemaker but grew confused as she looked from me to the clock. "Did you get out of your meeting early or something?"

"In a manner of speaking, I guess." I flashed a tired smile. "How's the coffee today?"

"Well, on a scale of one to ten, this is slightly above roofing tar." She shrugged. "In other words, pretty par for the course."

"No expense spared for our customers," I said dryly. "Could I borrow some of your creamer?"

"Well, you can't borrow it 'cause I don't want it back after you've drunk it." Cel's nose wrinkled with a grin as she turned for the break room. "But, yeah, sure. I've got two, which do you want—hazelnut or thin mint?"

My stomach dropped. I picked up one of the single-use creamers by the machine and shook it halfheartedly. "On second thought, maybe I'll just go with plain today."

"Uh, okay, if you're sure." She frowned. "Is something wrong? Nobody's been sending you wacko faxes again, have they?"

"Not faxes, no." The creamer lid didn't want to come off. I glared at it in frustration. "I don't really want to talk about it. I just want to forget it ever happened."

"Well, okay, but if you change your mind, I'm here." She lingered for a moment, still clearly worried but unsure of what to say.

"Really." I tried to force a little more warmth into my voice. "Go on. We on for lunch today?"

Cel slid into the break room. "You got it. See you then."

With a final tug, the creamer opened, spilling all over the counter in the process. It took every ounce of self-control I had not to swear as I grabbed a napkin and wiped it up, then started the process anew with a second creamer.

A mechanical chime beeped as another customer entered the lobby.

"Good morning!" one of the other employees called from her station. It was unusual to see her smile so genuinely at someone coming through those double doors. Anyone who worked on the teller line for very long had perfected the art of the fixed smile. "How can we help you today?"

"Oh, uh, hello. I was kinda hoping I could open a new account."

I whirled around at the sound of a familiar voice.

There, in the middle of the lobby, and looking immensely sheepish, was Henry. Since I had dropped him off at Kairos he'd changed into one of the outfits Teddy had bought him, a Henley shirt and corduroy trousers, and had somehow acquired a small bouquet of orange roses and tiger lilies. He held the flowers like he wasn't quite sure what to do with them, managing an awkward smile. "Hi, Ada."

"Henry," I breathed out.

His eyes fell to the floor. "Uh, did you mean to pour that on your shoe?"

Sure enough, a glance down confirmed there was a trail of creamer rolling across the toe of my pink high heel. With a sigh, I crumpled the plastic creamer and tossed it in the trash. "No, I didn't. But—what are you doing here? You were supposed to be going home."

"Uh, yeah, about that." There was a hint of shyness as he rubbed the back of his neck. "Listen, I was being a first-rate jackass last night. Things were, well, they were good, and I'm not used to that—"

I smiled. "You don't have to explain."

"No, I do," he insisted. "I've been looking for any reason to get sore. An excuse to leave. Don't have a chance to screw things up if I'm already gone, you know? It seemed easier."

"What's that?" I took a step toward him, trying to surreptitiously shake the creamer from my shoe in the process. "Do my ears deceive me? Is Henry Levison talking about doing something the easy way?"

His gaze flattened. "Yeah, yeah. Don't get too smug. Anyway, I'm sorry. I thought if I started a fight between you and your brother, you'd be happy to see me go."

"Siblings bicker all the time, you should know that." I wasn't about to mention that Teddy rarely stayed mad with me for more than a few hours, and that his silence that morning was already unusual. "Besides, I can't say I didn't deserve it."

"Still. It wasn't right." Cellophane crinkled as he waggled the flowers. "So, I brought you these as a peace offering. Please take them before I manage to destroy them somehow."

Suddenly, I was aware of the half dozen pairs of interested eyes observing us from around the lobby. Even Cel had taken notice of us, flashing a thumbs-up as she emerged from the break room. I dragged my attention back to Henry. "Thank you. I think there's a vase in my office."

Mercifully, the conference call had ended by the time Henry took a seat at my desk. He took stock of the room with an appreciative nod. "Nice setup, but I was expecting more marble and cigar smoke, if I'm being honest."

"The job's changed a lot since your time. The real moneymakers are in Richmond, and they only come to work when they feel like it. These days, I'm more of a glorified ringmaster, always chasing after clowns." I dug through cabinets until I found a crystal vase, a holdover from the manager who came before me. "So, how'd you get here? Kairos isn't exactly in walking distance."

He shrugged. "I hitchhiked."

It was hard to tell if I choked on his words or dust as I blew the vase clean. I coughed, fanning the air. "Henry, no! That's dangerous.

I know that was fine back in your time but there's no telling what kind of maniac could've picked you up."

"Hey, I made it okay, didn't I?" he asked before reaching into his pocket. "Besides, that's why I came here. Maybe if I open up a bank account, I can save up for one of those tuna cans you call cars nowadays."

I shifted my focus from admiring the bouquet in its new vase to the money he was sliding across the desk. My eyes widened. "Ms. Little's paying you well. That's more than two weeks' salary for me."

"It's more than an entire month's worth of protection money, hustling chess games, and Schlomo's bathtub gin operation put together, and that's just from orientation. Wait, I think I still got a silver dollar from beating that old man—" He fished a coin from his other pocket and flipped it onto the table. "There. That's all of it. So, what do I gotta do to open an account?"

"Well, I really shouldn't be the one to do it." I pulled up the bank's user interface. "It's a conflict of interest. I know you."

He leaned on the desk, both hands cupped around his face. "Doll, you know me, but I don't know jack about you. Your name's Ada Blum, you got a brother named Teddy, you can't cook for shit, and your favorite color is pink. That's not enough to know a person."

I glanced over at the vase. "And my favorite flower. I didn't even tell you that one. That's a fairly intimate detail to know about somebody."

"What, that?" Henry rolled his eyes. "Lucky guess. You and me, Ada, we're practically strangers."

"I guess I can't exactly pass you over to another personal banker," I said as I double-clicked the option to start a new account. "All right, then. I'm going to need you to answer a few questions."

"Sure. Ask away."

Together, we filled out the user profile. I was surprised when the bank's interface didn't immediately reject Henry's actual birth date, despite it being well outside the normal parameters. "What's your Social Security number?"

He looked up from counting his money for the third time. "My what?"

"Your Social Security number," I repeated, racking my brain for any other terminology it might've been called back then. "The government issues you a nine-digit number when you're born. It's used to identify that you're really you."

"Uh, I hate to tell you this, but I don't got one." The wad of bills slowly lowered. "The only thing I got issued when I was born was a slap on the tuchus, and I don't think that came from Uncle Sam."

Tabbing out of the bank's interface, I brought up a quick internet search. "Damn it. Social Security numbers weren't issued until 1935. I can't open an account without an ID number, the interface won't let me through to the next screen. We'll need to get you an ITIN somehow."

"What's an ITIN?" he asked.

The door opened. I looked up to see Cel waiting nervously in the threshold. "Hi, honey, I'm a little busy right now—"

"Yeah, hi, sorry to interrupt," she said, giving a quick glance behind her. "It's Officer Muffin-Pecs. He says it's urgent."

My heart hammered in my chest. I looked at Henry, then back at my head teller. "We'll have to cut this short. Send him in."

Henry smirked at me above steepled fingers. "Officer Muffin-Pecs?"

"Special Agent Rowland Fairchild, from the BTA," I hissed, but he only stared at me blankly. "The Bureau of Temporal Anomalies! He's here regarding an investigation into Sam. If he finds out you're a temporal alien, he'll deport you, and send me to prison."

"Shit." Henry turned around in his seat. "Should I go?"

"I'm afraid he'll see you." I rolled back in my chair. "Under the desk."

He stared at me. "I've seen schoolkids with more imaginative hiding places."

"Look, I'm a little short on ideas right now."

"Fine, fine," he groused, circling the desk. On hands and knees, he curled up in the kneehole. As my chair slid in behind him, Henry almost completely disappeared from view. "Just say 'olly olly oxen free' when it's clear."

I gave a cursory glance at my desk to make sure nothing looked out of place. Scooting the vase aside drew attention to the stack of money still spread across the table. "Henry—your money—"

"Oops." A hand reached up from the kneehole and blindly felt for the money, sliding out of view just in time as Rowland made his entrance.

The BTA agent was as gorgeous as ever as he joined me, shaking his perfect hair loose as he removed his helmet. "Good morning, Ada. It's good to see you again."

I settled into a practiced smile. "It's good to see you too."

"I hate to interrupt—your teller said you were with someone." He gave a brief glance into the lobby. "But I didn't see anybody leave."

"Oh, I was on the phone with a client." I was pretty pleased with that explanation. "No worries at all. I'll just call him back later."

He seemed to buy it, clearing his throat. "Speaking of phone calls, Ada, I was beginning to wonder if you'd lost my contact information. We could really use your insight on our investigation."

"My apologies." With a couple of clicks, I had saved Henry's half-completed account profile and had pulled up Sam's information instead. "I had a very busy night last night. It completely slipped my mind. But I checked into Sam's account history for suspicious activity, and I think there are some things you'd like to see. Before I show you, of course, there's the matter of client confidentiality. I assume you have a warrant?"

He nodded, reached into his motorcycle jacket to remove a folded slip of paper, and passed it over. "Of course."

"Thank you." Unfolding it, I read over the search warrant but found nothing unusual, nothing that I could use to stall. The printer whined on and spat out a few pages of scanned checks and ledgers. "Either Samson's ceased getting direct deposits or he's arranged to receive them at another bank, but he hasn't canceled his automatic payments—Penny's alimony, rent on the townhouse, miscellaneous credit card payments . . . that's why all his accounts with us are delin-quent. When he does try to pay off his negative balances, he does so in large sums of cash or personal checks from dubious sources."

Rowland's green eyes roamed over the documents one by one before returning to me. "But he's not making any progress."

"No. It's always just enough to keep his head above water and his accounts from going to debt collection," I explained. "Something's not adding up. Sam's always been terrible with money, but his law firm is still in business and he's still getting a senator's salary. Where's the money going?"

The BTA agent drummed his fingers on the motorcycle helmet with a thoughtful hum. "He's hiding it."

I nodded. "Or squirreling it away for some reason, but that seems unlikely. He's never had the willpower to save for a big purchase."

"You're right, Ms. Blum, this is rather suspicious," he said, folding the papers up. "But I'm not entirely sure how it fits into the temporal trading scheme. I'll need to investigate further. May I take these?"

"Of course." The knot in my stomach was slowly dissolving. With any luck, this conversation would be over soon. "Is there anything else I can help you with today?"

"There is one thing." Rowland paused in the middle of zipping his jacket back up. "If you could just get close to Senator St. Laurent with a wire, I'm sure you could get a confession from him. He'll open up to you. Would you consider that?"

I took a shallow breath. As much as Sam had hurt me, I couldn't turn on him like that. "No, I'm sorry. After everything that's hap-pened, I'd like to avoid anything that might put me back in the public eye. I hope you understand."

"Of course. But if you change your mind for any reason, you've got my contact information." He was almost out of the chair when he noticed the flowers. His lips parted in a dreamy smile. "It looks as though you've been upgraded from van Gogh's ugly sunflowers. Roses and—is that honeysuckle?"

"Tiger lilies."

"Right, of course." He stroked one of the petals with a finger. "I hope you didn't have to buy these for yourself. No girl should have to buy herself flowers, especially not one as lovely and intelligent as you are."

Under the table, Henry shifted his weight and stuck out his tongue, thoroughly unimpressed.

"That's very sweet of you." I smiled, willing myself not to blush. "They were a gift from my boyfriend."

At that, Henry perked up—and smacked his head on the table in the process. He winced, face going through a series of unpleasant contortions. I prayed Rowland hadn't heard.

"Your boyfriend?" If the BTA agent had noticed Henry's presence, he didn't show it. "Congratulations. I'm going to assume you've stopped using that time travel dating service, then. That's very fortunate, all things considered."

I blinked. "Beg your pardon?"

"Oh, it's nothing." Rowland shook his head. "To tell you the truth, it's just that I've always found services like that rather exploitative."

"That's the nature of time travel, isn't it?" I asked. "All of those science fiction writers who spun hopeful stories about exploring and learning from the past would be so disappointed. In the end, time travel is a money-making business."

"You're all too right." He sighed. "I've even heard about some people in the business smuggling temporal aliens in for cheap labor."

I felt like fainting. "Is that so?"

"Oh, absolutely. They smuggle in someone from a protected era and force them into long hours and unsafe work conditions." He shook his head sadly. "Seduce them with cash, a promise of a better life, but they have to keep in line or there's the threat of deportation."

"That's terrible."

"It is. It absolutely is." Rowland rose from his seat. "If I had my way, time travel would be outlawed. There's a certain order to things, the way they should be, and when you defy the natural order, things can go pear-shaped rather quickly."

"I see." I was almost breathing normally again. Despite the change in conversation, he didn't seem to suspect me. "You're more of a temporal purist, then. Things are set in stone, and they shouldn't be changed. Good to see your stance hasn't changed since our college days."

"Absolutely." He smiled, putting on his helmet. "That's why I joined the BTA—to fix the errors created by time travel. It's a much better use of my degree than sitting in some ivory tower, I suppose."

"We appreciate your service, Special Agent Fairchild," I said, mustering as much sincerity as I could. "I'll let you know if I discover any other information that I think will be useful for your case."

"Thank you, Ms. Blum." He pulled down the visor, obscuring his eyes. "Hopefully I won't need to pay you a visit again for a while."

The room seemed to breathe a sigh of relief as the BTA agent took his leave.

"Can I come out now?" Henry asked. "As much as I like staring at your gams, I'd kinda like some fresh air."

Just as I rolled to let him out, the door swung open again. Before I could process what was happening, I jammed the chair back into place, my knee connecting with Henry's forehead. He fell back with a muffled curse.

"It's not every day you're visited by two good-looking guys," Cel said in a singsong tone as she flopped down in the seat across from me. She dropped a package on the desk. "So, I'm familiar with Officer Muffin-Pecs, but who was the first guy? With the flowers?"

"That was Henry. You'll probably meet him soon." I nudged him gently under the table. "So, what's with the package?"

"Well, I know you've been busy lately, so I took the liberty of ordering our slutty tutus, and—ta-da! They came in today." Cel grabbed the letter opener sitting on my desk then tore open the packing tape.

Desperately trying to ignore Henry's snickering beneath the

desk, I flashed a smile as the vacuum-packed tutu was slid my way. "That was very thoughtful of you."

"Don't mention it," she said.

We opened our bags at the same time. As I lifted the gray tulle up to the light, my face fell. "Um."

Both tutus were comically too small. Cel stood to try hers on; grunting and straining, she could barely get it over her thighs—and she wasn't a big girl by any means. "Almost . . . got it . . ."

Cringing on her behalf, I peeked at the tag on the waistband of my tutu. "This looks like a child's husky size 3X."

She slumped into her chair, puffing. "Aw, man. I guess that explains why they were so cheap. The party's a week away—what're we gonna do for costumes now?"

"Well, we may not have matching ones this year, but I'm sure we'll come up with something." I glanced up at the clock. "Are you ready for lunch?"

"Oh, man, am I." Wriggling out of her tutu, she made a beeline for the lobby. "We can come up with more costume ideas over nachos!"

I watched her go, already dreading whatever bizarre matching costumes she'd come up with next. Once the coast was clear, I rolled aside so Henry could crawl out.

"Finally," he breathed, slumping into a chair. "So why do you need slutty tutus again?"

"There's this Halloween party at Cel's favorite club," I explained. "She wants me to go. I'm not really enthused about it, but it makes her happy. The tutus were part of the costumes."

"Oh." He stared down at his shoes. "Can I come?"

"Sure." I tilted my head, studying him. "No offense, Henry, but I didn't exactly pin you for the type of person who'd enjoy a Halloween party. Or any kind of party, for that matter."

"Yeah, well, normally you'd be right." He stretched out his legs. "But I've never been to a Halloween party, and hey, I'll try anything once."

"Well, I'm sure Cel will be thrilled to know you're coming." I picked up my purse. "Speaking of which, do you want to come to lunch with us? No pizza today, I promise."

"Nah, maybe some other time." Rolling up his sleeve, Henry revealed a slightly bloodied bandage around his biceps. "Teddy's right. Vaccinations make you feel like hell. Think I'll just go home, watch that *Superman* movie, and pretend I don't exist for a while."

I smiled.

He looked at me curiously. "What's with the grin? Is it something I said?"

"Home," I said. "You called it home."

"Huh." As he ran a hand through his hair, Henry was smiling too. "I guess I did."

20

I passed a trio of trick-or-treaters on the stairwell leading up to my apartment. The first two wore costumes I didn't recognize—probably some tween pop star or cartoon character—but the third was Superman, complete with cape and padded muscles. They toddled into the parking lot, striking poses and chattering excitedly while their mother tried to corral them into her SUV.

As they drove off, I peeked into my shopping bag one more time, making sure I hadn't forgotten any essential part of Henry's costume. A pair of plastic frames and a folded blue T-shirt marked with a red S stared back at me. I might have skipped the padded muscles, but I thought that he'd make an excellent Man of Steel regardless.

Rowland would've been glad to know I hadn't gone back to Kairos. Between the bank and helping Henry adjust to modern life, I didn't really have time, and as the days passed, my daydreams of marrying Mr. Darcy to escape it all started to feel silly and overblown.

Teddy was right, of course; he was always right, but my texts telling him as much had so far gone unanswered. I checked my phone one more time, hoping for a reply, before heading into the apartment.

The living room was dark. The plastic case for *Superman* sat open on the coffee table, but that didn't mean anything—since his initial viewing Henry had watched the movie almost daily. I set the bag on the entry table with the rest of his belongings then checked the kitchen, but he wasn't there either. "Henry? Are you home?"

There was no response. I made my way down the hallway. Henry was very fond of modern plumbing, but there was no sound of running water from the bathroom and the lights were off. It was possible that he'd had to work late, but his hours at Kairos had been shorter than mine while he was still in training, and he typically beat me home.

"I'm getting you a cell phone for your birthday," I said to the empty apartment before stepping into my bedroom. It wasn't a huge deal if he was running late—that gave me more time to drum up a Lois Lane costume from my wardrobe, since Cel had opted to go solo as "female Magnum, P.I., but slutty," complete with impossibly tiny jorts, a baseball cap, a salaciously unbuttoned Hawaiian shirt, and—most confusingly—a fake moustache.

To my surprise, there was already a costume laid out for me on the bed. I smiled with nostalgia as I picked up string after string of pearls and swaths of turquoise silk. A note was attached.

Working late, it read in Henry's distinct handwriting. *See you at the party.*

I picked up the dress Sam had given me, holding it against my chest as I looked in the mirror. Though I wasn't sure how Henry had managed to get his hands on it, especially since it had been surrendered as contraband, I had my suspicions. Any questions I had would have to wait for the party, though. For the time being, I needed to get ready.

"Hey!" A man in a rubber horse mask danced into my vision. He wore a noose like a necktie, the frayed rope bouncing with every gyration to the club music. "Nice costume. Guess what mine is. Go on, guess."

"You're hung like a horse," I said with a deep sigh.

"Damn right I am! If you ask nicely, I could show you later." At least the mask saved me from whatever suggestive face he was making. "My name's Brady. What's yours?"

I smiled sweetly. "Not interested."

For the record, I am not a fan of nightclubs. The Erstwhile Club was no exception. I wandered away from the smoky dance floor, scanning the crowd for Henry. Even if he had already arrived, I doubt I would've been able to pick him out from the other partygoers, a churning rainbow of face paint and glitter.

I did spot Cel across the room, though, her hairsprayed-to-oblivion bangs whipping back with a spray of water as she emerged from bobbing for apples. She sputtered, makeup slightly smudged, with nothing to show for her effort. She waved me down. "Hey, sweetheart! Still no sign of this elusive Henry, huh?"

"Not yet." I closed the distance between us, standing just to one side of the line forming behind her. "Knowing my luck, he hitchhiked and finally got picked up by a psycho. He could be halfway through a woodchipper now, for all I know. By the way, your fake moustache is slipping."

"Oops, thanks." She pushed it back into place and handed me her baseball cap for safekeeping. "On Halloween? Isn't that a little cliché?"

"Gonna give it a second go, Magnum?" one of the club attendants asked.

"You bet your sweet ass, buddy," Cel answered, cheeks puffing as she launched herself into the tub of water again.

"I don't think a psycho cares if it's Halloween or not," I continued as she floundered in the water. "I'm starting to get worried."

She held up an index finger, telling me to wait. Gripping both sides of the container, Cel scissored her legs in the air as she did a headstand, to the cheers of onlookers behind me. She made one, two, then three passes in the water before her teeth finally caught the stem of an apple.

"Ta-da!" The apple dropped from her mouth as she did a flourish for the crowd. She handed the fruit over to the attendant. "So, what did I win?"

The man turned the apple over in his hands. The number 19 had been written on the skin in black permanent marker. He gave a quick glance at a chart. "Looks like you get a free drink."

"Aw, man." She pulled the hat from my grip and fixed it on her head. "I'm gonna get that Hawaiian vacation one of these years, you just wait."

"Better luck next time, Magnum," he said, handing her a coupon.

"I swear the game's rigged," Cel muttered as we left the apple bobbing station. She glanced behind her. "Did you wanna try?"

"Not really," I admitted with a weak smile. "But I'll do it if you really want that vacation. Those were some impressive moves, by the way."

"I figure all those years of dance have to pay off eventually, huh?" Cel flung an arm around me and squeezed. "You're the best, but seriously don't worry about it. I wouldn't want the water to mess up your feather diddly-bopper—"

"That's a fascinator."

"I like 'feather diddly-bopper' better," she said with a grin, making the peacock feather bob with a poke of her finger. "Your costume is amazing, by the way. Blows slutty Bugs and Daffy out of the water. You look like you walked out of *The Great Gatsby*. I mean, it almost looks real."

"It does, doesn't it?" I tried not to look too guilty. "But I'm sure Bugs and Daffy would've been fun too. You want to get your free drink?"

"Yeah, might as well." Her arm still around me, we changed course for the bar. "It's a good way to pass the time until the DJ gets his head out of his ass and plays my song already."

"Or until Henry shows up," I murmured.

"Yeah, yeah, or pass the time until your man shows up." Cel rolled her eyes. "I love you, Ada, but I'm starting to get the feeling you care more about him than you do the Time Warp."

"You know, you may be onto something." I laughed.

We grabbed the last two seats at the bar. I ordered a strawberry daiquiri off the regular menu while Cel used her coupon to get a dry ice monstrosity served in a skull-shaped glass. For a while I forgot about Henry, talking to Cel about nothing in particular—her hypothetical Hawaiian vacation plans, the new girl at work and her chronic texting addiction, the memo corporate sent us to set up the Christmas tree first thing the following morning—until we were interrupted by another round of drinks, courtesy of a Bob Ross at the far end of the bar.

He moved closer as soon as a spot opened up. It quickly became clear he was interested in Cel, but I didn't mind playing wingman if it meant free drinks. I talked her up as best I could, but the conversation slowly left me behind. My attention shifted again to the dance floor. To my absolute nonsurprise, it looked like Brady's Horseman of the Bropocalypse schtick still wasn't working out.

It might have been my empty stomach or the heat from so many bodies packed in such a tight space, but as I drained my second glass, I started to feel uncomfortably warm. Tapping Cel on the shoulder, I excused myself from the bar and wandered through the club in search of a place untouched by strobe lights and overworked fog machines.

I found my solace in an outdoor courtyard marked by a few evergreen shrubs and naked trees. The carpet of stamped-out cigarettes told me it was meant to be a smoking area, but the cold, wet air had discouraged most of the partygoers from using it.

The thump of bass ebbed and flowed as people trickled in and out from the courtyard to the party—others in need of fresh air after one too many drinks or the odd couple looking for a discreet make-out spot. At first, I found myself glancing at the door every time I heard it swing open, expecting it to be Henry, but once another fifteen minutes had passed with no sign of him, I started to give up hope.

Taking a seat on a stone bench, I pulled out my phone and started to idly swipe through my camera roll. I paused as I came across a selfie I'd taken with Henry at the park the week before.

It had been several days since he had made his way into the present. His presence still felt surreal at times, but stranger still was how seamlessly he had become a fixture of my life, as though he had always belonged there. It was a sort of ease that I'd only ever felt before with Sam.

A shadow fell across my lap. "Hi, Ada."

"There you are." My smile grew broader as I looked up. "Wow."

A consistent sleep schedule and modern-day nutrition had transformed him into someone I barely recognized. His eyes were no longer sunken and dark rimmed, and his former corpse-like complexion had softened into a fairness that harkened back to Renaissance-period paintings—which was especially fitting considering the costume he had chosen to wear that night.

His dark-wash jeans and work shirts had been traded for buckskin breeches and a woolen tailcoat the color of deep water. His coal-black hair hung in soft curls and perfect spirals. I hadn't realized how severe the pomade had made Henry seem, but without it he became prince-like as if he had walked out of a storybook.

"It's, uh, it's not too much, is it?" The shyness in his voice shattered the illusion; he was no longer some long-lost prince regent but Henry in a costume. In a way, I preferred it like that. He sat beside me, watching the party through the glass double doors. "Admittedly, I'm kinda feeling a little overdressed here after I saw that guy with the rubber horse mask."

"No—it looks great," I said, almost breathless, toying with the handkerchief hemline of my dress. "But after finding this waiting for me at home, I half expected you to show up in a pinstripe suit. We could've been a gangster and his moll."

"Thought the whole point of Halloween was to dress up as

something you're not, yeah? Monsters and ghosts?" He looked away. "I'm a monster every other day of the year."

"Don't say that." I leaned forward, placing my hand over his. "You saved me. You came back when you had every right to be mad at me, and you saved me."

There was a flicker of recognition in Henry's expression, though he didn't reply.

"There's nothing monstrous about you." I squeezed his hand, half out of reassurance, half frustration. "I wish you could see what I see. It may take some time, but maybe I can show you."

"Yeah. Maybe." Henry's smile warmed, but it was short-lived. "So, uh, you enjoying the party?"

"It's—it's been all right, I guess," I said, faltering at the change in conversation. "I've never been a big fan of club music. Speaking of which, why did you bring your violin?"

"Uh, well," he started, suddenly interested in the laces of his riding boots. "To tell you the truth when you called it a club, I thought it was going to be more like the Palm Court and less like . . . well, whatever shenanigans are going in there. Something with a little more live music, I guess. If you can call what's going on in there music."

"Henry," I said, as my smile crept back into existence. "You were going to play?"

"Hey, maybe," he said in a small voice. "I mean, if they'd let me. But something tells me that the audience isn't exactly my kind of crowd, if you get my drift."

"They may not be, but I am. Why don't you play for me?"

There was a long pause—so long, in fact, that I began to wonder if Henry hadn't heard me. "Don't know if that's a good idea."

"What?" I laughed. "So you were fine with potentially performing in front of hundreds of strangers, but just one person, that's out?"

"It is if that person's you."

"Why?"

"Because," he said, swallowing hard, dark eyes darting around the courtyard as though searching for an answer. "Because I don't care about them. I care about you. If some asshole in a rubber horse mask thinks I'm lousy, who gives a shit? He's wearing a goddamn rubber horse mask. He's the idiot. But you. If you think I'm . . ."

He trailed off, jaw working but unable to say the word.

"Bad?" I offered gently. "Henry, I'm not going to think you're bad."

He straightened. "But what if you do?"

"But what if I don't? What if I think you're amazing?" Something in the warmth of my voice seemed to scare him, but I was undeterred. "In fact, I don't think so—I know you are. I've heard you play before. At the Bowery, remember?"

"Yeah, uh, well, that's plausible deniability," he stammered. "The door was closed. You don't know if that was me."

My shoulder crashed into his. "Come off it, already!"

"Hey, you don't know!" he insisted, the corners of his mouth twitching into a tentative smile. "I could've had a record player?"

"Oh, like you could afford one." Our eyes met and the laughter between us faded into a vulnerable silence. I ducked my head, smile softening. "Please play for me. Please?"

"I . . ." He debated for a moment before relenting with a hard swallow. "Yeah. Okay."

Picking himself up from the bench, he examined the instrument a final time, the way I imagine a knight might consider his sword, before tucking the violin beneath his chin. He took a last, wavering breath, placed the rosined bow to the strings, and then began to play.

As the first note filled the air, I found myself untethered from space and time in a way that Kairos and all its matchmakers could only dream of; a reality where only Henry, the music, and I existed. There was a motif in the song, lovely, bittersweet—and strangely familiar.

I struggled to place it, distracted by Henry's princely transformation. He seemed so different from the person I had smuggled to the present just a few weeks before. In my mind's eye, I could still see him surrounded by the thin walls and patched windows of his room in the Bowery—

The Bowery. That's where it was from. It felt like a lifetime ago but hearing the song a second time made the pain in my heart feel fresh.

The song came to a gentle close, like the dying embers of a fire. Henry's eyes opened and the instrument drifted to his side. His face was blank—like a man awaiting execution.

"That was—" I struggled for the right word as they all seemed too simple, too reductive, to describe what I had just heard. "Beautiful. What song is that, by the way?"

"It, uh, doesn't have a name yet," he said in a small voice before admitting: "It's for you."

"What?"

"I did say composing was frilled cravat kinda stuff, didn't I?" he said, tugging at the lace at his throat, still unwilling to look at me. "It's not much, I know. Can't get you pearls or a huge rock like Sam."

"That's—" I shook my head. "This is better. That song—it's you, Henry. That's all I've wanted."

"Yeah, well. Me too," he said, and looked like he wanted to say more but reconsidered it. He put down his violin to offer me a hand up. "So, uh, now what?"

"We could always go back inside." I was curious about what he was hiding but didn't want to press. "Cel would probably love to teach you the steps to the Time Warp."

"I thought a time warp was what got us into this mess."

"It's a dance," I explained.

He raised an eyebrow. "Thought we had already covered that I'm not much of a dancer."

"We did. We also covered that I'm probably worse." I took a step forward to toy with one of his curls, tucking it behind an ear. "The Time Warp is easy, though. It's just a jump to the left—"

I could have cringed myself to death in the following, awkward silence.

"Sorry, it was a joke," I said sheepishly. "But, really, I promise. Anybody could do it."

"Yeah, well, uh," he stammered, taking a step back. "I'm nobody, so there."

I was perplexed at his sudden need to put space between us. "Is there something wrong?"

"No, it's just . . ." He trailed off as he took a careful hand to his scalp. "I'm not used to people touching my hair, that's all."

"Well, of course not when it's covered in pomade." Moving closer again, I waited for Henry's permission before running my hand through his hair. "It's gorgeous."

"You, uh, you think so?"

"Mm-hm." I wrapped a dark ringlet around my finger, then uncoiled it. "A lot of girls would kill for curls like this. Me included."

"Well, don't start getting any ideas." The tension in his shoulders seemed to wane as he grew accustomed to my touch. "Always got teased about it when I was a kid. Then when I was older and got with the mob, I realized it was kinda hard to be taken seriously with a baby face and hair that looks like it belongs on one of Estelle's dollies."

"That's a shame." My hand slipped to rest on his shoulder. "You can wear your hair however you want, Henry, but I think I prefer this over the slicked-back look."

"Thanks." His hand trembled as he placed it around my waist. Staring down at our feet, his face pinched in concentration as he took a step to the right, then to the left. "I'll, uh, keep it in mind."

I lagged just behind him, stifling confused laughter. "What're you doing?"

"What does it look like? I'm dancing."

"This is more like swaying, really." I finally matched my footfalls to his, but we were still out of sync with the manic beat reverberating through the club's walls. "And this isn't exactly a song for slow dancing."

"Oh. How about this, then?" My skin registered Henry's barely audible humming long before my ears did, neck and shoulders buzzing with goose bumps. It was my song again.

"Better."

"Good," he said. "You know, I think about that night at the Plaza a lot. You, in that dress. The way you forgot to breathe when you saw the Palm Court. If I had any brains at all, I'd have let Sammy sleep it off and we'd have gone in."

"Things were different then," I reminded him. "I didn't know what to think about you. Telling me to leave and beating the shit out of my ex wasn't exactly a great way to start off a relationship."

"You're never gonna let me live that down, are you?"

I smiled. "Not in the foreseeable future, no."

Though it still wasn't what I'd classify as dancing, we found a sort of rhythm together. Things were going fine until Henry got ambitious and twirled me right into a stone planter. He scrambled to help me up. "Shit, I'm sorry—"

"No, no, it's fine." I pushed myself off the cement tiles with a laugh. "Just carrying on the proud tradition of crashing into furniture every time I get the courage to dance. At least this time I can blame the alcohol."

Taking my hand, Henry pulled me to my feet—a little too quickly, I found out, as I fell forward into him. He grinned. "You know, this is becoming a habit."

I was so close to him. "Well, everyone has to have their vices, I guess."

Henry made a noise that sounded an awful lot like a choke. "So, uh, Ada. There's something I've been meaning to ask."

"Yes?"

"It's just that—" He swallowed hard. "You keep saying things. Called yourself a moll, referred to it as a relationship. The time you told Officer Muffin-Pecs I was your boyfriend."

I winced. "Please don't call him that."

"Oh, what, does that bother you? Now I'm always gonna call him that." Henry's teasing was short-lived, his smile fading as his eyes met mine again. "What I'm trying to get at is—I mean, we met through Kairos—are we—aw, hell—"

He sighed in frustration, falling silent. A long black tendril drooped into his vision. Henry just stared at it in annoyance.

But even though he hadn't asked, I already knew the answer. With a smile, I pushed the hair from his face and kissed him. "I love you, Henry."

"Yeah." He squeezed my hand. "I love you too."

From inside the club, I could hear the whoop and applause of the crowd as the DJ made an announcement. I didn't give it much attention until I heard the squeal of the door behind us. Like two kids caught under the bleachers, we scattered, Henry dragging his mouth across a wrist to erase any evidence of my lipstick.

"Hey, I've been looking all over for you," Cel said, backlit by a storm of colorful club lights.

I tried to look innocent. "Sorry, I stepped out to clear my head."

"Yeah, sure you did. But, hey, at least it looks like you finally found your Mr. Darcy." She grinned toothily at Henry. "You guys wanna come in outta the cold? The Time Warp is about to start."

To my surprise, he answered, "Sure, why not? You wanna give it a go, Ada?"

"Can't be any worse than the dancing we did out here," I joked.

"Yeah," he said, "but now we got a captive audience. Witnesses."

"We'll be right there," I said.

As we headed inside, I spared a final glance at Henry. He looked through the glass doors with an expression that was a mix of mild terror and fascination. "Okay, what's the asshole in the horse mask doing?"

"That, Henry, is called a keg stand. It was invented slightly after your time."

He shook his head. "You know, for as advanced as the future is, you guys sure are backward."

I laughed.

In a way, Cel was right. I had finally found my Mr. Darcy.

21

"Are you sure you're comfortable driving?" The headlights blinked as I unlocked my car remotely. It wasn't too late yet—just past midnight—but that was still perilously close to my regular bedtime, and with two drinks in me I definitely felt it. As we wove through the parked cars out front, I couldn't tell the difference between my heartbeat and the distant thump of the club's bass. "I could call a cab."

"Hey, you said I need the practice, right?" Henry opened the driver's-side door, gesturing for the keys. I tossed them his way. "You sure you wanna leave now? Night's still young. You didn't even try your hand at bobbing for apples."

"It was very sweet of you to try to win that trip for Cel." I smiled, arms folded across the roof of the car. My feathered fascinator bobbed in my face like an antenna. "But, yeah, I think I'm ready. All I really want to do is eat Halloween candy and watch lame horror movies in my pajamas."

He grinned. "I swear, Ada, you're extra cute when you're zozzled."

"When I'm what?"

"Zozzled," he repeated, as though this was an expression I should know. He raised an eyebrow. "You know, corked? Canned? Ossified? Scrooched?"

"Tipsy?" I suggested.

"Well, yeah, but where's the fun in calling it that?" He ducked inside the car. "C'mon. If it's candy and bad pictures my cream puff wants, that's what she'll get."

Flushing with warmth, I climbed into the passenger seat. In true Henry fashion, the car inched from the parking lot, and my giggles turning into full-on belly laughs as he looked to the right and to the left of a nigh-empty stretch of road before cautiously merging. "At this rate, we'll be home in time for me to watch a Christmas special or two before they go out of season. The speed limit is forty-five here."

"Could you stop with the kibitzing?" he asked in feigned annoyance, turning on the heater. "You could be walking, you know."

"You wouldn't dare."

"How do you know? I'm a hardened criminal, Ada. Should I remind you I've already stolen one car?" He puffed up, shoulders squared, and gave me a dangerous squint. It lasted for all of five seconds before he exhaled into a slouch. "But you're right. I probably wouldn't."

"'Probably,'" I repeated with a smirk. As we passed by a shopping center, I jolted with a realization. "Oh shoot. I forgot to buy candy today. I guess I'll just have to settle for popcorn with my movies."

But Henry was already slowing the car—well, if it was possible to go any slower. "Uh, well, I'd stop to get you some, but I don't think there's going to be anything open at this hour."

"There's plenty of twenty-four hour stores nowadays, but really, don't worry about it." I brushed my hand against his, which was resting on the gearshift. "I don't need candy. This is already the best Halloween in recent memory."

He looked at me sidelong. "Listen to you. You can't say something like that and expect me *not* to stop and get you some. Besides, who said I'm not gonna skim a little candy off the top?"

"Well, that's only fair, I guess." I caught a glimpse of my reflection, ghostly and faint, in the passenger window. My hair was a frazzled mess and my makeup was totally ruined, but I looked surprisingly happy. "Take a right up ahead. That convenience store is still open."

The mini mart—a little BP station that seemed to be constantly changing hands—was a beacon of fluorescent light on the otherwise darkened street, its eaves and fixtures irrevocably yellowed with every new owner.

While I would have been happy to kill two birds with one stone, Henry wasn't entirely confident in his ability to pull near any of the pumps without setting off an explosion, so I was left to twiddle my thumbs and flip through radio stations after sending him inside with my debit card and the order: "Nothing with nuts. They're just obstacles to more chocolate."

After a minute, I noticed a buzzing from the purse at my feet. Guiltily, I ignored it since it was probably Cel begging me to come back to the club because her hookup had ditched her—and we both knew I couldn't refuse a request like that.

Instead, I watched Henry bobbing along the aisles of the store, black curls bouncing out of sight as he stooped to pluck several dark-wrapped candy bars and a bag of Jolly Ranchers.

He was a good guy, really.

I was distracted by my phone buzzing again. Mustering my most put-upon sigh, I dug it out. I'd at least humor Cel with a response, maybe an admonishment that she could do better than Bob Ross anyway . . .

DEEP SHIT PUDDINPOP

It was Teddy.

CALL ME WHEN YOU GET THIS

Puffing out my cheeks, I focused on the messages and tried to glean what could be wrong. It wasn't exactly rare for Teddy to type in all caps, and he usually wasn't big on punctuation, which left me with little to go on from the text alone. Still, I was relieved to hear from him at all after the radio silence.

Shaking my head, I brought up my contacts to return the call, only to nearly drop the phone with a start as somebody rapped sharply on the passenger window. I looked to my right, and my breath caught in my throat as I locked eyes with Special Agent Rowland Fairchild.

I swallowed and mustered the most natural smile—as devoid of mortal terror—as I could, rolling down the window to let a chill October wind gust in.

"Sorry if I gave you a start," Rowland said. "Enjoy the party, then?"

"Yes." I stopped myself. "Oh, were you there?"

"Only looking to catch up, really. Got something for you." His smile crystallized as he held up a silver dollar.

I eyed the coin with uncertainty. "I appreciate your efforts, but that isn't mine."

He shrugged, frowning at the coin in his palm. "Curious, then. Found it in your office. From 1922, and in *mint* condition—could be worth a lot."

Fighting to stop myself from looking into the store, avoiding drawing attention to Henry's presence, I feigned a laugh that I hoped sounded less nervous than I felt. "It wouldn't be the first coin dropped at a bank, would it?"

Rowland's humor melted as he looked me in the eye. His voice was low, almost apologetic. "I've already executed a search warrant for your office, and I've got another for your home."

I couldn't fight the tremor rising in my voice. "Why?"

The agent's eyes flicked through the window of the convenience store where Henry debated on flavors of soda at the cooler.

"At first, I thought perhaps your unwillingness to help in the case against Samson St. Laurent hinted that you were more involved with the senator's scheme than you let on, especially when I found the coin. So I did some digging," he said. I stiffened in my seat, hands curling into fists, but before I could protest, Rowland turned his solemn attention back to me. "Now, I don't like playing Bad Cop, but I've got two things for your boy in there, and which he gets is based on your response."

Tucking the coin back into his pocket, he held up a folded form. An arrest warrant.

"No! You don't—" I started, biting back tears, but stopped short as he produced a small leather booklet emblazoned with the silver seal of the US Department of Temporal Emigration.

"Samson St. Laurent has disappeared completely. We suspect he's hiding in another time period. You know him." Rowland wagged the temporal visa, cutting his eyes again to Henry, already at the register. The BTA agent leaned in, his voice an insistent hiss. "If you do the right thing—help us—then we'll get our man and I'll make sure that your boy there gets naturalized. Social Security number, a new identity, the whole package."

"And if I don't?" I asked, voice wavering.

"He goes back to his protected era. You go to prison." Rowland glanced at the phone vibrating frantically in my lap with another text message. "And so does your brother, for assisting and harboring an illegal temporal alien."

My throat felt hot with the promise of vomit. "Fine. I'll help."

"Excellent." Rowland stepped away as we both watched Henry pay for his purchases. "Go home and tuck him into bed, Ada. I'll expect you at the BTA headquarters in Washington no later than six a.m. Arrive promptly, or he'll have a very rude awakening come the morning. Do I make myself clear?"

I nodded. "Yes."

The only evidence of Rowland's presence at the gas station was a pair of red taillights growing smaller in the distance as Henry climbed back into the car. He smiled sheepishly over a grocery bag's worth of snacks. "So, I might've gotten a little carried away. I hope that's all right."

"Of course." I couldn't let Henry know what I had done. If I understood him at all, he'd turn himself in the moment he thought I was in any kind of trouble. I rubbed at my temples, feigning a pained expression. "Ugh, I'm sorry. I think I feel a headache coming on—too much to drink. Do you think we could postpone for tomorrow?"

"Oh, yeah, sure." He seemed unbothered, carefully backing out of the parking space. "I mean, it won't be Halloween anymore, so maybe we could swap the horror pictures for something else."

"*Superman?*" I gave him a knowing look.

"Hey, I can watch other movies, you know," he said, a hand to his chest in mock indignation. "But I mean . . . if you wanted to watch it again, I wouldn't complain."

I laughed, but it felt hollow.

In light of my pretend headache, we drove back in relative silence, which gave me plenty of time to assess the situation at hand. A few years before, I would've been able to tell Rowland exactly what Sam was up to and where he was going. I had been his confidant. But now he was little more than a familiar stranger to me, his motives unfathomable. Even the Sam I had met in the 1920s, the one who loved me and had given me his ring, seemed little more than a memory from a dream—someone who never was and never would be.

Henry cut off the engine in front of my apartment, breathing a sigh of relief as he unknotted the cravat at his throat. "I don't know how people wore this kinda stuff back in the day. A tie is one thing, but this is practically a noose."

I cracked a dim smile. "Believe it or not, Henry, but a lot of men these days would think the same thing about your usual taste in clothing."

"Yeah, yeah. Don't get me started on your generation's potato sack fashion," he said with a roll of his eyes. "Anyway. Heading in?"

"In a minute. You go on."

As I watched him climb the stairs to our floor, I cranked my seat back to stare at the ceiling of my car. I searched through every interaction with Sam, every conversation I could recall, hoping for something to stand out, but I kept getting lost in the phantom scent of his cologne and the way he looked at me in that cab back in 1922.

The cab.

I vaulted upright in realization. Digging through my purse, I found Rowland's card and quickly dialed his number.

"Fairchild speaking."

"It's me." I breathed in then out, heart thumping in my chest. "I know where Sam is. He's in Las Vegas. The 1960s. Old Vegas."

"Very good, Ada, very good," he said. "I'll have Research look through the databases to narrow it down further."

I relaxed in my seat. "Are we even?"

"Not quite." There was a note of apology in his voice. "Once we find his exact location, we'll need you to get information out of him to build our case. Please report to headquarters promptly tomorrow morning."

My heart sank, and I lowered the phone. I had hoped that would be enough. Waves of exhaustion washed over me. It had already been a long day at the bank and an even longer evening at the party. My vision blurred and readjusted, the last clouds of alcohol still fogging my brain. How was I going to do this?

The phone buzzed again, this time with a call. It was Teddy. I answered on the second pulse.

"Puddin' pop, I'm so sorry—" he began.

"I am too," I said, rubbing the sleep from my eyes. "For everything."

"What happened?" He was frantic. "There were legit, like, super-official Men in Black here talking to Antoine, and then they just left—"

"I know."

"Are you okay?" he asked.

"Yeah." I saw a light go on in my apartment. "I'm going to be fine, Teddy. We're going to be fine. This is my mess, and I'm going to get us out of it."

There was a long pause. "I love you, sis."

I smiled. "I love you too."

22

Dice rattled across the green felt of the craps table. The surrounding crowd erupted into applause and cheered congratulations as a stack of multicolored chips were pushed along to the winner. I used the flurry of activity to slip away, unseen, migrating to the next table. Maybe someone there would have some information about Sam.

"Isn't this tech contraband?" I passed by a couple of cigarette girls flitting between smoky poker games. They'd put a wire on me, masked by the twinkling crystals on my décolletage.

A second receiver was hidden in a set of sparkling drop earrings—my personal line to Rowland Fairchild as he mingled incognito at the bar on the other side of the hotel. "It's all a matter of perspective. Have you made any progress?"

I took a flute of pink champagne from a tray offered by a pretty blond. My smile dropped as soon as she was out of sight. I gave a sweeping glance at the tables again. "There was a tip from the roulette game that somebody matching his description was playing craps, but it was a false lead. No sign of him."

Rowland sighed in frustration. "Research said he would be here, so he must be. Keep looking."

I rolled my eyes, but the snarky retort I had been formulating died under the weight of an unfamiliar arm settling over my bare shoulders.

"Heya, doll." The man was a good ten years older than Sam and probably fifty pounds heavier, crammed into his too-tight suit like an overstuffed sausage. I felt like I had seen him before somewhere but couldn't place him. Probably someone from my high-school history books. "You having a good time?"

It felt like a trick question. I twirled my champagne flute. "Yes, thank you."

"Nah, I don't think you're having a good time." The grip on my shoulder tightened just as I tried to step away. "Relax, sweetheart. It's just a little unusual—a cutie like you without an arm to hang off of. What's the matter, not a gambling type?"

"Only over games of chess," I said in a small voice.

"Hard of hearing in my old age, doll." Cocking his head, he hunched until his drooping ear was uncomfortably close. "Say that again."

I raised my voice, overenunciating to be heard over the celebration at a nearby blackjack table. "My boyfriend's busy in the back room."

"Why didn't you say so?" His gaze lingered just a touch too long on my chest. I pulled at the neckline of the strapless gown, worried that he had somehow seen the mic. The graze of his tongue along his teeth said otherwise. "Let me walk you back there, honey."

"Very resourceful, Ada." Rowland buzzed in my ear. "I'm going to pay a visit to the sports book. Maybe Senator St. Laurent tried his hand at betting on the horse races. Let me know if you require my assistance."

My only response was to tighten my grip on the flute's stem until it threatened to crack in two. The older man led me out of the pit and to an opulent staircase made of curling gold leaves. A stone-faced man in a dark suit unhooked the velvet cordon for us. As we passed, I couldn't help but notice the handle of a gun tucked into the waistband of his slacks.

Each stair step brought up a new worry. Obviously, there was no boyfriend waiting for me at the top. That meant one of two things: either this man would realize I was lying, or it'd open the door for a round of drinks and teeth licking. Neither were very promising. Maybe I could pretend to twist an ankle and take a fall down the stairs as a means of escape.

"You work at the Flamingo, doll?" the man asked.

"No. Just visiting."

"Huh. Sorry." He ran a hand across the bald spot at the back of his head. "I took a pretty hard hit to the head when I was just a kid. Since then, faces sorta run together sometimes."

My heart slammed to a stop.

Frank.

This was Frank Kingston.

"Shit," I murmured.

He looked at me sidelong. "Told you, you're gonna have to speak up."

Tipping the champagne back, I drained it and handed the empty glass back to him. "I just realized I could use a refill."

Breaking into a toothy grin, Frank finally relinquished the death grip on my shoulder. "I like your style. You head on up. Get comfortable. I'll be right back."

Once Frank was out of sight, I hiked up my dress and bolted for the mezzanine, ducking into the first open door.

I was startled by the sudden crack as numbered balls scattered into the pockets of a pool table lined with half-finished drinks and full ashtrays. Cigar smoke blanketed the room. Bing Crosby crooned from a long, cherrywood stereo.

"Twenty says you're not gonna sink that four." A young man leaned on a pool cue, taking sips from his martini.

His opponent, a much larger and much more familiar man, circled the table looking for his next shot. The skinny blue plaid of his suit—very stylish for the time—was a perfect match for his eyes.

"Twenty-five says I will," Sam called back. Maple scrubbed against the gold of his ring as he drew the pool cue back.

I saw an opportunity, and I took it. "Hi, Sam."

He looked up at the moment of impact. The cue ball went wild, skipping over the edge of the table. It rolled to my feet. The man with the martini howled with laughter.

Undeterred, Sam straightened, giving me a sentimental smile. "You know, I ain't never been so happy to lose twenty-five bucks."

I weighed the cue ball experimentally, giving it a quick toss before catching it with satin-gloved hands. "I've been looking for you."

Pool balls scattered across the felt as the maple rod dropped to the table. The man with the martini let out loud curse at their ruined game, but Sam didn't seem to hear it. He ashed his cigar and left it smoldering in the tray as he took a tentative step toward me. "Ada—"

My stomach twisted into guilty knots as Sam scooped me up in an easy embrace, arm looped under my thighs as he spun me. I took a surprised breath. It was easy to forget how strong he was beneath his soft exterior.

"How are you here? *Why* are you here?" He set me down on the edge of the pool table. Though he drank me in, gaze lingering lovingly along my curves, there was something different from the way Frank had looked at me. Worry knitted his eyebrows. "You ain't in trouble, are you?"

"No," I said, but the lie in it made me hesitate. Taking his hand felt like a betrayal, but I wasn't sure who I was being disloyal to—Sam or Henry. "Everyone back home is worried. You just disappeared. You knew I'd come looking for you. Even if it meant chasing you across time."

He struggled to respond, brushing some hair from my face. "Been kicking myself ever since you left the townhouse. I shoulda canceled my plans with Penny. Lord knows she's got all the company she'll ever need with those two statues of hers."

I laughed, and before I could stop myself, I had wrapped my

arms around Sam for a hug. It was so second nature, even now, being close to him. The smell of his cologne made me feel safe.

The man with the martini took a loud sip. "So now that the game's over—we gonna do this deal or not, Sammy?"

"This is what we've been waiting for." Rowland buzzed again in my ear. "Don't let him out of your sight."

Sam nodded before turning his attention back to me. "There's something I need to finish up here, then we can catch up. Hear Frank Sinatra's playing at the Sands tonight, maybe we can catch it."

More drinks were poured as the two men settled into a pair of handsome leather chairs arranged around a floor-to-ceiling window overlooking the strip. I sat on the arm of Sam's chair, keenly aware of the briefcase on his lap.

"This is Jack Kingston, an associate of mine," Sam said, nodding at the man across from us. "Jack, this is Ada, the woman I was telling you about."

"The old flame." Jack nodded appreciatively. "Pleasure to meet you, Ada. Telling you, the man's yarns don't do you justice. They really don't."

I ducked my head, unsure of what to make of his words. "Thank you."

"Here it is." Jack slid a bundle of papers from the interior of his coat. "A cool one thousand acres of Bumfuck Nowhere, New Mexico. Bought under a dozen pseudonyms, like you asked."

Sam nodded. Cracking open the case, he slid it across the table for Jack's inspection. "Fifteen grand. That's just from the ones I've placed this week. You'll find an envelope inside with every winning bet for the next year. Horse races, boxing, the World Series—you name it, it's in there. Should be more than enough to cover the maintenance and escrow."

"I knew it. He's been using time travel to place winning bets," Rowland hissed. "But what is he doing with the land in New Mexico? Real estate fraud?"

Frank reappeared in the doorway, a crystal flute in each hand.

One had already been emptied. He smiled at me, swaying, but his expression soured as he spotted Sam. "Guess you found your boyfriend after all."

Jack sighed. "You better not be too sauced to count money, old man."

"Well, pleasure doing business with you folks." Taking advantage of the momentary distraction, Sam yanked the deed from Jack's fingers. "See ya again in about twenty years, give or take."

"Hold up, Sammy." There was a threat in Jack's voice. He settled back into his chair, legs crossed at the ankles as he thumbed through a stack of hundred-dollar bills. "Kooky Uncle Frank might believe you're some kinda psychic, but I don't buy it. I know what your game is. You make a bunch of lucky guesses, build up some cash, then sell us a book of phony predictions and skip town."

"Are you in danger?" the BTA agent asked, but I didn't dare answer.

Sam gave Jack a withering look. "You always treat your business partners this way?"

"What can I say?" Jack looked up from his folded hands with a razor-sharp grin. "If it sounds too good to be true, it probably is. You're not going anywhere, Dixieland. Not until we do a little renegotiation."

Sam's eyes slid to me, then back to Jack. He let out a slow exhale. "All right. I'm listening."

"I want in on this chronium mine." Jack stood from his chair and moved back to the poker table. He inspected his pool cue before chalking it idly. "If it's going to be so important in the future, there'll be plenty enough profits to split. Fifty-fifty."

Sam snarled. "Fine, but I don't like them numbers. Eighty-twenty."

"Seventy-thirty," Jack fired back.

"Sixty-forty and the girl," Frank interjected, grinning at me from across the room. "I want a night with her."

My stomach churned. "Please, no."

"Now that's enough." The grinding of Sam's teeth was almost

audible as he stood, towering over both Kingstons. "Like it or not, we made a deal, and it's already better than the one that you deserve. So you two can either learn to grin and bear it, or you can spend the night picking your teeth out of the marble once I throw your sorry asses down that pretty staircase outside."

"Ada." Rowland's voice was more urgent this time. "Do you need assistance?"

"Maybe," I murmured.

The room came to a standstill. Sam locked eyes with Jack, daring him to move. My shallow breaths sounded like the crash of a wave in my ears, the room was so quiet.

Then Sam took my hand and pulled me from the chair. He gave Frank and Jack a wide berth as he headed for the exit. "C'mon, Ada. Let's get out of here."

There was a swoop—and then a *crack*—as Jack swung the pool stick at Sam's back. Sam didn't even flinch under the blow.

"Give me that." Sam yanked the pool cue away from the younger man and broke it over a knee.

Jack grabbed one of the half-empty bottles of gin and smashed it over the table. He advanced on Sam, menacing him with the jagged edge. Sam froze.

A chair toppled as Frank dove for me. I pulled away but he managed to wrap his fingers in the hemline of my dress as he fell to the floor with a rattle of the surrounding furniture. He grabbed me by the leg with a drunken giggle. "Gotcha."

Wincing, I planted my shoe against his face to pry him off. "So help me, Frank, I *will* hit you with a shovel again—"

His dirty nails tore through my stockings and left angry welts in my skin as his grip slipped with each shove, finally popping loose along with my high heel. He stared at me, the glimmer of recognition in his eyes paling into something approaching terror. "Y-you're Levison's moll—"

I shook my head, but the desperation in my voice gave me away. "I've got no idea what you're talking about."

"It's *you*. Both of you, I remember now," he gasped. "But it's been—thirty, forty years—"

"Ada, are you there?" Rowland asked. "Do you require assistance?"

"Yes, for goodness' sake!" Searching for something within arm's reach to keep Frank at bay, I settled on a standing lamp behind me. The fringed shade swayed as I swung it between us, cord yanking loose from the wall. "I could definitely use some backup right now."

"Goddammit." Jack's head whipped in my direction. Seeing an opening, Sam hurled the splintered halves of the pool cue back at him. The broken bottle fell and shattered as Jack clutched at his eyes, howling in pain. "She's wearing a wire."

Sam looked at me, his expression a mixture of hurt and confusion. "We gotta get out of here."

"I'd stay put if I were you." Frank slowly crawled to his feet, teetering with inebriation. In his left hand he held a gun. "Don't know if you can shoot a ghost, but I'm not afraid to try."

"I'm on my way." Despite the proximity of his voice in my ear, suddenly Rowland seemed a thousand miles away. "What is your current location?"

Jack blinked a single narrowed, watery eye, a hand still protectively shielding the other as he got his bearings. "Take off the wire. Now."

Frank edged the gun toward me. Obediently, I slid the bejeweled disc from my neckline.

"Drop it." Jack watched it fall to the floor before nodding to Sam. "You, smash it."

There was a moment of hesitation, then a crack of plastic as Sam stepped on the listening device as hard as he could.

"Ada, don't—" I could barely hear Rowland's voice through the static roaring in my ears. Then, with a final pop, the clarity of the line was restored. "Which wing are you in? Please respond."

There was no point of answering him. He couldn't hear me anymore.

Frank nodded, satisfied. "Good. Now, get the money. We're going to go for a little ride before the Feds get here. Don't worry, doll—this time you're sitting up front with Franky, whether you like it or not."

The barrel followed Sam over to the briefcase. He picked it up, expression grim. We were shepherded onto the mezzanine, where Jack picked through a set of keys to lock up.

Sam looked at me sidelong. "I want you to know, no matter what comes of this, I still loved you, Ada."

I swallowed hard. "I loved you too."

Just as Jack found the right key, Sam slammed the briefcase into Frank's face as hard as he could. Frank's gun thundered once as it tumbled from his hand, the bullet crashing through a grand chandelier, showering the mezzanine with broken crystal.

Jack snatched for my arms, but I was better prepared than I had been outside Henry's run-down apartment in 1922—I brought the kitten heel I was still wearing down onto his instep, grinding it as I turned toward the stairs.

Briefcase still in hand, Sam started after me, but he didn't make it far before Frank snatched at the case clumsily. Despite his inebriated state, he grabbed the corner with a drunken grin.

"You're not getting away with *my* cash, pal," Frank slurred.

"Brother, you can *keep* it," Sam snapped as he shoved the case back at the elder Kingston, sending both him and the briefcase tumbling over the railing, thousands of dollars spilling forth like confetti all over the casino floor.

We didn't take time to dwell on what had just happened as we took the marble steps two at a time. Unfortunately, as suitable as my remaining heel was for self-defense, it did little more than hobble me on the fourth step. I lurched headlong, nearly plummeting after Frank. Before I could scream, Sam wrapped an arm around my waist and threw me over his shoulder in one fluid motion.

Above, Jack limped after us, shouting, "You rat bastard! I'll kill you! I'll kill your whole family!"

In spite of everything, a laugh bubbled in Sam's voice as he shot back, "Pleasure doing business with you, too, son!"

I could hear the man standing guard at the velvet rope shout at Sam as we rushed headlong down the stairs. "Sam, I think the bouncer has a gun—"

"Don't worry, sugar, the St. Laurent Express don't got no brakes." Sam dropped his shoulder and rammed directly into the thug. He sprawled into the railing with a grunt, dazed. "Choo-choo, motherfucker."

"'Choo-choo'?" I couldn't help but give an incredulous laugh as Sam set me on the other side of the velvet rope. "Have you been drinking?"

Letting himself through the rope daintily, Sam latched it behind him with a quirk of his moustache. "It's Vegas. Live a little."

The pit was in chaos, patrons making mad dashes both for the exits and for the money still fluttering to the ground around us. Nearby, Frank lay bleeding—probably dead—on the marble floor.

As we passed, I remembered something.

"What are you doing?" Sam paused, apprehensive as I stooped next to Frank's body.

"He's got something that doesn't belong to him." I couldn't even be sure, but if he was half as vindictive as I took him to be, he'd still have it.

With a grimace, I found it in his breast pocket. The monogram *H. L.* was nearly rubbed away from its silver casing. Henry's watch. I looked up to see more thugs pushing through the crowd, trying to find the cause of the commotion.

"We need to make ourselves scarce or we're gonna have half the cast of *The Godfather* on our asses," Sam said.

"Please, these clowns are barely *Godfather III* material." I tucked the pocket watch away in the most natural place I could—my cleavage—before we made a break for the nearby elevators.

"Sugar, you been spending too much time with your brother." Sam hammered at the Call button.

As we stepped into the elevator, I forced a sober smile. "Hardly enough."

"The Girl from Ipanema" filtered in through a small speaker as we rode to the fourth floor. If I hadn't known any better, I would've sworn it was following me. I looked at Sam, on the verge of cracking a joke about it, but his expression was stony.

"You didn't really come here to see me, did you, Ada." It wasn't a question.

"No," I admitted, cheeks puffing on an exhale. "I didn't. The BTA knows what you're up to. They enlisted my help in the investigation. There's more to the story than that, but that's probably all we have time for."

He nodded but said nothing else. The silence was infuriating.

"Why?" I pressed on. "You've never been good with money, Sam, but surely you haven't gotten yourself so deep you've got to collaborate with the mob."

We reached our floor, but Sam still didn't answer. Walking down a corridor lined with velvet sofas and glass tables, he took out his hotel key and unlocked one of the rooms. The door opened into a small suite that was tacky in its opulence, the floors and walls a vivid magenta and furniture upholstered with bright satin.

I followed him inside, anger building. "Is getting Penny back really worth jail time?"

"You're killing me, Ada." He dropped a suitcase onto the bed with a bleak laugh. "You really think this is about her?"

The question stopped me in my tracks. I stared at Sam, backlit by the vertical shades swaying in the room's air-conditioning. "That's what Rowland—Agent Fairchild—said. You're trying to get back in her good graces."

"Well, Agent Fairchild was wrong." His blue eyes were glassy with tears. Folding two shirts into the already-full piece of luggage, Sam slammed it shut. "I'm using the money to buy back the farmhouse. For you. For us."

23

"What?" I didn't know if I wanted to cry or throw up. A tremor started in my core, racing through my limbs. "Don't lie to me. I talked to Penny at the townhouse, she told me—"

"That we were working through things," he finished. "Been trying to buy the farmhouse from her for 'bout a year now. Finally got her to agree on an offer. At least, until she saw you. Once she realized what I was doing, she doubled her asking price."

I sank into an armchair, head in my hands.

"As much as I like to pretend, I ain't made of money," Sam continued. "With my bills, debt, Penny's alimony, there was no way in hell I could afford it."

"So you reached out to the Kingstons." I swallowed hard. "Exchanging 'predictions' for real estate."

He sat down in the chair across from me, taking my hand. "The price of chronium's gone up. I thought if I could cash in before it was discovered, we'd be set for life. I could retire early. You'd never have to work another day in your life, and I'd give you anything you ever wanted. It'd be exactly like I promised."

I smiled weakly, blinking back tears. "You, me, peaches, and a farmhouse full of spoiled rotten kids."

"It can still happen. I got the deed to what'll be the largest deposit of chronium ever found right here in my pocket. A thousand acres." His hands closed over mine. "I found your apartment key a couple weeks ago while I was cleaning my desk at the firm. You got no idea how hard it's been not to just show up with a ring and the keys to the farmhouse."

"So you really aren't my stalker."

He quirked a heavy eyebrow. "Somebody been stalking you? I thought the heat would die down after so long."

"It did for a while. But now it's back. Someone broke into my apartment. Twice. They know where I work. They sent me threatening messages—" I pulled my hands away from his. "That's why I can't do this, Sam."

Sam looked as though he'd been slapped. "But I can fix things. The farmhouse—"

"No," I snapped, voice quivering. "You *could* have fixed things once, and it wouldn't have involved buying me some extravagant apology present. All you had to do was tell the newspapers what we really were. I needed you, Sam, and you hung me out to dry because a couple of yes-men told you it was a good idea."

"I made a mistake," he said. "My career, Ada, I was just trying to do what was best for us—"

"I know, and that's why I'm not mad at you for doing it. Or maybe I'm just too weak to be truly mad at you." I stood and paced around the room, tearing my chignon loose with a hand. "Do you know how many times I've wanted to drive to the townhouse in the middle of the night? How often a bank customer has come in with your cologne and sent me into tears? I missed you."

"I missed you too." Sam rose from his seat, his arms outstretched to console me. A month before, this would have been everything I had ever wanted. "Please. I can change."

"I don't think you can." I thought back to our night at the Plaza. "In fact, I know you can't, because you don't. I've met a future you, Sam. Rather than set things straight, you just try to run away again."

"That's . . ." He shook his head, face pinching in confusion. "That's not fair, Ada. You're judging me on somebody I could be rather than somebody I am. And the person standing in front of you right now wants to change."

Something in his words stopped me in my aimless circles. He had a point. I hugged my arms, turning it over in my mind, but I already knew the answer. "No. I'm sorry. I just can't do this anymore. I've met someone else, Sam."

"What?"

"The harassment's gotten so bad I was using a temporal dating service, Kairos, to find a husband. Can you imagine? I was willing to marry a total stranger born centuries ago just to get away from it all." I offered him a fledgling smile. "That's how I met Henry. He's from the 1920s. You met him. Or, well, you will meet him. Or maybe you never will now. I'm not sure."

I decided it was best to skip the circumstances of their initial meeting.

"Oh." I had always thought Sam had aged well—growing more distinguished with the passage of time—but suddenly the man across from me looked every bit of his forty-eight years, and then some. "Is he good to you?"

"I think he's a good person."

"There's a difference between being a good person and being good to you." Sam took a tentative step toward me, judging my reaction before moving closer. "I think this conversation proves I'm not a good person. Politics will do that to a man. But I always tried to be good to you. What about him?"

When I closed my eyes, I could almost hear the song Henry wrote for me. "He does the best he can."

Sam nodded. "Does he know? Have you told him you love him?"

"We . . ." I bit my lip. "I haven't made it official."

He reached for my hand. "If there's anything I can still give you, let it be advice. Don't wait. Time goes by faster than you know."

My fingers laced through his. "I know you're right. I guess I was just scared of being hurt again."

A sudden crackle of static in my ears made me wince. "Think I've established your coordinates. I'll be arriving in five."

"Rowland," I hissed, eyes wide. "He's on his way. You need to get out of here."

Sam gave a resigned look at the window. "Let him come. I've spent long enough running from my problems. 'Bout time they caught up to me."

"Please." I squeezed his hand. "Please leave. Go. Anywhere but here. You can start again too."

"Ada . . ."

My voice was small. "For me?"

He looked away, shoulders dropping along with a defeated sigh. The thump of my heart counted the passing seconds.

"Never let it be said I didn't do everything you asked of me." With our hands still knotted together, Sam stooped to kiss me on the forehead.

Before his lips could graze my skin, I grabbed him by the jaw and brought his lips to mine instead. He swept me up in an embrace, strong, cocooning me in his warmth and his cologne. I tried to remember everything I could about this kiss, the softness of his lips, the taste of gin and cigar smoke, the tickle of his beard against my cheeks. In that moment he was Sam, *my* Sam, who'd carried me up and down stairs, always late but always prepared, who ordered too much takeout and listened to Peggy Lee. And I still loved him.

Our lips parted.

"Hell of a last kiss, sugar." He smiled at me. His eyes were wet, but they were also kind. He picked up his suitcase. "I hope he's good to you."

Rowland Fairchild found me sitting alone on the bed, looking out the open doors of the balcony at the cars rolling down the streets of the Las Vegas strip. He placed a hand on my shoulder. "He's gone, isn't he?"

"Yes." I didn't look at him for fear he'd notice the tracks of mascara on my cheeks, though I'd given them a hasty scrub in front of the suite's mirrored vanity. "I'm sorry."

"That's all right." He squeezed my shoulder once reassuringly. "You're not an officer of the law, you can't be expected to detain him indefinitely, especially if it puts you in another dangerous situation. My apologies for not reaching you sooner. Are you injured?"

"No." I brushed a rogue curl away from my face. "I know his game. He's invested in a chronium mine before it's discovered. He was funneling the funds toward buying back a piece of property his wife took in the divorce settlement."

"Would you be willing to testify once we apprehend him?"

I felt numb. "Yes."

"Good. I think you've earned this." Rowland reached into an interior pocket and removed a small leather booklet. He passed it to me. "There's some paperwork Henry will need to fill out, but once he does, he'll receive a Social Security number in four to six weeks."

I brushed my thumb against the seal of the US Department of Temporal Emigration. "Thank you. Thank you so much."

"Before we go, I want to make one thing abundantly clear. All citizens from protected eras are forbidden by law to know about the existence of time travel." He took the arrest warrant I had seen before and tore it to pieces. The BTA agent locked eyes with me, voice sharp with warning. "This never happened."

Shivering, I nodded.

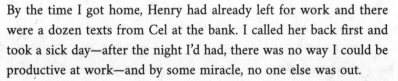

By the time I got home, Henry had already left for work and there were a dozen texts from Cel at the bank. I called her back first and took a sick day—after the night I'd had, there was no way I could be productive at work—and by some miracle, no one else was out.

After changing into my pajamas, I dozed sporadically on the

couch to some daytime TV, wrapped in the Disney Princess blanket that was part of Henry's de facto bed. I realized that was going to have to change soon, but I wasn't sure how he would feel about sharing a bed with me. While I was more than fine, maybe even a little excited at the prospect, a lot had changed about relationships since the '20s.

During the closing credits of *The Price Is Right*, I started to straighten up the living room. If the trio of brightly colored wrappers were any indication, Henry had broken into the Halloween candy and helped himself to a cup of coffee . . . and to most of the creamer. I took a bag of his dirty laundry and ran it through the washer, then vacuumed. All the while, my eyes kept coming back to the coffee table, where the visa sat, waiting.

I couldn't stop smiling.

As I was sorting through junk mail, I noticed his violin on the entryway table. He must have been playing it sometime that morning, or maybe he'd never put it away after the party. Either way, I was suddenly filled with paranoid visions of somehow damaging it during my house cleaning spree. Gingerly picking the instrument and bow up, I searched the room for his violin case. I finally found it tucked beneath the sofa.

The case felt strangely heavy as I pulled it out.

Everything about that moment felt wrong. My excitement had been replaced with a sense of dreamlike dread. A stench of moldering copper struck me. Old blood. A few flies, smaller than pinheads, crawled along the surface before flitting off.

The latch sounded like the fall of a guillotine as it opened.

Inside was a small bundle, wrapped in one of Henry's dress shirts. Dead flies fell from its folds as I peeled back layers stained brown with blood; huge, manic sprays of it, like a butcher's apron. I gagged.

I laid out the contents one by one. After the shirt, the next item was a photograph. A trio of faces smiled up at me, all with Henry's piercing dark eyes. His mother was strikingly beautiful, even in her plain, threadbare dress. A younger Henry, still growing out of his baby fat, carried a frail girl with thin, twisted legs. Estelle.

Beneath the photo was a gun. I stared at it for a long time until it became a vague, blurry shape that lost all meaning. Blinking hard cleared my vision, but the snub-nosed revolver at the bottom of the case never went away. I scrubbed my palms on my pajama pants.

It felt strange, almost out-of-body, as I got up and went to my purse. I don't even remember dialing Rowland's number.

"Fairchild speaking."

"Send him back," I said, teeth gritted to keep myself from breaking down. Everything inside me felt like it was unraveling. "Erase it. Erase him. Any memory I have of him. Send him back."

"I beg your pardon?"

"Henry killed Sam. He shot him at the Fulton Fish Market in 1922 and pushed him into the East River." My fist hit the wall so hard the pictures rattled. "Arrest him. Send him back."

There was a long pause. "I understand. I'll be there as soon as possible."

It was late afternoon when Henry came home. I had thought there would be something different about him once I knew he had murdered Sam—a cruelness around his eyes, something sinister and hungry in his smile. But he was unchanged. Somehow, that was even more disturbing.

He did a double take as he saw me sitting alone in the living room. As he kicked the door shut behind him, his eyes wandered to the clock, then back to me. "I know this is gonna sound stupid, but what day is it? You off today?"

"I called in."

"Oh." He kept stealing glances my way as he hung his coat in the entryway closet. "Uh. Is everything okay? Did I do something wrong?"

Looking down at my hands, I swallowed hard. "I found your violin case today."

The words struck him like a fist to the gut, and were punctuated by the slam of the closet door. He leaned against it heavily, arms bracing his head as he stared at his feet. "I never meant for you to see that."

"Of course you didn't. You knew exactly how I would react if I found out." The cold dread in my stomach flash boiled. I stood, shaking as though I was in the throes of fever. "Henry, you're a murderer."

"You know, it's funny. I've been telling you this whole time: I'm a monster." He shook his head, back still to me. "You were the one who didn't wanna believe it, not me."

"I thought you were starting over. You weren't busking that night at the fish market. You were there to get rid of the evidence. Funny how you knew so much about getting blood out of clothes. You should've followed your own advice." My breaths were shallow as I stared at him in cold fury. "I was trying to help you out of the hole you'd been living in. But you crawled right back in, didn't you?"

He snorted. "It was more like a nosedive, if we're being honest."

The dark humor in his tone only made me angrier. I stomped my foot and took a step closer. "Turn around. Turn around and face me instead of—of pouting in the corner like a petulant child."

With a sigh, Henry turned to face me, hands raised in surrender. "Listen. Let's sit down and talk about this. I didn't tell you because it was the only way I thought I could be with you. If you knew, you'd never wanna see me again."

"How could you," I whispered.

"I do a lot of bad things for good reasons." Henry's voice lowered to a register that made my skin crawl. "It's hard to do the right thing, so you gotta do the best you can."

"I can't believe you." Before I could stop myself, my palm struck his cheek. The sound echoed off the walls of the apartment. I stared at him, terrified he would retaliate.

He was stunned for a moment, gaze sinking to the floor. "A charity case. That's all I ever was to you. A Jewish boy with a violin case full of sad stories. You thought you could wash it right out of me, didn't you? Like pomade. Parade me around, show everybody what a good person you were—"

I shrank under the steady rise of his voice. "Henry, please—"

"And the worst part is I fell for it. I'm just stupid enough that I bought it wholesale." His shoulders heaved as he moved uncomfortably close to me. "I believed you when you said you didn't want to do the easy thing anymore, but when shit *actually* goes wrong, it's the same old song and dance, just like I knew it'd be. But I played along. I tried for you, Ada, because I love you."

A hand slid down Henry's arm, wrenching it behind him. His head whipped around, and he came eye to eye with Rowland Fairchild, emerging from the hallway. The lock on one of the handcuffs slammed into place. "I think we've heard enough."

Henry's face fell. "And here you said you weren't a setup."

I smiled at him sadly. "For what it's worth, I loved you too."

"Don't lie to me." Violent tears rolled down his face. The cold bark of his laughter filled every corner of the room. "You smell like Sam's cologne."

"Henry Levison, you are under arrest for traveling without a temporal visa and the murder of Senator Samson St. Laurent." Rowland secured the second handcuff. "You have the right to remain silent. Anything you say may be used against you in a court of law."

"Sure. I had it coming anyway." There was a flash of hurt confusion in Henry's features before his head dropped. "I was so close to it."

"It?" I echoed.

"Yeah." He gave me a watery smile even as Fairchild continued reciting his rights. "We were almost easy."

Rowland led Henry to the door but seemed reluctant to leave. "Ada, I hate to think that you've gone through all this trouble for little more than heartache. If there's anything I can do for you, please don't hesitate to ask."

"Though I appreciate the offer—" I paused, struck by an idea. "Actually, there is something you can do for me."

He smiled bleakly, pulling Henry back as he wrenched against his handcuffs. "Name it and it's yours."

24

My co-workers were wearing an assortment of silly party hats when I walked into the lobby. Foil letters stretched across the teller line spelled out *F-A-R-E-W-E-L-L*.

It was my last day at work.

I'd been cognizant of the date, circled in red on my calendar, sneaking up on me as I had rushed to get my affairs in order. In a way, I was thankful I had been so overwhelmed the previous few weeks, subleasing my apartment, converting what little savings I had into pounds sterling—adjusted for 1816 inflation, of course— and selling the belongings my brother didn't want or had no room for. It kept Henry off my mind.

The less I thought about him, the better.

"Hiya, bosslady." It was still strange to see Cel in anything but quirky sweaters, baggy skirts, and leggings, but once it was official that she'd be taking over my position, we'd decided she was in need of a wardrobe upgrade. As she came out of the break room, she looked so grown up in her pencil skirt and matching blazer. Her party hat was still on gangster lean, though. "Surprised?"

I forced a smile, looking beyond the former head teller to my office. The doorway was covered in a curtain of streamers and balloons. "It is surprising, yes. That is a word to describe it."

"You eat yet?" She bounced like an excited Pomeranian.

Thinking back through my morning routine, I shrugged. "Does a protein shake count as food?"

"Only if you're an old lady or a gym rat. C'mon, c'mon." Cel practically danced back into the break room. The lunch table was piled high with potluck staples. "Let's see. Trish brought the Crock-Pot weenies, you know, the kind with the grape jelly? Lindsey brought the seven-layer dip. Oh, and Heather brought the veggie plate, because Heather is a slacker and wants to be part-time forever—"

"I heard that," Heather called from the lobby.

"Yeah, well, I meant for you to hear it." Cel's head poked from the doorway as she shook a fist. "Consider it motivation, peon. Heed the words of your lovely sovereigness."

"It's good to see the promotion hasn't gone to your head." I scooped some potato salad onto a paper plate. "So, what did you bring? Let me guess: The drinks and plates? Again?"

"Hey now." She held up two fingers, folding them down one at a time. "First of all, whoever brings the drinks is the real MVP, 'cause you gotta get a variety, and that shit's heavy. Secondly, no. I happened to make a cake for the occasion."

Curious, I stepped over to the covered dish on the counter and pulled off its lid. The cake inside was not very pretty; it was uneven, with patches of crumbs visible in the frosting. A message was written on top in pink icing.

"'Remember to bathe,'" I read aloud.

"I mean, I was gonna write 'Sorry you are going to a place without flushable toilets,' but it wouldn't fit." Cel shrugged. "This seemed more helpful anyway."

I snorted. "Thanks."

There was a brief moment of hesitation from Cel before she leaned forward to catch me in a one-armed hug. "Thank you for being a great manager and—well, a great friend all this time. You let me know if you come across any other eligible time-bachelors, okay? Like, if you happen to meet a prince . . ."

"I don't know how many princes I'll come across in the Regency era. Just one, I'd imagine," I said as I finished filling my plate. "But I'll keep it in mind."

A flicker of motion in my peripheral vision caught my eye. The break room had a flat screen, always on mute. Usually, it was tuned to the teller line's favorite soap opera, but it hadn't come on yet. A news ticker at the bottom of the screen reported that Samson St. Laurent was still missing.

"Something wrong?" Cel asked.

I shook my head. "No. Why don't we eat on the teller line today? Just this once."

"I dunno." Cel's arms swayed with mock indecision. "That's pretty unprofessional. We might need to have an interoffice meeting to decide."

"Shut up and give me some cake." I laughed.

We took turns visiting the break room and covering the drive-thru as everyone got their plates. To my surprise, there were a few presents waiting for me between transactions. Most of them were short-term gifts—candy, a bottle of wine—but the last one, from Cel, contained two sticks of deodorant in both men's and women's scents.

"For you and that special someone in 1816, once you find him," she teased with a bat of her eyelashes. "His and hers."

"Cel!" My head fell in my hand as I collapsed into giggles. "This is contraband. I can't take this with me."

"You know, there's some things worth smuggling," she said.

It should've been funny, but I didn't laugh. I filled the awkward silence by pushing potato salad around on my plate while the other girls talked office gossip.

A customer came into the lobby. Cel hopped up from her seat. "I'll get it."

"No, that's okay, you're eating. Let me get it." I was already up before she could protest, smiling at the man slowly heading to the teller line. I was all too eager to distract myself with a transaction. "Hello, what can we do for you today?"

My smile fell as he came closer. His eyes were nearly swollen shut and the skin of his face was worryingly red, worse than a sunburn. With his good arm, he slid a check across the counter, the other—broken—was in a protective sling. I'd last seen that face unbruised and sweating as he'd grunted down a hallway with a statue of Sam's ex.

Trevor. I almost didn't recognize him.

I glanced down at the check just long enough to see Penny's signature and the date. Doing some quick mental math, it checked out. It had been written the night of the break-in.

Renewing my smile, I slipped my hand under the desk and pressed the silent alarm. "Our system's a little slow today. This could take a few minutes."

Blue lights flashed outside my office window. I watched a police officer march Trevor to a squad car, shoving him into the back seat without worrying about his broken arm. Trevor glared at me through the tinted window. I smiled and waved. All that, and I didn't even cash his check.

Officer Toussaint stepped up behind me. It could've been my imagination, but I thought I saw an inkling of apology in his eyes as he took out his notepad. "Found some more plaster statues in Trevor's car. They look mighty similar to the mannequin we found in your apartment, but we won't know for sure until we send 'em to the lab."

"It's Penny," I said. "Penelope Jackson. She's hosting a sculpting class right now. If you search her art studio, I bet you'll find a lot more evidence. She also had access to my apartment."

"We found a copy of your apartment key on Trevor's key ring, just like you said we would," he admitted reluctantly, jotting down another note. "The motive makes sense. Jealous ex-wife looking to punish the woman who broke up her marriage."

"I didn't break up her marriage." I opened a desk drawer and started to empty it into a cardboard box. "Penny ruined her marriage to Sam long before he ever met me."

His eyes flicked away but he didn't disagree with me. "You're not gonna see overnight results from this. Penelope Jackson's got money, and money means resources. You can bet she's going to hire the meanest lawyer she can afford."

"Either way, it's not really my problem anymore."

He nodded on his way out to the lobby. "We'll be in touch, Ms. Blum. You have a nice day, you hear?"

"I plan on it." Once the box was filled, I sealed it with masking tape and set it alongside the others. My office was officially cleared out.

A few minutes later, Toussaint was outside my window, climbing into the squad car. Sitting on the edge of my desk, I watched them drive away. I should have felt relief, but I didn't. Everything felt hollow. Opening my purse, I took out the permanent temporal visa Rowland had procured for me. With it, I'd be able to emigrate anywhere in time.

No marriage needed.

"So, uh, that was exciting," Cel said behind me. As I swiveled to face her, I noticed she was carrying our plates, both loaded with big, lumpy slices of cake. "Hypothetically, if I caught the guy who was harassing me to the point of mental breakdown, you know how I'd celebrate?"

"With cake?" I suggested.

"You got it!" Passing my plate over, she plopped down in my rolling chair and shooed me away. "Hey, get your tuchus off of my desk."

"Oh, come on, it's not your desk until the end of the day." Nevertheless, I slid into one of the chairs across from her. "By the way, whatever happened to Bob Ross? From the party?"

"Hm? Oh, him." Cel sighed. "Things were going pretty good until he went from painting happy little trees to wanting to do some hardcore anatomy studies, if you get my drift."

I smiled sympathetically. "Oh, honey."

"Eh, it's not a big deal." She shrugged. "We got free drinks, didn't we? Now, go on, go on. I wanna see you try the cake."

She watched with bated breath as I cut into the cake. To my surprise, the interior looked innocent enough—light and fluffy sponge cake sandwiched between layers of chocolate icing. I gave Cel a dubious look before bringing a forkful to my mouth. Then another. And a third. "This is actually really good."

"Hah!" Cel pumped her fist as she licked her fork clean of frosting. "Telling you, nobody can resist great-granny Estelle's cake recipe."

I nearly choked. "Wh-what did you say?"

"Great-granny . . . actually, I don't know how many 'greats' back she is," she admitted between mouthfuls. "But let's call her greatest-granny Estelle. This was her recipe. My mom can't cook for beans, so I took the recipe book when I moved out."

"I see." It was funny. People spent all this money trying to go back to the past when food was still the cheapest time machine I knew. "You're from Brooklyn, right?"

"Yep. Born and raised." She beamed.

For a moment, I thought about telling her everything, but I decided against it as my phone rumbled from inside my purse. I looked at the screen. "Sorry, I should probably take this. Maybe I can get that recipe from you sometime."

Cel waved me off. "Oh, yeah, sure."

I hurried out to the lobby, then to the parking lot. The rising winds had cleared most of the fallen leaves and the sky was the clearest blue, almost white. Across the street, city workers were stringing artificial garland between the lampposts.

"Hi, puddin' pop," Teddy said as I answered the phone. "How's your last day going?"

"It's been, well, eventful to say the least." The wind blew my hair in my face, plastering it to my lip gloss. I wiped it away with a sputter. "Maybe I can tell you about it over dinner. How's Kairos?"

"Oh, same old same old," he said. "You know, since you won't be using my employee discount anymore, maybe I should use it to go back in time. Find someone who's a little more mentally stimulating than Antoine."

I sighed. "Did he dump you again?"

"Not this time," he said. "I thought about what you said, and you know? I don't think he really makes me happy. The stupid fights and cryptic texts were fine when I was twenty, but I think it's time to move on. So I called him up and made our split official."

"I'm so sorry, cuppycake," I murmured sympathetically. "I know you're doing what you feel is best for you, but breakups aren't fun no matter what side of them you're on."

"Yeah, it sucks. I mean, I liked Antoine a lot," he said. "But, hey, maybe I'll find some Roman gladiator with a heart of gold."

"Here's hoping." I turned away from the wind, hugging myself. "But, speaking of time travel—"

"Mm-hm?"

"I know this has been a rough time for both of us. We're both starting new chapters of our lives and, well, it's mildly terrifying," I admitted. "I just wanted to say thank you for always being there for me. For letting me go."

"I'm sorry for being such a douchenozzle about the whole thing," he said. "You shouldn't have to live your life a certain way just to make me happy. I should know that better than anyone."

"No, you had every right to feel the way you did. After Mom kicked you out, I was the only family you had. And after the affair— well, I'm pretty sure she regrets ever having kids." I laughed and it only felt a little bitter. "I'll miss you so much."

There was a long silence. "Well, don't miss me too much. Because I'm going with you."

I thought I'd blow the speaker out. "What?!"

"Ninety-day visas are actually way easier to get than I thought," my brother explained casually. "Didn't have to sell a kidney on the black market or anything. Should be here in a couple of days."

"But, Teddy." My vision was already blurring from tears. "Who would ever want to live in a world without Netflix?"

I could hear the smile in his voice. "Puddin' pop, who would ever want to live in a world without you?"

25

"It's crooked, isn't it?" Though I couldn't see him in our unlit carriage, I knew that Teddy was already in the process of untying and retying his cravat for what had to be the tenth time since we had left the row house. "I know it's crooked."

"It's not crooked," I said.

"Yes, it is. It's *so* crooked." There was a shift of fabric. "You just don't want to hear about it anymore."

There were three problems with my new life in Regency-era London. First of all, while my savings ensured that I could live comfortably, though not lavishly, there was no way that I could keep up my lifestyle forever without taking up some sort of occupation. Needless to say, there was very little opportunity for a female banker, much less a lawyer. My other options—life as a governess or nanny—required references that I didn't have.

I decided to try a different tactic. "No one is going to be paying that much attention to your neck."

"Percy might," he insisted.

Which brought me to my second problem: the insular nature of Regency-era society. To my surprise, Teddy had an easier time integrating into 1816 London as a gay man than I did as a woman. While the places I could go without a male chaperone were limited, my brother had found solace in several molly clubs—the era's equivalent of a gay bar—and had met a new "husband," as the clubs termed it, in a man named Percy Sterling. He'd even entertained the idea of staying with me forever.

"I get the feeling he's going to be more interested in those buckskins you've crammed yourself into." Despite the chill outside, the air in the carriage felt uncomfortably warm and stagnant, almost swampish. I opened my lace fan.

"Oh god, let's hope so." He sighed. "I swear if they were any tighter, I'd be talking in falsetto."

I laughed. "They're not that bad."

"No, for real, I feel like if I have more than a sip of punch at this party, a button's gonna pop off and hit somebody with deadly force." I could almost hear the smile in his voice. "Maybe I can use it as a secret weapon."

"Like James Bond's pen gun?"

"Well, Bond never canonically had a pen gun. But, yeah, something like that." The carriage turned down a street lined with lampposts that briefly illuminated the cabin. Teddy's smile curled wickedly. "You're gonna want to fan a little faster in a sec."

"What? Why?" The smell suddenly struck me. For a brief moment I was worried for the safety of my eyebrows. "God, what have you been eating?!"

The carriage shook with my brother's crowing laughter. "I'm sorry! I'm still not used to Regency-era food, and everything has meat in it and—oh god, what if I fart in front of Percy?!"

Within just a few weeks, it had became quickly apparent that to succeed socially, I needed to know people, and I didn't, especially now that I was without Kairos's guidance. My new life story, that of a suddenly orphaned Yankee (I had learned not to bother with the accent), while plausible, wasn't appealing, nor did it leave me with many connections.

Thankfully, my dilemma had a solution. If there was anything that was in great abundance in 1816 London, it was house parties, balls, and most importantly, the rout—large and ungated gatherings that afforded every chance for Teddy to meet with Percy, and for me to ingratiate myself with the upper crust. Some nights, we would make our rounds to three, sometimes four of these soirees. All the while, I would take names, make niceties, and generally try to be as charming as humanly possible.

It was very much a typical season in London.

This, of course, left me with my third and final problem: I was still painfully clueless about nineteenth-century social politics, and I *still* didn't know how to waltz.

"Well, you'll need to get it all out of your system now," I said as the carriage slowed and the door to my left was thrown open. "We're here."

We disembarked and took the stairs to the two-story home arm in arm. The moment we were past the threshold, I was dazzled by the sudden light of two dozen beeswax candles, and Teddy was greeted by a group of acquaintances playing a game of lanterloo in the morning room. He grabbed me by the hand and practically dragged me in their direction.

He took a seat on a long bench and fired off the names of the others in rapid succession—far too fast for me to recall—but took his time when introducing the man to his right.

"This is Percy Sterling." Teddy's eyes searched mine for approval. "Mr. Sterling, may I have the pleasure of introducing you to my sister, Ms. Adaliah Blum?"

"A pleasure, to be sure," Percy said with a nod. His laugh and smile lines made him affable, the silver at his temples distinguished, and his square jaw and strong shoulders ensured he was absolutely my brother's type. "Mr. Blum speaks often of you—if you are only half as kind as his words paint you, then truly I'm in the presence of a saint."

"Hardly, Mr. Sterling." I shook my head good-naturedly and gave my brother a squeeze. "Theodore's known to tell some very wild tales from time to time. I'm sure this is no exception."

Teddy glanced up with a knowing smile. "Did I mention Mr. Sterling is a duelist?"

"Nothing so dreadfully serious!" Percy raised a gloved finger. "Fencing, rather. I spend an occasional evening at Angelo's school, nothing more than that."

"He's rarely ever beaten. Angelo's always congratulating his form." A few cards landed Teddy's way. He scooped them up but gave a sly look at the two of us. "He has a very exquisite sword collection."

"Now that, yes, is entirely true," Percy admitted. "I've recently taken a keen interest in Egyptian weaponry. I'll be traveling to Paris later this month to speak with a dealer who tells me he has a genuine khopesh."

"How very fascinating," I commented.

My brother beamed at me.

Percy looked down at his cards, then back at me. "Would you care to play, Ms. Blum?"

"Oh, thank you very much for the offer," I said to the whole table, already taking a step back. "Perhaps I'll return in a few games—for now, I think I'll see the rest of the party."

He nodded. "Of course."

As I walked away, I wondered for a moment if it was Teddy who'd been born in the wrong era, not me. Putting on my most fetching smile, I pushed the thought from my mind and wandered deeper into the townhouse.

Most of the furniture had been cleared away to make room for the overwhelming number of guests, though the walls were still dotted with the occasional chair. Music filtered through murmured conversation and the carpeting in the parlor had been rolled up, replaced instead by a lovely chalk pattern of stars and roses, to better facilitate dancing.

For a moment I stood, transfixed by my surroundings. It felt like something out of a Jane Austen movie. Except—I noted with a sniff—for the smell. With so many bodies packed in such a tight space, it was to be expected, but sometimes I really regretted not bringing Cel's deodorants with me.

I nearly lost my balance as a coltish young girl in a white muslin gown tore past me, still sucking cake crumbs from her fingertips as she galloped up the stairs to the second floor. Hot on her heels was another woman, closer to my age, though they had the same sort of happy, nervous energy. She stopped as she saw me, transfixed for a moment, before the slam of another door in the townhouse brought the realization she had allowed her quarry to escape.

"Ah, forgive her, and me as well, if you will—if she had not toppled you, I was about to, surely," she said. "And how do you find yourself this evening, Ms. Blum?"

Clearly, she recognized me, but for the life of me I couldn't place her. "Well enough, and yourself?"

"Fine, though I would fare better if my darling sister had not just absconded with an entire seedcake," she grumbled, wiping a single brown curl from her face. She took a breath, eyes darting to and fro as though to see if we were being actively observed by anyone else in the parlor before breaking into a conspiratorial grin. "Have you studied any of the men paying a visit this evening?"

How did she know me? I stopped and started. "No, but my brother and I have only just arrived, so I am unaware who is in attendance."

"Come, then!" She reached for my hand and towed me through the crowd. "There is one in particular I think you should see, and if you like him, we could see that you are introduced."

I murmured a string of excuses but none of them deterred her. Finally, I gave in to the whims of my mystery matchmaker, tugging at my skirts so I wouldn't step on them as we maneuvered through the crowd.

At last, we came to a group of men gathered around an open window, where a limp November breeze relieved some of the stifling heat of the crowded townhouse. A few of them sipped at cups of wine. One of them in particular looked my way.

My heart stopped.

He was beautiful. Dark, wavy hair, strong features, with a slight unevenness in his teeth that lent his smile a certain charm.

"That's Mr. Thomas Pickering." Her whispering in my ear was punctuated by a girlish giggle. "An eligible bachelor spending a season here in London—shall we make you acquainted?"

"There's no need," I said, feeling pale. We were already very acquainted with one another, but I thought that was better left unmentioned.

"Ms. Blum!" Mr. Pickering flashed a brilliant smile as he left the circle of men to approach me. "How good it does my heart to see you again. I am positively filled to the brim with envy that Miss Lovell discovered you first this evening and not myself."

That's where I knew her. Apparently, I had been introduced to Miss Lovell after all. My smile became fixed as I stared between the two of them.

Mr. Pickering glanced toward the parlor. "Would a certain Yankee lady care to dance? Or perhaps take a turn in the garden?"

The innuendo was still there. I could still taste the garlic on his breath, the way he greedily scooped up handfuls of my dress with so much hunger and so little regard. Still staring at him, I dropped into a quick curtsy, ducking my head.

"I am eternally humbled, Mr. Pickering, but I am afraid I must delay accepting such an offer, however generous, for another time." Maybe once hell froze over. I took a deep breath, ignoring the shocked look of Miss Lovell as I put distance between us. "I really must find my brother, Theodore. I hope you have an even grander time in my absence."

I raced through throngs of partygoers to the sound of Mr. Pickering calling after me.

Wasn't this what I wanted? Some roguish Mr. Darcy figure who would marry me without question, so long as he got to keep up his "diversions" with the hired help? I was thousands of miles and hundreds of years from home, where no one knew me or about my affair with Samson St. Laurent. It was everything, and yet nothing, that I wanted.

Teddy was exactly where I'd left him, playing cards in the morning room with a table full of mixed company.

"Adaliah!" His smile put me instantly at ease. He slid to the edge of the bench to make room for me. "Do you fancy that card game now? Another game is starting soon. I can teach you how to play."

I was all too glad to settle in beside him. He made quick work of showing me the rules of the game—it reminded me a great deal of poker—before we were dealt our first hands.

"Are you here for the entire season, then, Mr. Blum?" Percy asked. He took a single glance at his cards, brows furrowing, before immediately tapping out.

"Perhaps, perhaps," Teddy said. Examining his hand, he slipped one card out in exchange for another, gaze lingering meaningfully on the man beside him. "I have business to attend to elsewhere, but there are certain matters that could persuade me to tarry a little longer in London."

A young woman eyed Teddy, a hungry edge to her smile. "I wonder what sort of matter could possibly keep you here with us, Mr. Blum."

I straightened, eyes wide.

My brother seemed unbothered. "Good conversation and good company are always strong motivations for a man to stay in London."

Another man laughed and leaned in conspiratorially. "And we both know one can find those in a good wife."

"Perhaps, Mr. Hennicker. Perhaps." Teddy laughed, too, but it was hollow, and the smile did not reach his eyes. I dropped my cards and gave up the round. The conversation dwindled, allowing the sound of the parlor and its happy waltz to filter through.

"What lovely music." The woman across from Teddy sighed. "I'm sure it would be even more lovely with a dance partner."

"Absolutely." My brother nodded absently but didn't look at her.

Instead, he locked eyes with Percy, an unsaid question on his lips. "I couldn't agree more."

"Then, if we're in agreement, perhaps Mr. Blum would take Ms. Matthews to the parlor for a song or two?" Mr. Hennicker asked. "I believe it would do you both some good."

Teddy swallowed, hand slipping from the table. He formed a flinching smile.

"Of course. I would be honored," he said. "Shall we?"

They left with the other card players, leaving me alone at the table with Percy. There were a thousand things I could've said—I should've said—but no words could match the look on Percy's face as he watched his lover dance with someone else.

"He's a very remarkable man, your brother," he said to me in a low voice.

"I couldn't agree more," I said hoarsely.

"Intelligent and curious, but with a gentle soul." He picked up the scattered cards and began to shuffle them. "Any woman who finds herself on his arm ought to consider herself fortunate. I'm very thankful to call him my friend."

The word hung in the air like a gunshot.

"The feeling is absolutely mutual," I said through a tight-lipped smile. "I can assure you."

An eruption of applause signaled the end of the song, and with it, Teddy's dance with Ms. Matthews. I hurried to the parlor and absconded with my brother, complaining of some vague illness that surely could be remedied by the fresh air outside.

As soon as the shadow of the front door fell across us, Teddy slumped with a deep exhale. "Thanks for the assist there. She had just asked for another dance, and I had a sneaking suspicion that she wasn't going to appreciate my particular brand of freestyle moves."

"First of all, Teddy, *nobody* appreciates your twerking. Secondly"—I threw an arm out to point at the townhouse—"you didn't have to do that. You could've just said no."

"I can't say no forever." He ran a hand through his hair. "If anybody finds out about my relationship with Percy, they'd kill us or let us rot in jail. Besides, if I stay here with you, I'm going to have to get temporal citizenship somehow, and I can't exactly marry him."

"So you're totally okay with leading some poor girl on?"

"Are you even listening to yourself?" Teddy stared at me above his glasses. "It's fine if you bag some Mr. Darcy for temporal citizenship, but when I do it, it's wrong?"

"I—" I stopped and started, unsure of how to answer. "I know you mean well, but you can't just spend the rest of your life pretending to be something you're not."

"I dunno." His shoulders heaved with laughter, but it was bitter. "I did it for most of high school. I can do it again."

"You shouldn't have had to then, and you don't have to now," I said, tone growing firmer. "I won't let you."

He pushed his glasses back into place but said nothing.

"You're right. You're always right." The words flooded out of me. My breath shook. "This was a disaster. I hate London, I hate the parties, I hate petticoats and overdresses and chignon curls. I hate being chaperoned and being cooped up in the row house. I want an evening in my sweats, dammit!"

Teddy nodded. "Not gonna lie, I miss Netflix. And I almost miss Antoine."

I gave him a look.

"Almost!" he said meekly. "I said almost."

"At least you've got a life you can go back to," I said. "But I've run out of options. I've given up my job, my home, everything in the present. And even if I hadn't, everything there is a reminder of Henry—and I had just started to feel like I was getting over Sam. I can't believe I let myself get hung up on a monster like that."

"People are strange, honey. You never know who you can trust." Teddy looped an arm over my shoulder. "But we'll get through this. We'll figure it out together."

"Yeah." A heavy London fog was settling in. Suddenly I was

chilled. "I don't know about you, but I don't feel like partying any-more. Let's go back to the row house."

"Sure. Let me tell Percy," he said. "But I want you to know that whatever happens, I'm coming with you, whether you like it or not. Even if it means marrying the most insufferable beard I can find."

I stared at him, shaking my head in disbelief. "You really are the best-worst brother, you know that?"

He brought me in for a hug. "I try, puddin' pop. I try."

There was a carriage waiting outside our row house when we got home, an eerie black island rising above the ocean of fog. My steps slowed, and my grip on Teddy's arm tightened as we drew closer.

He noticed. "Maybe the neighbors are expecting company."

"Maybe," I said with a bleak smile.

But the neighbors' windows were dark.

With every exhale, I had to remind myself that there wasn't anything to be afraid of anymore. Trevor had been arrested, Penny was under investigation, and even if either of them walked free after the trial there was no way they'd have traveled back to 1816 just to torment me again. It was finally over.

Despite this small comfort, I clung tight to the wrought-iron fence that framed our modest front yard. It took every last ounce of self-control not to just bolt past the carriage to the safety that lay beyond the front door. Teddy's sympathy slowly turned into per-plexity as we walked on. The mist around us lifted to fully reveal the carriage—its handsome horses and the blue forget-me-nots painted on the side of the cab.

"Kairos?" I whispered.

I exchanged looks with Teddy, stepping closer. There was no driver but I could see the vague impression of movements through the curtained window.

The carriage door opened.

Teddy groaned. "Oh god."

I felt a tremble of a smile. "Sam?"

While he had easily blended in with the well-dressed suits of the '20s and the '60s, in Regency-era London Sam was, to put it mildly, an oddity. The cut of fall-front trousers and the many buttons that lined the front of his pale-blue waistcoat only drew attention to his generous middle, and it was comical to see him pull himself to his full height after exiting the relatively small confines of the carriage. Still, after my reunion with Mr. Pickering, Sam was an all-too-welcome sight. I rushed to hug him but stopped just short, fingers curling into fists.

"Evening, Ada." He seemed almost wounded, but he smiled nonetheless and nodded to my brother. "Good to see you, too, Teddy."

Teddy made a begrudging noise in greeting, arms crossed.

"I—but how—when did—" I stopped. "Why are you here?"

"Reckon I'm here because I need to straighten out a thing or two." He reached for my hand but hesitated. Shooting a warning glance at Teddy, I took Sam's arm, trailing down until our hands were intertwined. His ring was missing. "Ada, Henry Levison didn't kill me."

I sucked in a deep breath.

"Um, obviously," Teddy said. "You're here. Unfortunately."

Sam gave him a withering look but quirked a grin. "Well, what I mean to say is that he doesn't kill me."

"I don't understand. There was a murder weapon, his shirt—" I murmured, turning Sam's palm over as though I expected the ring to miraculously appear there like a magic trick. "Why do you—how do you know this?"

A second voice spoke up from the carriage. "Because I've got evidence, dear."

I blinked. "Ms. Little?"

It took a great deal more effort for the matchmaker to exit the carriage, carefully climbing down the few short steps until her slippered foot touched the cobblestones. She was apologetic. "I hope you don't mind that we've stopped by. Though after everything that's happened, I feel like I owe it to you."

My confusion only worsened as I looked between the two of them. "But I thought you banned Sam after the 1920s incident?"

Ms. Little pushed her fingers together ashamedly. "Well, I did, but I sort of thought you might take this news better coming from Samson. Besides, I just can't stay mad at him."

He chuckled. "What can I say? I'm very persuasive."

Teddy could not roll his eyes hard enough.

"It's the accent. I have a real weakness for genteel Southern gentlemen." She tittered before sobering. "Er—that is to say, Samson isn't dead because the man Henry murdered wasn't him."

Eyes fluttering closed, I could feel the beginning of a headache coming on. "Please explain."

"Oh! Right, yes." Ms. Little reached into her pocket to pull out a creased envelope. She held it out to me with a sad smile. "This was found in the pocket of Henry's Kairos overcoat by the laundry staff. I'm so glad they checked before washing it."

It was the letter Henry had written to his family. After we were abducted by the Kings, Henry had never gotten the chance to mail it that night.

A part of me didn't want to read it. The lack of closure between Henry and me had aided my healing process. Without hearing his side of the story, I had been able to villainize him more than I ever had Sam during our breakup. Any hope of Henry's redemption, even a small glimmer, was enough to completely undo what little progress I had made.

Reluctantly, I opened it and began to read.

Ma & Sticks (aka my baby sister, Estelle),

Wish I had wrote you more often. It might have made this easier, a single letter among dozens instead of the handful that I've dropped in the mail over the years. For what it's worth, I've written you a lot more letters than I've sent.

Please never think that my absence came from not caring. The truth is, I thought it'd be easier if I was gone. You could start mourning early, if you even had to. Hard to miss somebody you never really knew.

I did some bad things. Sometimes for good reasons, but others just because I could. I'm not proud of them, but if given the chance I would do them again a thousand times over.

I think everybody knew, deep down. No factory job pays that good, and I'd never make that much with my music.

Don't know which one of you found this first. If it was you, Sticks, don't read any further. Give the letter to Ma.

Until a few days ago, I was just a nobody, a small-time grunt doing petty crime. Was heading home when a Kings boy got the drop on me in Chinatown. He was there to rub me out. It was so fast. There was a gun. I knocked him down and hit him in the back of the head. He stopped moving, but I was scared. I just kept going. There was a lot of blood.

Took him to the fish market and threw him in the river. The cops would've never believed me. Not after the things I've done.

Never meant to do it, Ma. Know it's hard to believe but it's true.

Don't know why I'm telling you this. It'd be easier to just disappear without an explanation, but that's cruel. You deserve to know. You deserve to hate me. You'll miss me less.

I'm leaving New York. Don't know where I'm going and don't know if I'll be back. But Jake and Schlomo will take care of you. Things will be okay.

> *I loved you both. So much.*
>
> *Henry*

I slowly lowered the letter.

"He really didn't do it." There were tears in my eyes, and I wanted to crumple the note. The dull ache I felt whenever I thought of Henry flash boiled into anger, mostly at myself for assuming he was guilty, but there was a small bit reserved for him too. There had been a million opportunities to speak up as Fairchild arrested him, but of course Henry had stayed silent. He had always expected the worst, almost welcoming it like it was something he deserved. My nails bit into the paper. "Oh god."

Teddy wrapped a comforting arm around me. His face darkened as he read over my shoulder, hand slowly guiding my head against him as my tears turned into full-fledged sobbing. "Shh, no, it's okay, puddin' pop. You didn't know."

"That doesn't make it better!" I said. "If I had just asked him, maybe he would have told me—oh god. I'll never forgive myself."

"It's not too late, dear." The matchmaker's smile was fragile. "In fact, it's never too late with time travel. We can still set things right."

"Please." I peered at her through swollen eyes, voice thick with desperation. "I'll do anything. Just tell me what needs to happen, and I'll do it."

She stepped away from the carriage door. "First, we need to get back to Kairos. Climb aboard, my dears. I'll handle the horses."

"Teddy?" I glanced back at him meaningfully. "Are you in?"

He stared at the dark interior of the carriage before taking a long-legged step up. "It beats the hell out of marrying a beard."

"Like you're gonna convince any woman to marry you, Ted." Sam sputtered with laughter as he helped me inside. "You're about as good at being straight as I am at being skinny."

"I don't know. Considering you got a lady to marry you, I think I've got a fair shot," my brother said with a glare.

Sam just shook his head. "First of all, Penny was *not* a lady. Hell, I'm not entirely sure she was a human being."

"A perfect match, then." Teddy sneered.

"Come on, boys, let's not fight." I took the spot next to Teddy. The carriage door closed behind us. Even in a seat by himself, Sam looked cramped. I couldn't stop looking at the empty spot on his hand where his ring should've been. "But I'm afraid I still don't understand why you're here, Sam. You don't stand to benefit much from saving Henry."

"Yeah." My brother sucked a breath through his teeth with a cringe. "It's kinda like training your replacement, isn't it?"

But Sam just shook his head, settling into a patient smile. "I might not have a dog in this fight anymore, but I've exhausted my options. I tried to give you the farmhouse, but you didn't want that. I went back in time to try to prevent you from meeting the boy in the first place, but he knocked me out with a baseball bat."

"That was Schlomo, actually," I corrected in a small voice.

"Whatever. The blunt force trauma makes things kinda fuzzy." He rubbed his head in remembrance.

"So, you're finally my Sam, then," I said. "The one I met in the twenties."

He nodded. "I knew you were meant to love him, Ada, but I didn't think a last-ditch effort would hurt. But I know better now. I ain't gonna try to fight it anymore. What is to be will be—"

"—even if it never happens," I said in unison with him.

"I just want you to be happy, so here I am," Sam said, but as the silence dragged on his jaw worked guiltily with a confession: "Well, that and Ms. Little said she'd hide me from the Feds in exchange for a small cut of the chronium mine. I ain't got time to go to prison—the food there is lousy."

I laughed. "Now that's the Sam I know."

As the percussion of horses' hooves echoed outside and the carriage rolled forward, I finally felt like I was home. Whatever plan Ms. Little had, I knew it wasn't going to be easy, but that was okay. I was done with doing the easy thing, and this time there was no turning back.

26

Time was not on our side as we left the Manhattan branch of Kairos in 1922.

"Wouldn't it be a little, I dunno, *safer* to just bring the letter to the trial as evidence?" Teddy had chosen a charcoal suit that probably made him feel like a gangster, while Sam was back in his seersucker. "We wouldn't have to haul ass at the eleventh hour."

"But that's exactly what we're doing, dear." Ms. Little would have stood out the most among us in a white suit with contrasting black pinstripes, but her androgynous figure and buzzed-short hair served to diffuse any quizzical looks we might have gotten. Once she pulled the brim of her fedora down to hide her full lashes and lavender eyes, she looked like any other man on the streets of New York. "Trials work a bit, ah, differently when the BTA is involved."

"How so?" I found myself again in the jewel-toned dress Sam had given me. I still didn't know if I was wearing it out of misplaced sentimentality or the fact that I knew it fit. "That wasn't covered in law school."

"Let's just say that they've found a much more expedient way to dispense justice," she said.

"Okay." I focused on the plan—such as it was—trying to ignore the thundering in my chest as we moved into the midtown alleyway. "How are we getting to the Lower East Side?"

"I suppose we'll simply have to drive there," Ms. Little replied as she moved to a nearby car parked at the curb. With a smile, she passed the key to Samson. "It would probably be best if you did the honors, dear."

Sam didn't argue as he climbed into the driver's seat with a grin. "How'd you know I wanted to give it a try?"

I took the passenger seat, shaking my head, "Don't tell me you've never driven one of these things either."

"I've driven cars a sight older than I am, sugar—can't be much harder than an old Studebaker," he quipped back as he turned the key and stepped on the starter. The engine growled to life.

"I didn't realize they *made* cars back then, Sam," Teddy teased as he climbed in.

"Then it's settled," Ms. Little piped up as she took her own place in the back seat. "Let's go buy some fish, shall we?"

Not for the first time, I wondered if there wasn't something very wrong with the matchmaker.

There was no radio to fill the silence as we drove down Fifth Avenue. If I was being honest, the bile rising in my throat would have prevented me from holding a conversation anyway.

This was my fault, and I knew it.

Sam was somewhat notorious for trying his luck with speed limits, but that evening he thankfully showed some restraint. The last thing we needed were 1920s police officers stopping us for driving recklessly. I think he was more nervous than he let on, and that made him cautious, especially as we arrived at the Fulton Fish Market right as the sun was going down.

"We should probably keep the car, in case we need to make a getaway," Teddy noted darkly as we threaded through the narrow cobblestoned roads of the seaport, headlights dim beacons in the growing twilight.

"Of course we're keeping the car, dear," Ms. Little chided. "It's

Kairos property, you know. It's not as though we'll be driving it into the river."

"Still, we don't know where Henry's going to be, do we?" I asked, scanning the thinning crowds, eyes darting to the alleyways for any clues. The whole time, my mounting panic conjured images of BTA agents lurking around every corner to stop us.

But as we reached the south end of the road, we found nothing.

Puffing his cheeks in quiet frustration, Sam turned down the next street, moving northward. He reached over to pat my knee reassuringly. "Don't worry, Ada—we'll comb every back alley to find him."

The Model T rounded a stack of half-broken pallets, passing by the back door of the same cannery where Henry had helped me clean up. I half expected to catch sight of us through one of the windows, but they were dark and lifeless.

Even if it took a hundred tries, in a hundred different timelines, I knew we would find him. I had already committed one felony by bringing Henry to the present in the first place. A few more wouldn't hurt.

Sam brought the car to a stop, jarring me from my musings. From the alley ahead, I could make out the rear of a black truck with small windows reinforced with iron bars. The side read NEW YORK CITY POLICE DEPARTMENT.

Ms. Little leaned forward with interest. "That's the sort of thing the BTA would use to blend in, don't you think?"

The car crept closer, bumping along the unpaved road until we could see clearly down the alleyway.

The police van had been abandoned, but the occupants hadn't gone far. Opposite the vehicle, another alley opened into a narrow berth for smaller ships, which sat vacant save for a half dozen blue-uniformed officers in a semicircle, each armed with tommy guns, their expressions stone.

"There's so many of them," I murmured. "Why send out so many men for a single execution?"

"Those aren't men," Ms. Little whispered. "Those are ORAE. Order Restoring Autonomous Entities."

I stared. "So, the ORAE did get involved. I didn't think it was that serious."

"You're telling me." Sam gave a dark chuckle. "I sorta thought they were an urban legend, like the sewer gators."

Ms. Little nodded. "The ORAE may look like people, they might sound like people—they may even taste like people, though I'm a bit hazy on that one—but I assure you they are *not people*. In my time, they serve the BTA as foot soldiers and a sort of mobile courtroom. Judge, jury, and executioner, all in one."

I opened my mouth to say something but decided now wasn't the time for a Q&A session.

The ORAE stood guard over a pair of men at the water's edge. Both were black-haired and roughly the same age. They were even dressed similarly, in woolen suits, though only one had his coat on. Henry stared down the barrel of Fairchild's gun, unmoving.

"Henry Levison." As if on cue, the ring of officers spoke up, droning on in horrifying, robotic unison. "You are guilty of the crimes of extortion, grand larceny, illegal temporal immigration, assaulting officers of the law, and the murder of Samson St. Laurent. You are hereby sentenced to death. Commence execution in fifteen seconds."

"Oh my god," Teddy hissed from the back. "Are they really going to shoot him like a bad mob hit?"

"Commence execution in ten seconds."

"Not if I can help it," Sam said, laying on the horn, the angry sound echoing through the ghostly docks.

The uniformed officers didn't react. "Commence execution in five seconds."

"Stand down," Rowland said, annoyed, flashing his badge at the ORAE. The line of tommy guns lowered. Squinting against our head-lights, he tried to wave us away. "You there! Police business!"

I stormed from the car, anger bubbling as I headed down the

alley toward him. "No. No, this is *not* police business, Fairchild. This is murder. We have evidence that proves Henry's innocence."

Behind me, I heard the other car doors open as Teddy, Ms. Little, and Sam followed.

"It's too late, he's already been found guilty," the BTA agent said.

"Ada, let him." Henry's voice was haggard, just like it had been when I'd called Fairchild to haul him away. "You said it yourself. This is how I die."

"This is how it must be, Ms. Blum. He never belonged in our time. I'm simply restoring order to the timeline," Fairchild stated, his tone nearly reasonable. "I can think of no fairer punishment for his role in the murder of Senator St. Laurent."

"That's a hell of a charge considering I ain't dead yet, Officer." Sam corrected him as he neared the police line.

Fairchild seemed surprised. "Senator, you really shouldn't be here. There's a warrant out for your arrest and beyond that—this man has killed you before, and I doubt he'd hesitate to do it again."

Sam spread his arms with his most winning smile. "All right, then, why don't we come to a compromise? I turn myself in. The boy doesn't get to murder nobody, and he don't get murdered either."

I tensed, heart in my throat, but I couldn't argue if it meant saving Henry.

Fairchild seemed to consider the offer for a moment, his eyes flicking between Henry and Sam before he shook his head. "That only solves one facet of the problem, Senator. Historical integrity must be maintained. Henry Levison must die tonight."

Ms. Little stepped forward now, raising a hand innocently.

"If I may, Agent—Fairchild, is it? You do realize that not only are you failing to preserve historical integrity by executing Henry Levison like this, but you're *also* jeopardizing your agency's own interest by doing so at the expense of apprehending, goodness—" She paused, making a show of counting heads. "No less than four suspects for temporal crimes?"

Teddy frowned as he stepped up behind me and laid a reassuring hand on my shoulder. "Not to mention you're just being kind of a douchenozzle about this whole thing."

I sighed. "Good hustle, cuppycake."

"For fuck's sake, can we *please* just let Officer Muffin-Pecs kill me already?" Henry barked from the edge of the dock. "Don't I get any say in this?"

I took another step forward, threatening to break the police line. "Dammit, Henry, give yourself a chance. Why didn't you try to fight the charge if you didn't do it?!"

"Because." Henry snorted, looking away. "I did something just as bad. It seemed easier."

"What happened to doing the right thing?" I glared at him.

Rowland Fairchild's patience had run out. "All of you, that is *enough*. You are all about to be placed under arrest for obstruction of justice if you don't back down."

"Then add it to the list of charges," Sam growled as he stepped forward to break the police line. Strangely, the uniformed officers let him pass without batting an eye. In fact, their gaze didn't even move to follow him.

Fairchild stepped away from Samson, warding him off with his pistol. "Senator, I am warning you, this is not a situation you're going to be able to bluster your way through. Lay a hand on me and the ORAE"—he nodded to the line of silent officers—"will have you on the ground."

"It's a hell of a lot better option than watching you kill this boy." Sam didn't pause as he grabbed for Fairchild's wrist, but the BTA agent was faster—unnaturally so, nearly a blur—as he pulled away again and snap-fired.

Sam reeled back, a hand clutching his chest. He swayed on his feet for an instant before collapsing to the ground.

"NO!" The world seemed to slow as I dove down with a cry, cradling Samson's head in my lap. I cast around for something—anything—to serve as a bandage, my eyes settling on the handkerchief in his pocket.

Fairchild was clearly rattled, the barrel of his gun flitted to each of us tensely. "I *told* you all what would happen. Now *leave* and let justice be carried out."

His continued explanations became little more than background noise. My entire world was Sam, bleeding out on the cobblestones.

"Sugar, don't worry, I can barely feel it," he lied as he coughed up a mouthful of blood.

Teddy joined me on the ground, applying pressure. "Sam, could you shut up for once in your damn life? Talking's only going to make it worse."

"You really don't listen to yourself, do you Agent Fairchild?" Ms. Little put herself between us and the BTA agent, voice eerily calm. "You talk about fate and order and historical integrity but with time travel, every moment is what you make of it. We have more control over our world than we ever have. But rather than use the sum of our knowledge to build a better future, we cling to the past."

Fairchild growled. "I'm not going to listen to your revisionist propaganda. We are gatekeepers, not god."

"Are you?" She jabbed a finger at him. "A man lies here dying, and it was *your* devotion to maintaining history that did it. Are we not both playing god?"

Sam did his best to push Teddy and me away. "Dammit, both of you, get out of here before Fairchild gets trigger happy with you too."

I locked eyes with him. He was losing so much blood. "Sam, I am not going to just leave you to bleed out."

Sam laughed weakly, coughing up more blood. His eyelids fluttered. "Ada, you're killing me . . ."

I couldn't help but laugh through the tears as I held him to my chest. "Don't say things like that."

He didn't answer.

"Sam?" I pulled away, shaking him to try to keep him awake. When he didn't stir, I shook him harder. "Sam—"

"Oh shit," Teddy whispered, bloody hands cupping his mouth.

New York City seemed to fall silent as I watched Sam die in my arms.

"Rowland Fairchild." The tense silence was broken by a chorus of mechanical voices speaking as one. The ring of ORAE turned to face Rowland Fairchild. "You have been found guilty of the murder of Samson St. Laurent. You are hereby sentenced to death. Commence execution in fifteen seconds."

We all looked on, stunned.

Fairchild tried to back away but quickly found himself at the water's edge. His pistol clattered to the ground as he frantically grabbed at his badge, flashing it at the line of mechanical officers again and again. They were unrelenting. "No—no—this was clearly unintentional. Our records, the database says no crime was committed here. I did nothing wrong. ORAE, stand d—"

Henry hit the ground as the officers opened fire before Fairchild could finish. Within seconds, the BTA officer's torso was a bloody ruin dancing under the force of the rounds pumped into it. A moment later, what was left of Fairchild plummeted into the river, his expression frozen in silent horror.

I used the distraction of gunfire to try to drag Sam's body away, Teddy and I looping our arms beneath his shoulders. Ms. Little tutted sadly as she lifted his feet—single-handedly—as we carried him. "Well, I suppose in the end Fairchild got what he wanted. Justice was served and order was maintained."

Henry blinked at the ORAE. "Uh, thanks for your help, fellas."

There was a deafening click as they reloaded their weapons in unison.

He paled. "Aw shit."

The mechanical officers turned toward us as we retreated, speaking in unison again as they raised their weapons. "Adaliah Blum, Theodore Blum, Ellis Little, you are guilty of the crimes of temporal human trafficking and resisting arrest. Stand for sentencing."

"Oh, cherry tarts," Ms. Little said. "That's not good."

We rushed down the alleyway, ducking around the corner as the machines fired their guns again. Bullets chewed into the brick of the warehouses and sprayed the car, shattering windows and riddling it with holes as the engine wheezed to a stop.

Well, the Model T wasn't getting us anywhere anytime soon.

The ORAE began advancing up the alley toward us as we ran for the police van across the way.

"God, I hope this thing is armored," Teddy grunted as he tried the handle on the back doors. "Shit, it's locked."

I winced, ready for the worst, but it never came. A gun fired from the dock. Henry had taken Rowland's pistol and was facing down the ORAE. "Get the hell out of here. I'll keep 'em busy."

"So help me, I am *not* going to watch both you and Sam die tonight, Henry," I yelled, furious.

"Henry Levison." The ORAE split their attention now, half of the pack turning to Henry. "You are guilty of the crimes of extortion, grand larceny, illegal temporal immigration, assaulting officers of the law, voluntary manslaughter, and resisting arrest."

"Aw, c'mon, I didn't even *do* that one." From some place at the far end of the alley, Henry popped off another shot. It caught one of the ORAE in the head.

It fell to the ground with a crash, a spray of sparking wires and bright-blue hydraulic fluid. "St—by—for—sen—cing—"

Ms. Little, Teddy, and I dropped Sam's body and darted into the cover of the thick fenders of the police van, our every step dogged by rounds stitching across the cobblestones.

As the ORAE closed in on us, I pressed forward. The cab door was locked on the police van, though the window was open. I climbed the fender and heaved myself into the opening with an unladylike grunt. Ms. Little simply wrenched the far door open and climbed inside behind Teddy.

I stared for a moment in disbelief. "And you can't open a tin of cookies?"

"Now's not the time, dear," she answered. "Drive."

The key was still in the ignition. Jamming down the starter, I threw the throttle into high gear. The vehicle rumbled forward and crashed through refuse as we careened down the narrow alley, being peppered with gunfire all the while.

I hauled the steering wheel into a tight left.

Teddy slammed against me. "Where are we going?"

"Back for Henry," I snarled as I took another left. One more, and we were driving by the riverside, tearing through a stack of crates as I closed in on the small berth where we'd last seen Henry. I spotted him crawling away from the alley, the fallen ORAE's tommy gun braced against him.

"Hi, Ada." The cab was a tight fit as he slid in beside Ms. Little.

"Hi, Henry." I flashed him a smile.

It was all the distraction the mechanical officer at the end of the alley needed. He opened fire on us. I didn't duck in time, and a bullet buried itself deep in my shoulder.

With a cry, I slammed on the gas again and pulled out of the firing line.

Ms. Little was rolling up the sleeve on her right arm, revealing a thick metal bangle on her wrist.

"Not without Sam," I hissed through the pain.

Another burst of gunfire pocked the rear doors.

"Please, Ms. Blum. You're injured and the ORAE are highly unpredictable without a handler." The jewelry at her wrist glowed dimly with a tap. "There's no way we'll be able to retrieve Samson's body without losing one or more of our own."

I pulled another pair of tight turns, gritting my teeth as pain blossomed bigger and brighter from my shoulder. I could see Sam lying in the street, untouched by the madness of the running gun battle.

Just where I'd seen him when Henry and I had met at the Fish Market.

Levison's body was discovered in the East River on April 10, 1923, but contemporary records indicate that he may have gone missing as early as October 24.

Exactly two weeks after October 9, when I told Sam I would run away with him.

I pushed the thought from my mind as I accelerated, trying desperately to get to Sam's body.

The five remaining ORAE stepped from the alleys, guns raised, ready to obliterate the unarmored windshield of the van. "Stand by for sentencing."

"I'm sorry, dear," Ms. Little offered. "There just isn't time. Not now."

She tapped her wrist a final time and reached up to hold on to the frame of the car. Electricity arced from the bracelet, dancing along the interior of the police wagon. The guns ahead of us blazed to life and my world was filled with light and sound.

My eyes clenched shut against the assault.

It never came.

I let off the gas and blinked at my surroundings.

It was the same street, early morning, by the look of things. Sam's body was nowhere to be seen. There was no blood. No bullet holes marked the walls. No smashed or overturned crates.

The passenger door opened. Henry lurched out, paler than ever, as he emptied the contents of his stomach. "Did we just time travel? I think we just time traveled. Oh god. I hate it even more when there's no pod."

"Shit." Teddy tore a strip of his shirt loose with his teeth. "Ada, let me see where it hit you."

"No." I panted, already revving the engine. "We have to go back. Sam's body—"

"Is probably already gone," Ms. Little finished, looking at her bracelet. "The BTA keeps obsessive records of crime, dear. His body's likely already been collected as evidence."

Something in her words made the last bit of adrenaline in my body evaporate. I was pinned in place by pain and grief and loss, sobbing. My shoulder felt like it was melting, even as Teddy started to apply pressure. "Sam is gone. We have to fix this."

"We can try," the matchmaker said. "But it won't be easy. You saw how adamant Agent Fairchild was about the integrity of the timeline. His is not an isolated opinion. If you meddle too much or make too many alterations, you can bet the BTA will have something to say about it."

"But that's not fair." I gasped. "It was an accident."

"Of course it was," she answered, voice sharp. "Think about it, dear. If you have access to time travel, why isn't every premature death prevented?"

Wiping his mouth with a wrist, Henry weakly hung on to the frame of the car. "I messed this up for you, Ada. I'll help you fix it."

I let out a whine as the pressure on my shoulder increased. "Please, Teddy, you're hurting me."

"Suck it up, puddin' pop, 'cause I'm not stopping until we get you to an emergency room." His expression softened after a moment. "I know it's hard to think about right now, but would Sam even want you to change things? In the carriage, he seemed pretty aware there was no possibility of a life with you. He wanted you to be happy with Henry."

"That doesn't mean he had to die," I choked out. My throat felt like it was closing.

"Ms. Blum." The matchmaker touched my hand. "You're on the crux of making a very important decision, one that shouldn't be made while you are actively bleeding out."

I nodded, biting my lip. "We need to get back to Kairos."

EPILOGUE

"For years, the accepted narrative painted Blum in a manipulative and controlling light," the news anchor said. Her tone was as professional and boring as her pantsuit. "But in a series of emails uncovered during the investigation surrounding his disappearance, St. Laurent tells an entirely different story."

At first, it had been hard to stomach Sam's private correspondence being plastered across every news platform. It felt wrong, invasive. But as the news anchor read the words aloud for the fourth time that day, I could almost hear Sam's voice. "Ada is the love of my life. People make a whole lot of assumptions based on our age difference, the circumstances. They've got an idea of what love needs to look like, and we don't fit it."

My office phone rang. I muted the television and picked it up. "Hello?"

"Ms.—" The receptionist stalled for only a moment. "Blum. Ms. Blum, your six o'clock appointment is here."

I smiled. Close enough. "Good. Send her in."

While I waited, I toyed with one of my new business cards. ADA BLUM, MATCHMAKER FOR THE KAIROS TEMPORAL MATCHMAKING SERVICE, it read in stately, black lettering. WHAT IS TO BE WILL BE, EVEN IF IT NEVER HAPPENS.

I glanced up at the sound of the door, faint strains of "The Girl from Ipanema" drifting in from the waiting room. There was a look of apprehension on Cel's face but once her eyes met mine, she settled into a wide smile, plopping into the upholstered chair across from me. "Uh, hi bosslady! I thought by now you'd be up to your neck in hot Regency-era men."

"Turns out you were right—they were a little too smelly for my taste," I said, nose wrinkling as I slid a sleeve of Oreos across the desk. "Cookie? I promise there's no glitter in them."

"Uh, is there normally glitter in them?" She took one, scrutinizing it before taking a bite.

"Sometimes." I sighed. "Nothing's sacred anymore. How's life at the bank?"

"Same circus, same clowns," she said with a shrug. "I had to get rid of the new girl when she accidentally sent me a sext."

I cringed. "Ouch. Well, I guess that explains why she was always texting."

"Yeah." She popped the whole cookie into her mouth with a crunch, garbling around it. "So, you're working for Kairos now? Were you the one who sent me the coupon?"

"That's my employee discount." I straightened a stack of manila folders. "You said to let you know if I found any more eligible time-bachelors, and I think I've got a few lined up that you might like. No princes. Sorry about that. But how do you feel about 1985 Hawaii?"

"Hawaii!?" I thought the chair might give out under her as Cel started bouncing. "You're sending me to Hawaii? I FINALLY GET TO GO TO HAWAII?"

"If you want to."

"I look fine as hell in jorts and teased hair, I swear. This is the greatest thing ever," she squealed, flopping over the arm of the chair with giggles until another thought hit her. "Wait. He doesn't have a mullet, does he?"

"No." I wheezed with laughter as I slid one of the folders over. "I promise, no mullets to be found. Here's his dossier. We'll need to get you vaccinated first, though."

"Yeah, sure, of course. Ada, you're the best friend a girl could ever have." Cel hopped up from her seat, wiggling excitedly. She was just about to leave when the door opened a second time.

"Oh, there you are." I smiled. "Cel, Henry, you two remember each other from the party, right? Cel's the one with the cake recipe I told you about."

For a moment, Henry's dark eyes tried to parse her features, picking out the pieces of her that might still have some resemblance to his sister. He must have found it, and his face blossomed into a smile that threatened to make my heart burst. "Hi, Cel. It's nice to see you. You know, when you're not totally soaked from bobbing for apples."

"Not my best look." She tilted her head. "Your accent is familiar. Brooklyn?"

"Pretty close," he said.

"Henry's training to be a chaperone." I opened a drawer and pulled out a bejeweled corsage, passing it across the table. "Can you show her the way to First Aid?"

He nodded.

Cel picked up the brooch, turning it over in her hands, shoulders heaving in a relieved sigh. "Gosh, it's really good to see you again. We're gonna have to play catch-up when I get back. I missed you."

"I missed you too." I settled back into my seat. "Oh, and Cel?"

"Yeah?"

"Before you go, do you know anything about greatest-granny Estelle?" I asked. "Beside her awesome cake recipe, I mean."

Cel's eyes rolled to the ceiling in thought, clicking her tongue. "She was a dancer, I think. Ballet."

My smile broadened. "That's great. I hope you enjoy the bachelor I've picked out for you. He's every bit the hunkasaurus you've been looking for, and more."

She passed by Henry in the doorway. His jaw hung in shock for a full five seconds before he wandered into my office bewilderedly, heavy eyebrows knitted together, absently dragging a chair over so he could sit beside me. He started and stopped several times, trying to formulate a sentence before settling on a single word: "How?"

Opening another drawer, I pulled out a small plastic case. Inside were four small syringes loaded with a pale liquid. "I thought—maybe, tonight after work, we could go back."

He was quiet for a long time, staring at the floor to hide his growing smile. "I love you, Ada."

"I love you too." I leaned forward to steal a quick kiss, coiling a wild curl around a finger before letting it bounce loose. "Hope the chaperones are ready for Cel. After all the trouble I caused, I can only begin to imagine the hell she's going to raise in the eighties."

"Hey, it's not like you set her up with a gangster, right?" But Henry's smile dimmed as his eyes flicked to my television. A photo of Sam was plastered across the most recent news report. "Again, I'm really sorry for what happened."

"That has to be the twentieth time you've apologized. Please don't blame yourself." As I watched the footage of Sam play out, I smiled. "Things get a little easier every day. Time really does heal."

"I know. And I know you're still thinking about things." He squeezed my hand. "But whatever you do, I'll be with you every step of the way."

"Thank you." I glanced at my phone just in time to see 6:22 roll back to 6:21. I still wasn't wild about time travel. "You know, you could always go with her. Maybe they'll let you swap your uniform for a Hawaiian shirt, huh?"

He rolled his eyes as he trudged to the door. "Yeah, yeah. You'd like that, wouldn't you?"

"Oh, and a pair of board shorts." I grinned. "Put those pasty white legs of yours on display. Don't forget sunscreen. At least fifty SPF."

"I gotta get to work." Henry shook his head, but he was laughing. As he closed the door, I could hear him whistling my song from the hallway.

Opening up my appointment book, I thumbed through the day's matches. There was still so much work to do—I had so many questions for Ms. Little—but my heart just didn't belong to Kairos that evening. With a sigh, I picked an Oreo from its sleeve and considered it, but I didn't even feel like eating.

I reached for the chain around my neck and pulled out Sam's ring. The three diamonds sparkled in the low light.

I missed him. I missed him every single day.

"What is to be will be," I whispered. "Even if it never happens."

ACKNOWLEDGMENTS

Thank you, Mama, for sharing Grandmama's motto: "What is to be, will be, even if it never happens." Without her peculiar turn-of-phrase, this book may have never happened.

To Kenna, my best friend of twenty-some-odd years: thank you for all those lunch breaks you spent reading the first version of *Kairos* on Wattpad and for deciding that Sam was smooth peanut butter.

Thanks to all the unwashed deviants that came from Electrum City, from your lovely dread sovereigness. Through playing *Dungeons and Dragons*, I learned I had more than a couple good stories in me, and those stories should be shared. I love you all so much.

Larry, you are literally watching me type this, but know that the next book is for you. You are a beautiful gift, and my life has been improved by knowing you. Thank you for wiggling with me.

And Sei'ne—thanks for the adventure.

ABOUT THE AUTHOR

Banker, nonprofit worker, code monkey, private eye's assistant, Leigh Heasley has held a lot of interesting jobs, but her favorite one is storyteller. Her debut novel, *The Once and Future Fling*, has over 800,000 online reads, won a Watty award, and has been optioned for television. After the untimely passing of her husband and co-writer, Sei'ne, Leigh has promised that the world will hear all of their stories. She lives in a restored farmhouse in Virginia with her two dogs and too many wild rabbits to count.

The ONCE And FUTURE FLING

DISCUSSION QUESTIONS

1. Do you think time travel will ever be possible?

2. If you could go back to any era, which one would you choose and why?

3. If you could have dinner with five people from any time period, who would you invite? What would you talk about?

4. If you had to pick between the time periods in the book—Regency England, 1920s New York, or 1960s Las Vegas—which would you choose to visit and why?

5. Teddy tells Ada that she won't like the 1920s because there's no Netflix, and therefore no "Netflix and chill." What would you miss from the present? Why?

6. What would be the greatest drawback to being in the past? Why?

7. The matchmaker, Ms. Ellis Little, is an unforgettable character. Do you think she's from the past, the present, or the future? What intrigues you most about her?

8. If you had to pick one of Ada's dates—Henry Levison, Thomas Pickering, or Samson St. Laurent—who would it be? Why?

9. What do you think of Sam? He previously treated Ada badly—do you think he's really sorry when he first sees her again or does he gradually realize he made a big mistake? Would you forgive him?

10. What is the significance of the forget-me-nots on the Kairos logo and the jewelry they use to track clients?